NIGHT OF THE DARK FAE

THE COMPLETE TRILOGY

ANGELA J. FORD

Dust Jacket Design: Atra Luna Design

Chapter Header: Atra Luna Design

Case Design: Raven Pages Design

CONTENTS

PAWN

FATED

NOBLE

A day will come when curses will be broken, the lost shall be found, the found shall be lost, and the rift between mortal and celestial will cease to exist. The dragon queen of old will rise, freed but hidden in disguise. The last defender will come forth, and the sword of justice will purify.

— PROPHECY OF ERINYES

PAWN

NIGHT OF THE DARK FAE
BOOK ONE

I

DUNGEON OF THE DAMNED

Chains rattled against iron, and somewhere in the bleak darkness a banshee screamed. Its cry, like the sound of teeth grating against metal, high and wild, sent a shiver of trepidation down the spines of those who listened. A low growl echoed through the chambers, followed by a sharp bark.

A sword slid into a warm body, the hilt sinking into fur and withdrawing with a slight sucking sound. Moans were soft, aware of the coming inevitable sentencing, and doom was near for those unlucky enough to be cast into the Dungeon of the Damned. Little light poured into the blighted prison, hidden far under the fertile earth of an island and crawling with the souls of the pure and the damned.

The newest prisoner, Maeve, knelt on the uneven stone floor, aware of the grime that now stained her bruised, bare knees. When she'd arrived at this godforsaken place, the fae —her jailers—had stripped away her breastplate, sword, shield, and crown. Upon her capture, a simple golden collar had been placed around her neck.

Aside from the collar, she also wore a plain, sleeveless tunic that fell to her knees, leaving her long arms and legs bare to the elements. The tunic covered the pattern of brown ink that adorned her neck, chest, and upper arms. The patterns symbolized her heritage, a lost civilization, and even Maeve, the sole survivor of her people, did not know what they meant.

The destruction of her homeland, Carn, had happened only twenty-five years ago, when Maeve was five or six, but when she tried to think back, memories of her people evaded her, lost like the cool winds of winter burned away in the warmth of sunlight.

Cold air crept into her windowless cell. Stale seawater dripped off the stones, creating a pool of stagnant liquid in the corner, her only source of refreshment. A putrid smell came from it, but she knelt all the same with her hands clasped in front of her. In between sips of water, she rocked back and forth, her mane of dark hair gracing her shoulders like a halo.

Maeve's lips moved as she whispered the same prayer she'd repeated every day since her imprisonment. She kept her steely blue eyes closed against the gloom, unwilling to let in the nightmarish images. Today marked her thirtieth day in the dungeon, and although the shrieks of the damned filled her with terror, she knew her time would come. She resolved to face judgment with the same determination that had carried her through every situation life had dealt her thus far.

Her capture was an accident, a fate no one could have

saved her from. Not even him. The warlord she had fought and bled with. At the thought of him, she rocked faster. What had he thought when she did not appear after the raid? Did he see the jailers arrest her?

And then there was the thought she pushed to the back of her mind, the desperate wish that she had not argued with him, that their last words had been on kinder terms. He would have known something was wrong when she did not show up, but would he assume it was because of their argument, not a situation out of her control? Unless . . . no.

She did not want to think it, but the cold, damp, and loneliness pressed in, and she couldn't keep the horrific thought from invading her mind. Had he wanted the fae to take her and lock her away?

The jangling of keys grew louder until they were thrust into the lock of Maeve's cell. A bead of sweat trickled down her forehead and splashed onto a scarred stone. The muscles of her arms trembled as the eerie squeak of iron made her cringe. She remained in position, staring at the floor as the shadow fell over her.

"Get up," barked the rough voice of a jailer. "Hands behind your back. Don't try anything if you want to avoid the stocks."

Maeve took a deep breath, counting. They'd half-starved her and kept her locked up for thirty days, hoping to break her. But they hadn't, and the time had come to act. Another drop of sweat followed the path of the first and slid between her eyes to hang precariously on the edge of her nose.

In one fluid motion, Maeve pushed off her heels and

balanced on her hands, then swung her feet high over her head and slammed them into the neck of the jailer.

The assault took him by surprise and he fell with a shout. His hand fumbled for his belt as he stood, seeking the short metal rod with the glowing ember at the tip that burned the prisoners and brought them to submission, but Maeve was faster. She allowed her momentum to carry her through until she was back on her feet, upright. She kicked out at the jailer's thigh, then brought her knee up hard between his legs. He gave a muffled cry and collapsed to the floor again, holding his groin and swearing.

Keys clanged against the stones, but the jailer held them tight as he whimpered and then shouted, "Help! She's escaping! Catch her!"

Footsteps echoed off the walls. If she did not act quickly, she would be caught and locked up again.

Maeve placed her bare foot on the jailer's wrist and pressed down until his fingers came open and the keys fell free. Panic clawed up her throat as she bent to snatch them; they were warm and slippery from his sweaty hands. She made a face and leaped over the prone jailer just as a shock crackled through her right leg.

She spun, hair flying over one shoulder. The jailer sneered through his agony. He'd driven the rod into her calf, and a burning sensation had bolted across her skin like a hot knife being dragged up her leg. Gritting her teeth against the shriek in her throat, Maeve lashed out with the keys, dragging them across the jailer's face.

He screamed and dropped the rod as he pressed his hands

against his cheek to stop the crimson flow that trickled down his chin.

Maeve darted out of the open cell, dragging her burning leg behind her. A whip slammed into her and ripped open the back of her shift with its teeth.

Maeve grunted and spun to face whoever had whipped her. Blood boiled under her skin and the familiar haze of battle lust rushed over her, dulling all pain while she fought.

The fae with the whip was too far away for her to strike. He leered, showing off a row of crooked yellow teeth. He was a slim creature, tall and skinny, who looked as though his bones would snap in half if stepped on. Unfortunately, she was familiar with him and knew he would bend, not break, if she fought him. The prisoners called him Nathair, the snake. His head was shaped like an adder's—flat, with gleaming yellow eyes that were more reptilian than fae. The row of yellow teeth in his mouth were sharp and pointy, and when his mouth was closed, the tips of his fangs hung out, completing his sinister look. Despite his scrawny appearance, he was fast and his whip acted as an extension of his arms. He lashed out again, and this time the whip curled around Maeve's arm that held the keys. The teeth of the whip sank into her skin. Her eyes narrowed, and she charged Nathair, determined not to release her chance at freedom.

The whip fell away, leaving angry red welts crisscrossing up her arm. Her free hand curled into a fist and she leaped into the air, drawing back her hand for maximum impact. The air gave her strength, but as she followed through with the strike, Nathair vanished.

A sinking sensation twisted through Maeve, but she was

already airborne. She'd forgotten who she was fighting against and had failed to consider the tricks of the fae—namely, the ability to slip into the shadow world and reappear wherever they liked. Instantly.

A hand tipped her foot, and instead of flying, she crashed. She closed her eyes right before the impact and landed on her face. There was a snap and searing agony ripped through her nose as it broke. Warm liquid pooled from her face and her ears rang. She felt, rather than heard, the keys come free from her fingers and slide across the stone passage.

A sour odor hung in the air, and she realized it was her own vomit spilling from her lips. Her stomach convulsed again and again. Rough hands grabbed her, lifting and dragging her backward as she spit a mix of saliva and blood and bile.

Her mouth hung open, as the blood streaming from her nose made it difficult to breathe. She tilted her head back to stop the flow and gasped for air. A fist slammed into her ribs and tears sprang to her eyes. She bent over, coughing and hissing, but the jailers held her firm and pulled her back upright. Her arms were yanked behind her back and secured below the elbow with iron clamps, forcing her chest to thrust out awkwardly. She sucked in air through her parted lips while the jailers secured chains around her ankles, ignoring her pathetic struggles. Rage surged through her abused body and her stomach clenched as a jailer shoved her forward.

"Calm down, prisoner." Nathair's whispering tones made her shiver with revulsion. "You're to be taken to the Hall of Judgement."

Eyes wild, she tried to tilt her head to look at him, but a

slow clap rang from the shadowed edge of the prison hall. Heat flared around her neck as the golden collar came alive, reacting to the sound of its master.

Maeve gulped for air as the heat cut off her breathing. Her vision went dizzy, yet still she pressed against the influence of the spell with all the strength she could muster.

"Feisty as expected; I told you not to transport her without me," a cold voice scolded the jailers.

Maeve sagged in her chains as the heat became unbearable, then evaporated.

"Master," hissed Nathair, clearly surprised. He recovered quickly. "You saw what she did. I ask leave to teach her a lesson with my whip."

"From the look of her, you've already begun," the Master snorted.

Nathair uttered an oath and curled up his whip.

The Master's cold voice faded as he walked away. "Bring her to the Hall of Judgement. I want her unspoiled. Ready to work."

2

HALL OF JUDGEMENT

"The accused shall kneel," the warden bellowed. He had the head of a bull with dark rough hair and curved horns, and although his hands were manlike, his feet were hooves. A heavy musk came from his animal-like body. A minotaur. A lesser one, but a fearsome enemy all the same. He stamped his javelin against the stone and pointed it at Maeve.

Maeve lifted her chin and drew up her shoulders as best she could with the heavy chains weighing her down. Her battle rage had faded, leaving her with a weary exhaustion. To compound her misery, the thin golden collar around her neck continued to drain her energy.

Two swift kicks to the back of her knees brought her crashing down, adding new scrapes to her old ones. Keeping her chin raised in defiance, she glanced around the Hall of Judgement.

Thick black columns towered on either side, reaching to the inky blackness far above them. About ten feet over her head were yellow torches, the only light in the forsaken place. Jailers—some fae, others human—lined the hall, along with the court of the Master, made up of fae and beast alike. They had all come to witness and revel in the disgrace of their prisoners.

Memories flooded Maeve's mind, unhappy memories she'd long repressed. She'd assumed—wrongly—that the past lay behind her and a life of freedom was ahead of her. It had been a long time since she'd had a run-in with the fae, and to be back in their grasp was a blow to her pride. Strength was supposed to be her salvation—even though it was the fae who'd taught her how to use her abilities—but ultimately it had failed her. She closed her eyes, once again recalling the heat of flames and the searing pain as a blade drove into flesh over and over again. Screams and cries echoed in her mind, much like those she'd heard in her cell in the dungeon below.

A heady fragrance hung in the air, making Maeve's eyes water. She held back a sneeze to avoid doing any more damage to her broken nose. What she would give for a healer. Already, she could feel the swelling around her eyes. Squinting, she stared straight ahead into the darkness, which pointed like an arrow to the end of the hall, to the Dragon Throne. It was covered with bronze-colored dragon scales.

Some said that over five hundred years ago, the fae conquered the dragons, who had been intent on ruling the world. After destroying their civilization, the fae slew them all except the largest one, and used their black magic to force the last living dragon into an eternal slumber in the form of a throne. The intricate layers of the scales were so detailed, Maeve assumed the tale was true, but there was no possibility the dragon was still alive. For one, it did not have a head, and they would have had to kill it to force it to morph and shift into such an inert object. Because dragons had been slain hundreds of years ago, the tales about them often conflicted with each other, but everyone agreed that the race of dragons were dangerous, predatory, and untamable.

Maeve's vision swam. The Dragon Throne served as a reminder that she was in the home of monsters, the fae. Banished from the world above, they did not treat those who could walk in daylight kindly. There was no empathy in their hearts, only malice. Maeve suspected there was a bit of jealousy as well, though the fae could enter the world above during the night of the full moon, and that window of time was enough for them to carry out their wicked plans.

Maeve assumed, since they had brought her to the Hall of Judgement, they were not interested in forcing her into servitude in the lightless kingdom or executing her. Which meant the Master wanted to make a deal with her. A deal she would have to take, for escape did not seem likely. Not with the pitiless gaze of the warden on her. She could hear the rattle in his chest as he growled, and his hooves clopped eerily as he circled her, like a wolf around a fawn.

Maeve swallowed hard. Did they sense her discomfort?

"Enough," the Master called out.

He stood by the Dragon Throne, a shadowy figure, intentionally hidden from the light. He towered well over six feet, yet kept his form shrouded in a velvety black cloak and his face hidden behind a black mask. Only his eyes were visible, and they were nothing more than liquid pools of darkness with no irises.

The gleam of his gaze met Maeve's, and she suppressed a shudder. He'd attacked her thirty days ago, during the full moon. She'd had a sick feeling in her stomach all day, as if her body was attempting to tell her something was wrong and that she should call off the raid. But she'd been headstrong, determined, and angry, and when the Master had appeared to capture her, she was taken off guard.

His fingers were long and slender. Sharp claws appeared on the edges and retracted, like those of a wildcat. Maeve recalled his claws sinking into the skin of her arm, the snarl on his face, and the hint of fangs as sharp as a wolf's. Then he'd collared and dragged her to his dungeon.

"Maeve of Carn." His sinister tone echoed off the stones. "I will not mince my words. Your actions and your crimes against the Divine drew our attention. You are a warrior, defender, and champion, and yet you forsook your sacred oath of protection. Because of your dark deeds and your particular skill set, we sought you out. We have decided you will fulfill a quest for us. Upon completion of the quest, I will grant you freedom."

Maeve's ears burned at his words. Crimes against the Divine? Dark deeds? He accused her and pointed the finger, but she was no champion, no protector of the people. The people of Carn were gone, dead. It was up to her to find her place in the world. Yet, her skill with the sword had landed her in a few hairy situations, and even though she worked as a mercenary seeking out the not-so-innocent and forcing them to face their crimes, she'd gotten careless. When faced with difficult situations, she'd let her battle rage overrule her judgement and acted with violence, killing those who should live, simply because they were in her way. Deep down, she knew her actions went against the laws of the Divine, but she'd assumed her deeds would not be judged in her lifetime. She clenched her jaw so hard it sent a spark of pain up the side of her face. "I'd rather rot than work for you," she spat, shaking with hatred.

A jailer lifted a hand and struck her across the face. Maeve's head whipped back, jarring her broken nose. Pain blinded her and fresh blood spurted from her nostrils. She gagged as it blocked her throat and her chained fingers twisted, desperate to clear the fluid away.

After a moment, the sensation faded. When her vision cleared, she saw the Master had left his shadowed corner. His slippered feet kissed the stones as though he were gliding across a frozen lake. His lips parted, and she glimpsed his fangs poking out of the corners of his mouth.

"You have no choice," fury rolled through his words as he growled them. "This is a command. It is what you will do."

Maeve spit blood and examined her enemy. Her bruised lip curled. "Your offer is tempting, but how do I know you will keep your word?"

"Those who break rules do not get a choice," the Master rebuked her.

Heat flared up her neck, a reminder that he controlled her

through the magical collar and she was nothing more than a slave to his commands.

"Listen well, Maeve of Carn. I alone can release you from the collar that holds you. I alone can reduce your sentence and let you go free. But I know your kind. You are full of self-righteousness and believe everything you do has an excuse, a reason. You forget the fundamental laws that shaped the world in the beginning of time, and you believe you can escape judgement for your deeds. You are wicked, but I see the merit in your skills. You hold a unique power, and although you are not fully human, you can walk among them. Unlike us, you need not hide from the sunlight. We have decided your redemptive path. You will return to the world where the humans dwell and find the Seven Shards of Erinyes. Every full moon, an agent of mine will meet you to bring the shards here."

Maeve froze, a dull horror beating inside her like the wings of a trapped bird. She opened her mouth, closed it, and opened it again. When her voice came out, it was only a whisper, and she stared up at the Master as though she'd heard wrong. "The Seven Shards of Erinyes? They have been lost for centuries . . ."

"Yes, and now to be found again. A scholar will assist in your quest. We have discovered the rough location of each shard. You will find them and bring them to me. Time is of the essence, but because of the perilous nature of this quest, we will give you seven months to complete it."

Maeve sputtered. Seven months? But it was a chance to return to daylight, walk among the humans again, and flee the rotting pit. Her mind worked through scenarios and possibilities. She'd redeem herself and find him. Seven months would give her time to find out how to free herself of the golden collar and thwart the plans of the Master.

When she looked up again, the Master stood within arm's length in a pool of torchlight. The paleness of his skin and the sharpness of his fangs made her quiver, but she faced him nonetheless. "If you would send me on this quest, I will need my weapons and my armor back."

He flicked his fingers. "We have arranged it."

Maeve took a deep breath as boldness came over her. "You have collared me, which reduces my strength. If you would have me succeed in recovering the shards, I will need access to my full abilities."

The black pools of his eyes became deeper, and the Master bent over, bringing his face far too close to hers. Maeve wanted to shrink away from the scents of blood and decay that surrounded him. There was a sharp click as his claws extended, and he placed them under her chin. His aura surrounded her, and she felt as though she'd been dunked into a pool of darkness and it was him, and only him, that she could see.

When he spoke, his voice echoed both inside and outside of her head, ripping through all her private thoughts and shredding them. "Do you know why they call me the Master? I have seen civilizations rise and fall, and you are but a means to an end. Your power is mine, and until I see fit, you will wear the collar. If you think you can blindside me, betray me, and escape, think again. You have a fire in your soul, but I am the king of the fae. I can send you to eternal misery if you even think about disobeying me. I can make everyone and everything you care about suffer, and I can bend your will to servitude. That flash of defiance in your spirit will help you find the shards, but if you turn it against me, I will release the Underworld's fury on you. Now go—and remember, you wear my mark. Wherever you go, whatever you do, I will find you. If you haven't retrieved all seven shards within seven months, your life will be forfeit."

3

ISLE OF DARKNESS

Sunlight kissed Maeve's face as the portal spit her out on the island. She squinted against the light and waited, allowing her eyes to adjust to the brilliance. Despite the dark mission hanging over her, the fresh scent of salt-infused waves and the warmth from the sun gave a buoyancy to her attitude.

The fae, keen to stay away from the sunlight, had sent her through a portal instead of allowing her to use the tunnels to access the Isle of Darkness, the gateway to the fae's Underground. On the island, crumbling, sand-bleached towers had given way to overgrown grass and the occasional tree, and four statues, each standing over fifty feet high, supported each corner of the watchtower. The statue that looked north was headless, with long robes and a broken sword in his, or her, hands. The one that looked south was an angel with one wing; the other had been shattered. She looked fierce as she gazed, sightless, across the shore. The ones that looked east and west each had one hand bearing a javelin outstretched, as if preparing to throw it at those who dared attempt entering the Underground.

Maeve stood on the watchtower lookout, which allowed her to see down the cliffs to the sea, where wild waves splashed up at the shoreline, chipping away at the ragged stairs that led down. To her right, on a crumbling staircase, sat a human woman. At least, she looked human. She appeared middle-aged with strands of silver in her dark hair, which was piled in a bun at the base of her neck. She had an ageless, elegant beauty, and once might have been a noblewoman, though wrinkles now surrounded her gray eyes, which had a sad droop to them. She wore a simple black robe and gloves, and a bundle sat by her feet. In her lap was a book. She frowned, and her voice came out hard and clipped. "You must be Maeve."

"I am." Maeve narrowed her eyes. "Who are you?"

"Didn't they tell you?" she muttered darkly, glancing at the statues and down her nose at the sea. "I'm Sandrine. The scholar."

Maeve stared and almost laughed. "You? The scholar? I thought they would send a warrior."

Sandrine snorted. "One is enough. They don't want us getting any ideas."

Maeve chewed her lip and glanced out toward the horizon. It was midday, perhaps later. If they started now, they could reach the shoreline before midnight. "That means you know where we are going?"

Sandrine drew her thin shoulders up defensively. "I

would not be going with you if I did not know where to go," she snapped.

Maeve held out a hand, frustration mounting. "I did not mean to offend you. This is just irregular and unexpected."

Sandrine sniffed. "Irregular? Unexpected? Where do you think we are?"

Maeve had to admit she had a point.

"Are you going to stand there while the sun sets, or will you gather your things?" Sandrine snapped her book shut and pointed to a second bundle that Maeve had missed.

Maeve's eyes widened, and she dashed forward, giving a grunt of pain as the wounds on her face and arms protested her movements. There was her sword, tucked into its scabbard with the leather belt wound around it as though to protect it. The familiar weight felt good. One hand went around the hilt, holding the familiar fibers and the grip that had given her the calluses on her palms. Her hands had gone soft in the past thirty days, and she hugged it closer, her fingers molding to the familiar dips and ridges. Her hand clenched, and a ripple of anger passed through her, slight and small, just a hint of what she would do when she was free to fight as she wished.

She frowned, aware of Sandrine watching her. Maeve considered unsheathing her sword and striking the frail woman dead on the spot, then running as fast and as far as she could before the Master and the jailers caught up with her. With a sigh, she dismissed the thought. She was determined to turn over a new leaf. No more killing, harming of innocents, trickery, or betrayal. That dark life was over; if she wanted to escape the fae, she needed to change.

She began pulling on her armor. A breastplate, gauntlets for her arms and legs, and her leather sandals with crisscross straps that went up to her knees. Finally, she lifted her crown with its ruby stone. She held it for a moment, and her eyes misted over. Queen of nothing. The ruby crown, her birthright, had been passed from generation to generation—until an earthquake and a war wiped out the people of Carn, leaving Maeve to scramble from one hired job as a warrior to the next. As much as she hated to admit it, the Master was right. She'd committed many sins. Until now.

She slipped the crown onto her forehead and felt the warmth of the ruby. Her eyes flickered to Sandrine, who watched her with a critical eye.

Maeve buckled her sword onto her back and picked up her copper shield. If nothing else, she should be nice to the scholar. Someone wise to the world could turn into a powerful ally, unless the fae were holding something over her head. "Why were you in the Dungeon of the Damned?" she asked, as a way of making conversation and finding out more about her companion.

"You mean, what did I do? They captured me for murdering my husband. I was faithful and gave the bastard nine children, and then he cast me out, exchanging me for some whore half his age. Why should he have happiness when he made me miserable? I killed him for it. I'm not sorry, so they are forcing me to join you, which is punishment enough. I'd rather rot in the Dungeon of the Damned than be forced to travel with the likes of you." She sniffed.

Maeve's attitude soured. She'd have to work twice as hard

to gain Sandrine as an ally, for the woman seemed determined to keep Maeve at a distance.

Squaring her shoulders, she faced the sea. The crumbling staircase ran down almost to the water, and tied to a protruding stone was a boat. Maeve pointed. "Is that for us?"

Sandrine put away her book, threw her bundle over her back, and started down the staircase. "If you want to make the shore before midnight, we should leave now. I hope you have some strength in those arms to row."

Maeve frowned and followed. "Is this the sea I think it is?"

Sandrine gave a humph. "The Sea of Sorrows. Best to be away as soon as possible, before the shadow people take your sanity."

Maeve groaned and touched her face. Even though the fae had allowed her to clean the blood, it was still tender to the touch. The skin around her nose was puffy, and a dull pain thudded in the back of her skull. "When we reach land, I need a healer. Will you find one en route to the first shard?"

"I thought you'd never ask," Sandrine said. "When we get to the bottom, I will fix your broken nose. I assume you don't have any other complaints?"

"You're a healer too?"

"I dabble," Sandrine said, but there was a lighter lilt to her tone of voice.

Maeve did not respond, although she was relieved to realize the Divine was with her. Part of her prayers had been answered. Now they just needed to navigate the Sea of Sorrows before the shadow people attacked.

The Sea of Sorrows was named for spirits who had lost

loved ones and desired revenge. Instead of passing to the afterlife, they clung to their former lives and became half-alive; shadow people. They sought to take over the bodies of the living so they could enact revenge on those who had caused them misery. The fae had made their home underneath the island on the Sea of Sorrows to dissuade the living from visiting them. Only the desperate would navigate this sea, and often only with a powerful spell to keep them from being drowned by the spirits.

Maeve hoped the fae had seen fit to spell the boat that bobbed in the water. She was unsure how true the rumors about the Sea of Sorrows were, and she did not want to find out.

They continued down the old staircase, Maeve following behind Sandrine until they reached solid ground. The beach was sandy, and grit sunk between Maeve's toes. She eyed the sea with a growing sensation of discontent. Legend said that even a drop of water against bare skin was enough to send a vision of madness into one's mind.

"Come," Sandrine commanded, dropping her bag into the sand.

Maeve moved to stand in front of the shorter woman.

"Kneel." Sandrine pointed to the sand, her words ringing out with a strange power odd for someone so small.

Reluctantly, Maeve buried her sore knees in the sand. It caked on her skin, sinking into her pores and making her itch.

"Close your eyes. This will hurt," Sandrine said.

Maeve obeyed.

Sandrine's fingers touched the tender part of her nose. A slight pressure built until it became uncomfortable to breathe. Maeve willed herself to stay in place as the throbbing increased to a crescendo, and then just as suddenly melted away.

"That's better," Sandrine said, wiping her hands on her robe.

She picked up two oars and passed them to Maeve. "You'd better take these. I will navigate, but brute strength is your gift."

Maeve took them, slightly insulted by being called a brute. Gingerly, Maeve touched her face. The swelling had gone down and there was no pain. "Thank you," she said begrudgingly, and climbed into the boat.

It was a mere fishing boat, narrow and low to the ground, with a space in the bottom for their bundles and a plank of wood for each to sit on. Maeve dipped the oars into the water and planted her feet firmly on the bottom of the boat.

Sandrine sat down and leaned over to saw off the rope. It separated with a snap, and the vessel sank an inch or two. Using the oars, Maeve pushed away from the shore. The boat slid off easily, moving into the waves with surprising grace.

Maeve glanced down at the shimmering waters, and just beneath the surface she saw shadows glide by. The shape of a body coalesced and Maeve ripped her gaze away, focused on the horizon, and rowed as fast as she dared.

4
SEA OF SORROWS

Maeve pulled hard on the oars as her gaze focused on the low clouds gathering on the horizon. A storm brewed, and the air smelled like salt. Maeve licked her lips and wished the fae had given them a boat with a sail. The wind would blow them to shore much faster than she could row, especially given her limited strength. She settled into a rhythm, her breath coming short and fast, muscles rippling. Every now and again she glanced over at her strange companion, Sandrine.

The scholar held a pouch in her hands, and her fingers shook as she undid the knots. Her straightforward, brusque manner was still there, but her wrinkled face was pale.

Maeve followed her gaze. The shadow under the water swam closer, the inky dark splotch taking the shape of a human. Nay. Not a human. An angry soul. Maeve tried to steady her breathing as coal-black eyes stared out of the water, glaring at her. Anger rippled across the surface, and

Maeve's skin crawled as the sensation of fury came over her. She picked up her speed, but the shadow stayed with them, matching her strokes. Then a hand, pure obsidian, reached out to touch the hull of the boat and tip it over.

Sandrine's body jerked as she hurled a black substance at it.

The shadow gave a hiss and the hand dipped back into the waters.

Maeve puffed and panted. "What was that? Salt?"

Sandrine patted her bag. "Pepper," she grunted. "Salt would do no good. You are aware we are in the sea, which is made of salt? It would only encourage the shadow people."

Maeve nodded, ignoring the smugness in Sandrine's words. "How did you know it would drive them away?"

Sandrine pinched the bridge of her nose and huffed. "I'm a scholar. Are you done with stupid questions?"

Maeve pressed her lips together and threw her frustration into rowing. But it wasn't enough. The words buzzed on her lips, begging to be said out loud. She gave in, and through gritted teeth, growled, "You don't have to be unpleasant. We're stuck on this quest together without a choice. We don't have to be friends, but we can at least be amicable."

Sandrine snorted but said nothing else, keeping her gaze on the water.

Time dragged onward slowly. Maeve glanced again toward the horizon as the sun sank, casting a rainbow of radiance across the sky. Shadows trailed their boat, although the shadow people did not come closer. The wind began to whip up, shaking the waters and casting the waves higher.

Sandrine remained a hostile companion, her gaze straight ahead. "It should be here soon. Any moment now."

"Land?" Maeve gasped out. The speed she was rowing at strained her muscles, and her strength was fading into exhaustion. Curses came to mind as she thought of the Master, who had tampered with her strength. Without the golden collar, she could have rowed just as fast for twice as long without growing weary. Was this how humans felt all the time?

The last glimmer of light vanished and Maeve's senses heightened. The smack of the oars moving in and out of the water made her shiver. The wind caused goosebumps to pimple on her bare skin, and a flash of purple lightning lit up the sky, showing Maeve her companion.

Sandrine stood up, making the boat rock back and forth, and pointed with a crooked finger. She looked like a wild witch as the wind pulled her silver-streaked hair free from her bun and the brief flash of light made her eye sockets appear hollow. "There!" Sandrine's voice rang with triumph.

Maeve whipped her head around just as another strike lit up the sky. She saw craggy towers, sharp and wicked in the storm. Land. Shelter. The sight renewed her vigor, and she reached deep down into her core to pull the last strands of strength she needed. Her arms shook from the effort and her bottom was sore and numb from sitting so long on the wooden plank.

The boat shot forward, responding as though Maeve had spoken aloud to it. She closed her eyes and pulled with all her might just as a horrific clap of thunder vibrated through the waters and a cloud burst. A torrent of rain poured out of the night sky as though she had just rowed under the thunderous might of a waterfall.

The boat tipped precariously to one side, and the strength of the rain knocked an oar free from Maeve's hand. Uttering a cry, she reached out, her fingers snatching at nothing but cold air and furious rain.

Fingers cold as death wrapped around her wrist and tugged. Before Maeve could react, memories invaded her mind, but not her memories—someone else's.

She saw a child, a little boy or girl—she couldn't tell with the shaved head—but the child was no more than a few years old. A strength gripped her, a desperate desire to do anything to save the child. Two people held her arms back, and she fought, kicking, biting, and scratching. Reaching the child was of the utmost importance. It was a matter of life and death. Fury engulfed her and burned like a raging fire as the strangers dragged the screaming child farther and farther away. And then she was free.

Picking up a stick, she beat those who'd held her back, once, twice, thrice, then raced after those carrying away the child. Her precious child, who she'd carried in her swollen womb for nine months and birthed after long hours of agony and pain. When she'd finally held the wailing child at her breast, a fierce joy had overwhelmed her, forcing her to sob and hold the babe close, swearing nothing would happen to it. And nothing had—until now. Until warriors invaded, destroyed her village, and killed her husband. The child was all she had left. She would not lose it.

A bonfire lit up the shadows around her. Men ran, women screamed, and children wailed. Sword and shield clanged together, but she bolted through them. Her own life was not worth saving, but she'd gladly die a thousand deaths to save the child. When she reached the ones who had taken her child, their wicked knives glittered in the light and pointed first at her and then the child.

A horrible rushing came to her head, and she screamed with all her might as they drove the blade in over and over again. She was too late. Tears streamed down her face and she beat her breast, wailing in misery.

Desperate to avenge her child, she snatched up a burning branch and ran toward them. Something went through her, and in an instant, her body went cold. So cold. Her limbs. She could not feel them. Oh, Divine One. She could not move them at all. And then there was the child, her lost child. She needed revenge. They had to pay . . .

Something slapped her across her face and Maeve gasped, limbs flailing as she came out of the vision.

"Maeve! Fool girl, wake up and swim."

Pepper filled the air, and she coughed, thinking she might have swallowed some along with the salt water. Her insides burned and the rain would not cease. Purple lightning showed her Sandrine's white face. She was bobbing in the water and lifting her hand to slap Maeve again.

"Wait, no. I'm here," Maeve protested.

"Swim," Sandrine shouted. "They will return!"

5
BAY OF BISCANE

The full moon shone down on the beach as Maeve and Sandrine hauled themselves out of the ocean, gagging and spitting out mouthfuls of foul water. Vivid hatred still plagued Maeve's mind. She could not forget the vision of the woman, nor the child, stabbed before she could save it. Her limbs trembled. She tried to recall the men's faces. They had to pay for what they had done.

"Don't dwell on it. Whatever you saw." Sandrine knelt in the sand, sweeping strands of wet hair back into a bun. The moonlight revealed the quaver of her chin, although her gray eyes were cold.

Maeve rose to her feet, checking to ensure her weapons and armor were all intact. "It felt real," she whispered. "The woman. The child. The soldiers. It was awful. I never considered how someone else might feel. The victims."

"Because it was real," Sandrine said. "The memories you .

. . *we* saw were real. They happened to people like you and I. The only difference is, they also lost their lives. Terrible things happen in this world, and people like you can stop them if you stop focusing on quests that are self-serving."

The words burned, turning into fury as Maeve absorbed them, and then dust. Sandrine thought her selfish, consumed with her own self-serving interests. Her rebuttal died on her lips. It was true. Ever since she'd become a hired warrior—at times a bounty hunter—her actions had been selfish. She never considered whether her victims were innocent; instead she had focused on catching and turning them over for a pouch of gold. There was the father who had stolen a crate of goods from a merchant. She'd hunted him down and struck down the sons who tried to fight her when she'd captured the man. He'd wept, pleading his innocence, but she'd turned him over regardless. Then there was the thief in the citadel, hunted by the king's men. The thief had a camp of men, women, and children in a nearby forest. Maeve had joined the warriors who hunted the thief and turned him over to the king's guard to have his hands cut off for pillaging the kingdom. Those in his camp were imprisoned, perhaps executed, but Maeve had left with her bag of gold before finding out what happened to them. And the woman who had lived in a cave near the coast. She was a warrior, and had often stopped merchants who traveled along the coast, stealing their wares. Maeve had killed her, but before she died she begged for mercy. She did not want to leave her children alone, on their own. Maeve, who had never seen any children with the woman, hadn't believed her, and hadn't cared . . . but what if she had been wrong about each of those people? What if they had been innocent? What if they hadn't deserved the fate she'd doomed them to?

Her reflections returned to her argument with the warlord, Caspian, she had served until the night of the full moon. A familiar panicky sensation rose in her at the thought of him. Initially, she had thought he was like every other warlord, hardened and stubborn, desensitized from fighting the wars of others, claiming land, and stockpiling wealth. Their initial meeting was in the dueling ring. Maeve was between jobs and her coin was running out, so she'd resorted to dueling. The dueling rings were ugly, full of brutes and bloodthirsty crowds. Maeve had taken a beating more than once, but none could match her strength, and dueling often opened doors to more work for her. As it did with Caspian, who took note and invited her to join his warriors on their next task. It had gone well, and she'd worked for him ever since. However, things changed.

Six months ago, Caspian decided his warriors would stop fighting and thieving for the sake of wealth, and would instead aim for something greater, something noble. Maeve blamed the change on his visits to temples. He'd studied with a priest and priestess of the Divine. While he refused to take on vows, he sought to understand the deeper meaning of life, and he'd become enlightened to the struggles of the people around him and his unique ability to offer solace and release from the difficulties and sorrows humans cast on each other.

Maeve was unhappy with the way he'd changed, and so quickly. It wasn't that she did not want to help people, it simply seemed impossible for one warrior to make much of an impact, if at all. There were so many people in the world with power: kings, warlords, mages, priests, slavers, and the fae—just to name a few—plus the creatures, like orcs, who preyed on small villages. Caspian insisted that the way warriors and warlords treated the lives of others was not in line with the way of the Divine. Killing just to kill and killing for wealth was a sort of darkness. It wasn't that Maeve did not believe him—after all, she prayed to the Divine, when she had a need. But Caspian claimed there was more.

Now, as Maeve stood on the shore and listened to Sandrine's words, she understood on a deeper level what Caspian had tried to share with her. The memory hung, trapped in her thoughts, and she wondered how many lives she'd unknowingly shattered with her actions. Actions that had led her down an immoral path and into the hands of the fae.

"Where are we?" she asked to avoid the pricking of her conscious.

"The Bay of Biscane."

Biscane. The word sounded familiar.

Sandrine continued. "Biscane is known for the warlords who keep towers full of wealth on the island, away from the mainland. We've landed on the northern end, which means we should be unseen. The law of truce applies here; everyone minds their own business, and trading takes place in the Village of the Lawless on the northeastern side of the bay."

It dawned on Maeve why the name sounded familiar. Caspian had a tower, a refuge, on the southern end of

Biscane, closer to the mainland and the citadel. During the year they'd spent running from battle to battle, he'd mentioned it, but she'd never been there. He often sent his comrades off to store treasure there, though, and they had a hired a ship to take the riches across the King's Sea to his fortress. Maeve had been on the northeastern end of Biscane, to the outpost, also known as the Village of the Lawless. It was a haven for outcasts and warriors, a place to hide out, spend coin, or look for work.

She gazed at the wicked towers, glimmering like rows of knives in the white moonlight. Another full moon. She shivered, wondering if the fae were out, watching her progress.

A sudden hope beat in her breast. Would he be home? Lying low? Could she find him, seek refuge, and ask forgiveness for her bullheadedness? She fingered the golden collar around her neck, debating whether she'd tell him about her fate.

"We shall head toward one of the towers farthest from the outpost. A retired warlord, Lord Sebastian, dwells there, and you will find the first shard in his treasury," Sandrine said.

Maeve scratched her head. The fae expected her and a worn-out scholar to perform a heist in the middle of a highly protected bay, near an outpost where the only escape would be to dive into the Sea of Sorrows or—if they could make it to the eastern side—the Sea of Eels. "We will be caught," she frowned. "I don't understand how the fae expect us to penetrate a fortress on an island full of warriors. This is not my first choice. Do you have any ideas?"

Sandrine raised an eyebrow. Maeve thought if she were taller, she'd look down her nose at Maeve.

"Sleep and a full belly should give you some ideas." Sandrine jerked her chin north. "See the outcropping of rocks? There should be a cave where we can rest and hide for the remainder of the night."

Maeve shivered and rubbed her hands over her arms. Salt sloughed away from her skin. What she would give for a hot fire and a warm bowl of soup.

"It would be foolish to start a fire," Sandrine said, as though reading her mind. "The shores are guarded, and anyone who found us would not be kind to people who came out of the Sea of Sorrows."

Maeve nodded, aware that Sandrine spoke the truth.

Using the moonlight, they made their way up the sandy beach and around jagged rocks to the cliffs that shot out over the bay. Caves loomed like eyeless sockets, providing shelter from the bitter rain and the relentless waves. Maeve trudged with her head down, considering her unique predicament. She would not survive if she were caught hunting for shards in the Bay of Biscane. It was protected on three sides by water, and the fortresses kept the fourth side fortified against those who wished to devour the wealth of Biscane.

Not every tower in the bay was kept by retired warlords; there were plenty that manned ships and went forth to conquer villages and towns. Some were brave enough to weather the storms of the ocean and travel to the far north, while most went south.

After a few minutes, Sandrine found a shallow cave for them to rest in for the night. Without a word to Maeve, she stretched out on the hard rock with her bundle, as though she were not cold and drenched from their swim in the sea. Maeve bit her lip and resigned herself to a light sleep, waking fitfully as the waves crashed against rocks. When deep sleep claimed her, she dreamed of the woman and the child. Low moans and desperate cries echoed throughout her slumber.

6

WIZARD'S TOWER

A cloud of smoke bloomed above Imer's dark head, then caught the wind, which carried it up and across the battlements and into the serene blue sky. A sigh of satisfaction passed from his lips, along with another cloud of the semi-gray smoke. The rich smell of herbs and leather—a strange combination—passed under his nose, and he took a long whiff of the tobacco, drawing it into his lips and releasing it with his nostrils.

"Take it easy with the smoking, Imer," drawled a lazy—and slightly slurred—voice. "We have to leave in the morning."

One corner of Imer's mouth tugged up, and he rested his head against the stone wall of the tower, closing his eyes. "Aye, so ye say when you're drunker than a bamboozled wretch."

"Drunker than a man on his wedding night," the other voice snorted.

Opening his eyes, Imer raised an eyebrow. His brother, Ingram, sat across from him, his back propped up against the wall, legs spread, and a bottle of Fire's Breath in one hand. Ingram had coaxed the tavern keeper into handing the bottle of rum over for free. Ingram had a way with words, and his silver tongue and one eye often encouraged others to take some sort of pity on him. Pity he did not need.

Imer grinned at memories of how they'd duped others—all in good fun, though. Their last mischievous joke had landed them a bag of coins, which Imer had used to hire a tailor. He sat up straighter, admiring his new clothes. Imer and his brother were both dressed from head to toe in rich, elegant black clothes lined with red around the edges. Usually they wore hats to cover their features, which gave them away for who they were. Sticking to the shadows and blending in was the reason they were still alive. Although they called the wizard's tower home, they never stayed for more than a few months at a time. There were three homes they roamed between, returning to safety now and again when the direness of their situation forced them to seek haven.

"Master Ingram! Master Imer!" a panicked voice called from below.

"Bah," Ingram moaned, "can't they leave us alone? One last night in safety to celebrate, and still the orders come."

Imer took the pipe from his mouth and frowned, his ears picking up the sound of running. "It's the lad, Jordan."

"Jordan the messenger, all he brings is bad news."

Imer grinned at his brother's mopey demeanor. "Perhaps it is good news this time."

Ingram took another long swig of his drink before tossing the empty bottle over the edge of the battlement. He raised a dirty finger, partly covered with his gloves. “I wager it’s bad news. I’ll give you ten coins if it’s good.”

A crash sounded from below as the bottle shattered on the cobblestones. There was a cry and then the squawk of a chicken.

Imer snorted. “If you had coin to wager, I’d take you up on it, but I’m fairly certain you spent it all on drink.”

“I’m fairly sure you spent yours all on smoke,” Ingram returned.

“Hardly fair,” Imer protested, standing and patting his chest. “Look at our fine clothes, and the new feathers for our hats. I spent our coin on a worthy cause!”

“Master Ingram! Master Imer!” A lad dashed up the stairs, his short curly black hair wet with sweat and his long arms and legs pumping. He slowed down when he saw them, and relief crossed his brown face. “The wizard requests an audience with you. Before you depart,” he blurted out.

Imer stared at the lad. What pompous words from a youth. The wizard requested nothing. He made demands in exchange for protection, and those who sought shelter at the wizard’s tower obeyed his every word. Otherwise . . .

Imer shuddered when he remembered how it had been for him and Ingram before they found the wizard’s tower. Perched in a hidden corner of the known land, the tower was a city in itself, albeit a small one. The tower was surrounded by a high stone wall, and within the wall were the workers, those who lived under the shadow of the wizard, seeking protection while earning a living. On the outskirts of the area was grazing land for the flocks they kept, a place to plant gardens, and a place for the warriors to practice. They had a bakery, a blacksmith, a winery, livestock—chickens, cows, pigs, goats—and messengers who gathered knowledge from the world at large.

Imer shook his head to organize his thoughts. He and his brother had unique abilities. Others saw them as odd, or wanted to use them for their skill. After his experiences in the wider world, he knew it was better to trade service for protection within the hidden wizard's tower, a haven for mages. True, the mages of the wizard's tower had problems and politics of their own, but mostly, it was a welcome respite. When they grew antsy, the wizard sent them out on quests, usually to quiet unrest and keep chaos from coming to the tower's doorstep. It was astonishing how wild the world was with corruption, but it was more than that. Rumor had it the fae were taking people, and the actions of the fae would make the Prophecy of Erinyes come true. The wizard claimed that it was in everyone's best interest for the Prophecy of Erinyes to come true, and whatever they could do to speed it along would help.

Imer stretched in an attempt to sharpen his mind, then peered over the battlements, taking in deep breaths of the late summer air. The view from the top of the tower was nothing short of glorious. To the south lay a great body of water sparkling in the distance, while to the north was the mountain that hid the tower's presence. It was difficult to access the tower, and the mists that hid it from view and the way it blended in with its surroundings made it even more so.

Indeed, finding the wizard's tower was nigh impossible—unless one had magic.

Flexing his fingers, Imer took one last deep breath, then tucked the pipe away. "Lead on then, Jordan, we're coming."

The inside of the tower smelled like books, old parchment, scrolls, candles, and wax. The battlements were halfway up, the best place for warriors to station themselves should the wizard's tower ever come under attack. Inside though, winding staircases led all the way up to where the wizard held audience and kept his magic.

The first time Imer had entered the wizard's domain, he'd been mute with astonishment. Thousands of scrolls covered the walls, the books in the library were thick tomes full of secrets, and the uncanny scent of wisdom somehow filled the air. It was enough to breathe in the same air as the legends had and know he was in the presence of something much greater than himself. When he stood at the top of the wizard's tower, he understood the pull toward the sky, the move heavenward, and the desire to awaken the celestials and bring them back down to the land. Then, and only then, would there be an end to their suffering. No longer would they be hunted, and humans would not see them as oddities for use. Instead, they would see them for what they were: magnificent beings, full of old power, like the celestials.

A shiver of excitement went through him. He reveled in that, and in the knowledge that his actions would cause such drastic, life-changing events. By the Divine, if their efforts played a part in waking the legendary celestials, it would all be worth it.

Jordan, a young lad with entirely too much energy for the

late afternoon, dashed ahead of them up the winding stairs, past golden banners and tomes collecting dust. When they reached the upper atrium with the arched doorways and wide windows letting light stream in, Jordan came to a stop. He swung his brown arms and legs in a wide gesture, pointing toward the doors, then bowed and scurried away. Likely to continue on with his next message. He was a runner —the fastest Imer had ever seen—but other than being quick of foot and fast with memory, Imer had seen no other manifestations of the boy's abilities.

As soon as Jordan disappeared, the door to the inner chamber opened. A woman walked out, her hips swaying as she strode toward them. In one hand she held a long, unsheathed blade that caught the sunlight. She was dressed in simple garb: a short halter that left her belly bare and a long skirt that settled low on her hips, revealing even more flesh. Willow. Imer gave her a wolfish grin which, to her credit, she ignored.

"Don't take up too much of his time," she said in passing. She smelled like magic, raw and dangerous, and there was a wicked glint in her amethyst eyes.

She brushed up against Ingram and then turned around, pausing her departure. He gave her a cool, aloof appraisal, his usual distant greeting. Ingram had a stand-offish approach, while Imer preferred to flirt. It was more fun that way.

Her perfect nose wrinkled. "Are you drunk?" she asked, her eyes narrowing in disdain at Ingram.

Imer laughed, both at her disdain and the disgruntled look on Ingram's face. Ingram had the allure, the ability to pull people toward him, and most woman ignored Imer and fell in love with Ingram's hardened, stony demeanor. Not that Imer minded, he got in enough trouble as it was, but Ingram often had to deal with love-languished women following him around, and they often lost their wits after he bedded them. It was best to stay away from womenfolk, no matter how desirable and attractive they were. Besides, Willow spent so much time with the wizard, Imer knew she aimed to become the next wizard of the tower. There was a cold ruthlessness hidden under her beauty.

Ingram growled. "Are you judging how I celebrate?"

Willow took a step back and smiled sweetly at him. "Just insulted you did not invite me."

Ingram tilted his head back, studying Willow, then shrugged. "Find me later . . ." he said, but there was no promise in those words, mere jest.

Willow frowned, crossed her arms over her chest, then turned and walked away, her hips swaying from side to side. Ingram stared after her until Imer punched his shoulder. "Careful brother, you still have a priestess waiting for you in Isdrine."

"I haven't forgotten," Ingram returned, his voice low. "But don't you wonder . . ."

Imer sped up so he wouldn't hear his brother's words. Wonder. Of course he wondered what Willow knew. But getting her drunk and seducing her wouldn't be the best way to find out. He shot a side glance at his brother before they both stepped into the domain of the wizard.

Multi-colored prisms covered the hall, creating a myriad of colors so rich it was almost impossible not to cover one's eyes. In a moment, the flare of magic died away, and the wizard appeared, blowing on his wand.

Imer paused just inside the doorway, heart pounding as he crossed his arms over his chest and waited.

The wizard glanced at them and then strode over, his robes billowing out behind him. He was not a traditional wizard. Although he was old—in years—his hair was black instead of white, he did not possess a beard, and he had the spryness of a man in his youth. It was his eyes, deep and magnetic, that gave away who he was.

"Ingram. Imer," he said. His words came out rushed, as though he were short of breath. "The hunter has risen."

The rest of the wizard's words were lost as a sudden ringing came to Imer's ears. His blood ran cold, and for a moment he wondered if they should leave the wizard's tower after all.

7
SEVEN SHARDS

"Tell me about the seven shards," Maeve asked Sandrine the next morning.

There was nothing to eat as Maeve and Sandrine walked north among the rocks, though Sandrine said after midday the waters would be clean enough to fish from, or they could search the rocks for crustaceans.

Maeve wondered how Sandrine knew so much, but the scholar did not seem ready to talk about herself any more than she already had, and Maeve was growing tired of her pointed remarks.

"Ah. The seven shards," Sandrine's dry voice gentled with wonder. "Legend says thousands of years ago, before the angels fell from the Divine's grace, they lived above the world as celestial beings and worshipped the Divine in an ever-lasting paradise. The scrolls state that the souls of the right-eous rest with the Divine after death, although you need to visit a temple and speak with a priest or priestess to find the path of righteousness. Once you gain access to the heavenly kingdom of the Divine, wealth and wisdom are yours for an eternity, and those you lost in life will be with you, forever and always. That is a promise of the Divine.

"However, the angels, beings sworn to worship and protect the Divine, stole a relic from the Divine's treasury. It was a crown made of seven crystals with a bluish aura to them. When the Divine discovered the theft, there was a war among the celestials. Half were cast down to the Underworld, not to be mistaken with the fae's Underground. They are now called demons, and they seek to undo all that the Divine built as vengeance for being kicked out of everlasting paradise. It is said the Divine was not unkind, and he gave the demons many chances to repent, but they were headstrong and determined to become more than they ought to have been, to become divine creatures who ruled the souls of all. They walk the earth as they are able, seeking to corrupt humankind, darken souls, and drag all down to the Underworld, where everlasting torment awaits as punishment for their deeds. After the war, the crown was cast down by the Divine. When it fell to earth, the seven shards were scattered across our known world, and most of the relic's power was lost. But not all of it. Legend says, if one can find all seven shards and put them back together into a crown, the reconstructed artifact will have the power to break all curses simultaneously."

Maeve listened, her forehead furrowing at the story. She believed some of it, but other parts seemed outlandish, impossible. But the people of Carn were not human, and they boasted extraordinary powers—perhaps the powers of fallen angels? She was unsure, for that part of her heritage was missing. Dwelling on the past brought her no joy, and there was no reason to question what had happened to Carn. The land was in ruins, taken over by the orcs. She frowned, hoping one of the shards wasn't there, too.

"Why do the fae want the shards?" she asked, curious to hear Sandrine's speculation.

Sandrine's sharp gray eyes met hers. "You caught the fae's attention, which means you must be a warrior exalted above all others, but you'd be a fool not to see what they intend. The fae have been banished from the earth, and although they walk it every full moon, they want more. You've seen what they can do, and you've likely heard the legend of the Dragon Throne. What more could they do if they were free from the curse?"

Maeve's fingers touched the golden collar, which hung loosely around her neck. Its touch burned against her skin, and again the words came to her. *The power to break all curses.* If she had the seven shards, she could free herself. Yet, just the memory of the dark eyes of the Master made her go cold. He was also aware of that fact, and he must have known her thoughts would drift to double-crossing him. That's why she had seven months. The fae would cast a portal, come to her, and take the pieces one by one. She'd never find all seven shards before they were taken from her. She worried her lower lip between her teeth. She needed a mastermind, someone to assist her in figuring out the puzzle.

Glancing at Sandrine, she weighed the pros and cons, but soon dismissed the idea. Sandrine was not worthy. Knowledgeable? Yes. But too brusque to count on.

"Think, girl. If the fae can break their curse and walk

among us, even if they must hide from daylight, we will not survive. If you think they will honor the agreement they set with you, you are wrong. They have tricked me more than once; it is better not to hope, and I see the spark in your eyes."

Maeve grimaced. "How long have you worked for them?"

Sandrine scowled and walked faster. "It's best not to get to know each other. You'll be dead once you've outlived your usefulness."

Anxiety bloomed as she sped up, recalling how the fae had treated her as a punching bag. The crack of a whip. The snap of her nose. Did the fae even want her to succeed? They'd taken the one trait that gave her an advantage above others, her strength. Destitute and in the wild, the best plan she could think of was to take on a bounty to fund her quest for the seven shards, all the while considering a way to foil the plans of the fae.

8
MASTER OF THE FAE

The Master—King Mrithun of the fae—climbed the stairs, wide slabs of stones that wound in a spiral, taking him higher and higher, up into clear air. He enjoyed the sensation of being away from the smell of blood, the rot of prisoners, and the cries elicited from the tortures.

The court of the fae had fallen. They'd always been dark, hungry for blood and twisted, malicious acts, but now they were lost, corrupted, trapped in the dank, dark Underground. Often their actions were for sport, a way to amuse themselves during the long dark days when they longed for sunlight, starlight, moonlight, anything other than the stifled heat of the Underground. It was as close to the Underworld as they'd ever be. Their exile was payment for their sins, wickedness, and desire to rule the world. The curse had been a devastating blow. Time and time again, Mrithun had analyzed the details of the war. He'd led his armies to the height of civilization—the kingdom of Draconbane—only to be set back because he misunderstood how powerful the race of dragons were. He'd used his black magic to create a curse, and somehow, the curse reflected back on him and his people. The dragons were no longer the most powerful rulers in the world, but the fae were also banished from sunlight.

Salvation was nigh, and once the curse was broken, he would take the name of king again and rule the court with an iron grip. New laws would be applied, for he had plans for his court and plans for his queen. All those years ago, she'd beckoned, and he'd come running, besotted, but not anymore. She hadn't warned him about her sister, nor the dangers of her land. Forgiveness had been given, but just because he forgave did not mean he forgot. There was also the Prophecy of Erinyes to consider, and he intended to rise as the prophecy came true.

Ah, but the years had been long, and the remaining months were bittersweet. In truth, he missed the light of the sun on his face, the song of the bird, the cries of the night hunters and his castle hidden deep in the woods. He missed the freedom. But patience was his weakness; he had made missteps, and it was taking time to recover from them. It was a risk to collar Maeve of Carn and bend her to his will. But if all did not go well, he had contingencies, and his queen was smart, always thinking ahead. At times, he wondered if she meant to blindside him, and so he stayed alert, sharing much and yet still hiding some of his plans from her. He understood the need to play his hand and hold out in case she tried to overthrow him.

Deep in thought, he made his way to his chambers, shedding his robes as he walked. His queen preferred him without the mask he hid behind, and he knew why. Fae were known for their cruel beauty, sharp features, hard eyes full of depth, and lips that thinned and curved back to reveal fangs or a row of sharp, pointed teeth. The appearances of the fae varied; some were beautiful, while others dwelled in beast form, for their fae form was enough to make one lose their wits. The Master's own form was a cross between devastating beauty and horror, hence the mask he wore to keep from distracting others with his appearance.

He removed the mask as he glided up to the door of his chamber and entered. Shutting the heavy door behind him, he turned to take in his dwelling place. The rooms were spacious, with high ceilings, as close to earth as could be in the Underground. Torchlight lit up the interior of the room, and black and red satin drapery hung from the dark stones of the walls and ceilings. The first room was his bedroom, and beyond that were his work rooms, filled with old scrolls, weapons, and conquests of war—mostly bones and treasure. He bared his fangs at the sight of the delightful creature who lay on the bed. She rested on her side, facing away from the door, her golden wings folded on her back and her slender form covered in a silk dress, thin and as delicate as a spider's web. One flick of his claws would rip it to shreds, and he would relish the pleasures of her naked body.

She turned at his step, sitting up and dropping the scroll from her fingertips. A light came to her honey-colored eyes and dimples stood out on her cheeks. Her face was round, angelic, her skin pale, and a cascade of hair as dark as his heart flowed down onto her pale shoulders. The silk covering her showed off her heavy breasts, pointed nipples, and the curve of her belly giving way to generous hips. His angel. His queen. His dragon.

"Mrithun, is your business concluded? Did the warrior agree to search for us?" Her voice was breathy and whispery, like bells that chimed gently with wonder.

"Aye, my angel." He strode toward her, his feet sinking into the plush carpets he'd stolen from houses of wealth to provide comfort for his queen.

Business. Maeve of Carn would do his dirty work for him, although he would send his warriors out every full moon to make her path easier—or more difficult. If Maeve of Carn succeeded, he'd have more for her to do, and the golden collar was a guarantee she would obey his commands. He only wished he'd been able to control the warlord, someone he assumed she cared about. It had been a mistake he'd easily rectified, yet it was difficult to exert full control with only twelve nights of the year to watch Maeve.

Still, Maeve of Carn was a puzzle, and the Master wished he had more on her. Although he'd sent Sandrine, the scholar, to guide her for a time, he knew the old woman would not be able to sway Maeve to join the fae. Nor would Maeve be able to persuade Sandrine to help her escape. Sandrine was hardened and uncaring, and although she had some weaknesses—what was left of her family—they were of no use to the fae. She'd lost everything and had bent to his will like clay in his hands, although he allowed his queen to handle most of the dealings with her. After all, it had been his queen's idea to gather the Seven Shards of Erinyes. Once Maeve of Carn completed her quest and brought him the shards, he would use his black magic to put the pieces back together, set his bride free, and break the curse that kept the fae trapped in the Underground.

He sat down on the bed beside his queen and ran his fingers through her long, dark hair. She rolled her head back and closed her eyes. A sigh came from her lips, those rosebud lips that begged for his attentions. A strap of her gown fell down, baring a shoulder to his caresses. He pressed a kiss to her arm, then her lips . . .

Her hand come up, sliding under his cloak, seeking bare skin on skin. A throaty moan escaped from her, begging for more. Passion seized him, but he pulled back, calming his thudding heartbeat, the heart he made certain no one knew he had.

"Before the year is out, I will set you free, to return to flight. We shall walk the earth and become the gods of men."

"Promises." She smiled, arching her back.

He frowned at her disbelief in him. "Promises, nay, it is the prophecy," he scolded her.

Still, she smiled up at him.

Conniving. The word pierced his thoughts, and he picked up the scroll she had dropped. "What are you reading?"

The flirtatious smile fell from her lips and she sat up, a seriousness coming to her pale eyes. "My lack of knowledge has always been my folly, my downfall," she admitted, searching his face for understanding. "I have learned much from the scholar, which makes me believe I should continue my studies without her. If we succeed in gathering the Seven Shards of Erinyes and break all curses, we must be prepared. We are not the only ones who are cursed. I've read the

Prophecy of Erinyes in full, but I don't know what other beings we will set free if we succeed."

"Ah," Mrithun said as he smiled, his fangs on full display, although they did not frighten her. She loved the horror of who he was and admired his beastly looks and abilities. "You strategize to find out what we might be up against."

"You speak truth." She reached out a finger to touch one of his fangs. "We need a blade, one that can protect us. Do you think you can make one?"

He took her hand in his, passion swelling as dark thoughts twisted through his mind. "You need not ask," he told her, and reached out a hand to brush her hair off her shoulder, baring her neck to his gaze. The marks where he'd bitten her were still there, a reminder of intoxicating pleasure.

She poked him in the chest. "I see where your mind goes. Work first, then pleasure."

A low growl came from his throat. "We make our own rules here."

"Of course, Master." She dropped her gaze, her voice going husky and breathy.

The term, Master, seemed almost derogatory coming from her lips. Baring his fangs, his growl came again, louder, without restraint. He gathered her in his arms, determined to enjoy his pleasure to the fullest before setting to work once again in the endless night of the fae Underground.

9
Warlord's Fortress

"It's quiet around here," Sandrine said as they crouched behind a rock. "Much too quiet. I don't like it."

Maeve peered over the stones, eyeing the fortress that rose before them like a lion guarding its pride. "Have you been here often?" She glanced at her companion, searching for clues to fill in the gaps of who Sandrine truly was and how she had come by her knowledge.

"Enough." Sandrine shrugged. "Lord Sebastian is retired, but his warriors are restless. I expected to see them patrolling the island, riding their horses to the outpost or, if nothing else, fishing and loading their ships for another conquest. We have seen no one since we passed Lord Murphy's fortress, and I don't like it."

Maeve chewed her lower lip, unsure how to respond. The sun hung low in the sky, casting a red sunset across the beach.

"That's Lord Sebastian's fortress, isn't it?" Maeve's gaze flickered to Sandrine's for confirmation.

"Aye, that it is. The first shard is buried in his collection of wealth," Sandrine confirmed.

Maeve used the failing sunlight to study it. Rust-red stones had been cut into blocks and piled high, covering the coast in shadows. Gray rocks and jagged boulders, large enough to sit on, lined the uphill path, a mixture of dust and sand that curved to the fortress. The tower perched on a ridge, allowing those inside to keep watch on those who came and went. Nothing would surprise the inhabitants of the fortress, and Maeve considered her options as she examined it. Her shoulders slumped, and finally she admitted it would be best to walk up to the gates, posing as a warrior for hire.

Sandrine slung off her sack and dragged out the same thick book she'd been reading when she and Maeve met. She thumbed through it, wetting her fingers with her tongue to loosen the vellum, which stuck together. "Have a look, girl."

Girl. Some of Maeve's frustration slipped out. "My name is Maeve. Would it kill you to address me by my given name?"

Sandrine merely waved her hand, brushing away the words, and pointed.

Maeve leaned over to examine the pages. The first page displayed a drawing of the fortress, but the second was only lines, marked now and then by small words or letters.

"This is a map of the keep," Sandrine explained. "Each of the fortresses in this bay have a similar design, for the same master builder built them, one who later became an ally of the fae. He provided the blueprints for the fortresses."

Sandrine pointed to the bottom of the first page. "Here are the gates, which let you into the courtyard. There are several doors here that lead to warrior's quarters, staff quarters, the kitchens, stables, and the side armory. The main armory is inside the keep, here, close to the treasury. The main entrance leads you into the hall. The first level is usually where they eat. The second level is the lord's chambers. The third level is used for defense, in case there is an attack or siege. Both are uncommon here. The fourth level provides access to the battlements. There are two places where treasure is stored. The first, the true treasury, is underground; these trapdoors on the first floor access it. The second is on the fourth floor, so raiders have to cut through all the defenses to reach the treasure. However, treasure is heavy, and not all of the warlords or their men are willing to carry it to the fourth level. Some keep a share in the hall of lords or in their chambers. Given the peace in Biscane, the shard could be in any of these possible locations."

"By the Divine," Maeve whispered, her tone hushed in awe. "Do you carry the knowledge of the world in that book?"

Sandrine gripped the edges of the book as though Maeve might rip it away. "I am the scholar, and this is my life's work. I will reveal what you need to know when you need to know it. Do you have questions regarding the information I have given you?"

"No." Maeve glanced at the tower again. "What you have shown me is useful; I simply need to buy myself enough time to search all four levels. I will wait until sundown, enter the castle, and pretend to be one of Lord Sebastian's warriors. If that is not possible, I will ask for an audience with him to convince him to come out of retirement for a treasure."

Sandrine lifted a hand to stop Maeve. "Girl. I do not need nor desire to hear your plans. I provide the knowledge and you complete the task. How you do it does not interest me, I only care about the result."

Maeve leaned back as though Sandrine had slapped her. The scholar's harsh words reminded her she was alone. This was not a conquest like those she'd planned with Caspian; she had no one to talk through strategy and variations with should things go wrong. She needed to make those decisions alone. Maeve bit the inside of her cheek and glanced out at the sea. They were well past the Sea of Sorrows, and the waters of the Northern Sea were clear, reflecting the rays of sunset. It was said if one sailed north, they would reach the Sweet Sea, where the waters were delicious enough to drink and the creatures that dwelled within them grew abnormally large and had the most delectable flesh. For a moment, Maeve wanted to dive in the waters and sail out there. If she ran from the fae instead of completing the task, how far would they go to come after her?

Maeve squared her shoulders. Sandrine's bitterness would not get the best of her. "I see," she murmured.

"Good." Sandrine packed away the book and slung her sack on her shoulder. She hunched behind the rock, looking like an old beggar woman. "You are on your own now. I will meet you at the outpost and make arrangements for our next journey."

Maeve raised an eyebrow. "Don't you need gold for that? Where are we going next?"

Sandrine sniffed. "I will worry about that. Focus on getting that shard, unseen. You know well enough that if we start a war on this island, escaping will become difficult."

"Aye." Maeve's fingers went to her blade. "Where shall I meet you in the outpost?"

Sandrine raised three fingers. "Wildling Inn on the southern end, close to the sea. You have three days. We need to keep pace if we are to complete this task in seven months."

Ah. So, the fae had given the scholar the same time limit.

"I will meet you then," Maeve said coldly, although she wanted to ask Sandrine about the fae. What had they promised her? Why did she work for them?

Sandrine set off down the rocky path with a scowl on her face, leaving Maeve alone to face the tower.

A SLIVER of moonlight lit her way as Maeve strode up the rocky path to Lord Sebastian's fortress. The eerie silence unnerved her, until even the sound of the waves crashing against the rocks on the shore made her jump. Sandrine had been right. It was too quiet. She hadn't heard a single horse neigh, nor were there any sounds of warriors practicing or talking. There weren't even any warriors on the way to the seas to fish, and everyone knew the best catches would be caught after night fell, when the fish could not see the shadows of the boats.

Salty sea wind blew against her back as she reached the

end of the path and froze outside the gate. The impressive structure rose higher than her head, with heavy iron doors that would take a troop of men to pull open. The doors were likely controlled by a pulley system with chains, and often a door in the side of the wall was used instead of the gates for regular foot traffic. The larger gates were generally open during the day and shut at night, when the comings and goings were few.

Maeve's throat went dry as she stared at the open gates, wide enough for three men to walk in side by side. Was it a trap?

She held her breath and silently counted to ten as she listened.

Nothing, not even the sound of footsteps.

Drawing her sword, she slipped through the gateway, steeling herself for what might be on the other side. An empty courtyard greeted her—cobblestones, a group of wells on the far side, and doors to adjacent buildings that stood wide open, welcoming the night air into their secret hollows.

Maeve's gaze shifted, searching for archers and other warriors who should be defending the tower. The wind blew again, but the stone walls blocked out the sea air, and this time a foul scent wafted to her nostrils. She sniffed. Dung. Decay.

Something white flapped in the wind, nailed onto the main doors to the keep, which, according to Sandrine's instructions, she could use to access the four levels. Still expecting a trap, Maeve crept toward the doors. Rubble crunched under her feet, and she held her sword in front of her, fully expecting warriors to pour out of the door and take her down.

The white item moved again. When she walked up the four stone steps to the doors, she saw it was a scroll nailed into the arched doorway that framed the keep. The doors were cracked open as though someone had been fleeing and swung the doors shut behind them. Words written in ruby red blood were scrawled across the scroll. Maeve pinned the flapping end of the scroll down with her finger and read:

Twelve hours of moonlight was not enough.
Finish what we started . . .

A muffled cry escaped her lips. She pressed her hand against her mouth as bile rose in her throat. Eyes wide, she scanned the courtyard again, even though she knew it was in vain. The night of the full moon had passed. The fae had gone, but not before they spent twelve hours warring through the keep. They'd likely slaughtered everyone inside as they searched for the shard.

Anger seeped through Maeve. It was clear they had failed, but fully expected her to finish their dirty work. After all, that was why they'd captured her. The fact that they had come before her and attempted to find it for themselves ignited a fury within her. The Master had made a deal with her, but it was clear she was their last resort. They already had the knowledge of the whereabouts for the shards, collected over years, perhaps even decades. But only being able to search once a month was not enough for them, which was why they needed Maeve to find the shards. Maeve understood their reasoning, but they had made her situation more difficult.

What if someone saw the fae attack the tower? What if someone escaped and went to the nearest tower to raise the alarm, or to the outpost? If the inhabitants of Biscane had been roused, they'd soon arrive to pick over the spoils of war, and if she were caught in the crossfire, they would kill her. Unless—by a miracle of the Divine—she got out alive.

Maeve set her jaw and ripped the parchment off the door. With a cry of frustration, she slashed it in half and stomped on it. The message was clear. Gripping her sword, Maeve kicked the door open wider and ran inside.

Bodies lined the hall, some headless, others with slashes down their chests. Some still grimaced in anger, while others held their swords, death screams frozen on their dead faces. Arms, legs, even fingers were scattered across the floor, along with ripped clothing, streaks of blood, and black, bloodied weapons. Maeve averted her eyes from the death and winced as guilt buried into her flesh like a knife. Was this how she left people after killing them? After the devastation she wrought with Caspian and his mercenaries? Was this why she was being punished? Because her sympathies did not lie with the salvation of humankind and the beauty of a single life? But there was no time to consider her guilt, so she pushed those thoughts away and ran on.

The trapdoor on the first level was easy to find. A burning torch had been left and, not expecting any resistance, she sheathed her sword and took up the torch. The stairs were damp and slick, and Maeve descended tentatively, ready to use the torch as a weapon if needed.

The yellow pool of light was tiny in the immense underground cavern. She held it up, and a structure caught her eye, along with the glimmer of glowing coals. She held the torch over it and it lit up, shooting light across the walls. It was as though she'd set off a chain reaction, and the torches across the treasury lit up. Light bounced off the stone walls, revealing the cavern.

Maeve's breath caught and her face went hot. Treasure. More treasure than she'd ever seen in her life. What a find! If this had happened before the fae had captured her, she'd have taken it all, found a ship, and set sail for the north without a care in the world. But now . . . a curse left her lips. She backed away. The golden coins that covered the floor were from tipped-over trunks, and the silk gowns were ripped apart. The treasury had already been ransacked. If the shard was there, the fae would have found it.

Spinning on her sandaled heel, she took the stairs back up two at a time, careful not to slip on blood.

She dashed toward the second level, fully aware scavengers might interrupt her at any moment. She raked her mind. Where would she keep the most precious treasure of all if she were Lord Sebastian? The treasury was not safe enough; that was where he sent his warriors to hide the loot, and likely where he paid them. No. It would be sacred. Close to him. Perhaps somewhere on the second level, close to his chambers?

Maeve had heard stories about men who lost their souls to their treasure. They'd find a jewel that made their eyes gleam, their hearts beat just a bit faster, and they'd hoard it. Each day they'd take it out, stroke it, talk to it, treat it like a well-kept mistress. Was Lord Sebastian like that? Did he hoard his treasure and look at it with stars in his eyes? If he had one of the lost shards, it was not likely he'd told others about it. Maeve imagined he might have killed anyone who'd helped him find such a powerful relic.

She paused on the stairs, unsure whether to proceed to his chambers or go to the tower on the fourth floor. In the end, the fourth floor won. If Lord Sebastian had the tendencies she thought he had, he might have a secret place in the most fortified area of the castle. If her luck held, he'd have died close to that spot, unless the fae had taken him prisoner.

She ran as though the fae were at her heels.

10
THE FIRST SHARD

The fourth floor was devoid of bodies. Maeve passed one on her way up, but otherwise the halls lacked the display of violence on the previous three floors. It appeared the fortress had been taken by surprise, and all they'd managed was an unorganized rush to halt the fae.

But what if there were survivors up on the fourth floor? Would she run into a fearsome warrior set on protecting the last defenses?

Her muscles throbbed with tension as she made her way through the fortress. The tower was like a maze. She passed arched windows blowing in fresh sea air, the moonlight combining with her torchlight to help her see a few feet ahead. Each time she opened a door, her heart thudded so hard she thought it would burst, but when her eyes scanned empty rooms, she left in disappointment. Was it possible to find the shard in a matter of hours? The fae had spent all night searching, though she didn't know if they had conducted a thorough search floor by floor.

Finally, she opened the door to a room that looked promising. A high arched window let in a flood of moonlight, revealing a table against a wall with a wide plush chair. Papers and scrolls ruffled in the wind, and on the other side of the wall was a full suit of armor.

A sudden knowing struck her, as though she'd been there before, and knew this was where she needed to be. Relief seeped through her. The shard had to be somewhere buried in this room.

She set the torch in a holder by the door and walked into the room, lifting each paper and unrolling each scroll before turning her attention to the table. It was solid, without any cracks or slotted openings. It revealed nothing.

With a sigh, she knelt by the chair, using her sword to rip through the plush cushion. It gave way without resistance, and white gossamer feathers fluttered out.

Maeve ripped out the feathers, tossing them on the table, but there was nothing. She squinted at the moonlit window. How many hours had she been in the fortress? It was well past midnight, she assumed, and she hoped to be away before morning. Her reputation would not survive being discovered in a tower full of death. There was still honor among thieves, especially for warriors who wanted to work for warlords, and if her name became associated with this terrible crime, she'd never work again.

She lashed out, kicking the chair over. It landed on its side, and a hollow bang rang out. There was something under the stone. Dropping to her knees, Maeve shoved the chair over and ran her fingers over the stones beneath it. Sure enough, one was loose. Using the edge of her sword, she wedged it in the crack and pulled back to pop the stone out.

Holding her breath, she reached down into the hole. Her fingers wrapped around a shape; a box. She pulled it out, fingers tingling with excitement. Was this it?

She placed the box on the table where the moonlight allowed her to see it plainly. It was a simple box, hewn out of wood with a symbol carved into it that resembled an S with a line crossed through it. Maeve narrowed her eyes. She thought she'd seen the symbol before, but couldn't be sure. She'd ask Sandrine what it meant.

Her fingers fumbled with opening the box, and she quickly realized it was locked. Biting her lip, she debated what to do. If she smashed the box, she could end up shattering the shard—if it was inside. A broken shard would cost her, but she did not have time to search for a key, which would likely be with Lord Sebastian's effects.

By the Divine! Was nothing easy?

A silver glint appeared in her peripheral vision and she jerked back—just in time, as a knife sailed past her nose. It clanged against the stone beside her and fell to the ground.

Hot blood rushed to Maeve's fingertips. Snatching up her sword, she spun to face the intruder.

A man leaned against the door in the pool of torchlight. He had a long face, high forehead, and shoulder-length silver hair tied back with a small black ribbon. His eyes were narrow, squinty, and his nose hooked and long. His overall appearance reminded Maeve of a ferret. His clothing was rich but torn in places, and bits of dark liquid had dried on it. Blood, she assumed. Then she realized he was leaning against the doorframe because his leg was wrapped in a bandage. He spoke first, his voice deep like the waves of the sea crashing against the shore during a storm. "So. You have come."

Maeve straightened, noticing he was unarmed. Why would he throw his last weapon at her? "And you are?" she asked, more for clarification than anything else.

He touched two fingers to his forehead. "Lord Sebastian. Although I suppose you already assumed. I knew this day would come."

His voice had a sweet lilt to it, compelling, like honey.

Maeve tilted her head at him, but her fingers squeezed the box. "What day?" she whispered.

"The day you came to take the shard." He shrugged. "Not you personally, I wasn't sure who they would send, but someone."

Maeve made a small sound in her throat. He knew about the quest for the shards. That meant she had to kill him so he could not hunt her. The thought made her tremble; she did not want to kill him, but she also understood there could be no witnesses, no one who could link her back to the stolen shard and the destruction of the castle. Fear tightened in her belly. To buy herself time, she held up the box. "How did you find it?"

Lord Sebastian's gaze moved to the window, which faced north. "I sailed north and found the treasure of treasures." His tone went wistful. "I also found meaning to life and retired from my pillaging ways."

"There is no retirement for warriors," Maeve muttered bitterly.

"That's what you think," Lord Sebastian replied evenly. "Whoever sent you is relentless. Evil. I assume they promised you a reward if you complete their dirty work for them; perhaps they even have something on you, a secret, a knowledge, or they captured someone you love or admire. But you are sealing your own doom. The seven shards should never be put back together. There is a reason curses should not be broken."

Maeve scowled, her heart pounding in her throat. She had to admit, she was curious about Lord Sebastian and what knowledge he might have. But she also hated talking to her prey before she killed it. She grunted. "I'm afraid I don't understand."

He shook his silver head. "Nay, I wouldn't suppose so. Warriors like you are all the same. You fight, giving little thought to right or wrong, good or evil. Your lack of conscience is your problem. I was like you once, young and given over to battle lust. Life and longevity can teach you much, if you will listen."

"I don't have time to listen to you," Maeve snapped.

"Ah yes. Young ones. Always in a hurry." Lord Sebastian's deep voice went hard. "One day you will regret your actions, when you come face to face with judgement."

A strangled laugh left Maeve's lips. "Judgement? I already regret my actions. You presume to know much about me when we have only just met."

"You have not shown me reason to assume you are different from any other warrior." Lord Sebastian narrowed his eyes and limped farther into the room. "Are you?" he demanded.

Maeve took a shuddering breath. Why was it important? Why did she want him to know she wasn't like the others? She wasn't a mere warrior out for blood in exchange for gold coins, a full belly, and a night of endless pleasure. Guilt pinched her conscience. "I don't want to hurt you, but my master is powerful. I must keep my end of the bargain to regain my freedom."

"We all serve a master," he sounded sad as he spoke. "Some more ruthless than others, but if you think someone as powerful as your master will grant you freedom, you lie to yourself. The only freedom he will grant you is release from this life—in the form of separating your soul from your body."

Anger ripped through Maeve as he voiced her worst fears. Her free hand tightened around her blade and she brought up her sword. "Enough!"

Lord Sebastian's shoulders slumped and his face twisted in pain as he limped forward. "Kill me if you have to. But remember my words. We all choose. Some to do right, others to do wrong. People often believe they are backed into a corner and left with no choice. But the decision to go left or right, to let live or let die, is always yours. When you think you are stuck, it is because you are only looking in one direction. Look the other way. For that is where escape lies."

Maeve pointed her sword at his belly. "You don't look as though you want to escape."

He held his hands out, palms up. "I don't. I have lived. I

set the fires when I heard you reach this level. They will be here soon."

The fires? Maeve's gaze tore to the window, where the moonlight shone in the velvet blackness of night. Stars peppered the skies and, in the distance, she heard the unending crash of waves against rocks. In the darkness she thought she saw a faint glow.

If the fire was ablaze at the top of the tower, it would be a warning to the other warlords that there was trouble on the island and to be on guard against it. Whoever was closest would send a squad of warriors to investigate, and if they caught her here . . .

As Maeve turned back, Lord Sebastian pulled a blade from the suit of armor and faced her with it, swaying on his one good leg.

Maeve's voice went tight. "Tell me where the key to open the box is."

"There never was a key," Lord Sebastian said. "You must pick the lock."

Maeve's lips thinned. She'd smash the box if she had to, but she needed to be sure it was the shard. She did not know Lord Sebastian, and although his words had unsettled her, she also believed he wasn't beyond reproach. What if he was lying to her?

He advanced, and she rushed around the edge of the table, blade raised. They met in the middle of the room, blade clashing against blade.

Maeve met his gaze as they crossed swords, and she stood her ground, pushing her weight against his. A voice in the back of her mind screamed at her to make a different choice, to let him live, but she was committed now, all guilt pushed aside, pressed down under a twisted mist of fear and rage.

Lord Sebastian's face had turned to a murderous calm as he waited for the final blow. It was the look in his eyes that sent Maeve over the edge. Using only one hand, she held her stance, brought the box up, and hurled it at him. It glanced off his head, leaving a deep gash in his forehead. His eyes went wide, his grip loosened, and he stumbled, losing his balance. His arms waved wildly, but his backward momentum was too strong. As he fell, his head crashed against the suit of armor. It fell with an echoing din.

Maeve was on him in a moment. She leaped over his flailing legs, raised her sword above his heart, and brought it down hard. Her blade sank in until she heard the dull thud of the tip of her sword meeting the stone floor on the other side of his body.

He moaned and coughed. A stream of blood burst from his lips and dribbled down his neck. "You will pay," he whispered.

His head lolled to the side, his eyes rolled up in his head, and he went still.

Maeve pulled her blade free, hesitated, then cleaned it off on his tunic. Adrenaline pounded in her ears as she reached for the box. The bloom of blood on one corner made her wince. She'd been forced to kill him. Hadn't she? She had no choice. Her hands shook. Since when had she gone soft?

Pushing whispers of unease to the back of her mind, she moved back toward the table, found the knife that had been thrown at her, and used the sharp tip to pick the lock.

Her hands were sweaty and her vision kept blurring.

Every now and then she glanced up at the moonlight, knowing she needed to flee the fortress before she was caught. But first, she had to know what was inside the box.

At last, the lock gave way with a click. Tossing the knife down, Maeve yanked the box open.

Pale blue light shone out. Nestled in the box amid a bed of straw lay the first shard.

II

ROGUE OUTPOST

Two days later, Maeve stood on a grassy knoll looking down at the outpost beside the shimmering sea. The blue waters twinkled, as though the nightmares of the bay had never happened. After discovering the shard, she'd run as fast as her feet would carry her back outside. When she'd stopped to listen near the main gate, she hadn't heard footsteps approaching, so she went to the stables. Her actions were rewarded, for there were horses. She chose a brown mare, tossed on a saddle, snatched up a saddlebag with a pouch of gold coin, and galloped across the rocky landscape into rolling hills. Following Sandrine's instructions, she stayed close to the sea. During her two-day journey, she saw other warriors, but no one raised an alarm regarding Lord Sebastian's tower, and she assumed she was safe. For now. Still, she was eager to reach the outpost and blend in. She had a full day and night before she needed to meet Sandrine. She was curious where they were heading next, but the freedom of being on her own was intoxicating.

Maeve slapped the rump of the mare. "Go on then," she said, not wanting anyone to recognize it as one of Lord Sebastian's horses.

The mare nudged her shoulder and put its head down, grazing in the long stalks of grass that grew in the hillock. Maeve shrugged. "Suit yourself."

Slinging a saddlebag on her shoulder, Maeve strode toward the outpost, also known as the Village of the Lawless.

The outpost was a walled town full of inns, trading posts geared toward warriors and mercenaries, and training grounds. Some sport could be had there, and warriors often went there to lie low or look for another warlord to work for. There was another village on the southern end of the bay, but for those who lived on the island—and needed some entertainment—the outpost was prime territory.

Maeve took her time walking toward it, though she kept an eye on the sky. The gates were open during the day, but as soon as night fell, they were closed. Wild animals hunted the bay at night, and were often drawn to the outpost by the scent of blood. After one too many wild animals had enjoyed a meal of human flesh, the walls were put up. There was also a pervasive fear of the Sea of Eels, which surrounded the Bay of Biscane on the eastern side. Many believed sea serpents claimed that portion of the sea, and the serpents were blamed for hindering ship journeys to the Draconbane Mountains.

Even without the Sea of Eels to get through, few would likely have traveled to the Draconbane Mountains, as no one wanted to disturb the dragons. That is, if there were any dragons left. The fae had supposedly slain them all over five hundred years ago, but across the Sea of Eels to the east, the Draconbane Mountains still awaited. It was said fearsome beasts had taken up residence there when the dragons disappeared. Maeve had a sinking feeling that one of the shards was hidden in those mountains. The fae had not made her task easy.

Maeve was too weary to worry about such rumors. There was a hollowness in her gut and a blanket of discomfort hovered above her shoulders. She'd slept fitfully the last two nights and knew there were black circles around her eyes. A hot bath and warm belly might help her feel better, and with the gold she'd stolen, she could secure a room and hide until her rendezvous with Sandrine.

Prayers rose like swirling winds in Maeve's thoughts, but when she opened her mouth to say them, they dried like dust on her lips. She knew it was guilt that gnawed at her. It sat in the center of her being like a dark hole, sucking away peace and all hopes of happiness, leaving her with nothing. Nothing but gloom and despair at the darkness in her soul that she seemed unable to escape.

Once again, she'd added to her personal darkness by killing someone who did not need to be killed. A choice had been laid before her and, like always, she chose the easy way out, dealing death instead of mercy. Her future lay scrawled in front of her, sealed in stone. The darkness in her soul was what the fae preyed on. If she could not conquer it, she would be their prisoner forever.

Deep down, she knew why she'd given in. Standing victorious at the end of the battle, a quest, or a heist was what she lived for. Winning brought a rush of excitement that filled her like a cup brimming over with pleasure. The delight of it thrilled her, renewed her with the rebirth of conquest. But not today.

Shoulders slumped and heart crumbling with the guilt, Maeve crept through the gates of the outpost like a thief. She tilted her head to avoid meeting the eyes of those around her. They merely glanced her way, obviously noting her as a newcomer, but one who, like them, was armed to the teeth and simply there to meet someone, hide from the law, or conduct business. Whatever it was, they'd all done it before. This was the warrior and mercenaries' land of luxurious inns, flowing ale, heavy beer, sweet, intoxicating wine, and the ability to lie back, hide, relax, and forget.

Maeve's footsteps slowed, and she surveyed the path ahead of her. A mix of stone and wooden buildings from which traders shouted out their wares and duel masters called out bids for the fight that evening rose on either side of the winding road. Whores hung out of second-story windows, their bosoms spilling over their bodices as they made eyes at the men—and women—hoping for a romp of passion ending with a pouch of gold.

The outpost was a vibrant village, alive at all hours of the day and night and always filled with sound. It echoed with rough voices, drunken laughter, screams of passion, and the clatter of horse hooves and wagons against the cobblestones The stink of flesh, dung, and raw fish assaulted her nose the strongest, but underneath was the scent of beer and the delightful smell of meat being roasted. It would take a day to walk the outpost from end to end, and it would cost almost an entire pouch of coins to sample the delights awaiting those in need of a mental escape.

Boisterous cheering jolted Maeve out of her reverie. Toward the beginning of the village was its most popular attraction, the fighting rings. Warriors often went to duel one on one, practice their fighting skills, and get a taste for blood. The rules were simple. There was a fee to enter, and after a certain number of rounds, the winner would take away a pot of gold and bragging rights. Depending on what kind of duels they took part in—first blood, first broken bone, or to the death—they would also take a trophy that could be used to help gain their next meaningful employment.

Maeve's stomach heaved at the scent of blood, and she touched her belly in surprise. She used to enjoy the duels, both watching and taking part. There was something about the eager fever of the crowds and their lust for violence and blood that used to draw her. Now, as she turned away, heading farther into the outpost, she realized duels were the warriors' way of desensitizing their minds and spirits to the ugly reality of fighting. Perhaps the fae were correct. She'd done wrong and needed to atone for her sins. Would the Divine grant her forgiveness? Give her another chance to live a life without murderous intent?

Her fingers went to the golden collar around her neck. It hummed with heat, and a white spark made her snatch her fingers away. She'd do anything to get rid of it.

"Maeve?"

It sounded as if the wind had hushed her name. But there was a familiarity to it. The open spaces of the outpost angled off into rows of buildings with alleyways and wide streets covered in a combination of dust and sand. Maeve turned slowly, then backed up toward one of the alleyways. If someone recognized her, it would be wise to be on guard. In the alley, she could keep the wall at her back to avoid being unexpectedly stabbed. There was a reason the outpost was called the Village of the Lawless. The strong survived while the weak were often mugged, beaten, and left to die—unless they had allies.

"Maeve of Carn!" the voice shouted, and then she heard footsteps.

By the Divine! Had someone seen her leave Lord Sebastian's fortress? Ducking into the alley, Maeve pressed her body against the wall and put a hand to her sword. Sunlight still shone in the sky, but it was dim and cool inside the alley. Toward the end of the alley she saw a man stretched out, sleeping, but she decided he was too far away to be of harm. When she turned back, what she saw made her heart stop. Her fingers dropped from her hilt and her mouth trembled. She wanted to run, scream, and cry, all at once. Kneel on one knee and ask forgiveness. Her heart leaped and shattered in one instant, and she pressed her hands together to hold back the relentless wave of emotions.

It was him.

Caspian.

He walked toward her, confusion and questions dueling across his handsome face. He was a big man, half a foot taller than her, with hair the color of sunshine tied back from his face. The shadow of a beard crossed his dimpled jaw, but his face was free from scars, a wonder considering his lifetime of battle. But it was his soulful brown eyes, deep set and haunted, that had always struck Maeve.

She fell to her knees, head bowed as thirty days of pent-up emotions burst free and tears streamed down her cheeks. That familiar sensation washed over her like a jug of cool water poured over her head, refreshing her from the journey. Her fingertips tingled, and a warm glow settled in her belly. His presence made her feel as though she were wrapped in comfort, where no evil could touch her. She'd fought the feeling the first time she felt it, the connection to him, the yearning, and as she knelt in the dirt, she realized she was still fighting. All her life, especially after what had happened in Carn, she'd focused on fighting and pushing others away, always ending relationships and killing off connections after a job was done.

"Maeve." His hand touched her head, warm and comforting. "What happened? After the raid, I couldn't find you . . . I thought . . . It's been a full moon . . ."

Maeve's shoulders quaked, not with fear, but shame. It was his approval she burned for most, his admiration, even though she was headstrong and haughty when they quarreled. Their last fight, before she was taken by the fae, seemed foreign considering the predicament she found herself in now.

His fingers wrapped around her arms, and he pulled her to her feet. Using his knuckles, he gently tilted her face to his, brushing her tears away with the pads of his thumbs. "Whatever it is, you can tell me," he whispered, voice twisted with emotion.

Maeve bit her lip and shook her head. “I’m sorry,” she blurted out. “I’m so very sorry.”

Sliding her arms around his waist, she buried her head in his chest and held on as though he were the one thing that could save her from drowning. He smelled like the sea, a combination of salt and a fresh wind. The hardness of his armor pressed into her cheek, but beneath it there was warmth.

She inhaled, surprised at how much she’d missed him.

He returned the embrace, holding her tight, his chin resting on her head.

Maeve took one shuddering breath after the other, eyes squeezed tight as she tried to forget about the dungeon, the whip of the cruel fae, and the Master’s dark desires. The shards. Should she tell him about the quest? Could she drag him down with her?

“Maeve, you’re scaring me,” he murmured, stroking her back. “This is not like you. You are strong, brave, and I’ve never seen you shed a tear, not even when that overgrown worm bit you, or when that paladin wounded you during the raid at the citadel.”

Maeve nodded into his chest, although hope flittered away like petals on the wind. She wanted to stay in the warm safety of his arms, for it felt like the Master could not reach her there. Caspian had been like her, but he’d repented, changed his ways; he’d become a champion of the light, the Divine. He’d been right all along, and now she understood. Perhaps during her quest for the shards, she could speak with a priestess and ask about repentance. But how could she truly change her heart when anger sizzled in her very bones? It was built into her, into who she was. Could she rise above her past to become noble, like Caspian? A protector, a defender of righteousness?

Letting go, she met his gaze. When she tried to pull farther away, he dropped one arm, but kept the other around her waist.

"I was taken," she offered him, unable to hide from his searching gaze, "by the fae."

His jaw clenched and his brows lowered. A thunderous expression crossed his face. "What did they do to you?" he demanded.

Maeve flushed. "It is not what you think, they did not defile me that way, but . . . there is much to tell you." Regret crept into her voice. "I am sorry we quarreled. You were right, you've always been right."

Caspian sucked in a deep breath and glanced away. "Maeve. I . . ." He shook his head. "Come. I have a room at the Bawdy Sailor. We can discuss everything there, and I daresay you're in need of a tankard or two of ale."

One of his lips curved up, a shadow of his teasing grin. "Maeve, I thought you were lost to me. The Divine has blessed our paths to meet again, and for that I am thankful."

The gloom surrounding Maeve lessened, and her shoulders relaxed. They were in the outpost, of all places, but whenever she was with Caspian, she felt like she was home. The thought surprised her. Blushing, she glanced down the path and nodded. "I'd like that. It's been long since I had a drink."

"Good." He released her and they fell in step together.

"Why are you here?" Maeve asked him. "I expected you to

be on the mainland, or at least headed to the citadel or the wildlands. Why return to the Bay of Biscane?"

"I heard a rumor, and I had to be sure," Caspian said. "One of Lord Arnold's spies reported strange events taking place here. Shadows during moonlight, beasts drained of blood, and fortresses entered and searched, although it seemed nothing was taken, just destroyed. It's against the code here, and I wondered who could do such things. Especially here. Do we have an unknown enemy? And then last night, I saw that the watch fire of Lord Sebastian's tower was lit. Strange things are happening, and although it is not my responsibility, I am curious. Why target the warlords, and why now? The bay is rich with wealth, but there is enough for all."

A shiver went down Maeve's spine and her face flushed. She had answers for him, but would he like them? Would he help her figure out how to escape the fae? Lord Sebastian's words rang in her mind. Curses should not be broken. The fae should not get the shards, but how? How could she stop them?

A vision of the shard, of how the ethereal blue light had shone softly from the object, hung in her memory. It seemed so small, insignificant, just the length of her hand, and yet the potential chaos it could cause was inconceivable.

"I know why," Maeve said. "Caspian, there is much to tell you."

12

THE BAWDY SAILOR

Maeve hunched in a corner of the Bawdy Sailor, waiting while Caspian ordered from the bar. He had chosen the windowless corner wall. The inn was built into a series of connected buildings facing the street, with exits to the narrow alley that ran behind the row of buildings. It was a place where warriors could easily escape and thieves could hide in the shadows. The inside was loud, with men talking, a group of entertainers singing and carrying on, and the women from the brothel sneaking inside to try to woo men away to a night of lust and passion.

In the middle of the room was the bar, where frothy tankards of ale were brought forth and wine was poured. The barkeep sat behind it, perched on a stool, every so often hollering orders to the kitchen. A swinging door behind the bar connected to the kitchen, and a delightful fragrance filled the air, shutting out the hoppy, wheat-like smell of ale. If nothing else, the Bawdy Sailor was known for its pies: great flaky crusts stuffed with all manner of seafood, mostly thick cuts of white fish, and dripping with sweet gravy.

Maeve relaxed as she watched Caspian's broad back, his gray cloak tossed over one shoulder, arms crossed, and legs spread while he waited. That familiar stance that showed both total control and an alertness to any unexpected event that might crop up. She appreciated that about him, his keen sense of preparedness and protectiveness. Yet . . . should she tell him about the Seven Shards of Erinyes? If he were on a quest, she did not wish to add to his burden, and yet, there was no one else she could or would ask. She cursed, wondering why she'd allowed herself to have so few friends. True, the life of a warrior did not encourage friendship, but she had always held herself away, afraid of getting too close to those whom she would only fight with for a season. With Caspian, everything had been different. The way his presence had affected her made her want to stay, to gain his confidence and lean into him, no matter how short their time together might be. When he turned around, two brimming mugs in his hands, her resolve melted. She was too selfish to push him away.

He slid into the seat across from her, leaned over the table —more like a shelf, with only a foot of space between them— clinked his mug against hers, and winked. "To finding each other." He smiled, his voice filled with warmth.

Maeve wrapped her fingers around the cool mug and drank, the frothy liquid sliding down her throat before buzzing and tingling in her belly. The tightness in her muscles faded and she met Caspian's concerned gaze. There was a wary flicker in his eyes, but it disappeared as his fingers brushed against her bare arm. "Maeve, tell me what happened."

To give herself time to decide where to begin, she took another sip, enjoying the sensation the dark liquid gave her. Thirty days without proper food and drink; she had missed it.

Caspian's gaze dropped to her neck, and his eyes went dark. "Maeve. Is that what I think it is?"

Tears pricked, and she hastily blinked them away. A flush covered her neck as her fingers touched the collar. It was a mark, a sign of a slave, as insignificant as it seemed. She wished she'd worn her hair down to cover it. If Caspian noticed what it was, surely others would.

"It was that night," she spoke low, her words intended for his ears only. "After we finished fighting the slavers. I remember the moon was high, and I'd fought on, leaving the others behind. I know you'd warned me before about going off alone without someone to watch my back, but the slavers were dead and the prisoners were free. If someone sprang up on me, I thought I could take them. I was retracing my steps and leaving the prisons when I heard a low keening sound, a cry. I thought it was another prisoner, so I turned around to re-enter the building, and that's when they attacked. There were four of them, as silent as though they'd stepped from the very shadows themselves. I felt claws sink into my arm, and before I could bring my sword up the collar went around my throat. I . . . I couldn't breathe—I couldn't fight. My strength faded, and . . ."

The words tasted like dry ash in her throat. She trailed off as the memory of that night brought back a whirl of emotions. Panic, frustration, and shame shifted into something else. Anger. Fury. How dare the fae treat her like a slave, a pawn to use to fulfill their own wishes? Another part of her knew she deserved it, but she couldn't remember why. It hadn't been her first encounter with the Master, and she knew her mercenary life was somehow because of him. But she couldn't remember if she'd made a deal with him when she was young or if there was another reason. Something to do with the destruction of Carn?

She took another sip, waiting for the intoxication, the out-of-control euphoria, to ascend. "They locked me up in the Dungeon of the Damned for thirty days. That's why you could not find me. I did not leave because we argued . . . I was taken and held against my will."

He listened, nodding along, though his eyes were still dark with anger. "If I had known—"

Maeve held up a hand. "You could have done nothing. Not if you value your soul. They forced me to make a deal. Caspian." She held his gaze. "I made a deal with the Master. If I find and deliver the Seven Shards of Erinyes within seven months, he will set me free."

Caspian's breath caught, his face went white, and his hands balled into fists around his empty mug. He set his jaw and shook his head. "Maeve, I should have been honest with you sooner. You can't—"

"I can." Maeve interrupted, almost surprised by the firmness in her tone. "They sent me a scholar named Sandrine, who knows the location of all seven shards. I've already found one here in the bay, which explains the odd behavior you've heard of. The fae are one step ahead of me at all times, even though they only have those brief hours of moonlight each month."

Caspian turned, a frown on his face as he examined the room. "Where is the scholar now?"

"I am supposed to meet her at the Wildling Inn, tomorrow night. She will share our next location. Caspian, I don't have a sense of this mission, this quest. I don't know whether I should trust Sandrine. She's old and angry. I don't know whether she works for them or if she's simply a tool, like myself."

Caspian's fist slammed into the table, making the mugs jump and resettle on the wooden surface. The noise was lost in the din of the tavern. "Maeve, this quest, this task—it goes against the Divine, the laws of nature, everything. You must escape."

Maeve leaned closer. "I agree. I . . ." She paused. What would he think of her? She was damned, but she wanted, nay, needed him by her side through this. With a sigh, she related what Sandrine had told her and shared her encounter with Lord Sebastian.

He listened, fists clenched, a muscle in his jaw twitching.

She finished, barely daring to breathe as her final words left her lips. "I have it, Caspian. The first shard. But I don't know what to do. I have to continue on with Sandrine, but I need a plan, a way to turn this around on the fae. I don't know what they intend to do once freed, but we can assume they will walk this world and corrupt it with their soullessness. I know I haven't cared much for others, but now I see, I understand what it's like to have something precious snatched away. I want my freedom, I want my strength back, but at what cost?"

Caspian sighed and scrubbed at his face. "Maeve, this is a puzzle. We need more information from the scholar."

"We?" Maeve raised her eyebrows, careful to keep the joy from showing on her face. She had succeeded in tempting him.

He leaned across the table, his eyes flickering to the collar. He touched it with two fingers and then lifted his eyes to hers. They were intent. She recognized that look; the look of someone who would not be argued with. The heat of his breath brushed her lips when he spoke. "Maeve, regarding our disagreement, our quarrel, I must bring it up again. You see, I've been looking for a quest, a true quest, something beyond our . . . my . . . warring nature that wouldn't leave a blot of darkness on my soul. I want to do something beyond accumulating wealth, something purposeful, that matters beyond this life and makes a difference. I want to do something noble."

Maeve slumped in her chair. Did he have his own quest? Did it mean he wasn't going to come with her? Caspian had everything. He was a warlord with faithful warriors who respected him and followed his every command. Strife and competition among his warriors was rare. During the year Maeve had spent with them, she hadn't had to deal with the kind of cutthroat mercenaries that she'd met during her service to other warlords. But when Caspian changed his stance, he'd lost some warriors who weren't ready to follow him on his unusual path, on his mission to set things right and grow in the grace of the Divine. She was aware of the attraction between them, but Caspian had seemed determined to ruin it with his selflessness, with his desire to set the world right. However, she understood now. After all he'd seen, why shouldn't he try to make things right, even though it was impossible? And yet, despite the conflict in her heart, she forced the uneasy feelings down and listened, *really* listened, to his words.

"What I've done in the past, what *we've* done in the past, was wrong. I am done with the old life and our old ways; I've spoken with a priest of the Divine. It is a quarrelsome point between us, I am aware, but I need you to hear me, and know this. Despite our past, our history, I care deeply for you, more than you know. I would see you free again, and this collar destroyed. I would thwart the plans of the fae, not because they affect you, but they affect the world. So, I am coming with you. I doubt the fae will object to more warriors joining in your quest, and should they ask, tell them I expect payment in gold. We don't know enough, but there has to be a way to stop them and gain your freedom. We need to start with the scholar; she knows much more than we do, and perhaps there is a way."

Maeve flinched and focused on the ale as Caspian pulled back, giving her space, allowing her to think, breathe, and consider a response without overwhelming her with his presence. Desperation clawed at her—she needed a friendly face during her quest—and his words were not surprising to her. She had already sensed how much he cared, and their chemistry was palpable, but the fact that he would come with her both excited and frightened her.

Finishing her ale, she drummed her fingers on the table.

"Caspian . . ." She hesitated, torn. He was coming with her because he cared, but also because it would set his mind—his soul—at ease. He would fulfill a quest, and in stopping the fae, do something noble. Something she could be part of. All the pieces fit. Stop the fae, gain freedom, stay with her best friend, and earn redemption for her soul. Was she ready?

A lad walked up just then with two steaming seafood pies. Flakes of crust drifted onto the old wood of the table as he set the plates down in front of them. He was young and skinny with a pockmarked face, but his eyes were alight, glimmering with youthful anticipation of a bright life ahead of him. He clasped his hands in front of his chest and gave a bow. "More ale?" he asked.

Caspian flipped him a coin. "Aye, make it a double."

Maeve's anxious thoughts faded as she bit into the pie. Flavors of fish and crustacean, all baked in a thick white sauce, melted in her mouth. Food. She had not tasted such delicious food in over a month. She stopped shy of letting a groan escape her mouth. For the next few minutes, a silence stretched between them as she spooned mouthful after mouthful down her throat.

Two more rounds of ale were brought and Maeve sat back, buzzing from a slight intoxication and smiling at Caspian, who ate and drank vigorously across from her. The drink filled her mind, pushing out all other thoughts and concerns. The seven shards faded into the background until at last, when she stood to relieve herself, the world seemed to pitch and dance.

Caspian gripped her forearm to steady her.

A giggle escaped her lips. Her hand came up, flat against

his chest where she felt the quick rhythm of his heartbeat. Thud. Thud. Thud. Against her hand. Blood rose to her cheeks. "Caspian. I—"

He shook his head, steering her away from the table. "Come. Let's get you cleaned up."

13
ROOM IN A TAVERN

Maeve stepped from the bath and pulled on her shift. She felt clearheaded after bathing, although the buzzing sensation of ale lingered somewhere in the back of her mind. When she came around the curtain, Caspian was already in bed.

He lay on his back, one arm flung above his head, the other stretched out. Was it an invitation? Maeve felt bold. Reckless. This could end so soon, whenever the fae chose to activate her collar and drag her back down to their Underground. Trailing her wet braid over one shoulder, she sat down on the bed, her back to him.

A sigh left his lips. Encouragement? She lay back, barely daring to breathe, tucked her head onto his shoulder, pressed her chest against his side, and curled her legs next to his. His arm came down, pressing her close, protecting her. Maeve reached her arm around his hard, toned stomach, holding on, relieved to be somewhere safe. Finally. The long days and nights of her imprisonment drifted away. They'd left her raw with anger, starved for emotion, and frightened of the future. With Caspian, she could finally let that go, let the nightmares drift away, and rest. But there was still a question that left her uneasy. Six months ago, Caspian had suddenly become concerned with the darkness in his soul. Why?

"Tell me about the priest," she whispered. "What did he say about the Divine?"

Caspian lifted his blond head and eyed her. "Are you sure?"

"When I was taken, I did not know what to expect. The fae are cruel, and they put me in a hole. I starved, and I prayed, daily. Even though the fae seek to use my abilities for their own dark deeds, I felt as though my prayers were heard. Yet, I deserve nothing. I know what I've done. Tales say the only reason the fae can capture someone is if they see the darkness in their soul, and everything I've done—even some things we've done together—have created that darkness. I'm not sure if I'm ready to make it go away, but I can't keep on feeling like this, living like this, and giving darkness a hold in my life. I don't know if I am ready to act, but I can listen. Without arguing this time."

Caspian's deep brown eyes held hers, and something passed through them. Maeve dropped her gaze and tucked her head firmly against his shoulder to avoid the questions that lay there. It was easy to bare her soul with Caspian, sometimes too easy.

"Months ago, a misfortune befell me," Caspian began, his voice slow and rich. "I realized I had to change my ways or risk losing everything. I went to the Temple of the Divine in

Isdrine and spent thirty days there. It was enlightening, but what I learned there isn't something that can easily be shared. I don't know how to explain it, for it's more of a sensation, a feeling, a knowing in my head and heart. You want to hear, to listen, to understand, but understanding something as powerful as guidance from the Divine isn't as simple as sharing my experience. You must seek, discover, and experience for yourself. The priests and the priestesses cannot make you whole, they cannot give light to your dark heart; you must make the choice to have faith and change. I suspect what you feel right now is guilt for the things we've done. We killed people, allowed the wrong people to come to power, and destroyed families. We were lost in our lust for wealth, for passion, and for purpose, but when you take the time to dwell on all things holy, an understanding will come over you. And that journey you will have to take alone."

Maeve lay still and a cool sensation of numbness came over her. Even with Caspian right there, she felt alone, as though the warmth of his body could not touch her. Could not pull her back from the brink and redeem her. After a moment, she realized he'd fallen silent, waiting for her response. Her thoughts muddled and converged, and her limbs went heavy. Exhaustion crept around her, pulling her eyelids shut, dragging her down to a slumber of nothingness. "I don't understand," she whispered.

"I felt the same way when the priest spoke to me. We are warriors. Give us a plan and we can follow through, but spirituality and faith are ambiguous to us. We don't understand the spiritual aspect of life because we are so focused on the physical. That's why you have to discover the revelation yourself. I can tell you what it feels like, but you will never understand until you have that connection, that meeting with the Divine."

Maeve paused. "Meet the Divine? But that is impossible. The celestials are far above us in their paradise. Why would they pay any attention to this world and races who are so far beneath their notice?"

"The Divine is not as far away as you think. You said it yourself. While you were in the dungeon, you prayed for deliverance and your prayers were heard. You have many doubts, but you also have the most important trait. Faith."

Maeve considered his words, and yet they still made little sense to her. She opened her mouth, but his words floated to her ears before hers could escape her mouth.

"Sleep, Maeve. You've been through a lot and deserve a night of rest before we face thc many challenges to come."

There was a light pressure on her forehead, and then her eyelids closed and she faded away.

She floated in nothingness before sinking deeper into a dreamless sleep. Sleep rode her like the waves of the Sea of Sorrows, pushing her back up to the shallows where dreams of the child and the screaming mother plagued her mind. She woke, sweating, heart racing, and alone.

Maeve was lying on her back, taking deep breaths to calm her panic, when she noticed a blue glimmer out of the corner of her eye. Heart in her throat, she tilted her head back and saw him standing by the arched window.

Caspian had lit a candle, which gave off a small pool of light, but it was the item in his hand that gave Maeve pause. It was the shard. *Her* shard. The hairs on her neck stood up, and her body went rigid. What was he doing with it? And why would he go through her things?

He turned it in his hands, examining it from every angle before lightly placing it back in the box. It closed under his fingers; the lock made a light clicking noise. Standing, he dropped it with her armor and padded back toward the bed. His face was pale in the wan light and he scratched his chin. "Maeve?" he asked.

Maeve bolted upright, glaring, a thousand questions rising on her tongue. "What were you doing with it?" she demanded.

His eyes narrowed. "Does anyone else know about this quest? Is there anyone else who might search for the shards?"

Maeve swallowed down her fleeting anger. "Just the fae. Why?"

Caspian sat down on the edge of the bed, his hand resting near her thigh. "The fae gave you seven months to complete the task, an impossible task, of finding these lost celestial relics. They were careful and sent you a guide, but what if you're not the only one they sent out? The fae can appear once a month during the full moon, but they can use their portals to go anywhere they desire. It stands to reason this is not the first time they have sent someone after the shards, and it is not impossible for one or two to appear from time to time. Maeve, it . . ."

He paused and looked away, his jaw tightening as if he were considering something. Then his shoulders slumped and he turned back to her. "One of the shards turned up in the citadel in the king's treasury. I'm not sure if it is still there, but if the fae knew about it, they could easily find it and take it during one of their full moon rampages. Once they get all seven shards, you will be of no use to them, and we don't know what they will do. Time is working against us. You assumed they had no shards, but I believe they might have one or two, perhaps even a few, and you were sent on this quest to get the last ones for them. Which means time is working against us. We may only have three or four months to come up with a way to circumvent their plans."

Maeve rested her hands on her thighs, her foot tapping against the bedding and her fingers drumming. "You could be right, but why tell me this? And why now? Just because you saw a shard one time doesn't mean they have them all."

"I can taste it in the air. Something is off, wrong. Warriors have disappeared before, but the last three disappearances I can think of happened during the full moon. There is a restlessness in the air, a shift, and you know I always make a plan in case things go awry. I could be wrong, but my gut tells me I am right."

Maeve bit her lip and stared at the candle flickering and sputtering against the night wind. She squared her shoulders. "There is only one course of action. We need to find out what the scholar knows."

14
OUTPOST

Maeve's wariness of Caspian fell away the next day. The idea of him sifting through her things and picking the lock of the box that held the shard had sent pinpricks of doubt through her. Yet that morning, Caspian purchased a hearty breakfast for them and offered to follow her lead, and also apologized for upsetting her the previous night with his sudden idea. Because of their history, Maeve decided to push it aside. Having the big, bulky warrior at her side was a balm, leaving her with the sensation that they were invincible. Yet, time and again, her fingers went to the golden collar around her neck, each touch a reminder that her life was not hers anymore.

Striding through the outpost with Caspian was like old times. Almost. His presence was big, strong, and between the two of them they could outfight and outstrategize anyone and anything they came into contact with. Between breaths,

Maeve whispered thanks to the Divine for guiding their paths together.

After breakfast, Caspian sent a raven to his warriors with word of his whereabouts and latest quest. He noted to Maeve that, as they found more information, there might come a time when they needed his warriors to rally. Maeve outwardly agreed with him, but inwardly decided it would be too risky. It would be hard to convince Sandrine that she needed hired warriors to help find the six remaining shards—if there even were six shards left to find.

The outpost was crowded, and despite the proximity of the town to the sea, the sun beat down with too much warmth. Maeve wiped sweat from her forehead and toyed with the idea of removing her crown, but brushed away the thought and strode on, ignoring the heat.

Caspian set a quick pace, weaving through the alleys and broad streets as though he knew the outpost well. They'd never come to the Village of the Lawless together, but Maeve wondered if it was a town he'd frequented in his past. A past of violence, bloodshed, and victory. A past he'd left behind. His words of last night nagged at her. She'd have to find out for herself? What did that mean? How could she possibly discover what he had?

They left the buildings behind and continued onto a dirt road that led to the sea. Hills rose on either side, creating valleys that pointed down to the sandy beach and the sparkling waves of the deep sapphire sea below them.

Maeve lifted her face to the wind and inhaled, tasting freedom that teased at her, just out of reach. Maeve lightly ran her fingers over the collar, wondering if the fae could see and track her. Then a thought jolted through her like a bolt of lightning, so sudden and shocking she gave a sharp cry. If she could destroy the collar, she'd be free from the fae.

Caspian spun to face her, one hand out to steady her while the other fell to his hilt. "What is it?" His concerned eyes sought hers.

"It's no danger," she assured him. "I just had a thought. All this time we've been considering how to thwart the plans of the fae. I know we need to stop them from getting the shards, but you came to help me too. I just need this collar removed, and they won't be able to force me to help them."

Caspian's eyes fell to the collar. "The collar was likely created by dark magic. It will be difficult to release you from it without causing physical harm."

Maeve's face warmed under his gaze. Why did he dash her hopes so quickly? Didn't he want her to be free? "I am no stranger to physical harm, and I'll do whatever it takes to regain my freedom."

Caspian ran a hand along his jaw and glanced at the sea. "I've come across some situations now and again where someone was bound with dark magic. If we try to break you free of the collar, it will probably kill you. And Maeve, I'd rather not gamble with your life. If we find a way, we will take it, but I would not have you mangled and disfigured because we tried to use something we do not fully understand."

Maeve scowled. "It was just an idea," she said through gritted teeth.

"A good idea." Caspian touched her shoulder lightly. "But a risk we will only take if we have to."

Anger flared within, but Maeve pushed it away. Her

temper was strong, and at times she felt the fire within, all-consuming, driving her to react, strike out, use violence to gain what she wanted. But she knew there was a balance, and with the collar diminishing her strength, she had to be patient.

"Maeve?" Caspian's light touch at her elbow brought her back to the present. "This is it. How do you want to do this?"

Squaring her shoulders, Maeve stared up at the inn. It slumped on the edge of a hill, a weather-beaten two-story building that had seen better days. The entire building looked as though it would tumble down the hill, scattering shingles and tile into the sea and sand-swept meadow. The once white walls were gray, their edges softened by wind, rain, mud, and sand. Persistent wildflowers cropped up around the edges of the inn, adding color to the surrounding meadow.

Maeve frowned. Why had Sandrine chosen the most run-down place on the bay to meet? She sighed. "Let me do all the talking."

Caspian slowed. "I will follow your lead."

An odd phrase coming from his lips. Usually it was Caspian who did the leading and Maeve who backed up his plans, improvising as needed.

The sea wind ruffled the wildflowers and a slight hissing sound came to Maeve's ears. She stopped in her tracks, tilted her head, and cast an anxious glance at the sea. That sound. She'd heard it before, hadn't she?

"What is it?" Caspian turned toward the sea, scanning it before turning his gaze back on Maeve.

"I thought—" She shrugged away the thought. "It was nothing."

But it wasn't. She heard it again. A slight shifting in the waves, a rustle, a cry. Something was there and yet not there. A ripple went down her spine, and the door to the inn flew open.

A group of sailors poured out, their faces red and ruddy as they stumbled down the hill, making for the docks that lay just below where a group of boats were laid out on the sand. The men looked grubby, their skin was tanned and leathery, and their faces were hard. Maeve saw the whites of their eyes as they passed, a silent march down to the shore.

Caspian gave a low whistle after they had passed. "They dare to fish in those waters . . ." He shook his head.

Maeve glanced toward the shore. "What's wrong with the water?"

Caspian's brow wrinkled. "You don't know?"

The light wind ruffled his dark hair and a few strands came loose from his topknot. "The scholar will be able to explain the full history, for I am not sure what happened. Across the sea are the Draconbane Mountains—"

"I know," Maeve interrupted. From glancing at maps, she'd seen the layout of the country, the islands to the southwest, the king's citadel on the western coast butting up against the King's Sea. To the south and east of the citadel were obscure and unusual cities, towns, and kingdoms—however small the kingdoms ended up being. The Bay of Biscane lay north of the citadel, and across from the Bay of Biscane to the east were the Draconbane Mountains. After the fae defeated the dragons, no one went to the mountains, as some still believed a few of the dragons had escaped the fae and dwelled in the heights of Draconbane. In addition, rumors had it that the soil in the mountain range was putrid—ruined from fire—the mountains were impossible to scale, the storms were unceasing, and dark creatures dwelled there, morphed and twisted by their environment. The unconfirmed tales spread quickly, and the fear was enough to keep most away. Those who had taken on wagers to explore the unknown territory had never reappeared, and it was assumed they had found demons in Draconbane and given their souls to the reaper.

Caspian frowned at the interruption, or perhaps it was the sea. His gaze returned to the shining waters and Maeve shivered as she waited for him to continue. "It's the eels," he admitted. "They fill the sea, and while hunting them is a sport, many have fallen to their deaths when the giant eels appear."

Maeve raised an eyebrow and poked his shoulder. "Caspian? It is not like you to be frightened of anything, especially a sea creature such as an eel."

Caspian brushed loose strands of blond hair back from his face. "It is not fear. I've seen them before. Leviathans that come out of the deep, bigger than a ship, their bodies thick and impossible to pierce, not with spear or sword. Nay, it's not fear that warns me, but an appreciation of life."

Maeve's gut twisted, and she glanced from the sea to Caspian. A sinking feeling nagged at her. She tried to push the thought away, but it remained. What if her next quest was to go into the west? To cross the Sea of Eels and go into the depths of the Draconbane Mountains to find the second shard? It would be like the fae to send her into a wild land, the untried unknown to find something they could only search for twelve times a year. Would she be able to find it? Or would she become another useless slave, falling to her death while the fae captured another soul with darkness in their heart and forced that individual to do their dirty work?

Again, her hand went to her collar. If it was removed, she would be free, and then, like Caspian, she could focus on blocking the fae from achieving their goal of putting together all seven shards. She glanced at him again, with his thick arms, his set jaw, the angular curve of his chiseled face. His presence was a beacon of solace, and now that he was with her, a yearning rose, so strong at times she could not ignore it. Her throat went thick, and she blinked hard. A wave of exhaustion cascaded around her, and she whispered, "Caspian, what if . . . ?"

His eyes met hers, emotion hidden behind them. His face went still as realization dawned. "Maeve. I did not mean . . ."

"I don't know where they will send me next," she muttered, her words coming out harder than she intended. "You are free to go if you wish it. I asked for your help because it will be impossible to do alone, and better with your company, but if you are too frightened of the possibilities—"

"Maeve!" Caspian raised his voice, cutting her off. He gripped her arm before she could dash up the path toward the inn and gently pulled her back to face him. "Maeve, I did not think. There are many dangers here, but I will not let you face them alone. If we go, we go together, even if it is into darkness."

Maeve stared, at a loss for words. He would do this for her? Selfishness fled. "Caspian, I only thought of myself when

I asked you to join. You don't have to be caught up in this nightmare with me."

He opened his mouth, breath hissing between his teeth. "Maeve. Don't say such things. If it is a nightmare, we will handle it together, as we have done the past year. I lost you once, and I will not lose you again."

Maeve studied his stoic expression, trying to find what was hidden beneath it all. She suspected—aside from their ability to work well together—there was something else, but she dared not name it. She opened her mouth to respond, but he smiled, shook his head, and continued toward the inn.

15
Wildling Inn

The dining hall of the Wildling Inn looked just as bad as the outside, neglected and uncared for. Sand covered the floor and dirt piled up in the corner. Cobwebs hung from the ceiling and windows stood open, letting in a mix of fresh air while expelling the strange odor that clung to the room. The inn was aptly named. The characters that crossed the threshold were slipshod, bedraggled, and unkempt, with beady eyes and hands ready to fly to their knives at the slightest offense.

Maeve led the way into the hall, eyes scanning the occupants and landing on Sandrine. She sat alone at a round table, spooning what looked like watery gruel into her mouth. Her dark hair was pulled back into a tight bun. She sat on the edge of her seat, one leg jiggling up and down as though she were impatient, or nervous.

Crossing her arms, Maeve marched up to the table and

waited, towering above Sandrine, the shadow of Caspian behind her.

Sandrine's eyes shot up, and the barest hint of surprise registered on her face, quickly covered by a scowl. Peering past Maeve, she pointed an accusing finger. "Who is he?"

Maeve lifted her chin, eyes narrowed. "I had to hire some help. Due to the nature of our quest, it's not enough for me to go in alone, without help. I need extra muscle to ensure the safety of our items. I have worked with him before and he will be content to be paid in gold."

The spoon in Sandrine's hand clattered on the table, and she shoved thc bowl of gruel away. Standing, she yanked up her pack and glared at Maeve. All pretense of friendliness, if it had ever been there, was gone. "Maeve. A private word." She pointed farther into the inn, toward a staircase hidden in shadows. Then her eyes locked on Caspian's face, and she sniffed. "Hired muscle indeed. Wait for a moment like a good watchdog while we discuss."

Maeve flinched at the term: watchdog. How could Caspian stand there and take it? But he played his part well, and not a word left his lips. He sat down at the table, pretending to be dumb, while Maeve followed Sandrine toward the shadows. She glanced back at Caspian, mouthing the word "sorry," but if he saw his expression did not change.

The rafters above squeaked, and the air smelled musty and moldy. Maeve wrinkled her nose, reminding herself that nothing was worse than the dungeon. Sandrine led her to a corner next to the stairway, which curved upward into gray light.

"Are you daft?" Sandrine scoffed. "What does that man

mean to you? Who is he? Because whoever he is, you are giving him a death sentence."

Maeve leaned away from Sandrine's bad breath and the rehearsed words came tumbling out, "I told you earlier, I hired him to help. He's a warrior I've worked with before. He's loyal and does well with a blade, he can follow directions, and as long as he's paid in gold, he will not interfere with the quest nor try to take the shards for himself."

Maeve's thoughts rang as the lies slipped from her lips. They were harder to say than she'd expected, and for a moment her heart quailed. This was dangerous. Should she tell Caspian to run? If he were harmed or even slain because of this quest . . . she shivered and rubbed her arms, suddenly uncomfortable. The situation was terrible, but what else could she do? If she sent him away, he'd likely follow her. For him, there was more at stake than her freedom—he also felt a responsibility, a duty to the world and a calling from the Divine.

Miserable, Maeve looked away from Sandrine's penetrating gaze.

The scholar clearly did not trust her tale. She humphed and shifted from foot to foot. "You think this is a game, don't you? You've never interacted with the fae. You don't know what they are like, what they will take from you."

A flood of memories rushed to Maeve's mind. Her childhood. A kingdom by the sea. The loving voice of her mother and father, and then those bright tones that turned commanding. A sea of darkness overwhelming Carn, and then the earthquake, shaking the buildings down to their foundations, and then the invasion. An army had come with the quake. She had flashes of soldiers striking down everything in their way, burning, pillaging, destroying. She recalled running, fleeing among screams and shouts and the anger that spurred violence. And then came the memory she repressed most often, the one that made her shiver and if she thought too hard, gave her nightmares. She pressed her lips together, avoiding Sandrine's eyes, almost bodily turning away. She knew the fae, what they were capable of, what the Master was capable of. It was not her first encounter with him. That's how he knew how to collar and control her.

Their history went back further than she cared to remember. Emotions from her first encounter with the fae washed over her; the beauty and mystery of it, then the terror, threats, and empty promises. Finally, she had been left alone, freed to live as she wished. Warrior for hire became her stance, to focus on violence and to forget what it was like to be controlled.

She hadn't had faith then, for the Divine had not seen fit to intervene with her downfall, but now she realized she'd never asked for help. She'd assumed the Divine would not want to help someone like her. The Divine was not like her, and the ways of the Divine were not ways she could understand. She'd clung to her preconceived expectations and she had been wrong. The Divine did not think the way she thought. She had to adjust her mindset, but it was difficult.

"Ah." Sandrine's single syllable startled her, and she turned back to face the scholar. "He is someone you care about." Sandrine dusted off her palms. "You are planning something, aren't you? Something to surprise the fae and get back at them for what they did to you. Don't say I didn't warn you, but I won't interfere if you plan on stopping them, as long as it does not break our quest."

Maeve clenched and unclenched a fist, the familiar fire stirring in her belly. She needed a fight to sate her anger and frustration. She wished the inn would be taken over, or that a bar fight would break out, anything to keep her temper in check. A muscle in her chin jerked and her gaze went slack. She focused again on the scholar. "Where is our next destination?"

She almost held her breath waiting for the answer, knowing what it would be.

Sandrine smirked, as if she enjoyed delivering bad news. "I've prepared for our voyage across the sea to the Draconbane Mountains. We are going to the lair of the last dragon, and there you will find the second shard."

Maeve stilled her breath as her worst fears were realized. Not there. She backed away, shaking her head. "Do the fae want us to succeed, or do they want us to die before we have begun?"

Sandrine tutted. "I do not pretend to know their ways. Gather your warrior, lover, whoever he is. You can drop the pretense with me. He is solely your responsibility, but next moon, the fae will surely take him from you."

Maeve scowled, but Sandrine had already turned around, heading toward the exit. "Wait! What preparations? Where are you going?"

She'd assumed they would stay the night at the Wildling Inn, but from Sandrine's gait she'd assumed wrong.

Darting out of the shadows, Maeve returned to the table where Caspian sat.

He half rose. "What happened?"

Maeve glanced to Sandrine's retreating form and bit back her confession. If Caspian knew the secrets she kept, of her prior engagement with the fae, with the Master, he'd leave, thinking the worst of her. After Draconbane she'd explain, tell him what she remembered from her past, although all the pieces did not fit together. There were still gaps in her memory, things she could not recall. Why hadn't she returned to Carn? Why hadn't she tried to make sense of her past? She knew why—she'd been too young....painful—but she felt now as if her past might hold the answers they sought.

"It is as I thought." She beckoned for him to join her, and they glided from the inn. "Sandrine has arranged everything, and we are going to the Draconbane Mountains. She also warned me of something." This part Caspian had to hear, to understand, even though he would not relent. He was a hardened warrior, smart, and would not be swayed away from any battle. "The fae may come for you during the next full moon."

"If they do, it will be no surprise," he reassured her.

They left the inn, almost bumping into Sandrine, who stood just outside, hands on her hips, glaring down at the sea.

"You must be our guide," Caspian addressed her in light tones. "I am Caspian, a warrior—"

Sandrine sniffed and waved a hand, brushing his words away. "Don't pretend you don't know what this is about. I warn you, if you attempt to steal any shards, I personally will have your head, and I won't use my healing abilities to restore it to your body."

Caspian's initial surprise gave way to a rueful grin. He nudged Maeve. "She has wit. I like her already."

Sandrine rolled her eyes. "We may run out of provisions long before we reach the mountains, but there is no time for delays."

Maeve glanced toward the waves as she followed Sandrine. "How will we cross? Surely you know about the eels?"

Sandrine glowered. "Less talk, girl. I've said it before and I'll say it again. I will tell you *what* you need to know *when* you need to know it, and not a moment before. Useless chattering will change nothing. You forget, I am much older, and I have been in the service of the fae a long time. I know what power knowledge has, and I do not intend to share what I know with the likes of you."

"Not even to take down the fae?" Maeve blurted out.

Sandrine snorted. "If I thought that was likely, I would share everything I have."

Caspian touched Maeve's shoulder, his eyes warning her against saying anything else.

Sandrine led the silent party downhill, rounding the boulders toward the sandy shoreline. The boats from earlier had been removed, and in the distance, Maeve saw dots on the horizon, brave sailors fishing for eels, which would sell at a high price in the market. As life-threatening as it was, Maeve noted it was not much different from her life as a warrior for hire. Everyone had their vices and different things they were good at. Why did she judge how they preferred to spend their time or make their coin?

They continued down the shore as the sun set behind them, casting rays of glory across the waters, a sacred incantation of honor between sky and sea, like lovers joining to kiss each other. Such magnificence was lost on Maeve, however, and her heart thudded harder as they rounded the bend. An odd-shaped boat bobbed on the waters in front of them. Maeve opened her mouth, but Sandrine quickened her pace, heading straight for it.

16
SEA OF EELS

Maeve watched the sea as she followed Sandrine and Caspian toward the strange ship. The water was quiet, still, with no hints of shadows or devious souls hidden under the surface. The mirrorlike waters reflected the aging sunlight, a hint of promise, a whisper of hope. Hope of what? Maeve could not say. Out of the corner of an eye, she glanced at Sandrine, who had not slowed down as she made long strides toward the ship bobbing on the surface. If it could be called a ship. It was long, narrow, and appeared more like a floating log than anything else.

"Why is the ship shaped like that?" Maeve asked, more curious than frightened by it.

Contrary to her usual attitude, Sandrine did not sniff or offer a snide remark. She instead answered in a brusque and straightforward manner. "There are few warriors who are willing to cross this sea, and those who do demand a hefty fee. The brothers—Ingram and Imer—offered us passage across the sea in their closed ship. They claim it is impervious to any damage, but we shall see. If our luck holds, we will cross without issue. If it doesn't . . ." She crossed herself. "The eels take us. They are less dangerous than where we are going."

Maeve decided to dig for more information, using stupidity as an excuse to ask more questions. "Less dangerous? I thought we were going to the Draconbane Mountains? All the dragons are long dead, aren't they?"

"You assume too much. If you would know the truth, you must find out for yourself," Sandrine scolded.

"The brothers . . ." Caspian murmured.

Maeve noted his lowered eyebrows and hung back, falling in step beside him. "What is it?"

His hand dropped to his sword hilt. "I've had dealings with them before that went awry. Be on guard."

Maeve dropped her tone. "What dealings?"

Caspian's lips tightened, and his dark eyes narrowed. "Let's just say we did not leave on good terms."

Maeve's fingers tapped her sword hilt as a thrill rippled through her like a bolt of lightning during a storm. "If they try anything . . ."

"Ah." Caspian touched her arm, brushing her fingers away from her steel. "Remember, we need them to cross the sea, so we will stay on opposite sides of that boat . . . contraption . . . thing. No fights."

Maeve glared at him. "You are growing soft, aren't you? No fights? If they start something you have a right to defend yourself."

The corner of Caspian's mouth tugged back into a slight

grin. "Oh, Maeve," he sighed. "You've always been a fiery one. But no, we will start nothing now."

Sandrine's dry voice cut through their conversation. "Are you two done making plans yet? Moonlight won't wait, and neither will the brothers. Unless you'd like to pay their fee to move your feet faster?"

They walked up to the object that bobbed in the water. The outside had been sealed and painted with tar to keep it afloat, while there were two small round windows near the side facing the sea. Realization dawned on Maeve as she gazed at it. The ship had been made to look like a sea eel.

Sandrine led them around to the side where a rectangular opening had been cut, creating what looked like a narrow plank for them to walk on. Standing in the odd doorway was a rugged man, tall and slim with dark eyes, a mustache, a broad hat on his head, and sagging boots on his feet. He was dressed in black with accents of red embroidered across his tunic. One of his eyes was covered with an eye patch.

Maeve's fingers went again to her sword hilt. No wonder Caspian had spoken grimly of the brothers. They were pirates.

The man's gaze went from Sandrine to Maeve and Caspian. His jaw tightened. "Warlords? You must pay double for them. And no steel onboard."

Rage rose like vomit in Maeve's throat, but Sandrine raised a hand, halting any impulsive move on Maeve's part and thwarting the pirate's demands. Planting her hands on her hips, she stepped up to the gangway. "Ingram, since it is your vessel, we shall surrender our weapons until we arrive. And there will be no more coin. A deal is a deal."

The pirate scowled.

Maeve glanced at Caspian, but his gaze was locked on the pirate and his fists were clenched. He was the one spoiling for a fight.

"A deal, aye," grumbled the pirate. "We take you into certain death and you increase the risk by bringing them aboard."

"You'll have their weapons," Sandrine returned. "What harm could they be to you?"

It was both a warning and an accusation. If the pirate brothers weren't strong enough to take on two weaponless warriors, what kind of pirates were they? The pirate said nothing else, and merely beckoned them inside as he stepped back into the shadows.

Maeve followed Sandrine up the gangway, surprised at Sandrine's spunk. The weaponless scholar knew how to stand up for herself, and again Maeve wondered about her. Whose side was she really on?

The pirate kicked open an empty chest as they entered the gloomy ship. It tilted under their weight as though it would suddenly roll on its side if they shifted too much. The air was stale, dry, and even the slight breeze from the ocean could not refresh it. The pirate crossed his arms and grunted at the chest. Maeve paused before unstrapping her sword and dropping it in, steel clanging loudly against the wooden chest. Caspian followed her lead, adding his knives.

Sandrine stood to the side, watching the proceedings out of bored eyes, yet one of her feet tapped. With impatience, fear, or something else?

A rustling sound came from the forefront of the ship and

then a rough voice called out, "Are they here?" Another man appeared. He looked similar to the former, but smaller and leaner, also dressed in black with crimson highlights. Wavy dark hair was pulled back from his high forehead, and there was a mischievous curve to his wide lips. Instead of a mustache, he had long sideburns and the beginnings of a beard on his chin, and where his brother looked rough and rugged, he had an air of elegance, as though he would be just as comfortable in the court of a king. He grinned when he saw them. A grin full of mischief and misdeeds.

Maeve met his eyes briefly. They were the color of the sea during a storm, dark, misty, and full of secrets.

"I'm Imer," he offered after a beat. "Lord Caspian. No one said you'd be joining us." He gave a mock bow.

"Imer," the brother—who had to be Ingram—growled, his tone thick with disapproval.

"Listen, I'm part of this voyage now," Caspian said, his voice low and hard, his intent unmistakable. "I will have no quarrel with you as long as we are on this vessel."

Imer raised his brow, and a quick glance passed between him and Sandrine. It was a familiar look, as though they knew each other and could read each other's minds.

Maeve's back stiffened.

Imer lifted his broad head and ran his fingers through his waves of thick black hair. "You didn't tell them, did you?" he addressed his question to Sandrine.

Sandrine frowned. "I will share more information when I am good and ready. Now point me in the direction of the quarters, unless you'd like the eels to wash in here along with the sea water."

Maeve wanted to step in front of Sandrine and demand answers, but Caspian slowly shook his head, and Maeve realized that time would come. Currently, however, they needed Sandrine on their side. They needed the book and to know what she knew. Arguing in front of the pirate brothers would not go over well.

"I'll show you the way," Imer offered with another flirtatious grin. "But I warn ye, if any of you think of getting seasick aboard *Lucky Jane*, you'll be thinking again and cleaning up every last drop."

Ingram shut the gangway with a bang and began hauling on a rope. He leaned back, clearly straining, although his brother did not offer any help. Little by little, the trapdoor began to close, shutting out the light.

For a moment, Maeve was back in the dungeon, stuck in the suffocating darkness, surrounded by the screams from the unearthly creatures . . . and the waiting. The fae knew the waiting was the worst part. The gold collar on her neck burned, and then the reminder was gone.

Caspian's hand landed on her shoulder as they followed Imer and Sandrine into the narrow hall. "We must be careful," he whispered.

Maeve nodded. They would speak later, but for now, she didn't like the odds.

"What is this vessel? Is it a ship?" Maeve called out to Imer.

The boat moved underneath their feet, rocking back and forth like a mother lulling a cranky baby to sleep. The sense of staleness grew deeper as they walked. A delicate balance of mistrust and treachery surrounded them like an invisible spider's web.

"I'd have to kill you if I told you," Imer said as he chuckled, his laugh echoing off the rounded walls. "My brother and I like adventure, and no one has conquered the Sea of Eels save us. We built *Lucky Jane* with our own two hands, and she is a pleasure to sail. The eels do enjoy playing with her, but they haven't broken her yet!"

Imer's excitement carried like the crackle of lightning.

He was an adventurer. A daredevil.

"Interesting. And how many trips across this sea have you taken?" Maeve asked.

"Ah, distrusted by a warrior." Imer snorted. "I could only expect as much. Just wait and see my lady, wait and see." He wagged his head sadly and patted the wall, as though consoling the ship.

Maeve scowled, and then to her relief saw lights. A low glimmer came from the wall in the form of . . . streaks of silver? Her eyes went wide. How was it possible?

"Mind the walls," Imer called, as though he'd heard her thoughts. "We used jelly from stinging fish to create eternal light, but it still stings when touched."

"Will there be vipers at the end?" Caspian asked coolly.

Imer chuckled, but this time a dangerous note sounded at the end. "As guests on this ship, I'd appreciate a little more enthusiasm and less discord."

"They'll be quiet now and leave you to your work," Sandrine snapped, turning to glare first at Maeve and then at Caspian.

Maeve sighed as they filtered into a round room. The ceiling was low, forcing them to hunch over, but otherwise the room was spacious and would allow them to lie down with ease. There were ropes attached to the rear wall, bolted down by a large hook.

"These are your chambers for the length of the journey," Imer said as he grinned, standing on the outside while they examined the room. "I'll let you know when we arrive."

In one swift motion, he yanked on a chain and an iron grating came down, locking them in the chamber.

17

LUCKY JANE

"No!" Maeve shrieked, banging her fists against the grating. For a moment she couldn't breathe. Panic rose and her vision swam. The cold, the dark, and the dank smells came rushing back. "Why are you locking us up?"

"Sit down," Sandrine hissed.

"Maeve?" Caspian's hand rested on her shoulder, the familiarity just enough to remind her that she wasn't back in the dungeon.

Imer walked backward with his hands raised, a mocking grin on his handsome face. "You'll thank me later!"

And then he was gone, disappearing through the glowing jelly back into the shadows of the bobbing boat.

Rage surged through Maeve and she slammed her fist against the iron bars, even though it was useless. The pirates weren't coming back. At least, not until they landed on the far shore.

"You knew about this?" Maeve spat the words at Sandrine. "That the brothers would lock us in here?"

Sandrine shrugged as she backed into a corner, sitting down near the coils of rope. "It was the deal. We are going across the sea the safest way possible—aside from flying."

Maeve huffed but allowed Caspian to pull her away from the grate. Every time she took steps to secure her freedom, she ended up back where she started, and this hole made her shudder. Maeve crossed her arms, taking in their quarters.

The room smelled of old shoes and stale water. Gray and green shapes grew out of the curved walls of their prison, lacing themselves between slats of wood and iron, desperate to belong somewhere.

The floor shuddered and then pitched forward with a wild swing. Maeve was thrown against the back wall. She smacked into it with a grunt, Caspian right beside her, groaning from the unexpected violence.

Sandrine was securely tied to one side of the cramped quarters, and she glanced at them, emotionless. "Use the rope to tie up. It's not going to be a pleasant journey."

"You could have told us that sooner," Maeve complained, rubbing the back of her head. "What is going on? Are you ready to tell us?"

Sandrine sniffed. "Are you ready to claim he's not simply a hired hand?" she pointed at Caspian.

"What's it to you?" Maeve demanded, holding up a hand to ensure Caspian stayed silent.

"You don't know how dangerous this is," Sandrine said. Her gaze shifted to the iron grating, and she paused.

Maeve knotted the rope about her waist and waited. Was

Sandrine about to confess? But instead of going on, Sandrine pressed her lips together, as though she'd changed her mind, and closed her eyes.

Caspian sat down beside her, his presence a welcome distraction from the gloom and stink of the hold. She glanced at him and he met her eye, nodding his understanding. Regardless of what happened, they were in this together. Again, conflicting feelings rose. Should she have dragged Caspian into this? Was it too dangerous? Would the fae threaten him? Take him?

The ship shifted again and then rolled. Maeve's hands came out to brace herself, grabbing the wall on one side and Caspian's bicep on the other. She closed her eyes as a sensation of dizziness came over her. The ship tilted again, and distantly she heard the ringing of water washing over and around them. They were pushed violently to one side, then violently to the other.

Maeve bent over, no longer trying to brace herself, and wrapped her arms around her middle in an attempt to keep her last meal inside. Were the pirate brothers insane? Maeve's senses went dull as the pitching of the ship continued, knocking them from side to side. Vaguely, she heard voices, and then her eyes closed, casting her back into the same vision she'd experienced while crossing the Sea of Sorrows.

Two people held her arms back. Tight. They were hurting her, were close to ripping her arms out of their sockets. But the pounding in her chest would not let her forget her internal pain. She fought, relentlessly kicking, biting, and scratching. Reaching the child was a matter of life and death. Fury engulfed her and burned like a raging fire as the strangers dragged the screaming child farther and farther away. And then she was free. Picking up a stick, she turned on those who'd held her, bringing the stick around to smack the first one in the head. He went down, hands raised to ward off more blows. But she couldn't stop. She beat him again and again until there was nothing but red streaming from his crushed head. Her fingers shook, then surged with power, and she turned on the second one, screaming in rage as she raised the stick once, twice, thrice. Curses flew from her lips. Then she stopped. The child. She needed to save the child. Bright flames filled the air as she turned, moving past the broken stone walls to where the soldiers were dragging the screaming child . . .

The vision blurred, but the fear remained, real, hard, and red-hot. Something twisted in her belly and a sickness came over her. Her neck burned. The strength faded from her arms, and then she was back in the Dungeon of the Damned. This time she was tied up, unable to move or fight. She shook from the cold, the horrific screams echoing off the walls, and the deep musk of fear. Her shoulders shook, begging for freedom, but she was trapped by inaction. Her nemesis. She wanted to be out, acting, fighting, running, anything but this restrictive imprisonment. She opened her mouth and a scream wailed out of her throat, long, mournful, and heartbroken.

"Maeve!" someone called in the distance, but they seemed so far away. "Maeve! Wake up! It's only a dream. A nightmare. Wake up!"

Maeve opened her eyes, red-rimmed and glassy. Her neck ached from the awkward angle she'd slept in. When she looked up, the unexpected gaze of one of the pirates met hers. It was the younger one. Imer. He stood in the open space where the iron grating had been, staring at her. There was a darkness in his deep eyes, and a hardness. The glint of teasing was gone; all he did was stare, and a dark shudder went through Maeve. Something twisted in the pit of her belly, something dark and unexpected. A flush rose to her cheeks, and she struggled upward, fingers fumbling for the rope to take it apart.

"Maeve?" Caspian's steady voice broke the strange moment between her and Imer. "Are you all right?"

His fingers came to touch her arm, gentle, and yet Maeve shrunk away. She was a hardened warrior and did not succumb to feelings. She was self-sufficient, steady; she could handle herself. Although she appreciated Caspian's help, she did not want it when it came to her nightmares. Her thoughts flickered back. The dream. What was it? There was a ring of familiarity to it, but why? Because she'd had it more than once? But it somehow felt more intense than it had been in the Sea of Sorrows.

“I’m fine,” she whispered, letting go of the rope. She met his gaze. “Are we there?”

Sandrine’s voice rang out as she said, “Come along. Are you going to sit here all night?”

Keeping her focus on Imer, Maeve rose, somewhat unsteadily. Her hands reached out for the curved walls, fingers gripping barnacles and other sea-grown weeds as she swayed in place. Her legs shook, giving her the sense that they would not hold her up for long. Curses rose to her lips. Oh, by the Divine, why couldn’t she walk? Especially with that horrid pirate looking on.

Sandrine smirked from behind Imer, then turned and gingerly made her way down the jelly-lit hall.

Maeve realized Caspian was in the same situation. He stood in place with his arms spread out, balancing himself, a deep frown marring his handsome face.

A wave of nausea rode Maeve, a mix of the rolling feeling and the bitter taste of her nightmare.

“Draconbane awaits,” Imer said, his lip curling as the words left his lips. He spoke as if in jest, but there was a tightness in his face.

Maeve refused to glance at him again, even though she addressed him. “How long did it take?” she asked, more to adjust herself to what she’d see outside.

Imer folded his arms. “Last night and most of the day. We’ll be in full view of the dragons, if there are any left.” He snorted to himself, but his earlier joviality was gone.

Caspian began to pace back and forth, checking his footing. “You will return our weapons to us.” It was less of a question and more of a request.

Imer smirked. "Follow the path. My brother shall return them to you."

Maeve's eyes narrowed, wondering what Sandrine had in store for them. The questions of last night lay thick on her tongue. She wanted—needed—to know. Sandrine's method of dealing out information piecemeal was not enough. She needed to know as much as possible to have a hope of stopping the fae. Being locked in a cell with Sandrine had done nothing to loosen the tongue of the older woman, and Maeve bit her lip in frustration. Instead of sleeping, she should have pressed Sandrine for information. The key was in the book; it had to be. Perhaps she could steal it from Sandrine; she just had to make a plan with Caspian and take action.

"Maeve, are you coming?" Caspian's concerned voice floated to her ears.

Glancing up at him, she nodded, loosening her hold on the walls. "Go ahead." She gave him a small reassuring smile. "I'll be right behind you."

Caspian hesitated, then moved past Imer, out of the cell. Maeve watched his body language, his shoulders high and tight, his mouth set in a grim line as he stepped around the pirate, staying as far away as possible from him. Maeve cocked her head and took a step, relieved to find that her balance was back. When she had a moment alone with Caspian, she'd ask him what happened with him and the brothers. Whatever it was, it took place before she'd started working for him.

She kept walking until she was close to Imer. The iron grating hadn't been raised all the way, and she had to duck under as she walked out of the room. A hand came up, touching her bare arm, and she flinched, surprised to find Imer right next to her. He was a few inches taller than her with a slim, fit body and eyes like motes of light. They were so close she felt the heat of his body and saw the flecks of gold in his eyes. He lifted a hand, and she noticed that his fingers were long, slim, almost elegant, as though he did not use his hands for labor. She supposed from the odd shape of the boat, that could be true. He seemed a thinker, more willing to use his mind than his brute strength. Something inside her ached just from standing beside him, and an instinctual awareness rose. She pulled her arm away and glared at him. "Don't touch me," she whispered.

He responded with a quirk of his brow and answered in a low tone, "You're one of them. Aren't you?"

Maeve's guard went up and questions danced through her mind. What did he know? How much had Sandrine told him? Did he and his brother know about the fae? The quest? An uneasiness crept up her spine, and she shivered, swallowed, and answered, "One of who?"

His gaze was riveted on the ruby of her crown, and then his eyes swept down, resting on her collarbone, shoulders, and then breasts. "There are markings on your skin, aren't there?"

Maeve froze. "How did you know?" She racked her mind, thinking of past encounters. "Have we met before?"

The teasing grin came again, and he pulled back, his mischievous mask covering the former intensity of his stare. "I should say not. I'd remember if I'd met you before." He gave her a flirtatious wink. "Nay, you must be one of the lost Carnites."

Maeve's next words caught in her throat. Carn. No one talked about Carn, and none other than the fae had thrown that in her face. A sudden longing to know her history and to understand who her people were rose. It wasn't important, was it? The past was the past, but he'd brought it up.

Her fingers gripped his wrist, and now it was her turn to move closer. "What do you know about Carn?"

He pulled away as smoothly as an eel. "That knowledge will cost you," he said with a laugh, then started down the path, following in Caspian's wake.

Irritation sparked through Maeve, and she stared after him, at a loss on how to respond.

18
SHORE OF DRACONBANE

When they reached the end of the passage, the gangway to the strange boat lay open. Imer motioned to the chest, and Maeve bent to retrieve her weapons, grateful for the cold steel in her hands once again. A vibration went through her body, embers of a fire, a desire for a challenge, for an opportunity to wield her sword in battle once more. As she walked down the gangplank her eyes adjusted to the dim light. Evening shadows covered the shore, and other than the flickering torches Sandrine and the other pirate, Ingram, held, there was no light. Maeve's sandaled feet touched down on grit, something thicker than sand, likely a twisted bed of rocks and sticks, but it was difficult to see.

Behind her was the sea, the gentle waves lapping peacefully against the shore, and she wondered if the strange boat had bumped up against the eels of the sea as they traveled. It seemed an effortless trip, aside from the rocking, though it still felt like the ground was shifting under her. She turned slowly, taking in the vague lumps of something in the distance. Hills? Mountains? It was too dark to tell. She opened her mouth to speak, but Sandrine was faster.

"Right then, it's not ideal to spend too much time by the shore. We need to head directly inland and find a place to take shelter. At first light, we take in our surroundings and head toward the mountains."

Maeve froze, dread sweeping through her. She crossed her arms over her chest as a scowl came to her face. "What do you mean, we?" she demanded.

Sandrine gave her a penetrating stare. "Yes, we," she confirmed, her voice flat. "We are in Draconbane, one of the most dangerous places known to us. If, by chance, we come across dragons in our quest, the brothers are the best chance we have against them. Besides, you said you need warriors to assist you in your quest. Now you have three."

Irritation sparked through Maeve. Three warriors. Caspian, Ingram, and Imer? She could almost feel the vibration of Caspian's anger, forced to travel into certain death with two brothers he despised, and the unfriendliness of the pirates was unfortunate. There was no trust between them, and all warriors knew it was best to perform a task like this with someone you could trust, who would have your back should things go wrong. With present company, Maeve was worried about being stabbed in the back before she could find the next shard.

She stepped back and motioned to Sandrine. "May I have a word with you? Alone?"

Sandrine's lips turned up into a smirk, and she handed

her torch to Caspian and pointed toward the ship. "Back inside to the glowing halls. It's the only place for privacy, if you wish it."

Maeve backed up the gangplank, fury washing over her in waves. She took deep breaths to calm herself, and once the others were out of view, she whirled on Sandrine. "Why didn't you tell me about the pirates? If I had known they were coming with us . . ." she trailed off sharply, unsure what she would have done if she'd known in advance. Surely she wouldn't have included Caspian. Or at least told him, so he could have made a more informed decision. She wanted him with her, and yet confusion twisted through her.

Sandrine rested her hands on her hips. "You what? Wouldn't have included that warlord? Caspian? Like I said before, I will tell you what you need to know about this quest when you need to know it. For now, we are going to the mountains, and you need ruthless warriors on your side. There are fearsome creatures here, and I intend to stay alive. Ignore the brothers if you wish. They will guard me, and you can fend for yourself. But I warn you, should this quest go wrong, you will have the fae to answer to, as will I."

Maeve frowned, feeling trapped once again. "Not if I'm dead," she muttered.

"That would be your own fault," Sandrine snapped. "I did not invite you to bring a warlord who has a problem with my hired help. If they erupt into fighting, just remember: I warned you. He should not have come, regardless of how much gold you're paying him."

Maeve bit her lip. "Why did the pirates agree to this? Surely there's nothing in it for them?"

Sandrine shook her head. "This conversation is over. What you don't understand is that people have motives, needs. Once you understand them, it's easy to manipulate them. That's why I'm a scholar and you're a warrior. Because I know how to use my head and not just beastly violence. Now, come. If you don't want to talk to the brothers, walk in the back, but keep your complaints to yourself."

With that, Sandrine turned and left the ship, leaving Maeve fuming.

Maeve spun on her heel and followed Sandrine back down to the group. Tension lay thick in the air, and she felt like she could reach out and touch the line of animosity between Caspian and the pirates. Frowning, she fell into step with him while Sandrine took the lead with the brothers.

"How did it go?" he whispered.

Maeve shrugged. "Apparently she hired them before I ran into you. She's shrewd and thinks ahead, that's for sure. She knew we were coming here, to Draconbane, and decided I might need help. I'm sorry. I did not know before I dragged you into this."

Caspian set a heavy hand on her shoulder and squeezed. "It's not your fault; don't hold that over your head. I'm here because I want to be by your side and help you through this."

That last remark should have made her feel warm instead of wary. She couldn't lay a finger on why, though, so she dismissed her anxious feelings. Caspian wanted to help, and the fact that she didn't fully understand why didn't mean she shouldn't trust him.

She shrugged his hand off her shoulder. "What's with you

and the pirates? Why don't you get along? What did they do to you?"

Caspian went quiet, and even though it was too dark to see his expression, Maeve felt him close down and turn inward. She sensed his hesitation, and then he stopped walking, his eyes on the flickering torchlight ahead.

Sandrine and the pirate brothers set a quick pace through the darkness, as though they knew the land. The wind off the sea blew cold, and Maeve rubbed her arms as she stood there with Caspian, watching Sandrine and the brothers move farther inland.

Caspian waited just a beat longer and then began to walk, moving the torch he held from one hand to the other. "It happened a few years back," he began, his voice so soft the lull of the waves almost washed it away. "Three, maybe four years ago, during a heist for a high-profile warlord. It was back in the days when nothing mattered"—his voice went husky and then hard with regret—"except winning, being the best. We raided a temple for a holy relic and it went bad. It was my first heist with the brothers, Ingram and Imer. I should have known better; I should have used my own men, like I always do. When there's trust . . . there has to be trust among thieves. We didn't see ourselves as thieves back then, but that's what we were, taking what didn't belong to us for profit. Sometimes it was for the right reasons, but most of the time it was for the wrong ones."

A cold dread snaked along Maeve's spine. She spoke up, steering Caspian back to the story, back to what happened. "A holy relic? What was it?"

"Nothing unusual. It was a statue made of gold, decorated with gems. A replica of a divine being. I don't recall which one, but it was worth five hundred golden coins. Our goal was to retrieve it, leave the temple undisturbed, and take the item to a collector who would pay us well for speed and secrecy. After we snuck in, we discovered we had bad information; the relic was not where we were told it would be. Ingram offered to capture one of the priestesses to assist us. I was against it, but they overruled me. Ingram snatched one and his charms were effective, too effective. She became enamored and begged him to take her with him. After we found the relic, we headed for the location we'd stashed our horses in, and Ingram and Imer attacked me. It had never been their intent to include me in the deal. They took the treasure, the priestess, and headed off for who knows where. I still have the scar."

Maeve almost stumbled, stunned. "You never told me about this."

"There are many adventures that went wrong, and I haven't shared them all with you," Caspian said. "There is much about your past I don't know either."

Maeve glanced over at him, but his face hid in shadows. Maeve chewed her lips, at a loss for words. She recalled her transgressions of the past, the things she'd done that had likely led others to hold a grudge against her. If the Divine heard her prayers, regardless of what she'd done, couldn't the same be true for the pirate brothers? She was in an impossible situation. She didn't trust the brothers, and yet she had to trust them, and Sandrine. If they did not keep their word, follow through, she had nothing. She'd be locked up in the Dungeon of the Damned and the fae would have their way with her. Even worse, Caspian was wrapped up in the mess too, and could end up paying the price if they were betrayed. Again. She shuddered, unsure whether that meant torture or something else. Her fingertips touched her neck, tracing the line of the collar. Heat flared against her fingers, and again she recalled the Master explaining her fate.

Rage ripped through her belly and her fingers clenched into fists. There had to be a way to get free, to stop them. She couldn't be a pawn of the fae. Her strength thrashed inside her like a caged beast, fighting to get free. Resolve rose in her and she decided, come what may, she'd ask the pirate, traitor or not, what he knew about Carn. Perhaps the past held the key to unlocking her future.

19
ENCHANTED MISTS

The howls woke Maeve; long, drawn-out mournful moans that made the hairs on her arms stand up straight and goosebumps pebble up and down her bare arms. She opened her eyes, surprised she'd slept at all with those unknown terrors keeping up noise throughout the night. There was something about those howls she could not explain, something that made her want to leave, return to the odd boat, and take her chances with the eels. The eels who had been silent throughout their sea journey.

Maeve rolled on her side, putting her back to the rear wall of the shallow cave they'd discovered a few miles off the coast. Sandrine had pressed forward relentlessly the evening before, determined to find a hiding place before the night terrors took over. Once they'd arrived, Sandrine told Maeve to sleep, while Caspian and the pirate brothers took turns keeping watch. Maeve had meant to wake up earlier and take a turn at keeping watch, but her sleep was dreamless and she slept later than she intended.

Her head felt dull and her muscles sore. She rose gingerly, shaking the stiffness out of her arms and legs. When she turned around, Imer was staring at her. He'd leaned up casually against the entrance to the cave, arms crossed, dark hair covered with his hat and one boot tapping against stone as he waited. Past him, she had a view of the gray mist, which hung like a cloud suspended in the air, so thick it was impossible to tell where the mist ended and the sea began. She shuddered, both at the look in Imer's dark eyes and the unfriendliness of the mountains.

Caspian walked over to Maeve, blocking Imer's view. A spark of irritation flared, but when Maeve met his eyes, something inside of her relaxed. Caspian was safe; she trusted him, but she also did not understand why she felt conflicted. Her eyes flickered ever so briefly back to Imer, but he'd turned to address his brother, their low tones adding warmth to the coolness of the cave.

Caspian touched her arm briefly. "Are you ready?"

Maeve shrugged, then crossed her arms. "Yesterday, when we were leaving the boat, Imer said something about Carn, my homeland. I need to talk to him. I want to know what he knows about my land of birth, my people."

Caspian scrubbed a hand over his stubble, his jaw set tight. "After what I told you last night, you still want to speak with them?"

Maeve blinked, realizing he was forcing her to choose a side. "There is no harm in talking to a pirate. Remember why we're here—to gain knowledge, not hold on to old grudges. If he knows something about Carn, something that might help me, I need to find out what it is."

Caspian's expression gentled in light of her rebuke. "Forgive me if I am overprotective of you. I took my eyes off you once, and the fae stepped in and did this to you." He gestured to the collar. "My past dealings with the brothers make me want to strike them down, but I will hold off. For now."

Maeve opened her mouth, unsure of what to say. Caspian's words confused her, as did his grudge. When they were in the outpost, he'd talked about the Divine, but now he wanted vengeance on his old enemies. She supposed it made sense. If she were in his place, her desire for revenge would be the same. Again, she wished she were privy to Sandrine's plans; that would change everything.

Her eyes tore across the rough walls of the sloping cave. "Where's Sandrine?" she asked, whirling toward the pirates.

Ingram scowled and spat, then jerked his chin toward the mist.

"She's out there?" Maeve clarified. "In the mist? Alone?" She marched to the entrance, glaring at the brothers in turn. "And she hired you to be her protectors."

Imer snorted, a grin coming to his lips at her outburst. "You'll soon come to learn that she knows best. Besides, she's out there mapping our journey."

As Maeve brushed by Imer, his fingers touched her arm. They were warm and sent something like a shock rippling through her. "Find me sometime," he whispered, "and I'll tell you what I know about Carn. For a price."

Maeve's cheeks burned as she slipped out into the mist. He had her. He knew what she wanted and yet, as always, there was a price. She recalled the gold she'd taken from the warlord's keep. Would some of it be enough to keep him happy? He was a pirate after all, or at least masquerading as one. There was something odd about the two brothers, something she couldn't quite wrap her mind around, but thoughts of them disappeared as she stepped outside.

The whiteness hid the world from view, wrapping around her face like a cold and clammy hand. Then it faded, circling around Maeve as though she'd stepped into a portal and the light inside recognized her. A sensation of wonder filled her, and the eerie howling that had woken her faded away.

"You feel it too, don't you?" Sandrine said.

Mist circled around Sandrine like a whirlpool. She stood tall with her book open in both hands, her gaze riveted to it.

"What is it?" Maeve breathed.

"Enchanted mist," Sandrine said. "It is meant to guard this place and keep people out, I suppose. But if you know how to walk through it, like I do, you can see it for what it is."

Maeve studied her. "You're more than a scholar, aren't you? You're a healer too, and you know how to handle enchanted mists. I'm curious, what other powers do you have? Will you ever tell me your tale?"

The lines on Sandrine's face softened and her tone was almost gentle. "There is nothing to tell, girl. Not until we get out of here. I've found the remnants of the road we must follow. The mist will hide us for some time, but then we'll be out in the open. The Divine help us then. There are many foul rumors of what lies out here, but we will discover the truth. And the shard."

There was a glint in her eyes, and Maeve had the slightest sense that Sandrine was enjoying herself.

"Will you tell me more?" she pressed. "Which mountain range do we need to go up to? I know you said you'd tell me what I need to know when I need to know it, but what if something happens to you? Divine forbid it, and you have the brothers to protect you, but I must know what to do should I need to continue this quest alone."

The book slammed shut in Sandrine's hands so hard an inch of dust came off it. She glared at Maeve, and her voice was low as she said, "Failure is not an option. If anything happens to me, Maeve of Carn, the quest shall end and you'll be a pawn of the fae. If I face death, you will face it with me, or answer to the fae. And who knows what they will do with the likes of you. Besides, there is no guarantee they will ever set you free, even if you finish this quest for them."

Maeve wilted under Sandrine's fury, frustrated by the reminder of her complete and utter helplessness. She spun on her heel, throwing her next words over her shoulder. "I'll keep that in mind, just as I'll keep in mind the fact that dragons might be alive."

Sandrine said nothing in response.

20
Mountain Slopes

The next week was frustrating for Maeve. Sandrine stonewalled her, refusing to share her knowledge and keeping the book hidden at all times. Even Caspian's charms did nothing to thaw the scholar's icy resolve. The brothers seemed nothing more than silent shadows. They kept to themselves when the group made camp and spoke to each other in low tones. Every now and then she saw Ingram drink from a pouch and wondered if it was his secret supply of liquor. Imer did not seem keen on drink, but he was restless and seemed unable to stand or sit still for long. It seemed like he never slept. He was pacing when Maeve went to sleep, and regardless of how early she woke, he was already up and dressed, with a finger on the hilt of his blade. More often than not, his dark eyes met hers and then drifted down, as though he could read the markings on her chest, hidden under her breastplate.

The silent attention made her feel both uncomfortable

and desired. She'd had her fair share of dealing with men, but it had been a long time since a man made her feel wanted for more than her skills with the blade. That, added to his potential knowledge of the words inked across her chest, made her crave speaking with him again. Yet, despite her earlier conversation with Caspian, he always ended up in the way each time she had the opportunity to speak with Imer. While she trusted Caspian and valued his opinion, it was frustrating that he kept silently interfering. Was Caspian protecting her, or was he jealous of the looks Imer gave her? And then there was Imer himself. He hadn't made an attempt to speak with her again, always eyeing Caspian and moving away. But she couldn't forget the way his touch made her feel, for it was so different from Caspian's comforting presence. Why was that? Did she harbor some attraction toward Imer? But that was ridiculous, it was Caspian, had always been Caspian. In little more than a year Caspian was the one who'd been able to break through her defenses, encourage her to become part of a team, and fight together. Yet, just when she thought they might be something more, he'd thrown all that away for what? For a sacred path? Knowledge of the Divine?

One morning, she woke and tasted dust in the air. They'd camped near the slopes of a mountain range with gray peaks that shot up out of reach, some capped with snow far in the distance. The land was taking on some character, a change from the gritty brown landscape they'd passed day after day. Maeve sat up, taking in her surroundings. She hadn't expected to actually like the mountains, but there was something oddly surreal about their wild and craggy beauty. In some places, she could see for miles and miles, and it was intimidating; it gave her a feeling that the world might be much larger than she'd ever imagined.

They'd traveled directly east since landing on shore, and to the north she saw vague shapes, what looked like the ruin of a town. To the south there was nothing, although she thought she saw hints of green in the distance, though it could have been sunlight reflecting off the gray stones.

"This way," Sandrine called. She stood in a hollow between two mountains, where a flattened dirt path sloped upward like a secret, sneaking its way into the heart of the mountains. "It will be a long trek today."

Ingram took the lead, moving up the slope as though he'd done nothing but train to climb mountains his entire life. Maeve watched out of lidded eyes, curious about the brothers.

Who were they? Why had they built such an odd ship, and what did they want so badly that they would risk everything to join forces with Sandrine and lead a party into the dreaded Draconbane Mountains?

A shadow flickered over her face and she jumped, heart pounding in her throat. Her eyes tore upward, and high above, a bird wheeled through the air. White feathers covered its wings, which had a span of at least twelve feet. One fell, drifting back and forth before it came to rest at Maeve's feet. Without thinking, she picked it up and tucked it into her belt. When she looked up, Imer was staring at her. Again.

"Go ahead, Caspian," she called out, her eyes not leaving Imer's rugged face. "I'll catch up."

Caspian grunted as he passed her, concern on his face, but he started up the mountain slope without looking back.

Maeve walked up to Imer, who cocked his head at her. That old, dangerous, flirtatious grin was back.

"Will you walk with me?" Maeve asked.

Imer touched two fingers to his hat. "We are traveling the same path, and I've never turned down an offer to walk with a fair lady."

Maeve scowled. "I'm a warrior, not a fair lady, and you'd do well to remember that."

"One can be both," he rejoined, "besides, I'm curious about you."

Maeve's fingers twitched, but she recovered in time to keep from punching him in his side. "Why the looks?" she asked, lowering her voice. "Why the stares, when you could have talked to me?"

"And risk angering your warlord friend? I think not." Imer grimaced in Caspian's direction.

The path was wide enough to allow them to walk side by side up the slope. It flowed evenly, and soon the rocks were replaced with patches of light green grass that flattened under their footsteps. Uncanny silence hung like a threat in the air, like a trap waiting until its prey was in the proper place to release its fury. It was plain no humans had walked the path in a while.

"You know him from the past?" Maeve asked, trying to get some sense of the pirate's history.

"Aye." Imer touched his hat with two fingers again. "We've done a task or two together. Missions that always went wrong. He has some bitterness toward my brother and me, which I do not blame him for. We were in a difficult position, what was done needed to be done. But that is all in the past."

Maeve raised an eyebrow. Should she be surprised at his lack of apology? Or by the fact that he'd taken responsibility for his actions and admitted he did wrong by Caspian?

"Are you saying that to gain my trust?"

Imer smiled, but it did not reach his eyes. "Nay, fair lady. I would not try to gain your trust so quickly; I have done nothing to earn it. Besides, I am here to offer an exchange, knowledge for knowledge, nothing more."

Fair lady. Maeve wished he'd stop calling her that. "Speak plainly," she demanded, frustrated with his words and the mixed emotions he stirred up within her. "What do I have that you want?"

Imer gestured ahead to Sandrine. "The scholar. She gave us a compelling offer, one we could not refuse. But I know it's only a cover for why we are truly here. Adventurers come here from time to time to dig up what jewels they can find along the shore. So, we've been here before; it's a lucrative endeavor, ferrying people across the Sea of Eels. Plus, the eels catch a fair price in the marketplace. But no one has asked for an escort into the heart of the mountains."

Maeve went still, wary. Why did Imer want to know the truth? Would it frighten him away or make him even more interested in the quest? Again, she recalled Caspian's tale. The brothers had stolen a holy relic—and a priestess—but she was more interested in the part about the relic. If they had an interest in holy relics, the shards would greatly interest them, if only for the price they could catch at the market rather than their ability to break all curses. How much truth should she give him?

She turned from his watchful gaze and shrugged. "There is not much to share. Sandrine and I are bound by a monster who sent us to retrieve an item for him. Once the quest is complete, he will return what has been stolen from us."

"Curious," Imer said, but his light tone showed he did not believe her. "Quite a story to tell. And what was taken from you that is so precious you're willing to risk life and limb?"

Maeve's fists clenched and her feet came down hard on the path. She quickened her pace, growling, "My freedom and my strength."

"Ah," Imer said, his voice gentling. "See, that wasn't so hard. I would ask who your master is, but I believe I have an idea."

Maeve's eyebrows shot up, and she spun around, coming to a complete stop. "Who?" How many people knew about the fae and their growing influence?

Imer stepped in front of her, so close she had to tilt her head to see up into his gold-flecked eyes. Instead of the distant hardness she expected to see, there was a gentleness, a caring in his gaze. His hands came up to rest on her bare shoulders, his light touch making her shiver and crave more. A headiness came over her, like nothing she'd felt before, and involuntarily she leaned into the spell he cast over her. Who was he, this mysterious man that awakened things within her that shouldn't be awakened?

The warrior in her faded away, replaced with the lost youth of long ago, before she was hardened by the world and learned how to fight. Her eyes closed and her head fell back as a light wind played with loose strands of her hair. Warm hands drifted down her shoulders, touching the light brown runes on her skin. Her heart pounded in her chest, so hard she thought he must hear it, and a flush rose from her neck.

"May I see?" he whispered.

He smelled like the sea, wild and free, eager to go wherever it wished, do whatever it wanted. Like freedom. If she kissed him, would he taste like salt and sunshine?

What hold did he have on her? What madness? For she was giving in at just his touch, at the unexpected gentleness of his words. A desperate desire thrummed through her body to have more of his warmth, to envelop herself in him and forget about the quest, the fae, and the potential of dragons.

"Yes," she whispered.

His fingers undid the laces of her sheath, baring her upper chest down to where her breastplate covered her breasts and stomach. A lump settled in her throat as his fingers brushed against the swirls that decorated her collarbone.

"They are beautiful," he breathed, a light in his eyes, lost in awe. "Do you know what the runes mean?"

Maeve shook her head. "I know nothing of Carn, my people, or my parents. It was all lost so long ago."

His brow furrowed. "Do you recall anything? Do you remember those early days before it all went to ruin?"

Maeve could not meet his eyes. "Nay, there is nothing."

But even as she said the words, she recalled suppressed emotions. Fear. Terror. Heat. Pain. And screams of death. Her nightmare from the Sea of Sorrows came back, the sensation hitting her so hard she hissed and recoiled from Imer's touch.

"What is it?" he asked, his voice distant.

There was a keen howl, and then a terrifying scream filled the air.

Maeve jerked out of her reverie, her hands flying to her sword. "Did you hear that?"

Imer turned in the direction the others had disappeared in. "Sounds like trouble."

Bloodlust surged through her, and all thoughts of Carn and dark nightmares disappeared. Maeve drew her blade and dashed up the slope, with Imer right behind her.

21

BANSHEE SCREAMS

The path became steep then jerked sharply, weaving back and forth into higher peaks. Cliffs loomed up on either side like stone monsters leaning over to capture their prey. Then they backed off, giving way to an open plain. A raw wind blew through the plain, bringing smells of dirt, old rot, death, and danger.

Maeve came to a standstill, buffeted by the wind at her back. She examined the grass, noting the trail of crimson blood leading toward a darkness in the mountainside that rose on her left. A hole? A cave? Something else? It was too dark to tell, but the matted blood led that way.

On her right, a gentle hill sloped upward and opened up into a valley with a breathtaking view of how high they'd come. A lake glistened in the distance and hills and valleys turned into slopes of the lower mountain peaks. Farther away, she saw white peaks glinting in the sunlight.

"Something attacked them." Imer, barely winded from

their run uphill, pointed at the blood. His voice was full of concern. "They could be hiding, or whatever it was could be waiting to attack us."

As if confirming his words, another scream sounded, low and wild, the cry of a feral creature. Maeve's blood went cold, and for a moment she was back in the dungeon, where the banshees screamed. No—impossible. But she knew, deep in her heart, that anything was possible in Draconbane.

Her hand shot out and closed around Imer's upper arm, pulling him back. A fiery bolt of power shot through her, preparing her for action, and her fingers squeezed the hilt of her sword, a familiar comfort. She was strong, she could fight, and fighting was better than hunting for lost relics or attempting to remember her shrouded past.

"Imer, I've heard that kind of scream before. I believe it's a banshee. If so, we must tread carefully. They are merciless, and if it has captured our friends . . ."

Caspian. Was he all right? He was stronger than her, now that her strength was collared, and almost as good as she was with a blade. She could count on him to know what to do. The unknowns were Sandrine and Ingram. How would they handle an attack?

"A banshee? Are you sure?" Imer took a step back, glancing from her to the hidden recess.

"I'll lead the way." Maeve stepped in front of him.

"It is unnecessary, fair lady," he said, keeping stride with her.

"Please stop calling me fair lady," Maeve groaned. "I am no damsel in distress."

She caught the edge of his smile as a flirtatious grin

spread across his face. "Aye, you are a damsel in distress, a lady with no knowledge of home, but knowledge of dark creatures such as banshees. Pray tell, how does one slay a banshee?"

Maeve bit her tongue and swung her sword. "Banshees are spirits. There is no way to slay them. We have to outwit it and slay whatever monster it works for."

"Monster? Are they not free beings?"

Maeve followed the blood trail, narrowing her eyes. Her next words came out a low whisper. "From what I've heard, most are bound to monsters who use them as a lure."

"I know the tales," Imer rejoined. " '*When a banshee screams, your soul will rest in eternal dreams*'."

Maeve wished he had not uttered those words. Slightly frustrated, she waved her hand at him, motioning for him to stay silent as they crept nearer to the darkness. The mountainside curved inward on itself, creating a yawning mouth that sloped downhill. Maeve paused at the entrance of the cave, letting her eyes adjust to the dim light. She listened, but there was nothing aside from the odd drip of water. The scream had gone, and while the trail of red continued into the gloom, she could not see nor hear her comrades. She glanced at Imer, then recalled he was not familiar with raiding a place, nor did he know her habits. Caspian's unfortunate tale came to the forefront of her mind, although she had some trouble believing that Imer would double-cross her. In fact, he seemed more interested in her heritage than she was. Besides, his brother was missing, and so she set aside her concerns about him attacking her.

As soon as she stepped into the cave, her senses were

assaulted with the pungent smell of decay. Something had died recently, and its flesh was rotting and moldering in the cave. She pressed her free arm in front of her mouth while her eyes watered from the stink.

There was a rustle of wind, a low wail, and then, materializing out of the deepness of the cave, came a woman. She had long hair, wild and matted, that fell to her knees, and her bone-thin body was covered with dirty rags that swept the floor. Her face was hidden in the gloom, but she reached out toward Maeve and Imer. "Help me," she groaned. "Please. Help me."

Maeve hissed, and before Imer could step forward and gallantly offer to help, she pointed her sword toward the woman. "Who are you? Where are my friends?"

The woman shook her hands, lowered her head, and moaned again. "Help me. *Please*. Help me."

Her voice echoed in the cave, sending chills up Maeve's spine. She swallowed the lump in her throat, briefly closed her eyes, then dashed forward.

Imer let out a shout at her unexpected move, but it did not slow Maeve. She pointed her sword at the woman's chest and ran it through her heart.

Nothing happened. The spectral form remained frozen in place, but then the woman's body began to flicker. She pointed a finger at Maeve as she threw off her rags. A scream came from her lips, wild, frantic, and feral. The creature spun and hurled a violent windstorm toward Maeve, who lost her balance and fell.

Imer shouted again and rushed forward to attack the

creature, but the spectral woman vanished, leaving them alone in the cave.

"Divine save us," Imer muttered, wiping a hand over his head. "She's the banshee."

"Come on." Maeve beckoned, moving farther into the cave.

No sooner had the words left her mouth than a roar thundered from deep inside the cave.

Her fingers tightened around her sword and she moved faster, her feet crunching rocks and shaking stones loose. They tumbled and scattered around her. The walls loomed higher as she moved farther in, and the natural dimness of the cave grew nearly pitch-black. Maeve cast about for a light and, coming up empty-handed, finally paused and glanced back at Imer.

His jaw was tight, but even in the shadows she saw determination on his face coupled with a surprising calmness. He held a short sword in his right hand and in his left was an orb-like object that glowed. It appeared to be the same jelly-like substance they'd had in the boat.

Maeve opened her mouth to say something, but his gaze met hers. "I'll lead the way," he said, and the tone of his voice warned her against arguing with him.

Maeve followed Imer as the tunnel sloped down. She placed one hand on the wall to brace herself and took quick, tiny steps. The roar came again, but this time she also heard steel clanging against rock. Fighting. Heart in her throat, she quickened her pace. Caspian. He needed her help.

The tunnel leveled out and curved sharply, hurling them

into a cavern lit by flickering torchlight. In the middle of it was a bearlike beast. It reared up on its hind legs, reaching almost ten feet in height as it roared. Claws the size of Maeve's face slashed the air, coming dangerously close to Caspian and Ingram, who danced around the beast, taking turns slashing at it. The beast had a mane of shaggy brown hair, similar to a lion's. It foamed at the mouth as it fought, and its red eyes were unfocused, rolling around in anger as it snarled and slashed.

Maeve took a step back in alarm, almost bumping into Imer, who stood at her elbow. But it wasn't the beast that surprised her—it was Sandrine. The scholar was kneeling in a corner of the cavern, her back to the chaos, digging in a pile of rocks. She moved slowly and methodically, as if there was not a monster in the cave that could kill her.

The smell of death hung in the air. Out of the corner of her eye, Maeve saw a pile of bones, some with meat still on them. It was the carcass of a large—very large—animal. She shuddered. What else lived up here in the mountains? What other creatures would they run into?

She blocked the thought from her mind and returned her focus to the beast. Caspian and Ingram were doing a valiant job of distracting it, but the beast was too wild, too unpredictable for them to get close enough to kill it. If she could sneak up behind it and stab it in the back, the four of them would have a chance at taking it down.

It seemed Imer read her mind, or at least had the same intention. He moved to the left, holding his short sword in both hands. There was a tightness in his face and his eyes were wary, a sign he wasn't used to fighting in close quarters. Or perhaps with a blade. Maeve forced her eyes back to the beast, although she was curious about Imer's actions. When she first met him, she assumed he spent his time fighting and causing chaos, but the reluctance to fight now wasn't fear, it was something else. What was it?

The beast roared again, sending a fire of boldness up Maeve's spine. Her feet pounded the stone ground as she ran, then pushed off with her toes and leaped. In a moment, she was airborne. She whipped her sword around, aiming it between the shoulder blades of the beast. The sword sunk into flesh, going so deep Maeve thought it would come out the other end. The beast gave a low howl, first in rage, then it tampered off to a pitiful moan. It staggered in place before falling forward, its weight creating a cloud of dust as it hit the floor of the cave.

Maeve allowed the momentum of the beast to carry her forward until she was standing on its back. With one hand, she yanked her sword clean and wiped off the bloody blade on the creature's fur before meeting the eyes assessing her.

Caspian gave her an encouraging nod and dropped his sword arm. Ingram's lips thinned as he gazed from her to the beast, and then he spun around, heading in the direction they'd come from. He grunted, "Doubtless there are more around here."

Imer joined him, leaving Caspian and Maeve to guard Sandrine.

"What are you doing down here?" Maeve asked through gritted teeth, glaring in Sandrine's direction. Would the scholar ever be open with her?

"Got it," Sandrine announced and rose gracefully, as though there hadn't just been a battle to the death. She held something firmly in her right fist and moved toward the brothers.

"What is it?" Maeve repeated her question, even more frustrated at being ignored. Her heart thumped hard in her chest. Just when she thought her friends were in mortal danger, it turned out to be nothing. The stream of blood she'd seen earlier was likely from a dead animal, the latest kill of the beast.

In a surprising move, Sandrine pivoted and faced her, a calmness in her eyes. "It's a spell, the lure we need to find the lair in the Draconbane Mountains."

She held up the object, and questions poured into Maeve's mind. How did the scholar know these things? What else was she hiding? And when would she let down her guard so Maeve could get her hands on the book?

22
ELUSIVE DARKNESS

No matter how much Maeve pressed, Sandrine would not describe the object she'd found in the cave. Maeve had to accept that Sandrine knew what she was doing, and yet, as they traveled higher into the mountains, day after day, her frustration grew. Caspian was a friendly companion, but he was always on edge, always looking for battle and keeping an eye on the brothers. It was Ingram and Imer who Maeve was most curious about, and yet she felt reproached for her attraction to them. Caspian's cool gaze kept her away, and even Imer seemed to have withdrawn into himself, occasionally flashing her a flirtatious grin, one she came to know was a mask he wore to hide his true self.

The weather was extreme in the mountains. Even though it was late summer, the days were long and relentlessly hot. At night a chill swept over the mountain peaks, sometimes hidden in mist that stretched like fingers, reaching out to enwrap those who dared enter its vicinity. Maeve grew restless, and even when they found some shelter to bed down in, a sense of impending doom hung over her. There was something dark in the mountains, maybe a spirit or lost souls crying out, seeking vengeance. She didn't know what it was, but the darkness was almost palpable, and yet somehow elusive. Each time she tried to put a finger on what was niggling at her, it slipped away.

And then there were the nightmares. Over and over, she was the mother, desperate to save her child from the soldiers, the fire, and each time she dreamed, it became more real, frightening, terrifying, as though she were looking in a mirror, back into her past, back into the forgotten things that haunted her, things she had desperately tried to forget. Destruction. Fire. Bloodshed. Was there something symbolic there that she was missing? A message, a knowing, something that could help her escape from her prison?

The days ticked by, one after the other, and as Maeve walked uphill, her thighs sore, she realized the night of the full moon was less than ten days away. The Master planned to send a messenger to retrieve the shards during the full moon, and she was no closer to finding out how to evade them or escape the golden collar around her neck. Time was running short, and she did not have a plan.

"Hold," Ingram called from ahead.

He often led the way, with Sandrine correcting his path from time to time. They stood in the open near the granite peaks, and even though Sandrine had a spell that protected them from unseeing eyes, she couldn't help but wonder what hell would break loose in the mountain ranges if they were discovered by whatever lived here.

"What do you see?" Sandrine stood at his side and shielded her eyes with her hand, as though the added shade would give her eagle eyes.

Imer walked up on her other side and crossed his arms over his chest, as though his very appearance could drive horrors away.

Caspian moved to another boulder and peered out into the valley. Maeve joined him. Her hand went to her heart, and she took a breath of surprise as her blue eyes took in her surroundings. The tales she'd heard of the Draconbane Mountains had led her to assume it would be a cruel place, ridden with ashes, brown and barren, with sand blowing across the burned plains. But what she saw was no dark and deathly valley full of monsters, nor an impassable landscape; instead, she saw green grass and white flowers covering the slopes, their petals blowing in the ongoing mountain breeze.

There was something playful about the valley, and Maeve took a deep breath, tasting a hint of flower blossoms in the air, a sweetness, and something else. Her brow creased. It was tangy, salty, but unlike sea air. No, this was heat, fire, maybe ash. A warning made the hairs on her arm stand up, and the air felt electric. Her eyes scanned the valley again, trying to see what had made Ingram stop. Did he have the same vague sensation that all was not as it should be?

And then she smelled it. It was an old scent, rotten with layers of musk, like bodies pressed tight together day after day, rotting in their own filth. And yet they were alive, moving as one, a mountain of greed and desire, driving Maeve further into the darkness. The sensation came over her in a flash, and her fingers twitched. But no matter how hard she squinted her eyes, she could not see what it was, though her skin crawled with unease.

"Do you sense that?" she whispered to Caspian.

He glanced at her, his light hair ruffling in the breeze and thick arms crossed over his broad chest. The compassion in his eyes made her heart melt. How had she doubted him, her warlord, the one companion that made her feel completely at ease? A warmth washed over her, relief that he was there, with her, bearing the struggle together.

"I sense it, Maeve," he said as he frowned, unfolded his arms, and reached for his sword. "It's that darkness that's been following us since we stepped on the shore, the darkness Sandrine has hidden us from."

Maeve nodded. She'd thought as much, since she'd told Caspian about Sandrine having the ability to hide them within the enchanted mists.

"Either her strength has failed or we've come too far into the mountains to hold it back any longer," he went on.

"It's been weeks," Maeve confirmed, discomfort riding her like a beast tamer rode the back of a wild horse, clinging so tight it was painful. "We should be close to finding the next shard, wherever it is hidden. I should have a word with Sandrine before whatever this is attacks us."

"Agreed." Caspian nodded. "It is coming for us, and whatever it is will be relentless. We are lucky to have stayed hidden for this long."

Maeve turned her body toward Caspian, feelings warring within her, words struggling to become coherent so she could speak them. She didn't know what it was, but there was something there, something she wanted to warn Caspian against. She didn't know why, and self-consciously she touched two fingers to the collar. "Caspian . . ."

His rough hand covered hers, pressing gently. "What is it?"

She shook her head, suddenly uncomfortable with their proximity. "I don't know . . . it's just . . ." She struggled for words, and then they came out in a rush. "The night of the full moon will be upon us soon, and I can't help but worry about Sandrine's warning. What if the fae come for you?"

Caspian shrugged, his jaw working. There was a darkness in his eyes, and a sadness too.

He sighed. "We've been over this. So what if they do? What if they come for Ingram and Imer too?"

Maeve smirked. "You would like that, wouldn't you? But do you truly think the scholar would have hired them if she thought the fae would take them away?"

Caspian looked away, back out toward the valley. "I can't deny it would please me somewhat, but the past is the past. I should forgive them and move on."

Maeve shrugged. "I don't know what to think. The scholar plays a game of her own, and I cannot comprehend why she hired them. I spoke with Imer, weeks ago, but he's avoided me since. There's something he knows about Carn that he isn't saying, and I admit, I want to know. What if it helps with my past? With discovering the source of my extraordinary strength and knowing how to remove the collar?"

Caspian moved his hand to grip her upper arm, where runes rose on her skin, lost words and meanings. "Then you have to find out."

"Maybe if you stop glaring at him, I'll have a chance to find out," Maeve told him pointedly.

His voice lowered further. "Maeve, I have my grudge and my reasons, but if you are truly concerned about the fae, I can hide until the full moon is over with. They want the shards. That is all. When they get them, they will go back to what they were doing before."

"Hunting." Maeve stepped away, and a coldness went through her, like a mist from the sea wrapping its invisible arms around her bare shoulders. "They were one step ahead of me before, why should now be any different?"

"Have a little faith, Maeve," he said as he let her arm go. He paused, his eyes cloudy, and he looked away from her, chewing his lower lip as though deciding whether he should say more.

Maeve waited, but when nothing else was forthcoming, she nodded and walked away, surprised to see Sandrine had also turned away from the brothers and was striding in her direction. The two met in the middle, between the two boulders.

Maeve stood tall, looking down at the older woman, determined to be passive and not feed into her desperate need to know what was about to take place.

Sandrine opened her hand. A round, golden object lay in her palm. "Take it, girl," she said, holding it out toward Maeve.

There was something inside the object, pulsing with light. "What is it?" she asked, making no move to pick it up.

"The Finder's Stone. It is a tool used to find treasure. The closer you get to your goal, the warmer it becomes. It has led us true, for I believe the lair of dragons is beyond the valley. But once we are there, it will be too late to turn back, and my spells are failing. I don't have the strength to hide us any longer, and they will come for us."

"Who are they? What is coming?" Maeve whispered, barely daring to draw breath.

Sandrine glanced out at the valley, then back at Maeve. She leaned in closer, silver strands of hair falling out of her hastily made bun. "Goblins. Fierce little fighters with hearts for treasure. They are greedier than dragons, but were too frightened of them to take action when the mountains were alive with dragonkind. They will have taken up residence in the lair, and you must fight them. That's why I brought the brothers with us. They expect gold as payment, but they shall be lucky to escape with their lives."

Maeve swallowed hard as rage welled up within her. Was Sandrine double-crossing the pirates? Leading them to their deaths so she and Maeve could survive?

Words came out of her mouth before she could stop them. "What if we waited?"

Sandrine scowled. "Wait? Wait for what?"

"The night of the full moon," Maeve hurried on. "If there are goblins inside the dragon lair, then we need help. And if the fae are coming to take the last shard I found, then surely they will assist with driving away the goblins."

Sandrine scowled harder and her eyes turned dark. "Are you a fool, girl? They are our masters." She pointed at the collar around Maeve's neck. "If we wait until the night of the full moon to attack the goblins and the fae portal into the middle of a battlefield, they will believe we set them up for ambush. Do you want this quest to be called off? Do you want to rot forever in the Dungeon of the Damned?"

"Surely you don't think they would believe we set them up to be ambushed," Maeve pressed.

Sandrine took a step closer, almost poking a finger into Maeve's breastplate. "You don't know how dangerous they are. We do this the way I'm telling you, or I walk away and leave you and your warlord to die. The fae will find another way. They always have, and they always will. So, listen, and stop trying to deviate from the plan."

Maeve's temper rose. "It is not a plan, it's what *you* want *me* to do. Why won't you share anything with me until it's too late?"

"It's for your protection," Sandrine scoffed. "Now take this. Should worse come to worse, it will guide you to the next locations."

Questions rose on Maeve's tongue. "Where is the next location? How will this relic guide me? And how do you know about it?"

"Who do you think told me about this relic? Who had the time to spend days tracking it down?" Sandrine snapped. "The portals the fae use are not as potent as you assume. They can only open them on ground where blood has been spilled. There is much about them you don't know, so don't underestimate them, girl. The lost shards have a potent power, and they will stop at nothing to retrieve them. Why do you think they planned so carefully and chose you, specifically, to carry out their wishes? You may not know what they have on you, but I do. It is my duty to know the dark things, the hidden things, and there is a reason for everything that happens. The fae looked for something like you to help them, something with your strength and your abilities. They have done their research; they have searched this world in its entirety for exactly what they need. When the moonlight shines upon this world in full, the fae use their portals with a purpose, and they will not stand for trickery. If there was a way to take them down, I would have done so long ago."

Maeve's fury evaporated and her breath caught, torn between frustration and astonishment. "You would have taken them down? But . . ." she paused. How much could she trust Sandrine? "You work for them; how can I trust your word?"

Sandrine lifted her chin and thrust the oblong object into Maeve's hand. "I've said too much already. If things go wrong here in Draconbane, make sure you continue with the quest. There may yet be a chance for you. After you find the lost shard in the dragon's lair, head south toward the ruins of Carn."

Maeve froze, and everything within her screamed in rebellion. Carn? The lost ruins of her homeland? She'd never been there and with good reason. She had no desire to go back, to look on the scattered ruins of her people and knowledge that was lost to her forever. But returning to Carn might awaken old desires and bring her clarity. What if she could find knowledge that would free her from the collar? Her heart soared for a moment at the possibility of finding answers, but just as suddenly, her crown felt heavy on her head. Why did she wear it? What was the point? She was the queen of nothing, and her people were all dead. Gone.

"There's a lost shard? There?" she demanded in disbelief.

"Aye," Sandrine nodded. She turned, jerking her chin toward Ingram and Imer. "Why do you think I called on the pirates? They are fearsome warriors, but they also know about Carn. You should ask them what they know of its history when you have a chance."

"They know . . ." Maeve repeated, her fingers going to her lips. "You did this on purpose so I could learn more. Find out more." Her voice came out as a whisper. "Sandrine, what do you really know? Whose side are you on, because I am confused. At times you seem to speak out against the fae, and wish for their demise, and at other times, like these, it seems you're on my side, and you want me to win."

Sandrine's expression went blank, and she fixed Maeve with a fierce look. Holding up a finger, she spoke quickly, "Girl. Understand this now. I am on no one's side. I am too old for wars and betrayal and mistakes. The fae have me and I have nothing left other than to do as they wish. You'd better do the same until you find a way out. I'm just telling you what you need to know to survive, should things not go as planned."

Maeve pressed on, determined to get to the truth, "But you know what will happen. A horde of goblins will attack us as we search for treasure, and you expect that a few of us will die, and I must go on, complete the quest." Her fingers shook with frustration. "I don't like this any more than you do, but we are in this together. I hope. I pray."

Sandrine turned away. "Pray to the Divine if you must. The celestial beings have minds of their own, plans of their own, and I too hope they will stand up and defeat evil before it goes too far. In the meantime, think of what I have told you."

"Wait." Maeve stepped forward, her hand coming out to spin Sandrine around, but she drew it back at the last moment. For some reason, it seemed strange and wrong to touch the scholar even mildly violently. "What about this object, the Finder's Stone? How do I use it?"

Sandrine turned back and glanced at the oblong gold item. "Think on the item you desire, and it will lead you in the right direction. The pulsing lights will lead you straight and true until you find what you are looking for."

Maeve glanced down at her armor, looking for a place to keep the object. "It is curious," she admitted. "Why don't the fae have it?"

Sandrine fixed her with a look. "Do you think the fae could use such an object to find what they need in less than twelve hours of moonlight, twelve nights a year? Nay, they passed the knowledge to me."

Maeve understood. The fae used mortals for their plans. She took a step closer to Sandrine, extending the figurative olive branch. "Sandrine, if I ever find out anything that will free us from the fae, I will use it."

Sandrine stared at her, and although her face was still emotionless, there was a passion in her eyes. "That's what I'm counting on."

Maeve stood still, staring, as Sandrine returned to the pirates, her mind abuzz with thoughts. Sandrine had set this up to benefit her—the pirates, the Finder's Stone, everything—to help her destroy the fae. And yet, deep in her heart, she knew pieces of the dense puzzle were still missing.

She lifted her chin as she returned to Caspian's side. This time, when she looked down, she saw a sea of green, but not the green of grass nor the white of flowers swaying in the pleasant mountain breeze. Nay. The green was an off-color one, dirty and moldering, and it belonged to goblins with pointed ears and soiled loincloths moving toward Maeve and her companions.

Maeve's hand drifted to the hilt of her sword.

"What did you find out?" Caspian asked, his gaze intent on the disaster rushing their way.

"Enough," Maeve told him. "I know where we are going next, and I know we need to defeat the fae. The only outstanding question is how."

"How, indeed," Caspian replied.

And then the air was filled with the sound of footsteps.

23

HILL OF DRACONBANE

The Finder's Stone pulsed against Maeve's chest, where she'd tucked it into her breastplate, squashed between her breasts. She could feel it, like a beast, breathing and pulsing, pointing her toward the dragon's lair. When she looked across the valley, she saw an opening in the mountains, a gaping hole leading down into darkness where she imagined tunnels twisted.

She flipped her sword in her hand as the goblins raced toward her and her companions, frustrated with the seemingly insurmountable obstacles they needed to push through to access the dragon's lair. The goblins were many and ferocious, but—she hoped—also inferior warriors, for the sea that raced toward them was massive and overwhelming. She turned toward Caspian and stuck out a hand. "It has been an honor," she told him.

He shook his head, although his cheek curved up in a hint of a smile. "Maeve, why would you say such a thing?"

"Don't you see what's rushing toward us?" She pointed into the valley, which was no longer peaceful or beautiful.

Caspian shrugged, a foolish grin on his handsome face as he drew his sword. "Maeve, they are only goblins. As I always say, believe in the best possible outcome. We can take them."

Maeve shook her head. How? "A warlord to the bitter end," she murmured, a fire rising in her belly.

"A warlord to the sweet end," Caspian disagreed, and then he began to run.

Maeve wanted to scream, demand for him to stop, but then the fire rose within her too, engulfing her with a desperate desire for blood. She wanted—needed—to fight, to slay, to kill them all. A battle cry left her lips and, taking her blade in both hands, she ran down the hill toward the horde of goblins.

The melee spread about her and she dived in, cleaving head from body, limb from limb, and striking down knives, axes, and swords as the goblins surged about her. It was like an unending sea rushing down into a waterfall—waves crashing against waves in an unstoppable force. Pinpricks of pain shot through her legs, arms, and core as short knives drove into her again and again. But she refused to stop and kept moving forward until she reached the middle of the valley, slinging bodies across it as the rage within her let loose and she fought to reach the lair.

For a long time, there was nothing but cries and screams, death throes of the goblins and she knew not what else. Although the sun was bright and high, she lost track of Caspian and had no idea where the pirates were. Even Sandrine was lost in the cacophony of sound. There was nothing but the killing. She wished she could bring this kind of violence down on the heads of the fae, but since they weren't there, the goblins would have to be a substitute. But it wasn't enough; it would never be enough. Each kill should have eased her conscience, but she still felt the darkness in her soul. Sobs rose in her throat as she fought. She whirled, twirled, slashed, and slayed, the rage pouring through her as she fought. Pointed ears went down and goblins shrieked in agony, but each one that fell was replaced with another. Maeve raced through the valley, down the slope of flattened grass, and up through the white blossoms where they gyrated in a sort of dance, celebrating a victory that never came.

Maeve's legs moved faster as the snarls of the goblins and the shouts of her companions echoed behind her. She sprinted up the hill, her breath coming thick and fast until she arrived at the entrance to the lair. The yawning mouth of the cavern stood open, and on either side of the opening were chiseled stones with runes carved into them, words of an old age marking the spot.

If the battle rage hadn't been running hot through her veins, she might have been frightened by the sheer immensity of the lair. Instead, she dashed inside, her screams echoing through the tunnels. Darkness invaded her vision, but the Finder's Stone pulsed, faster than before. Maeve twisted and turned, moving deeper into the lair until suddenly, she was there, at the foot of the hall of treasures.

Precious jewels captured her vision. More jewels than she'd ever seen in her life, a pit of gold—a pit of desire—running deep into the mountains. She stared at it, aghast, spinning as she took it all in. The treasure of Draconbane, the lair of dragons. Wealth beyond her wildest dreams glittered before her eyes. There was a humming in her ears, a low pulse, a beat, a well of uncontrolled lust.

A raw scream came loose from her throat and she dashed down, spraying gold coins, rubies, diamonds, and sapphires everywhere. The jewels sprawled around her, and she could do nothing but leave them there, glittering where they lay. She sank to her knees in the middle of the treasure, a searing pain in her chest. This was the treasure she had searched for; this was all she needed. All her years of hiring out her skills, fighting for others, when the wealth of the world was in Draconbane. A heat rose in her cheeks and for a moment, her thoughts drifted in a haze of greed. The thought entered her mind abruptly: here in the dragon's lair, away from the goblins, away from the fae, she was free. What if she ignored the fae and their demands? What if she took the treasure and sailed north, sailed far, so far away that they would never find her and could never use the collar on her again. Would it work if she ran?

Maeve was lost in her own thoughts until a roar pulled her back into reality. She stood up, shaking loose coins off her knees, suddenly disgusted at her weakness. How easily the treasure had overwhelmed her and made her forget what was real.

The cry came again, and this time she recognized it. It was partly distressed and partly frustrated, but she dared not ignore it, for it was the voice of someone she knew. Someone she loved. The sound broke through her thoughts like sunlight shattering fog. The past year she'd warred with her feelings, and although she was still unsure whether it was brotherly love or romantic love, it didn't matter. She needed to help him.

Maeve spun on her heel to head back to the tunnels, toward where the cry had come from. As she did, a gold sheen flickered on the edge of her vision. High above her was a gilded cage, and within it knelt what looked like a woman. In the quick glance, all Maeve saw was the woman bent over an object covered in blue dust. Without a doubt, Maeve knew she needed to ascend to that cliff and speak with that woman, but she couldn't leave her companion to fend for himself. She'd return once she helped Caspian.

Jewels shifted around her as she ran, heart thumping, back to the entrance of the dragon's lair, where the sides of the mountain narrowed down to a passageway that curved and twisted like the body of a snake. Maeve tore around a corner, ignoring the way her minor wounds wept and burned as dust clung to them.

As she rounded a second corner, she came up short, taking in the backside of an oversize goblin. A layer of dust covered its green skin, dulling it in the shadows of the lair, and it wore what was once a white cloth around its loins. Other than that, it was naked, with gangly arms and legs. It lifted a mace in one hand and swung it, eliciting another hoarse cry.

"Aye!" Maeve shouted, scooping up a rock and hurling it at the broad backside of the goblin.

It swung around, its wide, conniving eyes bulging from its flat head while its sharp nose poked out like a blade from its face. Its face was skeletal and misshappen, and its thin lips pulled back, displaying a row of razor-sharp teeth. As its nostrils twitched, a low snarl came from its throat, and then a tail snaked out, so fast Maeve could not leap away in time. It wrapped around her ankle and pulled, hurling her to the ground. The breath whooshed out of her and she almost dropped her sword as the surprisingly strong tail yanked her forward. Dust flew up like a cloud, obscuring the goblin from her vision. Maeve scrambled, managing to bring the sword down where she thought the tail was. There was a cry as the goblin let go and stepped back with a hiss.

Maeve sprung to her feet, allowing the battle rage to take her. She lashed out with a cry, whipping her sword around to waist height, where she guessed the goblin would strike next. She was right, and her steel clanged against the mace the creature carried, but she was surprised at the strength with which the goblin pushed back. She whipped her sword away and slashed toward its heart, but the goblin was just as fast, anticipating her movements and striking hard again and again. Maeve screamed as she fought, a howl of rage gurgling up from within. She ignored the weariness in her arms, the shaking of her legs, the rawness of her throat, and the terror that gripped her heart. If Caspian was behind the goblin, mortally wounded, she had to kill it, save him, find Sandrine, and ask her—or rather, beg and demand at sword's edge—for her to heal him. The warlord had been her only friend through the last year, her best year, and she could not lose him now. Especially when it was her fault for asking for his assistance on her dangerous quest. With the goblin horde outside, and the monstrous gatekeeper—she didn't know how she'd missed the creature when she'd run inside—she finally understood the terror that the word Draconbane invoked in peoples' hearts.

The goblin shrieked as it fought, its putrid breath coming toward her. The air was sour and stank like rotten eggs. Sweat beaded on Maeve's forehead and she kicked, her foot smacking into the beast's loincloth. It paused and shuddered, and that shudder was just enough. Using both hands and cursing her lack of strength, she lifted her blade and sliced through the goblin's neck. There was one mournful moment where it swayed in place, its eyes bugging out of its head. And then the head fell back and a spurt of blood shot up toward the walls of the lair. Maeve sidestepped just in time as the goblin fell forward, right where she had been standing a moment before.

Wasting no time, she ran to the figure slumped on the ground behind the goblin.

"Caspian," she rasped.

Tears filled her eyes, blurring his face. He sat against the wall, where he must have dragged himself after she'd appeared to fight the goblin. There was blood all over his clothing, and he pressed his hand to a wound in his side. His mouth was bloody, his eyes cloudy, and yet one hand still held his sword, as though it were the only thing keeping him alive. Maeve knew it was likely because his fingers were wrapped so tightly around his sword that he could not have let it go if he'd wanted to. His blond hair was plastered to his head, which he turned slowly, eyes taking in Maeve and then shifting over to the goblin, as if he wasn't quite cognizant of what had happened. "Maeve," he whispered.

"Caspian." She bit back a cry and pressed her hand over his.

He winced in pain.

"Don't speak, don't talk, I'll find Sandrine and she'll heal you. You'll be fine."

"No," he gasped, trying to catch her eye. "Maeve. Look at me. It's over. It's a mortal wound." He paused, panting between words as though he could not get in enough air to speak. "My time has come. I've been forgiven. I know what the Divine wishes of me. Maeve. My bag." His eyes dropped to his pack. "It's in there. It's yours."

Maeve shook her head. "Caspian." She reached up to cup his cheek. It was warm, rough, and a tear slid from her eye. "Don't say such things. What will I do without you?"

"Go on. You are brave. Strong. Beat them. Finish this. It's in my bag. I found it." He stopped abruptly, his eyes clearing and widening for a moment. Then his hand went slack, his head fell forward, and his eyes closed.

"No," Maeve whispered, "no, no. Please, no. Caspian. Don't leave me here, not like this," her body shook and, despite the danger, the dark, the stink of the place, and the quest that waited for her, she gathered him in her arms and sobbed.

She wasn't sure how much time had passed when she finally let go, her throat sore and eyes red and puffy. A hollowness centered in her core, and numbly, she reached for Caspian's bag, pulled it off him, and folded his hands over his chest. It seemed disrespectful to leave him there, in the hall next to the broken body of the oversize goblin. Already it was beginning to stink. The mace lay a few feet away, where it had fallen.

Tears still streaming down her cheeks, Maeve stared down at Caspian again. She longed to give him a proper burial, a warrior's burial, but to do that she needed a slab of stone, an arrow, and fire. Her thoughts flickered back to the inner lair, to the jewels flickering in the light. There was light there. If she moved quickly, she might be able to find a torch and return to give Caspian a proper burial.

Pain tore at her legs and arms as she rose, and when she looked down, crisscrossed patterns covered her legs where they had been sliced again and again with thin blades. Her vision went fuzzy, and she knew she needed something, food or water, before she continued. She opened Caspian's bag and pulled out the waterskin, tilting it back and emptying the contents into her mouth. The liquid was warm, but she did not care; it went down smoothly, dulling the pain in her throat. Her heavy breathing calmed, and she tossed the empty waterskin away. Tears, again, pricked at the corners of her eyes.

He looked so small and lonely slumped against the wall. As she surveyed the area, she realized she was alone. The goblins hadn't returned to defend their lair. Why was that? And where were Sandrine and the pirates? She'd seen them fighting, she was sure of it. But why would they leave her alone, unless . . . unless they were dead too? They had all been overrun by goblins. Was it possible that she must continue on with her forced quest alone?

The thought jarred her, and she realized having companions had eased her burden. Who would she talk to? And who would believe that the fae were a threat, and she needed to stop them? If it even was possible to stop them. Her fingers clenched into fists. The odds were stacked against her and the one man she had counted on to assist her lay dead at her feet. Even Imer's words regarding Carn were insignificant. She was alone.

Her hand went limp inside Caspian's bag and her fingers touched something hard and long, like the stone that pulsed around her neck. She swallowed hard as she pulled it out. It was wrapped in cloth that fell open in her hands. Astonishment shot through her like an arrow, and she felt everything she thought she'd known falling, tearing, ripping apart. Her gaze went to Caspian, and she wanted to scream, wake him up, demand answers. How? When? Why?

The blue light shone off her face, revealing another shard, larger than the one she'd found in Lord Sebastian's fortress. Did Caspian mean the shard was hers? If so, when did he find it? Was this why he had been intent on coming with her? Did he have plans she knew nothing about?

She looked up and howled in frustration.

24
DRAGON'S LAIR

Maeve walked blindly down the passageway toward the lair where she'd seen the woman, if her eyes hadn't deceived her. She walked without purpose, a sheen of anger dancing on the edges of her vision. Her eyes clouded over again and again and there was a weight over her heart. A dread. An acknowledgement that something beyond her control was happening. Many things needed to be explained, and before she took another step toward helping her enemies and gaining her freedom, she needed answers. Answers she would choke out of the scholar on the edge of a knife if she could find the woman again. If Sandrine had been forthcoming, Caspian might not be dead. Yet the shard she'd taken from his bag threw her into confusion. He was part of this, fated, it seemed, but she did not understand why or how. Her memory returned to the night they'd spent in the Bawdy Sailor. He'd taken her shard, studied it, but why? What had he been looking for? What did he want with it?

A nasty thought crawled through her mind. For a year, she'd warred and served with Caspian. One year. But things changed. He went away for a time, claiming to visit a temple and study with a priest. When he came back, his goals were lofty, and he spoke incessantly about the Divine and becoming noble. He had still focused on finding treasure and making them wealthy, but he had also focused on other causes. For example, breaking up a slave trade, a mission that got her captured by the fae. Was that on purpose?

Her breath constricted in her throat and she reached out a hand, feeling the warm dust of the slick, smooth wall. Was Caspian working for the fae? Had he been captured by them and asked to find the lost relics? And then they decided he needed help and involved her? No. It couldn't be. She shouldn't think such things. It was terrible to think ill of the dead, and yet . . .

Or perhaps it wasn't what she thought, and only what the fae wished for her to think. What if they had chosen her because of her proximity to Caspian, one who already held a shard? But if they knew he had it, why did he still have it? Why let him keep it when they could have easily overpowered him? Unless they were playing some sick game with her, and the quest was more about her and less about the shards. And yet, the relic she was seeking had the power to break all curses. Not something to be taken lightly.

The pounding in her head increased until she pushed away the maddening thoughts. Thinking of such dark things would only drive her to the brink of sanity. Feeling hollow, she put one foot in front of the other until she reached the entrance to the lair, where jewels sparkled and light beamed, casting shadows upon the walls and conjuring magic tricks, making the area seem larger than it truly was, more threatening, shining with a deadly brilliance and encouraging trespassers to their deaths.

Maeve sensed the warning that hung in the air, the aura of doom, of blood. Was the treasure cursed? There was no way of knowing, and yet she feared so. The Finder's Stone pulsed against her chest, and suddenly her feet felt as heavy as the roots of the mountains. Much had happened in one single day. How could she find the willpower, the strength, to go on, when the things she valued, the people she cared about, were lost and tarnished?

Rather than giving in to another bout of tears, she lifted her head up and tried to find what she'd seen out of the corner of her eye earlier. The glimmer of blue caught her attention, and when she turned in the glow's direction, she saw, once again, the cage. It had gold bars and a domed top, large enough for a small person to stand up straight in, even though the woman inside knelt. Stringy hair hung down around her face, making it difficult to tell whether she was asleep or praying.

Maeve flashed back to her imprisonment in the dungeon of the damned and how she'd felt in her prison cell, waiting, biding her time until the right opportunity came along. Who was this woman and why was she locked up? Was she a prisoner of the goblins? Maeve shuddered at the thought, unwilling to imagine what kinds of horrors the woman may have been subject to during her captivity.

The light flickered, sending shadows dancing. Shapes of dark monsters rose from the walls and faded again, as though the light was sending her a warning. In that transition, Maeve saw stairs pressed up against the walls, leading toward the cage. And then she saw there was more than one flight of stairs and more than one cage. Most of them were empty, but she thought she saw stark white bones in one, and revulsion swept through her.

Caspian's death drifted to the back of her mind and she moved toward the stairs. A vast array of jewels lay in her path, forcing her to step on them, her feet sinking down slightly as the jewels crunched under her weight. When she first saw them, she'd thought of taking them, but now as she walked over the hoard, she realized it was all blood money. Treasure that belonged to the last remnant of a lost race. Who knew what atrocious acts had been done to collect such wealth? Perhaps those sins, those crimes, were the reason all the dragons were gone, and nothing but a murderous horde of goblins dwelled in the mountains.

Even as Maeve thought it, she saw a reflection in herself. The things she'd done in the past she'd weighed only against herself and her motives, but thieving and killing in exchange for wealth was wrong, wasn't it? Who knew how many untold hundreds had been damaged by her actions? She'd never thought of them; she'd only fought to complete her contract and get paid.

The weight of her guilt struck her again. This predicament was her own fault; she wasn't one of the innocents who had done nothing to deserve her fate. The fae had said as much when they captured her; they could only do so because of the darkness in her heart. That was why Caspian had changed. He'd seen the darkness in his heart and started embarking on quests that benefitted others to try and complete a few acts that would show the Divine his change of heart. But had that change of heart ultimately led to his death? Would he have been better off staying a shallow, simple warlord? It was maddening not knowing.

The stairs were rough, crudely hacked into the mountain-side, but clear of jewels. Maeve ascended quickly, determined to keep her feet moving, for if she slowed down, exhaustion would catch up with her and she did not know if she could move another muscle once that happened. The strenuous climb made her cuts reopen, and every now and then she felt blood trickle down her legs. By the time she reached the top, her legs were burning, but in front of her was the golden cage.

She attempted to catch her breath as she approached, eyeing the woman. Her chest moved in and out, signaling that she still drew breath, her filthy fingers were clasped in her lap, as though she were praying, and a threadbare cloak was laid under her bare knees. She wore a kind of short skirt that must have fallen mid-thigh when she stood upright, and a thin, sleeveless shift covered her body. It was so worn there were holes in places, showing skin covered with a layer of dirt.

Maeve took another step, swallowing hard. A blue item did indeed lie in front of the woman's knees. It was another shard, this one as big as Maeve's forearm and pulsing with an inner light. Her eyes were drawn to it and riveted there. It was beautiful.

She took a breath, unsure. The shards were holy relics—she had no right to touch them. What the fae were making her do was wrong. The crown should be left in pieces, and yet she wanted to reach out and take the shard for herself, put them all back together, and see what the crown looked like. Perhaps even wear it. Blood rushed through her ears, and then a pulsing came, a warning hum, and she faltered, taking a step back as fear gripped her. Such thoughts of greed had never entered her mind before; they were dark, unnatural, and although she was supposed to be a queen, taking a holy relic for herself was not right. If the Divine had seen fit to destroy it, it shouldn't be put back together.

Awareness of who she was, or should be, roared through her ears. Queen of nothing. Survivor of Carn. But none of that meant anything at all; not her supernatural strength, not her ability to fight and win—nothing mattered. All she felt was the crushing weight of guilt and sorrow. This was wrong. All wrong. Everything she'd done thus far had led up to this moment, a reaction to her actions. Blame the circumstance as much as she might, she realized it all came down to choice. She'd always had a choice, and she'd always chosen to go the corrupt route, to destroy life, to give in to her selfish desires and do nothing else. Everything she'd done in her life was self-serving, which is why she deserved what was happening to her now, happening not only to herself, but also to the world.

"It's not your fault."

Maeve's head jerked up and her mouth came open, the cry of astonishment dying in her throat. The woman had opened her eyes; they were reptilian, golden and lidded, giving her face an eerie look when she blinked. Her gaze was direct, penetrating, without mercy, and other than raising her head, she had not moved.

25
GOBLIN QUEEN

"Did you speak?" Maeve whispered, the power in the air stealing her breath away.

"I know why you are here," the woman went on, as though she hadn't heard Maeve's question. "My time is over. The night of the fae falls nigh. Kingdoms rise and fall, all in time, but it must be the right time, deemed so by fate."

Maeve shook her head in confusion. Was this woman mad?

"Not mad," the woman said, "but I have languished in captivity for too long. According to the Prophecy of Erinyes: '*A day will come when curses will be broken, the lost shall be found, the found shall be lost, and the rift between mortal and celestial will cease to exist.*' That day is coming and you can do nothing to stop it, only circumvent its finality."

Maeve stiffened. She found it disconcerting that the woman seemed able to read her mind. She shifted from foot to foot, trying to ignore the way her legs ached and burned. A drop of blood ran down her shin and weariness chipped away at her spirit.

"I have come for the shard," she said. "That is all."

The lips of the woman rose as though in a smile, but there was no smile on her thin cheeks, nor in her reptilian eyes. Reaching out, she picked up the shard in both hands and ran her fingers over it, stroking it lovingly, as though she wished never to be parted from it. "Listen, Maeve of Carn, and listen well. If you want the shard, you need to hear me out and understand what is beyond your control. Isn't that what you seek? What you desire? Knowledge, above all?"

Her tone was gentle, intoxicating, and wormed its way through Maeve's mind. Questions flittered away, and she found herself sitting down and crossing her legs, but not of her own accord. What magic did this woman have? What power over her? She desperately wanted to hear and understand, at last, the knowledge that had been kept from her. Did she have time before the goblins returned and hemmed her in with their sharp teeth, wicked knives, and nasty blows?

"If you want to understand what is coming, you will listen to me." The women spoke steadily, but her fingers never stopped stroking the shard. "My name is Ariefluer of Draconbane, and I am its last mage. My power lies in the mind, in reading auras and sensing thoughts. If your mind is open, I can read it, not that I need to, for I can guess at what you might think. People are not as complex as they think they are, and it's simple to unravel them once I've discovered what they desire. Your desire drives you; it's plain on your face. You want knowledge, you're tired of being controlled, and I sense a darkness within you, a desire for revenge that's deep and driving. Guilt weighs you down, but you should not dwell on it. There is no hope for me now, but there is for you. This is why you are here, why I've sat here, waiting for someone like you. It makes sense, now that I see you. The fae took you, threatened you, and collared you. But in seeking what they do, they will bring about their own ruin. Draconbane was conquered by the fae, long ago. They killed the last dragons, imprisoned me with a dark curse, and took my sister."

Sister. Some of the tension in Maeve's body eased. But Draconbane was conquered five hundred years ago; how was this woman alive now? Was her sister still alive?

Those golden eyes bored into her. "My sister is not what you would think. Unlike me, she is not gifted with magic of the mind, but we have one similarity. We are both powerful beyond measure when we are in our true forms, our second skin, but when the fae cursed me, they made a mistake. There was a weakness in their spell that allowed me to turn the curse on the fae themselves. If I cannot walk in the daylight, they cannot either, aside from the night of the full moon each month. If I am cursed, so are the fae, and so is my sister. Nothing can break our curse except for the Seven Shards of Erinyes."

Fear rippled through Maeve. A second skin? What was it? Were the sisters dangerous? Evil? There must have been at least a thread of darkness within them that brought the fae to them.

"My curse is to live my days out here, in this cave, without my power, but I've had years to think on my plight. Once I give you the shard, I will turn into dust, and once again my soul shall sing. I'll be free to fly."

“Why are you telling me this?” Maeve demanded.

The reptilian eyes blinked, a double lid coming over them, creating a film and then disappearing.

Maeve shivered under the glare of the woman.

“I tell you this because of my sister. Watch out for her. We were both wicked in our own ways, one just as bad as the other, but there’s a reason the fae left me here and took her as a bride. Yet, I don’t believe she was captured unwillingly—I think she wanted the fae, desired the king of the fae for some reason. Perhaps there is more to the story than even I know. That is for you to find out. But be warned: my sister stopped at nothing to get rid of me. I don’t know what she would do to others who stand in her way. Perhaps she is aligned with the fae, or perhaps she is using them.”

Maeve folded her hands in her lap, linking them together to hold on to some sort of reasoning, some stability. If what the woman told her was true, she was in deeper trouble than she’d ever considered. “Why the quest for the seven shards, then? Why send me here, when all they needed to do was open up a portal and take what you have kept all these years? How did they not know?”

This time the woman did smile, a cruel, haunting smile that revealed a row of sharp incisors. Her mouth was full of fangs, and for a moment Maeve thought her heart would stop. Was she talking to a demon? A fae? Was that the second skin the woman spoke of?

“My sister did not attend to her studies. She was intent on physical manifestations, so much so she forgot about the mind being a powerful tool. My ability to manipulate the mind made me great. I knew about the Seven Shards of

Erinyes because I studied. I found this shard buried in the treasury and swallowed it whole before the fae came. I birthed it out like a child and took care of it while I waited, knowing that one day my sister would find out and send someone to retrieve it. And I knew she had to send someone, because the fae cannot open portals into Draconbane. There are grounds where it is impossible for them to work their dark magic, which is why they need you."

Maeve held on to those words. Places where it would be impossible for the fae to reach her? Did the scholar know about these places and withheld that information? "Where else? What other areas are off-limits to the fae?"

The woman's smile faded, and she shrugged. "I know not. My sights were set on protecting my realm and interfering with the celestials; that knowledge you must gain from others."

Ideas were already forming in Maeve's mind. If the fae could not reach her here during the night of the full moon, she could hide and wait them out. The collar around her neck hummed, as though the fae could listen to her treacherous thoughts. "Do you have books?" she asked, breathless. "Old scrolls? Anything that I might read?"

The woman blinked slowly, her eyes drifting down to the shard, and then she thrust it toward Maeve. "Draconbane contains a wealth of knowledge. There are books, scrolls, and endless treasures here, but they are impossible to take because of my guard. From the looks of you, you fought through my guard on your way in."

"Guard?" Maeve faltered, although her fingers stretched out toward the shard.

"Goblins." The woman continued to hold the end of the shard, her odd eyes boring into Maeve. "I've done you a boon and saved this shard for you, and now it's time for one last favor."

"Favor?" Maeve faltered. The woman was in no shape to offer favors.

"Aye. The goblin horde worships me as their queen. As they should. I'm the only queen they've ever known. When I die, they will disintegrate into chaos as they hunt for another queen. I will give you my stone. It will not be effective long after I die, but as long as the link lasts and you carry it, the goblins will not harm you. Once my ashes are cool, the link will break and they will come after you, so if you want to live, you will go far away from here before that time comes."

Frustration ripped through Maeve, and she all but snatched the shard away from the mage's hands. "Why should I trust you?"

The woman shrugged, her thin shoulders moving up and down underneath her filthy gown. "I have told you many things; they could be false tales to mislead you, or they could be true. In the end, you will have to trust your heart, trust yourself. It is not up to me to decide who you should or shouldn't trust. Words carry no weight if the actions behind them are meaningless. Take this." She reached behind her, then held out a round object.

It was oval and large, like a melon. The color was off-white, and yet it glistened in the light. It looked like an egg. Maeve stared at it, eyes wide. If she had to guess, she'd say it was a dragon egg, cursed by the mage perhaps? A symbol of her power?

"Take it," the mage encouraged, although it was too big to fit between the golden bars of the cage. "Seeing is believing, isn't it? The rest you will need faith for. Faith. Something I've never been so fortunate to have."

Maeve hesitated, an idea coming to her. "I will take it, and protect what is inside if I can, but only if you tell me how to defeat the fae."

The woman shook her head. "You are a bold one, aren't you? But alas, there is no room for you to bargain. What is done is done. If you would defeat the fae, you must find your own way. If you recall, my kingdom fell to their rule, the greatest kingdom in those days, and if something so great can fall, what chance do you stand against them?"

A cry of rage burst from Maeve's throat.

The mage eyed her, considering. "You are desperate, aren't you? I sense the same feeling I had, years ago, when the fae invaded my mountains. When my sister turned against me. I would have done anything to survive, anything to stop them and go back to those days of glory. But I also recognized my thoughts had turned dark, and that I had aligned myself with evil people. I heard whispers, though one would need to speak to a scholar to confirm them."

Maeve's chest tightened. A scholar? The term was used widely, but her immediate thoughts flew to Sandrine, and a dark awakening stirred in her belly.

"A scholar to confirm what?"

"To confirm how to eternally banish the fae to the shadow world."

"But isn't that where they are now? Cursed? And if curses

can be broken, what is the point of confining them to the shadow world?"

"Ah. That you will have to discover for yourself. Like I said before, my quest to destroy the fae ended in bloodshed and sorrow. I've heard word that one must go north. I've also heard that one must go to the western islands. It is a quest you will need to take up on your own. My advice is, know your enemy. Discover their weakness and use that to bring them down. And above all, stay patient. Revenge is not for the faint of heart. Now. I've said enough, and my strength is waning. Hurry. Before the goblins return."

The woman sat the egg down and pushed it toward the golden bars. She took a deep breath, arched her back, and spread out her arms. Her lips moved soundlessly, reciting a spell, or perhaps a prayer.

Maeve held up her hands. "Please, wait. There is more that you know, isn't there? I still have questions. What about your sister? Does she still dwell with the fae? You said she did not study the world, but to know what she knows, would she use a scholar? Please!"

The woman ignored her and a smell like an iron forge burning filled the air. A mist grew in the cage and swirled around the woman, momentarily hiding her from sight. Then, before Maeve's eyes, her body turned to dust and whisked away in the air.

Maeve gasped and stumbled backward. For a moment, she thought she saw wings, massive and leathery with hooked claws on the edges, and then there was nothing. The cage disappeared, leaving only a mound of dust with the egg sitting in the center. Free at last.

Sounds echoed through the silence: the clacking of feet and the licking of tongues. Maeve straightened and took a step toward the egg, even as her vision swam. She wanted to scream, curse, beg, and plead. The woman had given her hope, and yet the hope invoked more fear than she'd ever felt. It was as though she was in the grips of something unknown with the strength of a waterfall, yanking her downstream to the mouth of terror and there was nothing she could do.

Tears poured down her cheeks as she reached for the egg. Its heat surprised her and she almost dropped it, crying out at the instant pain that ripped through her fingers. She scanned the area, surprised to see that the ragged cloak had somehow survived the transformation of the mage. She used it to pick up the egg and turned toward the stairs. Caspian. She had to give him a warrior's salute before the goblins returned.

26
BEYOND THE VALLEY

Tears streamed down Maeve's face as she buried Caspian. She'd taken him to the treasure room and laid him in an alcove after sweeping out the mound of treasure. When the time came to cremate his remains, her heart stopped her. She just couldn't. Besides, his face looked so peaceful lying there. The creases were gone from around his eyes, his lips had relaxed, and it looked as though a sweet dream filled his thoughts. Silent tears rolled down her cheeks and dripped off her chin. Without bothering to wipe them away, she folded Caspian's cool hands on his chest.

"Caspian," she promised, "dear Caspian. I don't know what happened nor why you carried one of the lost shards, but I promise to find a way to stop the fae from taking and destroying. I will make you proud and discover what it means to be noble."

She lifted her chin as the words left her mouth and her

blue eyes flashed in defiance. She would do this for Caspian, and nothing would stand in her way.

Taking the bundle of rags in one hand, she stood tall. Time was short and the stomping of feet warned her the goblins would reach the treasure room soon. Would the woman's claim about the egg ring true? Part of her wanted to curse, rage, and wail, especially at the loss of all the knowledge the mage had collected. But there was nothing for it. Even if she could find a place to hide until the night of the full moon, she'd have to deal with the goblins eventually.

Stepping out into the passageway, she began to run. The bloodthirsty cries of the tireless creatures chased her. Yet as the cries rang on, Maeve recognized a sorrow in them, a deep and mournful note, as if they knew the prisoner they kept in a gilded cage had flown, escaped, and there was no queen to worship anymore.

A flash of green reared up in front of her and the reek of unwashed bodies assaulted her nose. Maeve took long strides and held her sword in one hand. A recklessness washed over her, tugging her to let go of her restraint and run into the multitude of goblins to see what they would do.

A high shriek pierced her eardrums when they saw her. They surged toward her, like the current of a mighty river. Battle rage boiled in Maeve's belly and her eyes sparked with hate. She lifted her sword, ready to give in to her emotions, to demand blood for blood. But as she reached the first segment of goblins, they sprang away, shrieking. Maeve halted, heart hammering in her throat. She took a step. The goblins scattered, as though her aura were holy and they were not allowed to approach. She took another step, and another, growing bold as the goblins scattered away, some hissing, others bowing, but none daring to approach her. Slowly, she slid her sword back into her scabbard and held the egg in front of her with two hands, lifting it high as she strode boldly out of the lair.

The low light of the dying sun made her blink hard. As she descended into the valley, she saw dead goblins lining the slope. There were charred remains on their clothing and some of them were still smoking. She sniffed. Aside from blood, there was a charred scent in the air, and a dark smoke so intense it made her nose itch. What was this? Who had done this? She hadn't recalled the smell of fire before as she fought her way to the lair, but then she'd been enthralled in her battle rage, which led her to forget about anything and everything else.

She scanned the hillside, wondering where Sandrine and the pirates were, if they had made it through alive. Come to think of it, they hadn't followed her and Caspian into the lair—of that she was sure. It was like the first shard; Sandrine had chosen to stay out of sight while Maeve faced trouble alone. A sudden bitterness rose through her, tasting sour on her tongue, though perhaps that was the bile in the back of her throat.

Her legs ached as she climbed the hill and exhaustion set in. She hadn't realized how hard she'd fought and how emotionally spent she was. The words of the woman echoed in her mind, and while she wanted to make sense of it, she also needed to get as far away from Draconbane as possible. Although it was the only true safe haven from the fae she knew of, it could only be a last resort.

"Maeve."

The hushed whisper of her name, nothing more than a question in the wind, made her open her eyes. She hadn't realized they were closed until she opened them and looked up. On the crest of the hill stood Imer, his clothes ripped, his fashionable hat gone, and his boots covered in a slick substance that might have been a combination of blood and guts. It looked as though his clothes were burned, and his face was covered in soot, like he'd been through a fire, though the skin showing through his clothing was hairy and unblemished by flame.

Maeve stared at him, unsure what she should say or even do. "Where are they?" she croaked out.

There was a haunted look in his dark eyes as he dropped his gaze and ran his fingers through his dirty, slicked-back hair. "Is Caspian . . ."

A bolt of rage flashed through Maeve, instant and shocking, like a flash of lightning. "Don't you dare speak ill of the dead," she snarled. Just as quickly as it came, her anger faded, leaving a hollowness so gaping she thought she'd fall into it and never find herself again.

"Come," he held out a hand, his fingertips stained with ash. "You've fought hard enough. Come, rest."

His face blurred in her vision as tears swam in her eyes. She forced her unwilling legs to the top of the hill, even though they felt like lead. Imer's hand closed around her arm, so warm it was almost hot to her skin. But his touch was comforting, and she leaned into it, willing to give up the struggle, give in, rest, and let her mind drift.

As Caspian always said, problems were best solved when

given a night of sleep, for sleep was healing, and when refreshed and in full health, solutions were always found.

Caspian. He had been a positive influence in her life; solid, steady—a home. What would she do without him?

Maeve vaguely remembered being led to an enclosure between the mountains, where a stream flowed through the stones, creating a pool shaded by fir trees. Imer helped her wash the blood off her legs, refilled her waterskin, and told her to rest as he tucked her underneath a tree branch and she snuggled up against a brown trunk with moss as a cushion for her head.

When she woke, hours later, a sliver of the almost-full moon hung in the sky, lighting up the shadows with hues of silver. She glimpsed a hint of beauty in the twinkle in the starlight, the magic in the moonlight, and the way the pool glittered underneath it all. It was as if the pool allowed the moon to shine its face upon the surface of its water and worship the lake.

Maeve propped herself up on one elbow, and as she did, the egg rolled away. She'd slept with it tucked against her stomach, and the sight of it brought back the memories of the day. The magic in the moonlight faded and the loss of Caspian threatened to flatten her. She scooped the egg up and sat cross-legged with it in her lap. Leaning back against the tree, she closed her eyes and recalled the conversation she'd had with the mage. Even though the goblins had overrun the lair, a spark of hope lit up in her. Perhaps there was a way to hide the shards from the fae. If they could not enter certain places, she needed to find one of those places and hide. If she were hidden—with the shards—they could not find them. And then it struck her like a blow to the chest.

The fae did not know about the shard Caspian carried. As long as she kept it hidden, apart from the others, she could keep them from completing the crown, keep them from taking over the world. Hope surged within her. It would not all be for naught. She would find a way.

Satisfied with a solution to her dilemma, she squinted in the moonlight, searching for Imer, Ingram, and Sandrine. She did not recall seeing them earlier, but the pool was quiet and the surrounding area dense and wooded. Perhaps she was alone, left to herself after securing the shard, but something about that did not make sense.

Sandrine wanted the shards, and surely she would have appeared after the battle, crudely reminding Maeve it was time to continue to the next location. Sandrine the scholar, whose book Maeve intended to steal. The need had become more urgent, dire even. Sandrine's book might contain the location of places where the fae could not open portals. She needed to find one as soon as she was able. As long as she kept Caspian's shard separate, when the fae came for the others, she could hand them over, and they would suspect nothing.

At the thought, the heat of the collar did not flare up, nor did the faint echo of the Master's words. She'd discovered a way to combat them, and while she did not want to hide for the rest of her life, she would do what she had to do to save the world. Even Caspian would consider it a noble act.

In remembrance of him, she rocked onto her knees and folded her hands in front of her. It had been weeks since she whispered prayers to the Divine, and yet on such a moonlit night it felt right. She closed her eyes, lips moving in a murmured prayer. A peace overwhelmed her, closing around her, softening her sorrow and reminding her she had a purpose, a place. It was all right. Everything would work out as the Divine intended.

Relaxing, Maeve lay back down against the tree trunk and returned to her slumber.

27
Wizard's Sanctum

Hushed whispers broke the silence of the inner sanctum, and Jacq the wizard stood up straight, letting his heavy robes hang off his shoulders. He lifted his hands, palms upright, and closed his eyes, listening to the voice of the winds. Some days, the whispers of the wind were easy to decipher, but others, it was blurred, like reading the future while looking through a marred mirror. He sensed the strange cadence in the voices, the sign that something had changed, something had happened. But what? He needed knowledge, information . . .

"Jacq."

A feminine voice interrupted his meditation, and he opened his eyes, purposefully keeping his feelings from displaying on his face. "Willow," he said, studying his apprentice, who stood in the doorway.

She was striking, with the shades of her dark skin offset by the long-sleeved, form-fitting red dress she wore. Its silk skirts, laced at the end, swept the stone floor as she moved. Her black hair was unbound and flowed in a collection of waves and curls down to her waist. As always, she looked beautiful, wild, intoxicating, and dangerous.

When she first arrived at his hidden village, Imperia, more commonly called the wizard's tower, he'd recognized their kindred spirits. At first, he tried to keep her at a distance, but quickly realized her power called out to his, and that he could not hide from a powerful mage like Willow. Instead, he began to teach her. Mages came and went, but it was Willow who stayed by his side. He saw her as his successor, but he was aware she saw herself as more, so much more than a mere keeper of power, instructor of mages, and next in line to guide Imperia.

She stepped into the room. The sanctum was a circular structure at the summit of the tower with walls made of high windows that ran from the floor to the ceiling. A cascade of golden light made the room shimmer, and often it seemed as though Jacq could see the power around him manifesting as words and visions dancing in the daylight. The stone floor was covered in runes and patterns that only added to the enchantment. The sanctum was where Jacq came to meditate and listen to the whispers the wind carried to his ears. Whispers of change and disruptions in the land.

"Forgive my intrusion, but Kel has returned," Willow said. She did not look sorry at all for interrupting him, and a slight smile played around her lips.

Jacq folded his hands together. Kel was Willow's white hawk, with which she shared a magical bond. When asked, she'd send the bird out to fly across the land, bringing back news of what it saw. The connection between Willow and Kel was potent, unusual. Jacq had never heard of a mage who could send power into a creature without turning it into a monster.

"Proceed," Jacq encouraged her.

"Ingram and Imer are in the Draconbane Mountains, with three others."

Three? That was unusual. He had only expected two others to join them. "Are they being followed?"

Willow shook her head and pursed her lips. "Not yet."

Relief surged through Jacq. "Good. Our diversion was successful and the quest still stands."

"But the night of the full moon is near . . ." Willow trailed off. She moved closer to Jacq and lifted her eyes to the doomed ceiling. Light danced across her face and bare throat as she breathed in. "I sense a change. . ."

Finally. Willow had never read the winds before, nor sensed a change. If she could feel it now, it meant either her power was growing stronger or what had happened was so strong it impacted the elements. But what was it? That he could not gain a sense of, but perhaps she could. "Still your mind," he coached her. "Listen to the whispers of the wind. What does it tell you?"

Willow listened, head thrown back, taking slow, shaky breaths.

Jacq watched the smooth skin of her neck throb as she swallowed, and then her eyes met his, dark and intense. "Do you remember?" she whispered, as though not to disturb the whispering voices in the sanctum. "When you first taught me of power and helped me understand the rush of emotions that twist through me? You told me the power of a mage is always strongest when united with others. You also told me about the Prophecy of Erinyes. When it comes true, we will be seen not as corrupt souls with powers that should be controlled, but the saviors of the land." Her eyes changed, widening in awareness. "But you never told me you were cursed, bound to this tower, which is why you need others to do your bidding for you. When the prophecy comes true, you will be free too."

He nodded in encouragement, afraid to break the spell of knowledge with his words. His heart beat faster, hoping she would go on. Was his prodigy becoming stronger than him?

"But you aren't like the cursed ones." Her hands reached out, catching his own and holding tight. "Because you don't want to rule the world—you want to change it. The prophecy mentions 'the lost' who shall be found, but there's more to it, isn't there?"

He looked down at their joined hands, and a hum of power cut through the whispers in the wind. "Aye, there is more to the prophecy. A day will come when curses will be broken. The lost shall be found, the found shall be lost, and the rift between mortal and celestial will cease to exist. The dragon queen of old will rise, freed but hidden in disguise. The last defender will come forth, and the sword of justice will purify."

The hum grew louder as they held hands, locked in a rush of power that whirled around them like a windstorm. Jacq studied her eyes, watching as they grew wider and as more and more power shimmered behind them. She felt what he felt, their union, strengthened as they held hands until it became overwhelming. With a cry, Willow let go and spun away, breathing hard.

When she regained her breath, she said, “When our hands were joined, I heard the whispers in the wind clearly. A queen of old was freed from a curse using the power of death, yet her spirit lives on. The last defender has been found, but has not come forth.” She turned back to Jacq, her eyes imploring as she took one shuddering breath after the other, like one recovering from the heights of pleasure. “I thirst for knowledge, like you do. I can see your mind, your thoughts, your desires. But I don’t know why. Not yet. Tell me more, teach me, so that we shall be ready when the curses are broken.”

Jacq caught her hand in his and pulled her back toward him, his mind churning with her words. A queen of old freed. Ingram and Imer in Draconbane. The last defender found. They were close. So close. “Willow, stay with me for a bit longer, and I will share with you all I know. Listen to the wind. The night of the full moon is near. We need to know about the shards and the sword.”

“We need to prepare for war, we need alliances and armies, but we are the hunted,” Willow puzzled. “How can we fight when there are so few of us?”

Jacq wrapped his arms around her, relishing the power that twisted around them when they touched. “In days of old, the mages fought together, and so we will strategize together and find a way. But first, we need to know more. I have done research, but it is not enough. We must be prepared when the shards are restored into a crown, and all curses are broken.”

28

FOREST OF PINE AND FIR

When morning dawned, they were all there. Imer was wearing his hat again, and he'd washed the soot off his face, although his clothes still hung in shreds, showing off glimpses of his lean, hard body. Maeve could not deny the gravitational pull, the slight attraction toward him, and yet her sorrow masked all other feelings. Questions rose on her tongue when she saw Sandrine, bent over, looking grayer and more tired than she'd ever appeared. Yet her chin was lifted, and she carried the book in her hands, arms wrapped around it as though she could protect it from the elements. Ingram lagged and there was a slight limp to his step. What had they done out here in the valley? Clearly, they'd fought to save her from something, but what? Did she dare ask? In spite of her curiosity, Maeve held her tongue, knowing she carried secrets of her own that would not be pried from her lips. Sandrine gave her nothing but a brief nod. "Do you have it, girl?" she asked, her voice hoarse and rough.

Maeve nodded once.

Sandrine pressed her lips together and took the lead, weaving past the pool and heading directly south. Maeve followed while Imer and Ingram moved to the back. There were no questions asked about Caspian, and Maeve assumed Imer had told them. She swallowed a sob, burying her feelings with dogged determination. She would see this through and make him proud. If his spirit rested above with the celestials, perhaps he would look down upon her, follow her progress, and know his sacrifice was for the greater good.

They trudged through the forest of pine and fir trees in silence, each lost in their own thoughts. The path they followed was wide open, leaving room for three to travel abreast. It twisted and turned, leading them to the crest of hilltops only to dive back down into deep valleys. All the while, the evergreen trees hid the view from them, and hid them from any hostile creatures they might encounter. The pace was slow, strenuous, and often they paused, allowing Sandrine a moment to huff and puff, and then carry on as though it did not matter. Maeve glanced at her now and again, wondering how strong the woman was. Her determination was boundless, but would her body fail her?

It wasn't until late afternoon that Maeve gave voice to the question that had been running through her mind. "What happened?"

The wind rustled in the trees, threatening to send her question dancing away with the breeze.

Sandrine glanced back at her and grunted. "Answers are given in exchange for answers."

Maeve shrugged. Instead of angering her, Sandrine's

taunt was expected. “What do you want to know?” she replied evenly.

Sandrine allowed Maeve to walk alongside her. They were in the flatlands now, without a hill in sight, which made it easier to walk and speak at the same time.

“Who did you see inside the lair?” Sandrine asked matter-of-factly.

Maeve almost paused. *Who*? Did Sandrine know who was in there? Questions raced through her mind and speculation mounted. Was it possible that the scholar, in all her wisdom, knew exactly what situation Maeve had walked into? She swallowed hard, but saw no reason to withhold the truth. “A woman in a golden cage. She had the shard.”

“Did she speak to you? Explain her history?” Sandrine asked.

Maeve detected just a hint of something else in Sandrine’s tone. Anticipation? Anger? Excitement?

“Aye,” Maeve confirmed. “She claimed she was the last of her kind, the sole survivor after the fae invaded Draconbane and killed all the dragons.”

“Eh,” Sandrine grunted. “Did she speak of her sister?” she asked sharply.

Maeve reached out a hand to touch Sandrine’s shoulder. “Sandrine.” She searched the scholar’s eyes, seeking truth. “What do you know? Why are you asking me these questions when you already know the answers?”

Sandrine stared back boldly, her emotions hidden behind her wrinkled face. “It is a confirmation of the truth, for you have no reason to lie to me.”

“Then why do you withhold truth from me?” Maeve’s

frustration leaked out, and with every word she squeezed Sandrine's shoulder harder. The sorrow ate away at her patience and her anger became impossible to control. "I have asked you time and time again, and it's like a puzzle, but you won't reveal the truth to me until I'm too close to it, and I can't see what this game is. Why Draconbane? Why did you send me in alone? Why didn't you save Caspian? You are a healer, you should have been there. And why are the pirate brothers still alive?"

Sandrine's hand came up so suddenly Maeve almost missed it. A bolt of lightning went through her stomach, and she was hurled backward so violently the breath whooshed out of her. Too startled to respond, she could only glare up at Sandrine in shock. As she did, she realized she'd left a bruise where she'd gripped Sandrine. She felt a sudden urge to scream, tear up trees by their roots, and rip everything apart. But it wouldn't help anything nor solve any problems. Taking a deep breath, she tried to focus on her breathing to calm herself. Stay calm. Ask questions. Discover knowledge. She would not resort to violence again.

"Ask me more," Sandrine demanded, her gray eyes alive with fury. "Ask me why I serve the fae or why I am still alive. Ask me why I warned you against bringing that warlord, or why I gave you the Finder's Stone. Ask. You are a clever girl, strong and clever, and there is a reason you, specifically, were brought on this quest. You were chosen because of who you are. Your heritage. Maeve of Carn. Perhaps it is time to tell you the truth. Perhaps I have spared you long enough. You've begun to suspect, so get up, girl. Stand on your own two feet and accept responsibility for what I am about to reveal to you.

When I end my tale, you might wish you had been left in the dark to mope in your frustration. Knowledge is the ultimate source of power, but it is sharper than a double-edged sword. You've faced sorrow, but the knife I plunge into your heart will not be easy to pull out again. Are you sure you want to know?"

Maeve's jaw hung open at the ferocity of Sandrine's words, and she simply lay on the ground, legs spread, staring up at Sandrine.

A warm hand touched her bare arm, and she felt a presence beside her. Imer. "Come on," he persuaded.

Maeve allowed him to guide her to her feet. Then he turned to Sandrine. "We will scout ahead. Call if you need us."

"Go ahead," Sandrine confirmed, jaw set.

Once the two brothers had gone a good bit down the road, Sandrine turned to Maeve. "Well?"

Maeve took a step toward her, breathless. "Tell me," she whispered.

"It all began here, in Draconbane," Sandrine said, her voice taking on a singsong quality. She began to walk, and Maeve fell in stride with her. The wind rushed around them, as though blessing Sandrine's words. "Old tales confirm that this used to be the land of the dragons. Stories often speak of their beast-like appearance, but the dragons were more like us, smart, intelligent, with the ability to shift between a dragon form and a humanlike form. The dragons were ruled by a ruthless king, Belroc, and a cunning queen, Drakaina. Word of their ferocity spread far and wide, so far and wide that the term Draconbane was used, for to awake the dragons meant to invoke the demons, and all who came to this land perished because of the dragons.

"One day, Queen Drakaina had a daughter, named Ariefluer, who became known as the Goblin Queen. The creatures were drawn to her and obeyed her wishes. The Goblin Queen became the pride of the kingdom, for she knew the way of the mind and was a great scholar and strategist. Although the king and queen desired a male heir, the power of their eldest was strong, and thus the kingdom flourished. When the second sister, Drakai, hatched, she did not live up to their expectations. She was not a scholar or strategist, nor did she have the power to read minds. She was, however, known for her quick tongue and violent temperament. Eventually the king and queen died, leaving the sisters to rule Draconbane in their place. There is much speculation about what actually happened to the king and queen; whether they died during a battle or if something happened within the mountains is unknown. It is only said they were killed and given a great burial, and while dragonkind do not live forever, it was known that the king and queen had died young. Too young."

Maeve recalled the flashing eyes of Ariefluer and the cruel smile on her face. Was she the cause of her parents' death, or was it her sister?

"After the king and queen died, Draconbane became wealthy, the capital of the known world. Until the night of the fae. They opened a portal a ten days march away from the city and slipped into Draconbane. Blending into the shadows like they do, they came and destroyed. Legends claim they were after the wealth Draconbane offered. Others claim they were after dragon fire, but either way, they wanted power, and with the corruption of Ariefluer, the Goblin Queen and Drakai, the Dragon Queen, they saw their chance. They took Drakai as a bride for the king of the fae and cursed Ariefluer, but the curse rebounded upon themselves. After their great victory, the fae were banished.

"While there was still awe and fear, freedom gripped the land. Slowly but surely, the legends died away, and the fae became known as nothing more than a terror during the full moon. But the fae found a way. They discovered that wicked people with evil in their hearts and murder in their eyes were easy to pull in to their domain and control. They also found that portals could not be opened everywhere, especially not in holy places. But people were predictable, and the fae found that with promises and threats, people could be controlled and bent to their will. And that is where I come in."

Sandrine trailed off, her eyes vacant, staring ahead.

Maeve stayed silent, giving the scholar space to continue her tale, although her mind whirled with questions. Why did the fae attack Draconbane? It seemed they could have made a deal with the two treacherous queens. It did not add up that the fae would attack the greatest civilization just to secure a bride for their king.

"I killed my husband. Someone I promised to love. Forever." Her words were matter-of-fact, as though she'd relived that moment over and over again, until it had lost its horror and potency. "I had a reputation in my kingdom; I was a healer first and a scholar second. I had a great library full of books I pored over, and some I wrote myself. I knew histories, languages, and lore. I went by many names in that life, and many came to me for wisdom. I had fame, I had everything, until that fateful night. If I had been a commoner, my sins might have been overlooked, but I was in a line of royals—royals who do not forgive or forget. My children were safe, but I was thrown in prison to await execution." Her hand went to her neck. "They were going to behead me, although hanging is a more common practice now. It just so happened that the night of the full moon came before my execution. The fae came to me and offered me a deal."

Maeve squeezed her hands into fists until her nails bit into the palms of her hands. This was the moment. This was the truth she'd been waiting to hear.

"My heart was full of vengeance and regret, so I took their deal to save my skin. After all, they needed a scholar with skills like mine, to dive into the histories, discover legends, secrets, relics, curses, and so I did. But not because I serve the fae—I care nothing for their kind. I serve the queen, although she is not their queen. She is Drakai, the Dragon Queen, and when the curse is broken, she will be set free."

Maeve's fists came loose although her heart pounded against her skull. This was what she'd feared, and yet also what she'd expected. Someone greater than the fae was behind this, and once she was set free, what would happen? Was she repentant, like her sister? Would she restore Draconbane to its former glory? Or was her heart bent on malice? Would she try to rule the world?

"Why?" Maeve asked, her voice barely above a whisper. "Why do you work for her? What has she promised you? What will you get out of the bargain?"

"It is ironic that you ask that, when you know why you

are here, why you still work for the fae, even though you could flee and go where they cannot find you."

"I don't have a choice," Maeve retorted. "They control me; they collared me. If I don't do what they say, I'll never be free."

"Aha." Sandrine jabbed Maeve's arm with a pointed finger. "You long for freedom, which means you will do whatever it takes to restore your freedom—unlike your former friend, the warlord Caspian. He was not like you."

Blood rushed to Maeve's ears. She turned, her heart frozen with terror. Her lips trembled as she spoke the next words, already afraid of what the answer would be. "Speak plainly. What do you mean?"

Sandrine held out a hand and took a step away from Maeve. "Do not take your anger out on me. I had nothing to do with your capture."

"Tell me," Maeve growled, rage boiling in her belly again.

"You were not the first one chosen," Sandrine told her. "It was Caspian. Half a year ago, the fae decided because of his deeds, he would be worthy to take up the quest to find the seven shards. They captured him and made demands, promising to destroy everyone he knew if he did not comply. It started well. He went out on his own, found the first shard, and then hid in a temple. A holy place. The fae could not reach him there, and when he left, he was so changed, they decided to take you instead, because of your heritage. They decided you would not fail them, not Maeve of Carn."

Tears spilled down Maeve's cheeks. So, Caspian had been trying to save her from the trap he'd fallen into. But she'd fallen nonetheless, and now he was gone, and it was because of their dark deeds that the fae had taken both of them. The darkness in her soul had called out to the fae, and they were able to twist and manipulate her because of it. She turned away from Sandrine, no longer feeling the need to strike her companion. Briefly, she wondered if she, too, could take the shards and hide in a temple until the fae forgot about her.

"What about Carn?" she asked, voice quavering.

"I am old," Sandrine said. "My family has been kept safe because of my service, and yet my grandsons—Ingram and Imer—are blessed with extraordinary powers, which makes them hunted and desired at the same time. I brought them on this quest because I know my time is failing, and you will be safe in their hands. They will take you on to Carn and help you understand. But beware. The next shard lies in Carn, and if anything I have told you has made you unhappy, what you find out there will be devastating."

A rushing came to Maeve's ears as the words, the knowledge, seeped inside, like a river brimming over, filling her, drowning her. She fell to her knees and wrapped her arms around her waist to give herself an anchor, but it wasn't enough.

A sob wrenched itself from her lips and she rocked back and forth, crying until she had no tears left. Fear, anger, rage, sorrow, and vengeance all twisted in her, emotions so powerful they poured out in a warring cocktail. But when her fingers twisted around her sword hilt, tightening, she knew, beyond a shadow of doubt, that she would stop at nothing until the fae were destroyed.

29
Night of the Full Moon

The next nine days passed swiftly, and Maeve looked at her companions with new eyes after Sandrine's revelations. Sandrine the scholar, who had fallen from a house of wealth and wisdom and was using her skills to protect her family, all the way down to her grandchildren. The fae must have had something to do with her mortality, for although she was an older woman, she had not aged as she should have. Meanwhile, the pirate brothers remained the same—they were quiet, kept to themselves, and showed no hints of extraordinary power.

Maeve, lost in her grief, sometimes wondered if she could not see clearly because of her inward focus. Her desire for freedom overwhelmed all other thoughts, but she could sense, even in her desperation, that it was akin to how the fae felt, and how the lost sister of the Goblin Queen felt. At times she peeked over at Sandrine, wondering about what the woman had said. She had not shared her vision for the future, and had only spoken of what Maeve would discover in Carn. What did it mean? Did Sandrine want her to stop the fae from breaking all curses? Was Sandrine on her side, or was she simply doing what needed to be done to stay alive, to protect her family? Sandrine had answered many questions, and yet created many more, leaving Maeve second-guessing herself.

Each day took them deeper into the land but farther from the Draconbane Mountains. White birds flew ahead, calling out to each other, and the scent of water increased as they moved south. Maeve sensed the change in the richness of the air and the growth of the trees that spread above them, larger than before. They began to see animals again. After the barrenness of Draconbane, it was a relief to see fluffy white bunnies running through the thicket, squirrels chattering as they climbed trees, birds chirping and flirting with each other, and occasionally deer, their eyes wide and solemn as they stood in the shadows, watching invaders trudge through their land. Faintly, old memories began to resurface. Maeve remembered when she was a child running through the woods, shouting and calling out, and then the calm, the quiet, the stealthy movements as she hunted. It all seemed so long ago, before . . .

Maeve opened her eyes. It was late again, and they'd reached a quiet area with woods on one side and a grassy opening on the other, overgrown and sloping downhill.

"It is time," Sandrine said, pointing to the hilltop.

"Time?" Maeve asked.

"It is the night of the full moon," Sandrine said. "Come. We will go to the hilltop and wait for the fae."

Dark visions flashed in Maeve's mind. Her fingers went to the golden collar, thin but strong, holding her captive. She couldn't refuse now; there was nowhere to run, nowhere to hide. Her salvation was the extra shard, but the fae knew that Caspian took one of the seven shards. Would they assume she had picked it up? She hadn't shared the knowledge with Sandrine, out of hope that the fae would assume that the location of the shard died with Caspian.

"I don't have to go with you," Maeve protested. "I can give you the shards, and you can take them to the fae."

Sandrine glowered. "Are you a fool, girl? After all I've told you, don't you understand why the fae are coming here? They need reassurance that you are on their side, that you haven't deviated from the plan and won't go rogue like Caspian did."

Maeve wanted to retort that there was no point, the fae would never trust her, nor would they ever relent.

Shoulders slumped, she followed Sandrine across the plain, heading toward the hilltop. When she glanced back, the brothers had disappeared. "Where are they going?" Maeve kept her voice low.

"I sent them away. They have no business being here." Sandrine shrugged. "After we meet with the fae, take the road south toward Carn. The Finder's Stone will lead you."

THE FULL MOON loomed bright in the sky, hovering over the empty glade and illuminating the silver blades of grass and the uncanny emptiness of the field. Maeve stood an arm's length away from Sandrine, arms crossed over her chest, the bag of shards in one hand. At least, two of the shards were in the bag; the other one she'd tucked into her breastplate, where she could feel the cool hardness between her breasts, a reminder to hold firm, hold steady. Too late, she'd thought about hiding the shard elsewhere, or even swallowing it like the Goblin Queen had. But it was too large, and she did not possess the magic necessary to force it down her throat. The Goblin Queen must have been desperate.

The egg was also in her pack, slung over her back along with dried food and waterskins. She doubted the fae would have use for it but all the same, she put the Finder's Stone on top. If asked, she could explain that it was given to her by Sandrine, to help complete the quest. Although she did not understand why Sandrine was leaving her so soon. Hadn't the fae promised her a scholar? Why would they take her away now, after only thirty days when she had another six months before they would demand her debt fulfilled?

A sound whispered through the meadow, followed by a dim roar. Clouds rolled across the sky and a mist with purple swirls filled the air. A hollow whistle sounded and with a sigh the portal opened on the hilltop. It appeared like a storm, a vast whirlpool, and out of it walked four shapes.

Maeve's heart quailed at the sight of them. Reflexively, she straightened her shoulders and set her jaw. She would not be cowed by the fae, not again. A reminder of the dungeon flashed before her eyes. She was upholding her end of the bargain; they needed her, and they would not send her down to the depths again.

When the mist cleared, her heart sank further. The Master was with them, clothed in his dark shroud with the cowl of his cloak pulled low over his head. He'd brought with him the lesser minotaur, who snorted and tapped his javelin against the ground. Surely, he preferred to be at the scene of a battle instead of acting as a guard overseeing the delivery of the shards. With them were two other fae that Maeve did not recognize; tall, stout creatures with gleaming eyes. One had leathery wings folded neatly on its back, reminding Maeve of a demon. Demons were ruthless villains, not unlike the fae. They had a thirst for death, blood, and deception; not that Maeve had ever met a demon, but rumors were enough to confirm the threat.

The Master's dark eyes roved over Maeve, and then he turned to Sandrine. "Sandrine the scholar, well met. Your presence is requested at court until the next full moon, at which time you will return to this quest. All is in order, I presume."

Sandrine did not cow before him as Maeve expected. She merely fixed him with a look. "I would not be the scholar if it were not as I had said. After you have finished here, I will return with you."

The Master lifted a hand, letting his claws display in the moonlight. A silent threat. "We do not need your presence for this exchange. You will return now."

He waved a hand toward the entrance of the portal.

Sandrine took a step toward it as the purple mist drifted over it. "As you wish," she said, bowing her head. Whether that was a sign of goodwill or submission, Maeve was unsure.

Despite her explanations, Sandrine remained a mystery,

and with each step that Sandrine took, a bit of Maeve's hope disappeared. The mist swallowed her whole, and then the portal snapped shut, leaving Maeve alone with the fae.

Suddenly the full moon seemed ominous, and while Maeve knew she simply needed to hand over the shards, she wished the pirate brothers were standing with her. Anything was better than facing the fae alone. Again.

Silence crawled through the glade. Even the wind stilled, cowered into submission. The Master held out his clawed hand. Maeve had to take two steps forward to reach him, stretching out her arm to hand him the bag.

He took it with a mere glance at her and opened it. The two shards gleamed, casting blue shadows across the glade as the Master held them to the moonlight and examined them.

Their beauty struck Maeve. They awoke a longing, deep within, that made her want to reach out and snatch the shards back for herself. Such holy relics did not belong in the hands of the fae. She sucked on her tongue to keep the words that were building in her throat from coming out.

"Two shards," the Master mused as he examined them, "one from the warlord Sebastian. We were there before you, but left it to test you, and you succeeded."

Maeve wasn't sure if there was admiration in his voice, or merely observation.

"One from the lair of dragons, in the Draconbane Mountains. But." His liquid eyes turned on her, so dark and depthless she felt as though she were drowning in them. "Where is the third?"

Maeve's heart froze, but she had expected this. She was ready. "Third? I don't know what you mean—"

The pain came suddenly, a searing agony flaring up her neck, rendering her speechless. The collar around her neck tightened, cutting off her breathing and blurring her vision. Eyes bulging, Maeve gasped, her hands going to her neck, as though she could pry away the collar. It burned her fingers when she touched it, but instead of crying out, only a gurgling sound came from her lips. Her knees gave way, and she fell to the ground, kneeling in front of the Master.

As quickly as it came, the pain faded, leaving her gasping in the grass, eyes wet.

"Restrain her," ordered the Master.

The minotaur pointed his javelin at Maeve while the winged fae and the wingless one came up behind her, ripping her arms from her sides and tying her wrists behind her back. They pulled hard until the rope bit into her hands. Writhing in place, she tried to rise to her feet, but a blow struck the back of her head. Her vision went white and she fell forward, head ringing with pain while they bound her feet. But now the fear was gone, and only fury remained, surging through her. If only she had her strength, she would make them pay, tear their eyes out of their faces and break their limbs. The battle rage rose in her and she struggled, although the bonds were so tight she barely moved.

Then the Master was there, lifting her face by the roots of her hair, forcing her to stare up at him. "Maeve of Carn, you were warned once, do not try my patience again," he snarled, his fangs too close to her face, too near her neck.

"I don't know what you are talking about," Maeve

protested. “It’s been thirty days; I’ve only had the chance to gather two shards.”

The Master traced a claw from her eye down to her lips, the sharp edge touching but not breaking her skin. “It is only a warrior’s nature; you plot against me, you scheme, but remember who is in control here. Your warlord is dead and he left you his shard. You have chosen not to reveal the location of the shard, and with that choice comes punishment. I will not warn you again.”

His claw hovered over her lip, and then with one quick movement, he slashed. Maeve’s cry was muffled as her lip split open and blood dripped out.

“Search her,” the Master growled, stepping back.

Maeve wanted to speak, to tell him where the shard was, to cave, to give in, but the fire on her mouth would not allow words to come out. She shuddered even as her crown was ripped off her head. The butt of the javelin bit into her side as it pushed her over, and then the fae were upon her. One sat on her legs, ripping off her sandals while the other undid her breastplate, tearing it off, wickedness in his eyes. His tongue came out, forked like a snake’s, as he examined her. Maeve was all too aware of the shortness of her shift and then a curved knife came down, ripping open her tunic from the top to her navel. Her bare breasts spilled out, along with the shard. It rolled once it fell into the grass.

The Master snatched it up and then raised his hands, stopping the fae from doing any further damage. He stood in front of Maeve while her shoulders heaved. Her face bloomed with embarrassment and shame. She should have hidden the shard elsewhere, but her anger and grief had made her careless. And now she was truly afraid, laid bare before the fae.

"Disgraceful," the Master snorted. "I had higher hopes for you, Maeve of Carn. The next time you disobey, I will bring the master of the whip with me. He shall enjoy doling out your punishment. This is not over, and I need you prepared to work, but you have shown your aptitude for trickery. Know that your punishment is not your own; the scholar will share in it, and her family."

"Please," Maeve managed to call out, despite the searing pain on her lips. "It was me, only me. The scholar knew nothing. I accept it all."

She didn't know why she was protecting the scholar, but there was something, a reason why she could not let others pay for her sins. Although if it had been thirty days earlier, she wouldn't have said a word.

"Master?" the minotaur asked, a hint of malice and delight in his question as he awaited the bloodletting.

"I shall speak with the scholar, but mark my words, your punishment is only delayed." The Master snapped his fingers.

A cold wind blew on Maeve's bare skin, and mist gathered, creating a portal for the fae to walk through.

"Untie her," the Master ordered the minotaur.

"With pleasure," it snarled.

And then the great hulking beast stood over her, his musk filling the air with a potent, animal odor. He kicked, his hoof smashing into the softness of Maeve's belly. A scream tore out of her lips as her stomach cramped. She writhed in pain, feeling like a gutted fish, still drawing breath with nowhere to go. The collar flared up, burning her neck, shutting down her breathing. She lay gasping as the minotaur cut the binds on her hands, allowing her to curl into a ball to protect herself from any more abuse.

Instead of striking her again, he cut the rope that bound her legs and disappeared into the portal. It closed behind the fae, leaving Maeve bleeding and alone on the hilltop under the light of the full moon.

30
ORC HILL

Maeve lay in the grass until she recovered enough to breathe without pain. Although the minotaur hadn't kicked her hard enough to draw blood, she knew she'd have bruises on her stomach in the coming days. She praised the Divine that he hadn't kicked her in the ribs. The intent of the fae was to frighten her, not keep her from completing the quest for them. She sat up to take in her surroundings and reached for her sandals. Some of the straps were torn, but they were still useable. She almost cried when she picked her crown up out of the grass and untangled it from the weeds. Opening her bag, she added the crown to the pile and checked over her things. They were all there, including the Finder's Stone.

She rose with a grunt and lifted first her sword and then her breastplate. The movement caused her stomach to cramp and her lips still burned, but she would not feel sorry for herself, not this time. She turned and saw that down the slope of the hill was a river, wide and shimmering in the moonlight. Glancing around again to ensure she really was alone, she headed toward it.

The riverbank was quiet. One side of the river was open to the field, but the other side, just a short swim away, butted up against the forest. Trees with upright branches and what looked like hair sweeping down toward the water grew there. Weeping willows. A sigh escaped Maeve's parted lips. With trembling fingers, she set down her sandals, bag, breastplate, and sword on a nearby rock. Wiggling out of her torn clothing, she waded into the water. It was cold, and the shock of it almost made her cry out. She wondered if the river came from the snowy mountain peaks, and the run-off of snow kept it cold. The fall weather meant she might catch a chill, but suddenly she wanted nothing more than to be rid of the feeling of the fae holding her arms, kicking her, abusing her. She dived, surrendering to the cold arms of the water. Eyes closed, she let herself drift down, where the water flowed smoothly around her, then pushed herself back toward the surface.

Goosebumps rose on her arm as she floated to the top of the river. Lying on her back, she closed her eyes, allowing the cold to numb her body, numb her senses, and let her forget the predicament she was in. But when she closed her eyes, a vision of Caspian rose before her, his blond head thrown back, laughing as they clinked mugs of ale together, celebrating another great victory. Drunken laughter echoed around them. The memory was from back in the early days, when they sought treasure above all with their rough and tumble crew of motley characters. Adrian, with the scar on his face and dark hair in two braids, was closest to Caspian and handy with a knife. Merloke, a stout man who was always eating. He kept most of his head shaved except for one long braid that went halfway down his back. And Timothy, keeper of the gold, a shrewd man, lean and tall with nimble fingers.

Caspian's hand had rested on her thigh that night—the first time he'd alluded to what was there. Maeve remembered the fire in her belly, the desire for more after a conquest, and yet Caspian had denied her, again and again. It was true he cared for her, but he had never pushed beyond the confines of friendship, of brotherhood.

Tears fell down her face and froze on her cheeks. Now she was alone. Alone in the Draconbane Mountains on a dangerous quest that would destroy the world. Then, suddenly, she was rushing out of the water to the shallows and kneeling in the mud. Stones poked at her, but she folded her hands, bowed her head, closed her eyes, and prayed under the moonlight.

Oh, Divine One.

Grant me mercy.

If you listen to the cries of those below you.

There's nothing left for me here.

I don't see a way out of this.

Every action I take hurts another.

I need relief.

I need mercy.

I crave forgiveness.

Show me a new path.

Show me a way.

Help me stop this madness.

Halt the rise of the fae.

When she lifted her head, ice-cold hair brushing down her back, she saw a stag upon a hilltop with antlers that pointed upward toward the heavens, but it was white as the feather she'd found during her first week in Draconbane. A rarity. A sign. She pressed her hand to her heart in acknowledgement. The pain in her chest, the frightened desperation, faded away, and peace—a peace she could not understand nor comprehend—swept through her, as though a presence filled her. Although she was still in the same predicament and no flashes of light had come from the sky, she felt something shift. She rose to her feet and iron determination rose in her core.

She had nothing to lose—aside from her life—and everything to gain from taking down the fae. Throughout her warring career she'd risked other lives, and now the stag seemed to agree, it was time for her to face the consequences of her actions and risk her own life. It's what she wanted, but more importantly, it was what Caspian would have wanted. Something noble.

A slight wind blew as she stood there, naked, and then a chill swept over her body. A cold warning. Shivering, she reached for her tunic and whatever spell lay over the hillside snapped.

Run.

The voice seemed to be in her head, and she glanced up toward the stag. Its dark eyes peered at her, and then it turned and started running south. But the voice—where had it come from? Why was it in her head?

With shaking fingers, Maeve dragged her torn shift over her head. Her stomach protested when she reached for her breastplate, but she pulled it on with some difficulty, her cold fingers hindering her progress. As she dressed, she heard a snapping sound and then muffled grunts. Snatching up her sandals, she wrapped the torn leather around her legs, willing herself to move faster. Something was out there; it would take too long to pause and look around, but it sounded like it was coming from the other side of the river, in the dense woods where she could not see. And she was standing there in the moonlight, a clear target for any arrows. Her tongue went dry. Her hand wrapped around the hilt of her blade and tugged it free of the scabbard, then she tossed her bag on her back and began to run alongside the riverbank. South. It was difficult to hit a moving target, and she hoped she was moving too quickly for whatever was out there.

Her mind raced, and although she knew it was unlikely goblins were around, there were many foul creatures that called Draconbane home, and she was alone. A curse passed over her torn lip, but the numbness of the water had not worn off yet and the fire building in her belly kept the pain at bay.

The grunt came again, followed by a loud snort. Maeve heard footsteps, and although she knew her focus should be solely on running, she wanted to know what was chasing her, so she glanced back. There were two creatures running on the opposite side of the bank. They were big, taller than her, and bulky, more brute strength than anything else. They were dressed in rags with gray skin and bloated, ugly faces. Her heart pounded in her throat. Orcs. By the Divine. Orcs were chasing her. But there were only two; she could take them.

Her foot snagged on a root and she went down hard, catching herself with one hand while her sword went flying, landing a few feet in front of her. Maeve scrambled to her knees just as the bulk of something slammed into her side, bowling her over. Lashing out, Maeve kicked and scratched at the creature. Rough black hair came away in her hand and a sour stink—like rotten eggs left out in hot sunlight—filled her nostrils. Bile rose in her throat as she scrambled toward her sword, but the creature was not far behind her. It snatched at her hair, forcing a cry of frustration from her lips. In her haste, she hadn't braided her hair nor tossed it on top of her head. Now, free and wild, it was a danger to her. She hooked an elbow back, hoping to catch the creature in the eye, but the fist holding her hair was strong and did not let go. Something warm moved over her legs, holding them down, pressing her into the mud.

Maeve wiggled in frustration and stretched out her arms. Her fingers grazed the hilt of her sword and she struggled under the weight of the creature, determined to reach her blade. The hand pulled on her hair, dragging her head back. Legs kicking feebly, Maeve realized its intention. The creature meant to bare her neck and slit her throat, leaving her blood to drain out by the riverside. She struggled as the weight pressed down, tears leaking out of her eyes from the pain in her skull. Oh, Divine One, not like this. She couldn't die face-down in the mud, attacked by orcs because she forgot to watch her back.

Rearing back in frustration, a cry of rage poured out of the pit of her being. Startled by her movement, the creature lost its tight grip, and that was all Maeve needed. She snapped her head back, her skull colliding with the hard face of the creature. It grunted and let go of her completely, giving her the leverage she needed to reach her sword. Her fingers closed around the blade and she twisted around, screaming as the movement wrenched her bruised stomach, for her legs were still held fast by the creature. She came face to face with the orc sitting on her and slashed at it. The creature rolled off her, holding its cheek and wailing.

The knife it carried dropped to the ground and Maeve snatched it up in her free hand. First, she rose to her knees, then she gingerly stood up on her feet and glanced around. The other two orcs were midway across the river, roaring as they pointed their blades at her. A knife whirled past her arm, clanged against her breastplate, and bounced off. Checking to ensure her bag was still on her back, Maeve took off, running uphill, desperate to leave the orcs behind.

Shadows rose and fell on the grass, and the moonlight was not bright enough to light her path. Twice she stumbled and almost fell while the orcs came on, grunting, their breathing loud and coarse. Maeve didn't know where she was going, other than south, and she was unsure where she should hide. Eventually she'd become winded and have to stop, and while she didn't know if there were more orcs in the area, she did know the ones following her would alert any others if there were.

Her breath came short and fast. Before the fae, she'd been able to run and fight almost indefinitely, but the collar lay heavy around her neck, sapping her extraordinary strength away. Oh, how she hated the fae for what they'd done to her. Emotions tumbled through her; rage, anger, grief, and then guilt. They came in waves, but it was the guilt that overwhelmed her as she dashed through the long grass, legs burning as she gained the hillside and followed the slope back down. The river disappeared, hidden behind more hills, and the forest loomed ahead, thick, wooded, covered. A shelter. Her heart pumped hard and fast in her chest, blood rose in her throat, and her sides ached, crying out for relief, especially after the beating she'd taken earlier. The grunts of the orcs came closer; they were gaining on her, their legs fast, built for speeding over the hilly terrain.

The trees rose in front of Maeve and she stopped, ready to make her last stand. Twirling the sword and the stolen knife in her hands, she spun to face the orcs, and to the surprise of both, dashed straight toward them, blades out. The orcs paused, only for a moment, but it was enough. Maeve whirled past them, lashing out with her blades and striking true. She heard them roar as the blades found flesh and there came a ripping, tearing sound. Grim satisfaction rolled through her as she spun around and dashed back toward them. This time the orcs were ready, although black blood rolled down one's shoulder. Baring rotten teeth at her, they charged, blades swinging.

Before she were collared, she wouldn't have worried about taking down two orcs at once, but it took all of her wits to duck, bob, and weave between the two creatures, trading blows with them. They were both strong, and despite their bulk, fast. Maeve's heart quailed as she fought, giving up ground as the two orcs edged in on her, blades whirling, tongues out as they saw their kill.

A blade cut across her forearm and she hissed, fire raging in her belly. She struck out with the knife, catching the first orc in the neck. It roared in surprise and anguish, both hands going to its neck where black blood spurted out. The other orc roared at the loss of its comrade, but Maeve stayed patient, blocking its blows—which came with increased fury—until it made a mistake and Maeve saw her chance. She brought her blade crashing down on its arm, which came off, leaving the orc howling. The creature dropped its blade and charged her, splurging blood across her breastplate. Maeve kicked out, knocking it back, and then swung her sword with pleasure, bringing the blade straight down into its heart. There was a sickening crunch and then the orc lay still. Breathing hard, Maeve wiped her sword on its clothes and stood tall, chest heaving as she caught her breath.

A sound made her turn and take another gasping breath. On the hilltop, dark shapes were gathering. Orcs.

31
GOBLIN QUEEN'S GIFT

Maeve bolted into the sparse wood, using the muted light of the moon to guide her way as she dashed, heart pounding in her throat. Pain from fighting the orcs faded away, leaving only the maddening sense that she had to escape, to outrun the horde of orcs that were coming for her. All reasoning fled and bitterly she considered whether the fae had alerted the orcs to her location just to toy with her. But why would the fae continue to plague her when she was working for them and doing her best to find the shards within the time limit they had set? It was madness to assume they also wanted her dead. But did they? Was there someone else they could use to find the shards? Or was Sandrine correct? Did they really need her, specifically, to complete the quest?

A tree branch whipped across her face, the sharp ends slapping against her bruised lip. Belatedly, Maeve cried out and raised a hand to shield her face. The next moment she almost cursed at her mistake. Surely the orcs had heard her, and now knew where she was in the wood. Setting her jaw, she shoved the pain to the back of her mind and pushed on.

She wasn't sure what time it was when the trees thinned and opened up to a glade. She glanced back, but it was too dark to see in the wood. When she looked up, she noted that clouds were gathering across the sky, clouds that would hide the moon and momentarily give her shelter. Squaring her shoulders, Maeve took a deep breath and started across the glade, running as fast as she could, sword in hand in case any creature threatened her during her mad flight. Instead, she felt something move, something on her back, and a distinct cracking sound came to her ears.

The egg! But not here. Not right now, in the middle of her flight. She did not have the time to stop and deal with whatever was in that egg. Her stomach twisted with horror at the thought of what it could be. Spawn of the Goblin Queen; what did it mean? What was the true nature of the Goblin Queen? A goblin, a human, a mage, a dragon, or something else?

A second crack came to her ears, and the bag on her back shook. Curses came to Maeve's mind, but she kept moving, determined to reach the shelter of the trees. Then a pain seized one of her legs. Maeve went down hard, holding out her hands to keep herself from smashing her face on the ground. A low whistling sound came and Maeve saw an arrow whoosh a few inches over her head. Eyes wide, she began to crawl on her elbows and knees, staying low in case more arrows came.

How foolish of her. She should have kept to the trees

instead of dashing across the glade. She didn't know the terrain nor where the orcs held camp. What if she were dashing into their midst? She'd blindly assumed the orcs at the river had come from a camp and were perhaps scouting, but now she realized her lack of knowledge could be her death. When she fought with Caspian, they always had scouts to go through an area first, report back on stations, changing of the guards, and all other details that might prove useful. But out here, she was in wild lands where dangerous creatures roamed. Alone. It was hard not to consider the fact that the fae had set her up for this. Perhaps they truly were finished with her, and an ambush by orcs was how they meant to get rid of her. Although it would have been much faster for the minotaur to slit her throat.

But there had been that moment by the riverside when peace invaded her being, peace she'd only felt one other time, and that was when she prayed to the Divine. It was a sign that there was a way out of this situation; she just had to be mindful. Resolve swept through her. Gritting her teeth, she crawled faster, trying to ignore the whistles of more arrows and the grunts as creatures came out of hiding spots, dashing to where she'd gone down. They must have thought they'd gotten her and the trees were close, oh so close.

A high-pitched shriek came from her bag and then it began to wiggle in earnest, as though there were a creature in it, fighting for escape. The spawn of the Goblin Queen had birthed, and it was loose in her bag. A real fear settled in the pit of Maeve's stomach. What was the creature in her bag? Although it was small and newborn, she could only assume it was something dark, something dangerous. She crawled faster, curious to see what it was, and yet dreading the fact. For all she knew, she could be carrying a demon in her bag, and its cries were drawing the orcs.

As soon as Maeve reached the line of trees, it seemed as though her bag came alive. The cries of the creature inside reached a new pitch as it fought to escape. The sounds were like the cry of a baby bird, high and wild and insistent, demanding nourishment. Maeve flung the bag off her back and set it gently on the ground, watching it move under the weight of the creature. Behind her, she knew the orcs snuck closer, and the clouds were nearly done passing over the moon; soon it would be light again, and while she needed to run on, her breathing was becoming labored, and she knew she needed to slow down, regain her breath, figure out what was in her bag, and get ready to fight again, if necessary.

Holding her sword in one hand, she tipped her bag on its side and opened it. Then she stepped back, eyes narrowed, and waited to see what would come out. The fury of shrieking calmed down as the creature found the opening. It gave a little cry, and then Maeve saw a long snout peek out. She held her breath; it was hard to see in the low light, but out came clawed feet, sharp like a cat's, and then a body that looked like it was covered in a tough hide, scaly and long with an almost orange sheen to it. Maeve gasped when she saw the thin layer of skin on its back in the shape of . . . wings? Were those wings? It was difficult to tell, but from everything she'd ever heard, it seemed she looked on a baby dragon.

Her fingers tightened on her sword hilt as decisions warred within her. Witnessing the birth of a dragon was a miracle, and yet the beast was dangerous. It should be killed before it could become like the others, an abomination. What if it was like the Goblin Queen? One who held magical power? Would it shift and take on human form? Aside from what Sandrine had told her, she did not know much about dragons, and what she'd learned led her to believe they were greedy, evil conquerors. She should probably kill it, and yet she longed to know more. A dragon. She had a dragon! What if it grew? What if it could be controlled? What if she could use it against the fae?

There was a snarl, and she realized the orcs were still coming. If she were smart, she would cut off the head of the dragon and run on. Taking a step toward it, she lifted her blade. Golden eyes stared back at her, unblinking. There was something within them that gave Maeve pause. Uttering a cry of frustration, she reached out a hand toward the creature. It was a newborn, and she'd hastily promised the Goblin Queen to take care of whatever was inside the egg. If it proved to be a threat, she would kill it later.

The dragon took a step and sniffed her fingers. Its tongue came out, warm and coarse, and licked her hand. Then it looked up at her and squawked. Maeve almost laughed. Gently, she reached for her bag and turned it over. A liquid poured out of it, hot and hissing. Egg shells drifted out along with a sour smell; the stink of birth.

Maeve groaned. The waterskins were okay, but the dried meat was soured. Quick as a flash, the dragon leaned forward and snapped up a piece of dried meat, then spit it out and squawked in Maeve's direction. As soon as she shook off the orcs, she needed to hunt both for herself and the little beast. Still questioning her decision, she reached for it, fingers closing around the scaly body. The scales almost bit into her, but ignoring that, she lifted the lizard-like creature to her shoulder, glanced back toward the glade, and set off deeper into the forest. The dragon gave one last squawk and then fell silent as they ran, as though it knew of the danger.

The trees grew close together, and there were dense bushes and undergrowth, making Maeve stumble as she fought her way through. The trees rose uphill and inclined sharply in places. But just when she thought she was rid of the orcs, she came to the crest of a hill that dropped away into an orc camp. Cursing her luck, she backed away, wondering how she'd missed the smell of campfires or the yellow light shining off the various structures and tents where the orcs lived. Several were patrolling the area, and she saw some butchering carcasses of dead animals. There was a scent of blood in the air, and Maeve desperately hoped the dragon would not give them away. If it opened its mouth, she would kill it.

Taking a deep breath, she began to back away, determined to skirt around the edge of the camp and make her way off into the forest, all the while hoping against hope that she would not meet any scouts along the way.

"Maeve." The whispered word invaded her ears, and she startled, upsetting the dragon.

32
INTO THE WOOD

The dragon's claws dug into her shoulder, making her wince. She turned toward the voice and a volley of emotions rose at who she saw. Imer crouched mere paces away from her, his dark clothes blending into the ever-changing shadows of the forest. He lifted a hand and put a finger to his lips before motioning for Maeve to join him.

Maeve's fists clenched tight, and she was unsure whether she felt relief or anger. A warning twisted through her gut, and as much as she wanted—desired—Imer, she was left with an odd sensation when it came to the brothers. Could she trust them? They worked with Sandrine, and ever since the scholar had disappeared through the portal, Maeve had been fighting off a sinking, queasy feeling. Caspian, the only person she truly trusted, was dead, and his death had revealed an ugly secret. He'd had his reasons, but there was no getting around the fact that he'd hidden a shard from her. But right now, it was the orcs or the brothers, and the brothers were the lesser of the two evils. She took a step toward Imer and the dragon squawked.

A curse rose to Maeve's lips, and she froze, glancing down at the encampment. The orcs continued about their nightly duties; some had paused to look up, but most kept working, skinning animals and cutting off chunks of meat. It was likely they were used to odd sounds in the night. Swallowing hard, Maeve inched her way toward Imer, who rose, standing tall and squinting as he looked at the creature on her shoulder.

He shrugged and then said, "Follow me." He turned, silent as the shadows, and slipped through them.

Maeve followed, relieved she had a companion, even if she didn't fully trust him.

They rushed through the trees, Imer setting a quick pace. Maeve managed to keep up, although her leg burned and she felt warm liquid running down to pool in her sandals. When Imer stopped, Maeve felt light-headed and dizzy. The dragon clung to her, whimpering in her ear, and she knew its claws had pierced her skin for she felt the blood dripping down her back.

"Come, Maeve," Imer said at just above a whisper. "Rest here for a time."

"Did you find her?" a low voice called. Ingram. He carried a blue light as he walked out of what looked like a tunnel. The trees were dense at the top but wider near the bottom, creating a strange sort of enclosure. It was much darker here, as they were in an area the moonlight could not penetrate.

"Aye, wandering near the orc camps. She has a creature with her, I think it might be hungry."

Ingram grunted in response, but Maeve did not see where

he disappeared to. She reached out a hand for a tree, suddenly feeling as though she would vomit.

"Wounded, eh?" came Imer's gentle voice. "Here. Sit, catch your breath. I don't think we were followed."

Maeve sank to the ground. It was cool and hard, but it was a relief to be off her aching feet. She sensed the dragon leave her shoulder, claws wrenching out, leaving her flesh punctured and broken.

There was a clicking sound, and she opened one eye to see Imer holding out strips of fresh meat to the baby dragon. It crawled toward him, snatching up the meat in its powerful jaws.

"By the gods, is that a dragon?" Ingram's deep voice came.

"I believe so," Imer agreed. "Odd, isn't it? But we are in Draconbane."

Ingram swore. "It's as the prophecy foretold, isn't it?"

Silence reigned as the brothers watched the dragon eat. "She looks bad. You should tend to her wounds," Ingram suggested. "I'll keep watch."

"Take the dragon with you, will you?" Imer asked.

Maeve closed her eyes again, listening to the low murmurs. Somewhere, she heard the nocturnal creatures of the wood rustling through the thicket, calling to each other with snarls and sharp barks. An owl hooted, a mouse screamed, and the cycle of life continued. Maeve took a deep breath, her feelings aligning with the mouse. She felt as though she'd been caught in the claws of a predator and escaped, but just for a little while. All too soon a reckoning would come, and she did not see a way out. Not yet.

"Maeve." A presence came near, and a hand lifted her head. "Drink this."

Maeve opened her eyes. There was a blueish light, like the jellyfish lights they'd kept in their ship, *Lucky Jane*. Imer hovered over her, and again she was struck by the gold flakes in his eyes, and the compassion she saw there. Was she wrong to feel the way she felt? The connection to him, the longing? All resistance faded away when he touched her. Was he blessed with a spell to make her forget her wits?

"I know it hurts," he went on, lifting a cup to her lips, "but this will help."

Her eyes narrowed just the slightest bit; what did he know about pain? But she lifted her head all the same, parted her torn lips, and drank, blinking to keep the agony at bay. The substance was warm and slipped down her throat, numbing the pain.

"I'm not the kind of healer Sandrine is," Imer admitted, though his voice seemed far away, "but I do know a thing or two."

Something touched her lip, a kind of paste. She pressed her lips together and earned a chuckle from Imer. "Don't eat it though, it won't taste too good."

She tried to smile at him; why was she smiling when she was exhausted? And where was the dragon? What was Ingram doing with it? "The dragon?" she whispered.

"We will take care of it, my fair lady," Imer quipped. He moved down to her legs and deftly removed the sandals, then began cleaning her wound. "You should rest so we can travel on tomorrow. You got lucky; the arrow barely nicked you. If it had gone straight through, you might have been out of a leg for life." He gave a wry chuckle, but Maeve closed her eyes, unused to his jesting.

As though sensing her attitude, Imer continued to work in silence, binding her leg just below the knee, where the arrow had bitten off a chunk of flesh. He moved around to her shoulder where the dragon had sat, tsking as he applied a paste. "My lady, it would be better not to carry a dragon on your shoulder until you have a perch for it. I had a friend who had a hawk, a common practice among lords who hunt. I will make something similar for your dragon friend once we leave this place."

His fingers went to her breastplate, rolling her onto her side so he could undo it. Maeve reached up, placing her fingers on his wrist. His body was warm, almost hot to the touch, and she wondered at the heat he gave off. What was the power Sandrine had spoken of? She'd seen no clear signs of it. "Why are you doing this?" she asked.

She caught the cocky smile, the mask he hid behind. "A beautiful woman in need of my skills? How could I resist?"

"No." Maeve held on tighter. "Why?"

The smile fell away and his dark eyes grew somber. "Some evils should not exist," he whispered. "I've studied the scrolls, the prophecies of old, the legend of the fae, of dragons, and of celestials. I sense a change is coming, but it all began with Carn. You have to go back, go back to your roots, and find what was hidden there."

"Carn," she whispered, and she closed her eyes, shutting out Imer's questioning look.

What was in Carn? What memories had she repressed all these years? She remembered her homeland in flashes, and yet she couldn't help but sense that the vision she'd seen in the Sea of Sorrows was somehow connected. The woman screaming, the child being stabbed to death, and the world burning, burning, burning around her.

"Rest, Maeve," Imer murmured. "We'll talk during sunrise."

33
FAE UNDERGROUND

To her credit, Sandrine the scholar showed no fear, nor remorse. She stood with her arms crossed around the book she carried everywhere with her and her pack still slung over her back. Mrithun watched her calmly, clicking his claws, debating whether he should punish her. They were alone in a small chamber that contained books and scrolls. It was where Sandrine went about her work, and where Mrithun and Drakai watched over her, ready to pore over every scroll and book she found. Often, she requested raids on cities with libraries, and although many old scrolls and books were stored in holy places, the fae had their way of manipulating others to do their bidding. Thus, the library had grown, the knowledge of the seven shards had fallen into the hands of the fae, and Drakai had taken a keen interest in learning from Sandrine. In part, the reason Mrithun wanted to punish the scholar was because of Drakai. The two had become close, and at times he suspected they planned without him, telling him only what they wanted him to know. Alas he had no proof, but if and when he got any, his fury would know no bounds.

His thoughts changed as Drakai walked into the room. She wore a sheer gown, and her long hair tumbled around her folded wings. She glided through the doorway like a beast of the night, her eyes alighting only on Sandrine. "Sit," she encouraged the scholar, "tell us what happened."

"All goes according to plan." Sandrine sniffed. Her voice never failed to be grumpy, as though she were displeased at the life she'd been fated to live.

Drakai shook back her hair, and her honey-colored eyes flickered with interest. "Tell me about the warrior. Maeve of Carn. Will she be a problem for us?"

Mrithun waved his claws in dismissal. "She is controlled through the collar, my angel. You need not concern yourself with her."

Drakai tilted her head, eyeing Mrithun with displeasure. "I asked the scholar. I am well aware of what you have done, but you used dark magic, and perhaps a curse, to collar her. I need to know if she can be turned, if she will be on our side when the curse if broken. For if we are free, she will be too, and she could be our greatest ally or fiercest enemy. I know she is a Carnite, perhaps the last one."

"She will not be turned," Sandrine spoke quickly and clearly. "Her mind is made up to betray you and escape as soon as she can. It would not surprise me if she went to hide in a holy place."

Drakai held Mrithun's gaze a moment longer, and then a wicked smile made her lips curve up. She barred her teeth and then addressed Sandrine. "But your grandsons will ensure she does not."

"They will go to Carn," Sandrine said, "which will be emotional for her. My grandsons will be there to comfort her."

"Comfort," Drakai purred. "Now you see, Mrithun? When a woman is in trouble, she cannot help but fall for a man who is there to assist her. So it shall be with Maeve of Carn. You may bully her if you wish, but she is a warrior—she can take it. The greater evil is for her to fall in love with someone who is not who she thinks they are."

Mrithun scoffed. "How do you know that she will not persuade them to join her?"

"Because of the Prophecy of Erinyes," Sandrine spoke up, lifting her chin. "More than anything, they want it to come true. But when the Seven Shards are put back together, chaos will reign, and the land will become a bloodbath. So prepare your armies; prepare for the worst."

"A bloodbath." Drakai grinned and a light came to her eyes. She rose to her feet, stretching out her golden wings. They were thick, leathery, and did not stretch out all the way before she folded them on her back again. "I am ready, the sword is ready. Let chaos descend."

34
BROTHERS OF FIRE

Nightmares plagued Maeve's rest. She dreamed of the woman screaming after the child, and then the fire morphed and shifted, shooting out of the mountains and the goblins poured forth, screaming and running from the fire. The fae rose, tall as giants, their impossible figures blotting out the sky while full-grown lizard-like creatures—dragons—roared behind them, ripping up mountains and tearing about the skies.

A scream tore out of Maeve's mouth as she sat up. Sweat rolled down her neck and her breastplate slipped, sliding off her torso. But someone thoughtful had placed a blanket over her and she snatched at it, grateful for something to hold on to.

Looking around, she realized she was not quite alone in the room. Beside her slept the dragon, curled up with its tail next to its head. Reaching out a finger, she stroked its head, marveling at the smoothness of the scales. Despite the ferocity of the creature and the future devastation it could wreak, she felt drawn to its wild, animalistic nature. She wondered if she should name it. It's what others did with the creatures they kept, horses, hawks, sometimes stray dogs even. But perhaps it was best not to get attached.

Close to the dragon was food and a waterskin. Unconcerned about modesty, Maeve reached out, suddenly realizing how hungry she was. Her lip protested slightly when she opened her mouth, but the paste Imer had put on her wounds had seemed to take away all pain. Perhaps he was a healer after all.

As she ate, she studied her surroundings, taking in the way the trees pressed close together and let in only a little light from the sunrise. A glimmer of pink showed through the trees, a bloodred morning, and she shivered at the thought. There were shadows near the entrance to the grove of trees, shadows she assumed were Imer and Ingram, keeping watch while she slept. She wondered if they'd taken turns throughout the night checking on her and ensuring the orcs stayed far away. A spark of gratitude filled her heart, and for a moment she was taken aback at her reaction.

After eating, she put her breastplate back on and reached for her sword. Blood had ruined her shoes, but her feet were tough and she was sure something makeshift could be found in the surrounding wood. Eventually, she'd need to find new clothes that weren't ripped and bloody. She was running her fingers through her tangled hair, trying to make sense of it, when a shadow grew larger and Imer walked into the enclosure.

His brows lifted, a question in his eyes as he glanced to

where the food had been and the sleeping dragon. "My lady, how are your wounds?" he asked gently.

Heat flared in her cheeks and, letting go of her tangled hair, she dropped her hands to her sides. She'd never been shy, but Imer's presence made her feel something different; not shyness, but a desire to please. His taking an interest in her made her want to hold it, keep it. Besides, he'd seen her wounded, vulnerable, and instead of taking advantage, he'd helped her. She rubbed her hands on her thighs and then sat on the makeshift bed. "Much better, thank you. You are a healer, aren't you?"

"Yes and no." He shrugged, moving closer to her. "I used rare herbs, as healing power does not come naturally to me."

Maeve raised her head to study him. "But you have innate powers, don't you?"

His smile froze on his lips, and a hint of darkness flashed through his eyes, so quick that Maeve almost didn't see it. "What makes you say that?"

Now it was Maeve's turn to shrug. "I sense it. Besides, Sandrine . . . er . . . the scholar mentioned it."

Imer's lips thinned and then he sat down, crossing his legs in front of her. "That she did. Listen, Maeve, there are many things we don't know about each other. I must admit, I wasn't prepared to care until I learned you are of Carn. But now I've seen you fight, lose someone you cared deeply about, and still, your determination drives you. I am not asking for trust, only a bargain. Ingram and I are in a bit of trouble, so when Sandrine asked us to join this quest, even though it's through these wild lands, we agreed. It's important we lie low for a time and stay away from crowded cities.

When Sandrine told us where we were going, I must admit, I became interested. I've wanted to return to the ruins of Carn, where I understand the next shard is hidden, for years; but it lies through orc land, as you have seen for yourself."

He dropped his eyes, gazing at the ground as though it would give him answers. His focus shifted to the slumbering dragon, and a light came to his eyes. "Regardless, traveling with you has been an adventure. There are dragons again, and the time is coming when the prophecy will come true. Will you come with us to Carn?"

City of ruins. Thoughts of Carn flitted through her memory and her fingers shook. She was afraid. Why was she afraid? She took a deep breath, wondering if she should trust the brothers, but after all she had learned, there seemed no other option. She leaned forward and felt the heat from his body. A tingling sensation started at her fingertips and wormed its way through her. His scent floated to her, warm, like a fire on a cold day, a beacon of hope. He held out a hand, reaching up to cup her cheek, and she did not slap his hand away. Instead, she leaned in to his touch and closed her eyes, feeling the smoothness of his fingers, the warmth in his hand, as though a fire simmered within him.

"I will come with you," she whispered, opening her eyes to meet his. "No other option lies before me, and I've lost everything."

There was sympathy in his dark eyes, and understanding. He brushed her cheek with his thumb, a soothing motion that made her heartbeat quicken. "Losing everything does not mean the end. I think going back to the beginning will reveal the key to your freedom, what you have been missing."

"But why? And what about the Prophecy of Erinyes? What do you know about it?" She studied his face, as though it would give her answers, his high cheekbones, the impudent twist of his mouth, his deep-set eyes, and his thick hair, neatly brushed back from his forehead, as though he'd taken the time that morning to work on his appearance.

He moved closer to her, dropping his voice. "The Carnites were the protectors, the last defenders of kingdoms. They were not human; they were a mix between celestials and human, born to guard our world. According to the Prophecy of Erinyes, when Carn was destroyed, the last defender would have the chance to save the world from those below and those above. When I learned of Sandrine, I looked into the lore of the world. You have a chance to become the last defender, but only if you remember what happened in Carn and take up the power that still rests there."

Maeve stopped short of biting her lip and reopening her wound. Disappointment swelled in her breast. "So, you want something from me too. They all do." She turned away and his fingers shifted, slipping down to brush her neck. "I am not a protector, defender, or hero, I just want to be free."

"There will be no freedom if the world is in bondage," Imer countered, "and you are not alone, not anymore."

He let go of her and rose to his feet, shaking back his thick hair as he did. His ears sprang up and out, pointed ears, unnaturally large.

Maeve gasped. No wonder he wore the hat and kept his hair over his ears. He wasn't human either. He was . . . no. He couldn't be, and yet there was no other explanation. But how? How did it happen? How was he walking in daylight if he was fae? She scooted back, scooted away from him, but he wasn't done yet. With a snap of his fingers, his hand burst into flames and his skin glowed.

Understanding washed over Maeve, but she could do nothing but stare at him, heart pounding in her throat. Fire. The goblins had burned; that's how they'd escaped. She didn't know whether to laugh or cry; surely the Divine was toying with her. She'd been fighting so hard to escape the fae, and yet she'd ended up with fae brothers after all. Is this what the king of the fae intended? Did he and Sandrine manipulate her into joining with the brothers on purpose?

Imer waved his hand and the fire disappeared, leaving white smoke drifting off his fingertips, his hand just as smooth as before. A rogue smile came to his features, and then he saw the horror on Maeve's face. Instantly he was beside her, kneeling in front of her, his heat almost unbearable. "It's not what you think, Maeve of Carn. We may have fae blood, but it is not born of darkness and evil deeds. We were born of love and light, to defeat the dark fae. That is our course, and now you know our secret. We are the brothers of fire. Whether or not you want to come with us is still up to you. But, like I said, you are not alone anymore."

"It's all too much," Maeve gasped. "I don't understand."

He nodded as he took her hands in his. "You don't have to. You just need a bit of faith."

Faith. The sentiment rang a bell. Caspian had reminded her, many times, about faith. She had to find a cause, a quest, a reason to be noble. She thought back to his death, his desire, and the secrets he'd kept, perhaps to save her, although it had done nothing good. What would Caspian want from her now? But she knew, even before she opened her mouth, she would go with the brothers of fire. She would walk with them to Carn, and understand her past, her heritage. And then together, they would work to stop the fae.

Tears swam in her eyes for a moment. She would stay on guard, stay wary of the brothers and their true motives. They were dangerous, but if they could help her, she needed to take a risk and learn how to trust again. She squeezed Imer's hands and looked him in the eyes, noting the hints of gold, fire, that danced there.

"Aye. I'll come with you."

FATED

NIGHT OF THE DARK FAE
BOOK TWO

I

Wild Lands

"You shouldn't have told her," the hushed words filtered through the trees as Maeve prepared for travel.

Moments ago, her conversation with Imer—one of the pirate brothers who, as it turned out, wasn't a pirate after all—had revealed a shocking and somewhat disturbing surprise. The brothers not only carried the blood of the fae, they were also brothers of fire. Fire mages. She'd never heard of such beings, although her strength was in fighting, not in knowledge, but all the same, it worried her. Then there was her surprising connection, albeit attraction to Imer, the younger brother, who was handsome, rueful, and made her feel like no one ever had before. Her skin still tingled from his touch as she checked the straps on her breastplate and fussed with her leather sandals. Broken and unusable. Just like the fae had left her—battered, broken with her clothes in ruins.

But as she buckled her sword around her waist, flares of anger and rage did not rise. Something had changed.

Imer's quiet tone interrupted her musing. "I had no other choice, if she is to come with us, she must feel like she has some sort of trust."

Ingram snorted. "Did you tell her the Hunter is following us?"

A beat of silence and then, "Nay, that is our battle to face."

"How is there trust if you share one secret but not the other? I would have preferred that you say nothing. After all, we don't know who she truly is. A pawn of the fae, nothing more."

"And a Carnite," Imer persisted. "That means something, you know it does. She's fated—"

"You would damn yourself and you well know it. We shouldn't have come here. After leaving the tower we should have stayed in hiding in the temple or by the Sea of Eels. We'll catch our death out here in the wild lands with the orcs and the Hunter on our trail. It's a miracle we escaped Goblin Hill and now Sandrine is missing."

"Not missing, returned," Imer rejoined. "But we have a chance Ingram, a chance to make things right, to stop hiding and walk in freedom with our powers. Doesn't that give you hope?"

"I care nothing for hope," Ingram said. "We should have set sail to the north years ago. I hope you know what you're doing out here and I would remind you, I don't care who you are falling for. The secret is ours, never tell anyone about our skill set, or I will have to take drastic measures."

"Bind me and toss me in a ship again? I know your ways, brother, and I'm just as stubborn as you."

"I'll watch your back, as always." Ingram's voice was cold with warning. "But Divine help us if you fall for her, we can't cross paths with the dark fae and if the prophecy is true . . ."

They must have moved away, for their voices faded into indescribable hushed tones. Maeve frowned, unsure what to think of their words. She'd spent her years warring in the company of warlords. She was used to the craftiness of others to serve their own motives, but this felt different. In her loneliness she craved trust and communication, something she'd had with Caspian. *How had it only been ten days since his death?* It felt like much longer.

Scooping up the slumbering dragon and deftly avoiding its claws, Maeve followed the openings in the dense wood out to sunlight, where the brothers stood. Their backs were to her, but they stood side by side, arms crossed, Ingram staring up and Imer shading his eyes to peer through the blended shadows.

Ingram was the first to turn when he saw her. "Ah, I hear my brother persuaded you to join us."

The words were not encouraging, but Maeve also did not get the sense that he meant to drive her away. Briefly he glanced at the dragon, then adjusted the pack on his back and led the way, moving among the trees as though he were a forest elf.

Imer gave her a rather sheepish smile, as though she'd caught them talking about her. "After you, my lady," he swept his hand out and gave her a mock bow. Then he put a finger to his lips. "We know not what is in the woods. It's best we travel quickly, and silently."

Maeve closed her mouth, understanding his meaning perfectly. If there was more to discuss, he was not interested in trading words.

Still, she caught his wink as she moved in front of him, her blood soaked sandals flapping as they walked.

Questions filled her mind as they moved like creatures of the night, silently gliding through the twisted trees and stunted underbrush. The air had a metal tang to it and there was something off, something odd about the wood they traveled through, as though it had been tainted by evil and would never recover.

Maeve's wounds did not bother her anymore. There was a hint of soreness, but the pain from her night of horrors had faded because of the paste Imer had used to cover her wounds. Even the dragon seemed content to sleep on, silver wings folded on its orange-colored back as Maeve carried it. Occasionally a lidded eye would open, glaring up at her and then around at their location. The pink tongue would flicker in and out, and then the dragon would sleep again.

Maeve caught Ingram glancing back at it occasionally. Both the dragon and the brothers were born of fire. Did they feel the connection? The desire to watch a flame burst into life and consume all it touched? Maeve's thoughts flickered back to her earliest memories, something so terrifying she'd tried to forget. But before she could repress her memories, the vision she'd seen in the Sea of Sorrows came sweeping in.

Burning. Burning. It was all burning. Red flames shot high into the sky, blending with other colors, red, orange, and blue. Heat seared her face, her cheeks melted, the skin giving way as the fire ate it up, licking up everything in its path. A moan came from her lips, the cry of her soul, and her tears hissed, evaporating under the heat of such intense fire. When she looked up, the night sky was blurry, covered with billowing clouds of smoke, so dark she could not see the starlight. Her fingers closed around a burning branch as the flames licked her body. An overwhelming grief surged through her, stronger than the violent pain that drowned her. Looking down, she saw a blade sticking out of her chest and she knew blood covered her garment. Again she saw the soldiers take the blade and drive it into the child, again and again. Those wild screams filled the air. Her daughter needed her, and she'd failed to protect her. Lips moved in silent prayer. Oh, Divine One. Save my daughter. Save Maeve.

The day vision faded under the noon sun. Maeve staggered, disoriented, reaching out a hand as a wave of nausea came over her.

"Maeve?" Imer whispered, reaching out to steady her.

She leaned into his gentle touch, her mind reeling with impossibilities. *Was it true? Could she have been the child that was stabbed?* But she had no memory of it. Her early days were a blur of fear. Fighting to survive, training with the other children, all orphans who fought to live. She'd stayed in a city near the sea and she recalled the kindly man with the long white beard who'd taught her first how to use a staff, then a knife and finally, she trained to use the blade. But then there was her supernatural strength which caused great interest and forced her to run away, to escape those who would use her, and in the running she'd run straight into the arms of the fae. The Master insisted he'd saved her for a reason . . . could it be that she was the child from Carn who'd survived the massacre of her people only to become a pawn of the fae? And what of the soldiers? Imer had told her that the Carnites were the defenders, protectors. Were they destroyed so that their land would no longer be protected? Protected from what?

"Maeve?" Imer whispered again, his tone insistent. "We cannot stop here; we are too exposed. Sundown will be soon. Can you make it a little longer?"

Face white, she looked at him, her fingers curling around his arm, desperate to know. "My memories of Carn are coming back, slowly but surely. I need to know more."

He nodded, his face calm, passive even. "All in good time. Come, let's find shelter."

The loss of Caspian continued to haunt Maeve as they continued across the rolling hills of the wild lands, sometimes traveling through thick forests, other times hiding behind the swell of a hill. Ingram was an excellent tracker and although they neared orc camps, he took them around, steering clear of the creatures.

As the days passed, first one, then several, Maeve emerged from her fog of grief. Although it was still there, like a distant memory, something she tried to forget, for there was no going back, only forward. The passage of time did not lesson the blow, only changed how she perceived it, even though, more than anything, she wished she'd known more about Caspian, the warlord she'd sworn to follow.

With the grief clearing, she could pay attention to how the landscape around her changed. The uneven ground beneath her feet, her all but ruined shoes, and the quick, almost panicky pace the brothers set. At night, Ingram would stand, listening, or sneak further ahead or behind, watching, examining the ground. He often came back with game, food for them to share, although Maeve was unsure how he caught it, since he carried nothing more than a short blade—no bow or arrows. If he was mysterious, Imer was even more mysterious. He spoke with Maeve, talked about the patterns on her chest and shoulders. There was even one on her hand that he admired. Yet she realized he said nothing more and nothing less about him and his brother. A puzzle, a mystery. And then she realized it was because she did not have their trust.

One night she sat under the starlight, her back pressed against the back of the hillside which rose steep and high.

Ingram fed the dragon raw stripes of meat while Imer paced, and then he gasped and pointed.

Maeve followed his finger and saw a dark figure perched on a hilltop. A cold shiver went up her spine and a fear like she'd never known before gripped her in its clammy fingers. Was it the Hunter?

2
THE HUNTER

"What is that?" Maeve whispered, following the direction of Imer's finger.

Everything within her quivered at the sight of the vague creature on the hilltop, although her voice remained firm.

When Imer turned around, his eyes were so wide she could see the whites of his eyes in the starlight. His arm came down and his glance flickered to his brother, seeking . . . encouragement? "This is the closest it has gotten . . ." he trailed off.

"It's the old vibe of this place," Ingram added, stroking his jaw. "It pulls evil toward it. I'm surprised we have seen nothing else out here in the wild lands."

Maeve tore her eyes away from the thing on the hill and lightly rested her hand on the back of the dragon. It sat straight up, ears raised, tail moving back and forth. Aware. Alert. "But what is it?" she repeated her question.

"I'm afraid we haven't been entirely honest with you," Imer spoke quickly. "There are ancient spirits, beings, the closest thing on this land to demons."

"Demons? As in something worse than the fae?" Maeve's breath caught in her throat.

For the past sixty days all she'd thought about was the fae and the way they captured her, collared her, and forced her to hunt for the seven shards of Erinyes on pain of death. If she succeeded within the next six months, she would earn her freedom. Again. They claimed it was her past, her wicked deeds that allowed them to pull her into their dungeons, a lair of intricate tunnels underneath an island, an old watch-tower floating in the Sea of Shadows. There were other races who dwelt on the land, humans, orcs, goblins, and then the darker creatures no one named for seeing them was rare.

"Dark fae," Ingram corrected, a growl in his tone.

Maeve sucked her cheek, noting the rebuke. Earlier she'd learned the brothers had blood of the fae, a thought that terrified her. How did she know that not all fae were evil and drawn to darkness? And yet the brothers walked in daylight, something the dark fae were cursed to abstain from. The brothers claimed to be born of light. But how did she know?

"One could call it a type of demon." Imer shrugged. "It feeds on outwardly powers, such as ours. When we left our haven, it started following us again. It doesn't like to be around people and prefers the darkness. When we reached the Bay of Biscane it was easy to blend in. Water confuses it. During the past few weeks we have had the protective mists, but after the battle in the Draconbane Mountains, we noticed it on our trail again. It's likely when we used our powers against the goblins, it found us again. But now we are in the wild lands, it will not be so easy to shake it off."

Maeve glanced from one brother to the other, but their faces were hidden in shadow, masking their feelings. "What does it want?" She stood to her feet, voice hollow.

"It's hungry," Ingram said, a strange tone in his voice. "It wants, nay, needs to feed, on magic." He took a step closer to Maeve, his broad shoulders giving off an air of hostility. "And that's what we have. Deep, powerful magic. A feast for the creature. We call it the Hunter. Now and then something else piques its interest and satisfies it, but it is nothing to what we have. There used to be more Hunters, back when there were more people with magic. Power. The defenders of the land. The Carnites. They were destroyed, and the Hunters disappeared."

Terror surged through Maeve, like nothing she'd felt before. The dark fae made her feel defiant, but this—an old creature, hunting, feasting on magic—made her blood run cold.

"What about the dragon?" she demanded. "Does the Hunter want a race that should not exist anymore?"

"Aye." Ingram's one good eye narrowed, and he took a step toward the dragon. "We are a dangerous group, for the Hunter wants Imer and I, but if it catches you or the dragon, it will feast."

Maeve's fingers went to the collar around her throat. "But I don't have magic and my strength has been collared . . ."

"Ingram." Imer's tone was sharp. "You are frightening her."

"Good." Ingram crossed his arms over his chest and

glared at his brother. "She should be frightened. We could die out here in the wild lands, a fate you cannot protect her from."

"I am aware of the seriousness of our situation," Maeve snapped, suddenly angry at Ingram for his attitude, and talking about her as though she were not standing right in front of him. "I don't enjoy being caught unawares but I can handle myself, after all, I am a warrior. If we need to run, then we run, but running will only work for so long. At some point we need to face the Hunter and kill it. With your powers it should be possible."

Ingram shook his head, but Imer held up a hand as though to keep his brother from arguing. "You speak some sense. It is only fair that we stand and fight. But the Hunter is not like any other creature; it is nigh impossible to kill without the right tools."

Maeve glanced again at the hilltop where the Hunter perched, examining its prey. A coldness swept over her, holding her tight in its clammy fingers. "What tools do you need to kill the Hunter?"

Ingram sighed and turned away, a curse leaving his lips as he crossed his arms. "You've told her everything else, go ahead and tell her this last secret."

Maeve frowned at his attitude, balled up her hands into fists, and then loosened them. They were all in the same predicament together, and it would not do to lose her temper.

Imer turned away, putting a fist to his lips as he considered.

A sinking sensation passed over Maeve. It was Carn,

wasn't it? The brothers were using her just like the dark fae were using her. True to their nature, they were devious, dark, and only looked out for their own wellbeing. She was the one who would walk into danger, take the risk that they might live. Her eyes shifted back to the shadowy form of the Hunter, silent, almost invisible and yet there all the same, watching, waiting.

"The blade of a celestial will slay the Hunter," Imer said finally, his shoulders slumped as though he'd let go of a great weight.

Maeve's brow creased. "Where will you find one?"

Imer let out a deep breath and faced her. "Ingram and I are searching for holy relics. Where one is found, perhaps there will be a broken blade, remnants of old wars before the rift between mortals and celestials was created."

Maeve's mind spun as the realization crept over her. The brothers were searching for a relic to protect themselves, which explained the negative experience that Caspian had with them. They weren't out for money and profit as warlords and hired mercenaries, they simply want to protect themselves from the Hunter. Maeve could have wept. *Why the secrecy? The twisted tales and hostile attitudes?* But even as her mind reeled she understood that they were protecting themselves from the world, from those who would hunt them and use their abilities. If she were in their place, she would do the same. Her supernatural strength was not something she boasted about, only an ability she used as a warrior, a skill that made her the best of the best. Until the fae collared her.

She lifted her chin and addressed Imer, determined not to

be disappointed by his answer. Just when she was beginning to enjoy his company. Speaking with him was calming, much different from her conversations with Caspian, although there was not the warmth, the familiar sensation of coming home, as it had been with Caspian. True, she recognized her own grieving and an awareness that no one would replace Caspian. Yet there was something compelling about Imer that made her feel connected to him. "Are we going to Carn because there is a holy relic there? One you need my help finding?"

Imer shook his head as he closed the distance between them. He placed his hands on her shoulders, squeezing gently but firmly. His eyes went dark and earnest. "It's not always all about you. I know you were taken, used, but Ingram and I are not like them. I've always been curious about the history of Carn and now our paths have aligned. You seek the shard, and we seek a blade. Nothing more, nothing less. There is a small chance a celestial blade is there, after all, Carn is a place of old power."

"Oh." Maeve's voice went small and her face flushed with embarrassment. Again, it was all too easy to assume that everything was about her and her plight; she tended to forget there were others in the world with separate goals. Her selfishness made her feel ashamed that the brothers were going out of their way to assist her when their needs might not be met.

"If we are to travel together, we will need to trust each other, do you agree?" Imer leaned closer, his fingers tighter about her shoulders.

Maeve's heart fluttered and her breath came short. It was

his proximity. Aside from Caspian she was not used to the closeness of a man outside of combat, and there was something heady and intoxicating about Imer. His lips were close to hers as his eyes searched her face. Heat flowed from his body to hers and her skin tingled under his touch. What was it about him that set her on edge? Made her forget her woes and wish for something she could not have? All her life she'd known she was different, unique, and it was her strength, her abilities that set her apart and forced her into a life of violence, fighting, and stealing—taking from others for her very survival and then comfort.

It was the kings who married queens, the lords and ladies who ensured they had children to continue their line of nobility, and the peasants who made sure they had plenty of children to help with the daily chores. There were farmers, tradesman, craftsmen, warriors, priests, priestesses, and other stations and classes which required the partnership of one to another. But there was no space for romance, nay, love in Maeve's nomadic life. There was only the blade, blood, and wealth. Nothing else.

But as she stood under the starlight, with the knowledge that the Hunter—a malevolent presence seeking their demise—watched them, something within her twisted. Oh Divine, was she losing her senses? Was she indeed falling for a fire mage who also happened to be fae? She should flee, run away from this madness, grieve for Caspian, and ponder the words of the Goblin Queen and Sandrine the scholar. Instead she leaned into Imer, craving his touch. Her lips parted.

Ingram's rough voice ruined the moment like a bucket of cold water dumped on her head. "Kiss her if you wish, and then let's go. The more distance we put between ourselves and the Hunter, the better."

Imer dropped his hands and Maeve's face burned as she stepped away. What had she been thinking? Imer and Ingram were fae, she needed to be more careful.

3
ROAD TO CARN

"Why doesn't it attack?" Maeve asked a few days later.

Ingram had picked up the pace, allowing them only a few brief hours of rest during the night. Otherwise they moved on to stay ahead of the Hunter, although Maeve felt its presence —dense and dark—as it followed their trail. Her fingers itched to take up her blade and charge at it, screaming as she drove her blade through it again and again, not understanding why it would not work. It frightened her and she wanted to face it instead of running like a terrified rabbit into a burrow to hide.

Ingram frowned. "It will. In its own time. The hunt is part of the game and there are three against one. It will wait and plot until we are weak and unthinking, and then it will try to pick us off, one by one."

"We are about to cross orc territory though," Imer spoke

up. "The time to attack is over. For now. Once we pass through orc land we will be in Carn."

Maeve swallowed hard. "I don't understand, I thought we were already in orc territory."

"We are in the outlands," Imer spread his hands to indicate where they walked. "Orc scouts are set up along this range, as for why they are here is unknown. Closer to the city of Carn is where the main army of orcs dwells. They will not take kindly to strangers scouting their outer realms. They took this land as their own, and are likely assuming that others will desire to take it back from them. After all, on the other side of their encampment lies Carn, a lost city." Imer's voice trailed off in wonder as he spoke of Carn.

A shiver went through Maeve and a niggling pricked her mind as though she'd caught a glimpse of something that connected to her past. The orcs. They took over the land. But when? "How do you know these things?"

Imer struggled and gave her a coy smile. "Some of it is known by those who study history. Mapmakers will tell you the tale, especially if you choose to travel into dark and dangerous places like the Draconbane Mountains or the Ruins of Carn. There is no reason for you to know these things, unless you worked with a warlord who had reason to travel this way."

Maeve bit her bottom lip; she knew it was true. If someone asked her about Contresea, the Kingdom by the Sea, she would know a lot about it for she had worked there, particularly along the sea and the tunnels there. Yet there was something deeper behind Imer's words, something she could not quite grasp.

"It sounds as though the orcs are guarding the city and its ruins, lest anyone go there."

Ingram shrugged, his voice harsh. "Look at what happened in the Draconbane Mountains? The goblins guarded the hidden treasure of dragons, is it any wonder that the orcs are guarding something?"

Carn. But what was so special about Carn? When Maeve closed her eyes she could almost see it, but the pain of her memories made her choose to forget. Knowing what she knew now, it was important for her to push through the pain, to understand why the fae were doing this and how she could beat them at their own game.

If anything, she'd learned from the night of the full moon that the fae were ruthless and did not care what happened to her. She needed a plan, a way to escape from their grasp, but who would help her? Could she trust the brothers to turn their backs on Sandrine?

As they traveled together, her desire for Imer only grew in magnitude, giving her something to look forward to. Each morning when he woke those dark eyes met hers, and a flicker went through her breast, causing her heartbeat to speed up. She began to look for the quiet moments when they might be alone, rare as they were. Even since finding out the Hunter was on their trail, Ingram had taken to hunting less, always staying in view and regarding her with an arrogant smile, as though he could read her thoughts and knew what she wished. And then there were the jibs, quick reminders that they were not alone, but it wasn't jealousy. It was something else, as though Ingram and Imer had a wager and Imer lost, allowing Ingram to resolutely make fun of him.

The morning mists gave the air a dream-like quality, as though it were a frost mother, breathing the chill through their clothes. Maeve would shiver, aware she was not adequately dressed for the coming winter. The time would come to raid the orc camps for clothes, but in the meantime, the heat of Imer's whispers and the warmth of his body drew her in. It was like a sweet wine, intoxicating, heady, and so difficult to let go. Maeve tried to fight off her attraction to him. By the Divine, he was fae! But he was curious, adventurous, and far different from any man she'd met. With Imer she felt strong, confident, as though she could conquer the dark fae, collared as she was, and yet, even greater than the confidence was the hope that she might be forgiven for the wrong she'd done.

She'd been taught to do terrible things without remorse, but with Imer she felt compassion, the need to care and let go of selfishness. Was it his presence? Some other kind of magic? Was it because he did not know her past and only saw the best in her? The version of herself that she wanted to be seen with in his eyes? He thought her strong and brave, ready to face the fae and do what it takes to regain her freedom.

Even though she should resist, fight him off and focus on how to stop the dark fae from reaching their goal, the distraction was a blessing. The priorities blurred and she took to letting Ingram take the dragon more often, feeding it, carrying it. It seemed to like him, and Maeve wondered if fire was drawn to fire. Regardless, on the road to Carn, she determined to take advantage of the brothers' help, and the solace she felt when she was with them. Perhaps Carn would be the answer to everything she sought, the key to her freedom.

4

EARLY TRAGEDY

"There it is," Imer said, his voice hushed in the early afternoon breeze. Tiny snowflakes floated lazily out of the sky, a reminder of winter and the coming cold.

Maeve paused on the hilltop, her feet sinking into the wild grass that sprung up from the fissures within the rock and broken ground. The landscape descended into rolling hills and from the height at which she stood, she saw a glimmer of blue and white. Water? Were they close to the great ocean? At the height of one hill, a plateau rose out of the ground and giant stones blocked the view of water. She saw sharp edges and rounded corners, a collection of columns, walls and buildings, all broken down, the remains of what used to be a great city, taken down by an earthquake, war, and then decay. Carn. Her first sighting of Carn since the day she'd fled. The sole survivor of her people. Tears misted her eyes and she swallowed hard, surprised at her sudden emotion.

"It's not what I expected," she admitted, blinking away the tears. "I thought it was all gone, destroyed."

"It is destroyed, but not gone," Imer said. "The structures still stand, although the foundations were shaken. It was twenty-five years ago, and the buildings are covered with grit and dirt. It's been raided time and again by the orcs who live in the vicinity, but I warn you, there might still be skeletons."

Old bones. Maeve shivered. As a warrior she fought the living and hadn't had to contend with the dead, she wasn't sure if she was ready to enter Carn, but regardless, the Finder's Stone pulsed against her breast. Besides, the next shard was buried in Carn and it was up to her to find it.

Imer's hand touched her shoulder, hesitantly and then settled. Maeve allowed herself to lean into the warmth, to take solace in the minor comfort of his presence. Despite her proximity to him, she couldn't but let her eyes drift toward Ingram who stood a few paces ahead at an angle, a scowl on his face. His outright disapproval of her and Imer's growing closeness gnawed at Maeve, although she did not understand why she craved approval, blessing. Although it seemed everything she'd done in life had been a mistake, a failing that led her down a dark path, she also sought forgiveness and acceptance. Forgiveness for the error of her ways, for allowing the darkness to sway her actions, and acceptance for the choices she made, the way she sought to make things right, to walk in the light. It started with the brothers, brothers of fire as she liked to think of them. It was clear there was something different about them, unlike Caspian and his choice to step away from evil and focus on doing something noble. No, whatever the brothers had was shrouded in mystery and

Maeve wanted to know more. She leaned into Imer's touch, aware of the weakness that flooded her body, a desire for his fingers brushing against her skin, the warmth of his lips pressed against hers, and the rhythm of their bodies moving against each other. What would it feel like to give in and take Imer as a lover?

"Are you ready?" Imer asked. "I know this is your homeland, and perhaps you cannot be ready to enter the ruins, but I will be with you. And if your memories return, and what you find in Carn brings you grief, remember that we will get through it. No matter what comes."

Maeve chewed her lower lip and then tore her eyes away from the ruins. When she met Imer's penetrating gaze, her heart flip-flopped. "We." She repeated the word. "We barely know each other and yet you are so confident . . ." She trailed off, unable to pull her eyes away from the magnetic gaze of Imer's dark blue eyes and the flecks of gold that danced there.

"It is because we are fated," his eyes went earnest and his hand trailed down her shoulder, fingertips brushing her arms until their palms met.

A sensation of anticipation went down Maeve's spine as their hands joined. A moment later, a ripple of warmth went through her, perhaps an effect of Imer's power of fire.

"We are supposed to be here, on this quest. Our paths aligned, perhaps they were meant to all along. Regardless, we are here and we will see this quest through."

Maeve froze at his words. *See this quest through.* A warning buzzed in her mind and she pulled away, stung, as terrible thoughts rose. What if the brothers of fire, given the fact that they were fae, also wanted the Prophecy of Erinyes to come true? What if, for some unexplainable reason, they also worked for the dark fae and were simply in disguise, meant to show her a gentle side of the fae while working to ensure the seven shards were found and returned to the dark fae?

Suddenly, it hurt to breathe.

"What's wrong?" Imer faced her, even though Maeve tried to shy away from him and the hurt in his dark eyes. "What did I say?"

"It's just . . ." Maeve trailed off, staring again at the ruins, trying to decide whether she should be truthful. But it was her own imagination, wasn't it? As a warrior she did not trust easily and was always looking for someone to blindside her, trick her, and judge her. If she stayed with her old habits, how could she change and move forward? She shrugged and faced Imer. "It's my own fears getting in the way. My mind is starting to play tricks on me."

Imer looked over her shoulder at his brother. Something flashed in his eyes, and then it was gone.

Heart hammering in her chest, Maeve moved toward the rutted path that led toward Carn. "We should go and get this over with."

"Keep your sword drawn," Ingram warned, joining the conversation. "The orcs are near and burning them would only bring more."

Clouds of dust billowed around the broken-down road and the air stank, a mix of moisture and something old and foul. Maeve imagined it was the sour smell of death, old bones, and orc hides.

At first, they were quiet as they moved quickly downhill, toward the ruins of Carn. Even the dragon was silent as it perched on Ingram's shoulder, watching its surroundings out of lidded eyes. Around each boulder, Maeve expected to see orcs and her fingers gripped and re-gripped her sword in anticipation. Finally, just to take her mind off her surroundings, the proximity to her homeland, and her thoughts that tried to trick her, she turned to the brothers.

"Will you tell me more about you? How are you fae? Especially because the fae cannot walk this earth except for the night of the full moon."

Ingram snorted and quickened his pace.

Imer fell in step with Maeve, his voice gentle, patient. "We are only part fae," he explained. "As she likely told you, Sandrine is our grandmother and she descends from a noble family in Contresea, the Kingdom by the Sea. She had many children but only one discovered where she came from and attempted to rescue her from the fae."

"Your mother," Maeve interrupted, her ears pricking with curiosity. Sandrine seemed relentless, hardened, and uncaring. Was it because her daughter had tried to save her and failed? "Go on," she breathed.

"Reika was a scholar but she was also a warrior, and although she was the youngest of nine, she was independent with a mind of her own." Imer's tone turned wistful. "She had high hopes and dreams."

Maeve gathered that Reika was dead, and something inside of her deflated.

"She found out about the fae, the watch tower, and how to access the Fae Underground. She went alone, because no one would help her and she thought she could sneak in and out undetected. But her plan did not work. One of the fae discovered her and, instead of turning her in, agreed to help her. He hid her in his rooms but before they could find Sandrine and escape, they were discovered. The fae tossed them into the Dungeon of the Damned to await judgement. The rest did not go well." Imer shrugged and stared off toward the ruins, his eyes misting over a bit. "By the hand of Sandrine, Reika escaped, only to discover she was pregnant. She couldn't return to the Kingdom by the Sea, no noble would take her in as she was, disgraced. So she went to the temple in Isdrine and waited. There she had Ingram and before he was a year old, she had a visitor. It was the night of the full moon and, unable to sleep, she'd left Ingram with one of the priestesses and went for a walk. The fae who had helped her had found a way to escape. After that first visit, it became tradition for him to return on the night of the full moon. Month after month he returned until one fateful night, he decided to stay. But when the sun rose in the morning, it burned him to ashes."

Imer went quiet, as though the words choked him. Maeve kept walking, unsure what to say as she thought of the horror of it. The sun rising out of the sky in all its glory and burning someone to death. No wonder Ingram and Imer were brothers of fire, perhaps it wasn't inherited, only fated because of their father's miserable death.

"I was only a year at the time, too little to remember. Ingram was two," Imer went on, a hollow ring in his voice. "Our mother was devastated but she went on until she contracted a rare disease and died not a year later. It's ironic. The fae should have killed her and yet they allowed her to escape, allowed her to live. It is rare that someone escapes from their prisons without incurring death. The fae enjoy a hunt, the scent of fear and terror draws them, as does darkness. I don't recall being let outside during daylight, but one day, Ingram and I were playing hide and seek with a novice and we ran out into the courtyard. It was, perhaps, our first time in the sunshine. Because of our fae blood the priest and priestesses were terrified we would burst into flames. Like our father. I recall the warmth of the sun and the way heat rose in my belly but it wasn't until later that the fire came. Instead of being cursed, we were gifted."

Maeve stared openly at him, the swagger in his step, the curve of his jaw, and the determination on his face. Tragedy had befallen him and his brother early and yet his spirit was still light. How had he kept from giving in to the darkness in his soul? "I'm sorry," she offered, surprised at her own empathy. It was unlike her. "For what happened to your mother and father."

Imer shrugged. "Thank you. Don't you see now, we all have stories, pasts, be they uncomfortable and sad, they make us who we are and yet still leave us with a choice: how to react when devastation and darkness threaten us."

His words stung as though she'd been slapped. Her past was dark, sad, and full of devastation. She'd reacted badly. And yet, according to Caspian, there was still forgiveness, still hope for her. Her fingers tightened around her sword just as a dark shape stepped into their path.

5
ORC AMBUSH

For one panic stricken moment, Maeve thought the dark shape in front of them was the Hunter, at last coming to terrorize them before they reached Carn. But it was only an orc, dressed in armor from head to toe that looked as though it had been burned to a blackish char. The orc stood at least a head taller than Maeve and was all thick muscle and brawn. It had ash-colored skin and held a club in its thick, knob-like hands.

"Divine save us," came Imer's whispered prayer.

Maeve's eyes darted around and her heart failed as more armored orcs stepped out from behind boulders, menacing shadows as they moved onto the road. Even before she tilted her head to glance behind, she knew they were surrounded. The creature in front gave a roar, and before Maeve could take a step back, it charged. She was barely aware of Ingram and Imer moving beside her, one protecting her back, the other her side. With a lunge she stepped forward, swinging her sword at the orc's head. A familiar sensation of blood lust and battle rage surged through her and as she found her footing, the movements of fighting came back, as though she'd never lost them.

Maeve studied the orc, taking in the coverage of armor and where the weaknesses might be, and then she struck. Blade out and pointed toward the throat, she aimed to strike the orc's neck, but it moved, anticipating her blow. Forced to pivot, Maeve slapped at the sword striking out for one of her arms and whirled. Kicking out with one foot, she caught the orc off guard and followed up by sweeping it off its feet and plunging the sword into its jaw. The sickening crack and death gurgle that followed felt good, and an odd sort of power tingled within Maeve.

She recognized it in an instant. Her collared strength begging for freedom, seeking escape anyway it could, to fight alongside her and rend the world from evil. But there was no time to dwell on it for another orc rushed up, heavy footed, and growled as it dashed toward her, hands out to grab her around the waist and smash her to the ground. Maeve took a deep breath and rushed toward the orc, moving just out of reach at the last moment, slapping its back with her sword and then driving it into its side right where the armor was weak. The orc fell with a startled grunt, sending a spray of blood into the air. Flecks of it dotted Maeve's cheeks but she felt a grim madness taking over. Battle rage.

The next group of orcs moved toward her. Unsure of where Ingram and Imer were, she moved ahead, whirling, striking, kneeling, and sinking blade into skin and bone again and again. Fighting was like a dance, and when she knew the steps and was in tune with herself, there was no way she could lose. There was a reason they called her the best of the best, a warrior of warriors. Darkness seeped through her, clutched her soul with relentless fingers as she fought on.

A steady stream of orcs flowed from each direction until a horn was blown, somewhere, and Maeve paused, sweating hard, suddenly aware of how hard her heart beat and how the orc blood, dark as night, stained her breastplate, arms, and face. She held up her sword, watching the blood move on it, dripping off onto the ruined ground, drop by drop. The ground which used to be her home. It flashed before her so quickly she almost lost the vision. Homes instead of orc tents, roads instead of rivers of blood and mud, and people living in the outlands instead of orcs. The knowledge struck her like a hand to the face. This was Carn. Not the city, the capital of Carn, but the outskirts, the place where the poorer people lived, in freedom and in awe of the great city of Carn. This was where the outcasts dwelled and they had been the first to fall.

How did she know that? Maeve could not understand for she'd been so young, surely her memories did not invoke that kind of knowledge! Confusion muddled her vision, and when it cleared, dead bodies lay around her, but before her stood a lone orc. He was about her height, not particularly frightening, and dressed only in robes with no armor. Golden eyes gleamed at her and then the orc grinned, a wolfish sort of grin, revealing his sharp, yellow teeth.

Maeve lifted her chin and whipped her sword through the air, a silent warning as blood flew off her blade, covering the ground with splatter. The orc sneered as it watched the blood, then moved its hands together as though it were rolling a ball of dough. Maeve sighed, it was clear this orc was not here for battle, perhaps just one of the cooks who thought he could do a thing or two while the warriors were out fighting. Well, Maeve would provide some clarity for him. She swung her sword as she stepped toward the target, just a few more steps and she could strike him dead, probably a blow to the neck, neatly looping off his head. As she brought her other hand up to grip the hilt of her sword, the orc released what it had been holding. A ball of fire slammed into Maeve's chest.

Her breastplate took most of the force of the blow, but she was still bowled backward, and nearly knocked off her feet. A cry of surprise burst from her lips and her vision went hazy. When she recovered, she saw the dumb cook was raising another ball. A faint shimmer of blue glimmered in his hands and then he hurled it, letting loose another ball of magic that slammed into Maeve's shoulder. This time she screamed as pain rocked through her, momentarily slowing her down until it evaporated. Whatever this magic was, the cook did not have full control over it. It seemed to slow her down instead of causing true pain.

Grunting, Maeve straightened and watched, stepping closer as she studied the hand. This time when the orc let go, she brought up her sword, blocking the flow of whatever it was. Still, she felt it go down her blade as though the sword were absorbing it, and her hands trembled on the hilt as though there were something inside, fighting to get out.

Frustration mounted before rage took over and she dashed for the orc like a roaring bull, out of control, gritting her teeth against the pain that rocked through her as the creature threw invisible magic at her. She whirled her sword for the neck, just like she'd originally planned, and to her surprise, the beast ducked, as though she was moving in slow motion.

"Maeve," a voice shouted. Imer, she thought, but it seemed so far away as though the echoes of the tone were nothing but memories. "Step away," the voice demanded, an order so strong, so vicious it almost knocked her away.

Pain fired through her head and distinctly she heard the maniacal laugh of the orc as it toyed with her. Somehow, she found herself on her knees, and when she looked up, the orc's head burst into flames.

She leaned back, watching while the orc burned, disintegrating into dust with the heat of the flame that seared its body. Smoke stung her eyes and the scent of charred flesh went up her nostrils. For a moment she was suspended, as though she were outside of her body simply watching what took place. And then it came, the realization that she was in a battle, on her knees in the dust. What was she doing? Why wasn't she fighting?

She stretched out a hand, shocked to find that her sword lay by her side. The orc burned and her vision went blurry as a sudden pain hit her temples. Lifting her hands, she pressed them against her head as though it would make the pain stop, make it go away.

Raw screams came out of her throat and there were hands on her shoulders and a familiar voice calling her name. "Maeve! Maeve!"

And then the sensations faded and nausea boiled in her

stomach. She gasped as though she'd been choked and stumbled to her feet, snatching at her sword and spinning around widely.

"Maeve, it's me, it's okay!" Imer stepped back, hands held up, and concern flickering in his eyes. "That orc did something to you," he pointed at the smoldering ashes behind Maeve.

She spun to look at the gray ashes, eyes wet, and then faced Imer again. "What was that? It felt. Horrible!"

Imer shook his head. "Some kind of magic, I haven't seen anything like it before."

Maeve noticed that the tips of his fingers were black, charred.

Ingram walked up just then with the dragon on his shoulder. He touched his eye patch and grunted. "Magic. The orcs have magic, that explains a lot." He fixed Maeve with a curious look. "What did it feel like?"

"Pain, sudden pain that quickly faded." She met his gaze, surprised at his interest.

"Sandrine would know more but I've heard about strange shadow magic of the orcs. They use a spell of weakness to slow down their enemies, allowing the weak to defeat the strong. Imer got to you just in time." He held her eyes for a moment, then moved away. "More will come when they see the dead bodies. We should keep going. Stay here while I scout ahead."

He moved off down the road. Imer made to follow him and Maeve took a step and then paused.

"They came in ships," Maeve breathed as she studied a

fallen orc. The sight of its helmet with a crude symbol, a black circle with a white swirl in the middle of it.

It was that sign, that symbol that awoke a memory from the past. The orcs had come on ships, and she recalled seeing their flags from the capital city of Carn, the black dots moving in the water, the swirls that made her think of whirlpools, an endless swirl of death. Why had they come? And was that why she'd been sent away? Because of the creatures who would swarm the capital? Did the king give his queen and his child a head start to outrun the madness? But why?

"Ships?" Imer spun slowly, ensuring they were free from orcs. For the moment. "I assumed the orcs were from here. What brought them across the sea to us?"

Maeve shrugged, a cloud of worry and unhappiness settling upon her like a dark shroud. "I don't have answers, only more questions. This is what I've been afraid of, returning to Carn only brings unhappiness, and more questions I don't understand nor know the answer to."

Imer leaned over and squeezed her shoulder. "There is a reason for this all," he said. "The people of Carn were a great nation, a powerful civilization, and yet they fell because of the orcs, the dark fae, and an earthquake. I believe it was to keep a prophecy from coming true. From age to age and nation to nation, there is one truth, one reason why all wars start and end. There is an ongoing struggle between good and evil, light and dark, and it will continue until the celestials return. All of this leads back to the Prophecy of Erinyes."

Maeve blinked, a sudden surge of coldness going through her. There it was again. That odd sensation she felt whenever he mentioned the prophecy, as though there was something he wasn't telling her. Could it be that, for some reason, he had a different view of the prophecy? He'd alluded to it before and yet, lost in her attraction to him, she hadn't asked outright. But darkness surrounded her as they moved toward the heart of Carn, and she wasn't sure she wanted to know the answer, especially if it would make her more unhappy than she already was. She bit back the question, knowing she should ask it, and lifted her eyes to the sky.

The dragon flew unsteadily in a crooked line, almost smashing into a tent as it landed awkwardly. If she hadn't been so lost in thought, Maeve would have thought it was humorous.

Ingram returned from scouting, glanced at the dragon, then scowled. "There's another orc party up ahead. We can move in, but we need fire to stop them."

Maeve noticed he only looked at Imer, as though the two had a moment of silent communication, using only their eyes.

Imer chewed his lower lip then tilted his hat up. "We are leaving a clear trail for the Hunter. I don't like it either, but what is our other option?"

Ingram folded his arms across his chest. "This is dangerous, we'll stay out of sight as much as possible but there are too many of them, we have to fight. And now we know we need to beware their magic."

The golden collar sat heavy around Maeve's neck and she touched it, recalling the weight of the quest that had been forced upon her. "Would you still go if not for me?" she asked, hating herself the moment the words came out.

Ingram glared at her, echoing words Imer had spoken

earlier. “Everything is not about you,” his voice almost a low growl. “We need something too, and yes, we would still go.”

Imer grinned, suddenly. “This isn’t the first dangerous situation we’ve been stuck in and we will do our very best to come out of it alive, as we always do. Don’t you think the Sea of Eels was dangerous? And walking into the Draconbane Mountains where the goblins nearly took us down. But we are still alive, along with the last dragon.”

Maeve glanced at the dragon at those last words and sure enough, it was stuck in a tent, making high keening sounds as it tried to wiggle its way free.

Ingram shook his head and headed over to free it, knocking over scattered bits of orc armor and buckets of food. “Since we are here,” he called, “we should loot the bodies and see if there’s anything useful before we move on.”

Looting. Maeve sucked her cheek. It was exactly what the mercenaries she worked with used to do. Although it was gruesome work, she’d gotten used to it, stealing from the dead who no longer needed their goods in order to live. She hated the orc clothes but there was nothing for it, she had to stay warm to if she were to survive Carn.

6

Memories of Carn

Days they walked through orc land, sometimes fighting, other times hiding. But the thing that stayed with Maeve as they traveled was the magic. She couldn't comprehend it and it seemed something learned, not innate. Why the thought came to her, she could not explain. But it seemed like something she'd seen before, a swirl of patterns, the dancing of fingers and hand, and then a blue shimmer that could change people. Who did that power belong to? Had the orcs brought it from across the sea, from whatever they were fleeing? Or was it of Carn, part of her birthright?

Words that Sandrine had told her came whirling back. Yes, one of the shards was in Carn, but there was another reason Sandrine had wanted her to go there. To find what was lost, to learn about her past, and use it to change her future. What if her past included magic?

Ash drifted through the air like the slow fall of a first winter's snow. Maeve tilted back her head and closed her eyes as though she deserved the kiss of fire against her skin. Grit covered her clothes and her skin crawled with dirt. It had been long, too long since her last bath. But as she stood in the land of Carn, physical sensation faded and memories rose. The vision she'd had in the Sea of Shadows returned. Except this time, she was the child.

"Maeve!" a whisper hissed next to her ear, jolting her out of sleep. "Wake up, we have to go, we have to run."

"Mama?" She opened one eye and peered up at the worry in her mother's face. "Are we safe?"

Mama shook her head. "They followed us here, it is only a matter of time. Someone will give us up if we don't run . . ."

Her words were cut off as a violent shaking rocked the room. Mama fell forward on the bed, almost smothering Maeve who clutched at her, even as the shaking threatened to tip the bed over and throw them on the floor. Aside from the bed, the room was not furnished, but in the distance Maeve heard the sound of glass cracking and shattering, the heavy thump of furniture being knocked over, and screams and cries as the unfortunate who were crushed or trampled in the quake.

Mama managed to right her and clasped Maeve hard against her breasts, mumbling prayers. "It's the wrath of the Divine, for the wickedness of our ways. When the earth quakes, Carn will fall into the sea and will be no more. Oh Divine. Save us!"

The quaking went on and on and on, knocking over candles and lanterns. At some point, Maeve smelled fire, around them things were burning and there came a heat, so intense she thought it would consume them. "The strength of Carn fails," Mama wept and then the shaking stopped.

The silence was almost more terrifying than the shaking. Maeve clung to Mama, hands balled into fists, her heart thudding so hard she felt the blood rush into her ears and tingle against her fingers and toes. "Mama," she whimpered.

Mama pulled back, wiping tears from Maeve's eyes, her strokes gentle. "You must be brave, my child. Can you do that for me?"

Maeve nodded, although her lips trembled. Mama had said those words many times in the past month. Everything had changed so quickly. They used to live in the palace overlooking the sea, until word came that an army was coming, an army of humans and orcs, joined together in one terrible goal to bring Carn to its knees. Papa had convinced Mama and Maeve to flee, after all, he was the king of Carn and must lead his people, while they were the bloodline and had to go into hiding. Mama had shaved Maeve's head and dressed them in the garb of peasants to blend in, but despite the disguise, they were still recognized. Some aided while others reported sightings to scouts and they were forced to keep running from village to village. But once again the soldiers were coming for them, and once again, they had to run.

"Yes Mama. I will be brave."

"Here," Mama slipped something into the inner pocket of

Maeve's dress. "Keep the crown with you, they will not think to search a child for proof."

Maeve smiled through her tears. The crown with the ruby on it was her mother's and when they lived at the palace, she loved to wear it. Now, knowing it was hidden inside her dress made her feel brave. Strong. She squared her shoulders and stood, took Mama's hand, and then they ran.

All the bravery Maeve felt inside melted away in the dark as they ran through the ruined streets. The yellow cobblestones were cracked, buildings toppled and gray rubble filled the streets. Maeve saw a bloodied leg sticking out from under a boulder, a man with sightless eyes, a child coughing up blood. Rancid smoke filled the air and everywhere she looked was a nightmare of blood and destruction. But worst of all were the sounds, screams and wails. In the distance blades clanged and men shouted. They were coming.

Her feet pounded the ground as they ran and her hand went clammy in Mama's hand. The rubble shifted around them, moving and falling as people dug through it, searching for loved ones. Others used their powers to help but it was awful, oh so awful. At one point, Maeve recalled pausing while Mama told her to catch her breath. Breathe. Just breathe. Even though the air was foul as though it was poisonous. Her chest rose and fell. Shudders shook her body. But when she looked up she saw the moon was full. An innocent hope rose in her heart. It was so beautiful, a pure light cutting through the black smoke, through the fear in her heart and the terror that something awful was about to happen.

And then it did.

A shrill scream split the air and then came the pounding

of feet. Maeve shrank back against Mama but not fast enough. A herd of spooked horses galloped through the street, threatening to trample Maeve underfoot. She screamed and reached out blindly, but after the horses came a crowd of people, running for their lives, shouting for others to move and screaming in a combination of fear and pain. For behind them were the soldiers who did not hesitate to thrust their blades out, impaling the people of Carn.

The next few moments passed in a blur of breathless running, trying to keep her feet and almost being swept away, until strong arms circled her waist and bore her upward. She kicked and screamed as she recognized the armor of one of the soldiers. He stank of blood and bile and panic overwhelmed her until she felt it like something growing inside of her, struggling to get free.

The solider lost his grip for a moment and Maeve squirmed free and turned to search for Mama. Instead, she saw a vortex whirling in a distance. Brilliant colors, purple and gold, almost assaulted her eyes and she lifted a hand to her face as creatures walked out of the vortex. Some were tall and magnificent, with long hair and slender limbs, others looked like brutes, a strange combination of man and beast with claws on their hands and fangs curving out of their mouths.The name for such creatures escaped her and she stood, frozen, staring at their brilliance as they poured out of the vortex, lifted their blades, and began to destroy everything in their paths.

A cold sweat came over her and young as she was, she knew she needed to flee, but when she turned back, two of the creatures had Mama by the arms. Maeve screamed, but she was lifted off the ground and carried away. She fought, biting and scratching, but whoever held her was too strong, and then an intense pain made her go numb. A blade slid into her shoulder and came free with a terrible ripping motion. Vaguely she heard screaming and wasn't sure whether it was her own or Mama's, and then the blade came again and again, and the world turned black.

MAEVE BENT over as blood rushed to her head and awareness pulsed deep within. She was the child who had been stabbed over and over again. She remembered even though she'd been so young, only five or six at the time. But the memory had been so horrific she'd lost it, or blocked it out somehow. She took deep breaths to keep the panic from clawing at her throat. The fae had been there all along. They'd come for her the night of the full moon. How did they know who she was? And more importantly, why were they interested in her?

As she caught her breath, misery changed to rage and her fingers balled into fists. She wanted to hit something until her knuckles were raw and bloody and scream until she was hoarse. Something within swelled, like a dragon rearing its head and pulling back to blow fire from its belly.

More memories rose, hazy as though she were looking into a dirty mirror.

Living in the palace and a bearded man, tossing her in the air, making her laugh.

The crown on Mama's head, the ruby bright against her dark hair.

A flash of blue being secreted away into a treasure chest. Was it the shard?

Mama weeping as she cut off their hair and long locks of black hair flew free in the wind, taking their identity with them.

The scratchy clothes of a peasant, so different from the smooth silk of royal clothes.

And then after she was stabbed and taken, waking in a cold sweat to a kind woman who bathed her wounds and whispered kind words over her. A healer. Maeve bore no scars, which meant it had been a very talented healer, either that or the wounds were not deep. But something else had awoken after the destruction of Carn. She had come of age and discovered her strength.

No wonder she'd turned and let darkness seep into her soul.

Rage poured out of her, for she could hold it back no longer. She fell to her knees, crying out in anger and frustration. Her hands sought the ground and she squeezed the rubble into her fists, ignoring the pain that sliced her palms. Her vision blurred and she saw nothing but red. Anger compelled her to rise and then she was running through the ruins, screaming and hurling stones out of her way as memories flooded her. Vibrant, colorful, full of life and love and only hints of darkness around the edges. They were there, executions, death, murder, darkness floated all around but she'd been protected. It hadn't touched her life for she was too young, shielded from the edges of insanity that brought down her people. They might have stood a chance if not for that fateful night, first the earthquake, then the soldiers, and finally the fae. And when they were all gone the orcs had taken over the land and there was nothing left but ghosts of the people of Carn. A strong race, ruined by . . . her breath caught. Ruined by the same thing that had ruined the race of dragons. Greed. Darkness. But ultimately the fae. It had been them all along, drawn to darkness, determined to find what they wanted, the shards, which eluded them each time.

The revelation threatened to knock Maeve over and she came to a stop, out of breath, alone. Every great civilization that had fallen was due to the fae, but not anymore. She would destroy them, even if it cost her soul. They took and took and took. But she was done being a pawn of the fae. It was time for them to face judgement for their deeds.

7
PATH OF DEVESTATION

"Maeve," the male voice called out her name as though it belonged to one lost in a cave. Faint echoes of it came to Maeve's ears.

The jagged edges of her memories faded as she blinked in daylight. She stood in the ruins of Carn, full grown, no longer a child who lived through those hideous last few days. But her heart still beat as though she were back there, still in the middle of panic, fear, and endless pain.

Heart thudding in her throat so hard she thought she'd vomit, she turned, limbs trembling, to take in the form of the brothers. Ingram and Imer were far behind her, and it was Imer who called out. Even from a distance, she knew those dark eyes would be full of concern, making her heart flutter with a desire to give in to him. But ugly feelings twisted inside of her and a wetness stung behind her eyes. She knew that if she went to Imer right then and there, everything inside of her would break. But she did not want to give in, did not want to break. Anger sizzled through her like meat roasting over a fire.

She wanted, nay, needed to be alone to work through her feelings. If Sandrine were still with them, she would have left Maeve on her own to seek the shard, only telling her where to meet once the lost treasure had been retrieved. But the brothers haunted her steps. While she understood that the ruins of Carn were dangerous, she also wanted to have time with her lost memories. Time. Alone.

They were intruding on her homecoming and she both desired them there and wished them far away, so they would not bear witness to her grief. Not only her grief, but also the knowledge that she grew up under the shadow of what had happened in Carn, forgetting the reasons why and yet recalling who she was and why her people had been destroyed. The Carnites brought it upon themselves, with their wickedness, their dark deeds. But who allowed the fae to judge the world and bring civilizations to their knees?

With a grunt of frustration, she tried to thrust the swirling thoughts from her mind. She faced the waters and recalled white sea foam splashing up on rocks, and the dull roar of the tides, lulling her to sleep each night. The seat of power, the castle, had to lie by the sea, and it was there she would find the fourth shard. Even as she thought it, she looked down, and the Finder's Stone pulsed, emitting a low light. It would grow stronger as she neared the coast, but how far would she have to dig to find the shard?

"Maeve," Imer shouted again.

Ingram and Imer had come to Carn for a different reason: to

find the sword of a celestial. Trust faded into anger, not directly at them, but the knowing, deep in her heart, that the brothers were interested in Carn for personal reasons. The people of Carn had the blood of celestials. The brothers wanted to search through the treasury for something that would help them kill the Hunter.

Maeve shivered as she considered the Hunter. Ancient power. Malevolent fear. Pure terror went through her at the thought of that predatory creature, but it was after the brothers of fire for their magic, not her. And with that decision she decided to run.

The rage inside of Maeve spurred her on. Ignoring her instincts and the shouts of Imer behind her, she ran. Her heart settled into the steady beat as her feet pounded the ground—a mixture of dirt and pavement. The crisp cold wind blew back loose threads of her braided hair while ash spun, whipping past her face.

A path of devastation led the way toward the shore. White bones stuck out of piles of rubble. In a blur she saw long bones that must have belonged to a leg or short bones of a hand hanging over a column, as though seeking to climb out of the void below and find help. The wind blew hard, and the smell of decay gave way to the dampness of water. There was a purity about it, as though the waters sought to flood Carn and wash it clean of impurities.

Maeve continued uphill—forcing her tired legs to keep moving—and down into valleys—ignoring the way blood pulsed hard against the back of her throat. She saw stone statues torn down and the remnants scattered and softened as the weather wreaked havoc on the ruins. The wind howled against her face like an angry monster, determined to deter her steps.

It wasn't until the sun began to set, shooting rich colors of red and purple across the horizon, that Maeve's hurt, anger, and rage faded, burned away by her run.

Chest heaving, Maeve paused on a hilltop. Sweat slicked her chest as she slid to her knees. In the faded light, out by the water, the shape of a ruined castle sprawled. She'd come so far and yet it seemed even further still. Night would be upon her and she was alone, without the brothers of fire, the dragon, or her rage. It was just her, the sole survivor of Carn.

But as she caught her breath, something else happened. Something Maeve did not expect. A spark of hope lit in her heart and, as she watched the sun set on Carn, she realized there must be a reason she, alone, survived.

"Oh, Divine One," she breathed. "Hear my prayer. Why was I saved? What am I to do? My life has been wasted as a warrior, seeking to only keep myself alive. But that has changed. I want to leave my darkness behind. I want to do something noble, and I am beginning to see what it might be: save others from the fae and what might happen should the Prophecy of Erinyes come true."

And there it was again. A peace, deeper than anything she'd ever experienced, filled her. How could she feel such hope, such peace, when around her was darkness, death and destruction? Caspian was right, the Divine was on her side, just waiting for her to ask. She didn't know how or why or what she was going to do next, but the knowledge that she was not alone sank in. She closed her eyes and let the sensation flow through her.

A THUNKING SOUND woke Maeve and she sat up, disoriented, surprised that she'd fallen asleep on her knees. Her muscles cramped and cried out against her movements but she stayed low, straining her ears for the sound that had woke her. There. It came again. A *thunk, thunk, thunk,* and then a scraping sound as though metal were being dragged against stone.

Maeve's hand went to her sword hilt and her fingers tightened around it. What was out there? More orcs hidden in the ruins? Perhaps wolves or other scavengers, although the destruction of Carn was over two decades ago, she doubted there was anything left to eat in the ruins.

The sound came again. Even though her muscles cried out, Maeve rose to her feet, peering into the darkness. Starlight had faded and the moon had withered into nothing more than a slice of nothingness. The blackness was absolute, making it difficult to see even the gray rubble beneath her feet. Indecision tore through her. Should she call out and see if the brothers of fire were near? But no, an oppression hung thick in the air. Dread crept around Maeve's heart, like cool fingers of death encircling her neck.

The *thunk* faded away, leaving only an eerie silence in its wake. Maeve's skin crawled in the uncanny silence. Even the wind was still, giving way before a malevolent presence. Her grip tightened on her sword hilt, even though her hands were sweaty and it seemed, suddenly, heavy. Fear twisted up her spine and she opened her mouth, taking shallow breaths as a wave of dizziness passed over her.

Before Maeve turned around, she knew what stood behind her, waiting to drain her of strength, of blood, and of life. The peace she'd experienced before she fell asleep evaporated but instead of the familiar battle rage sizzling through her belly, there was only a heaviness in her heart, as though she'd known and had been waiting, understanding this was the end she was fated to experience.

Intense darkness faded and she could see, albeit, poorly, yet somehow it was brighter than it had been when she first awoke.

She blinked rapidly to clear her vision, and there it was. A creature stood ten paces from her, its body shrouded in a dark cloak with the cowl pulled over its head. From its proximity to her, Maeve guessed it stood about seven feet tall, and she had to look up, even as the breath stole out of her body in a hard whoosh, for there was no face that she could see hidden beneath the depths of the hood. Air became hard to breathe, whether from poison or fear, she did not know. Her fingers were cold, shaking as they held her blade. It was a fear she could not grasp for she'd never been so frightened. What was it about the Hunter that set her on edge and made her forget her training? She searched for courage deep within her as the Hunter dragged its sword across the stone. The blade was about four feet long and a foot thick, a blade made for cleaving heads from bodies and limb from limb. Maeve gasped as light glinted off the Hunter's blade. With a sudden surety, she lifted her own blade.

She would fight with all her strength, for fighting was all

she knew, and with that single thought she mustered all the courage she could find, took a deep breath and focused, waiting for the Hunter to make the first move and display its strength or weaknesses.

The Hunter held up a hand which looked as though it were made out of iron. Its fingers clinked together as it pointed toward her and in a swirl of darkness, lunged. Its hand pointed toward her bare neck while the sword arched toward her waist to slice open the skin of her belly and bare her innards to the Hunter.

Maeve's breastplate protected her from the blow, yet she still felt the strength of it and heard the steel clang against steel with an awful scraping sound. Blood rushed to her ears as she leaned away from the onslaught, and tried to breathe, tried to steady her nerves. First rule of fighting: fear was the enemy, always. She had to be in control. It was only with confidence that she could hope to win.

She backed away, her movements light and quick as she swung her sword through the air with one arm and slammed the blade into the Hunter's blade, blocking its next blow. The impact jarred her, as though she'd slammed her sword into a solid wall. She almost cried out as pain shot up her arm into her shoulder and her teeth rattled.

Before she had time to recover the Hunter lunged again and the blade sliced toward her neck. Maeve threw herself backward, out of the way only to be tripped by the Hunter's booted foot. She fell back, one hand squeezing her sword while she snatched up gravel in the other hand and hurled it toward the shadowy face of the Hunter.

With a guttural grunt, the Hunter backed away, head

down as though grit had stung its eyes. Maeve took the opportunity to leap to her feet and strike out at the Hunter, slashing again and again, even though each blow was blocked and the strength of the Hunter rattled up her skull.

The dance of death continued as the Hunter circled her, waiting until she was off guard and then striking, a flurry of blows coming so fast, Maeve hardly had time to block them. She moved in sync with the Hunter, leaning into her sword, following her instincts as she blocked and parried. Panic caused her breath to come in short pants, bursting from between her lips like plumes of smoke. Sweat glistened on her forehead and dripped down her arms as the relentless onslaught of the Hunter continued. She went down again, and barely had time to move out of the way as the monstrous blade was driven into the ground beside her. She rolled on her stomach, almost crying as the sword came down again. Rolling to her back, she kicked out, striking the Hunter's legs. It ignored her, as though its legs were tree trunks without feeling.

Maeve's sword smashed into the Hunter's shins with a loud crunching sound, but the Hunter was prepared. In one move, it kicked her sword aside with its foot. Its blade came down, so fast Maeve let go of her sword and rolled out of the way. As soon as she did, she realized her mistake, for the Hunter pivoted at the last second, spun, and landed where she had rolled. The seven-foot-tall monster stood with her between its legs, covering Maeve in a cloak of shadows. Her hands came up and a scream left her lips as she was plunged into inky darkness, so black she could see nothing. Whether

her eyes were open or closed did not matter, for there was nothing but pitiless darkness.

A weight settled on her chest. Maeve thrashed, but it was useless. Boney fingers touched her neck and the scream died out of her throat as she lay struggling in the rubble of Carn. So this would be her demise? Her bones laid to rest among her people. It was the fate she deserved, after all she had done.

Even though her mind gave up, her body continued to fight, fingers clawing at nothing, and feet kicking, often coming into contact with the ground but nothing more. She squirmed against the weight on her chest, but it would not let up, and the bony fingers began to squeeze.

8
SENSATIONS OF DOOM

A scream, high and thin, pierced the air. A beast cried out, yet its voice was not strong enough to carry the ferocity of its cry. At first, Maeve thought the sound came from her throat, a last cry of dismay and despair as the Hunter searched for her strength and began to withdraw it. Cold lips pressed to her neck and a rough tongue licked the spot where no doubt, a pair of incisors would sink through skin to suck away her lifeblood.

Suddenly, Maeve heard a crackling sound, but not from the Hunter. She went rigid under his touch just as a flaming ball of light filled her vision. Darkness melted away like snow under the intensity of a blazing hot sun. The rough tongue withdrew, the bony fingers disappeared, and the pressure on her chest lifted. Maeve sat up, sucking in great gasps of air as warmth returned to her body. She snatched at her sword and, still in the clutches of panic, kicked out, aiming to strike the Hunter, if it were still in reach.

Instead, there was a groan and then the sizzling of flames. Maeve scrambled to her feet, sword in hand, just as the ball of flames exploded across the Hunter's shrouded face. The inferno curled around the beast, embracing it in the warmth of fire while the dark shroud burned. With a hiss of anger and a cry of frustration the Hunter spun toward its new assailants. But a winged creature flew in its face, shrieking and crying as its small claws rent through fabric.

With another snarl of frustration, the Hunter whirled and fled into the night, the flames licking at its clothes as it went.

Maeve's shoulders slumped and a sigh of relief passed between her lips as she watched the Hunter escape into the night. He'd almost consumed her. Her shiver of revulsion choked her. She'd been foolish, so foolish.

Hurried footsteps crunched through the rubble and then Imer dashed up to her, dark eyes wide as he examined her. "Maeve," he whispered, his voice like velvet. "Praise the Divine we found you before it took you."

Maeve almost recoiled at his words. Praise the Divine. No scolding? No shouting at her for deviating from their plan and running off on her own. In retrospect, if it had been Caspian, she would have received an earful, knowing full well it was her fault for placing herself in a perilous situation. She, of all people, understood that warriors worked better if they watched each other's backs. But the kindness, the worry on Imer's handsome face was surprising. He ran a finger through his dark hair, and she saw where his other hand was slightly singed from the fireball he'd thrown at the Hunter.

"Thank you," she breathed, her heart still thudding in her throat. "He would have taken me if you hadn't shown up. I did not think . . . my memories of this place began to return and I had to run, had to get away from them."

Imer rested a hand on her shoulder before touching the spot on her neck where the Hunter had licked her. There was a slight sizzle at his touch, and then, nothing. "Are you wounded?"

Maeve shook her head. "Nay, remember, I'm a warrior, Imer."

His teeth flashed white in the darkness. "Aye, this I know, Maeve of Carn. Just the last time I found you after fighting alone in the darkness, I had to bandage up your wounds."

Was he joking? At such a time as this? Again, Imer's lightheartedness and his lack of scolding threw her. Maeve did not know how to respond. She sheathed her sword, the movement causing Imer to step back.

"Thank you," she said again, wanting to draw closer to him, feel his warmth, unlike the frightening touch of the Hunter. Although it was unlike her to crave human contact, again and again she could not help but notice there was something about Imer she was drawn to. Despite the fact that he was fae. Or was it because he was fae? She reached out, her fingers brushing his shoulder and she stepped closer to him.

There came a whirl from ahead, like wings beating the wind. Looking up, she saw the dragon circling them.

Imer pointed toward it. "The dragon seems to have your scent. Even after we lost you it continued to fly straight and true, following as though it knew. I believe you have a protector."

The thought made Maeve feel lighter. "The gift of the Goblin Queen is helpful after all," she said.

Imer gave her a quizzical look, and at the same time his arm circled her waist, drawing her toward him.

"Where is Ingram?" Maeve asked, hesitant, yet desiring to be in his arms.

"Watching, always watching," Imer said. "Does it bother you?"

"Not if it doesn't bother you." Maeve met his gaze and nothing but relief swept through her.

She leaned into his embrace, resting her head on his shoulder. Why had she run away, when the comfort she needed was right here? Imer's other arm came around her waist and his broad hand rubbed her back, soothing her nightmares away.

"Imer," Maeve whispered as her heart continued to pound, but this time it wasn't from the near-death encounter with the Hunter. It was from Imer's proximity, the way his hands felt on her body made her crave more. She wanted to taste him, feel his lips pressed against hers, and then devour him, bodies intwined, naked as they explored each other.

She blushed hot under the idea of them making love to each other, but it was tempting. Although her mind told her they needed to move on, be gone from the cursed spot, her body leaned into him and she tilted her head up at him. The words she was going to say drifted away, unsaid as she stood in the cool night air, engulfed in Imer's warmth.

His hand caressed her cheek and then his lips were on hers, a slow, warm kiss, as deep and as bold as a dark red wine.

Maeve swam in a river of bliss where pleasure was the only escape. Her lips parted and she kissed him back, one hand pressing against his back until their bodies were lined up, limb to limb. His tongue thrust into her mouth, imprudent, demanding, taking and giving pleasure in a tug-of-war fashion. The peace that had so evaded Maeve when the Hunter appeared returned, filling and emboldening her. A low moan came out of her throat and a tingling sensation began in her loins, but before she could push further, Imer pulled back.

Her eyes came open and a current of rejection flowed through her, halted by the mischievous look in Imer's eyes. One of his hands drifted lower to touch her bottom and then he let go.

"Not here, Maeve of Carn," he whispered, tugging one of her curls with his finger.

His hand brushed over her lips, sending a tingling sensation across her bare skin. It took all of her willpower not to succumb to his potent pull. He was intoxicating, enticing, and the small taste left her yearning for more.

Her fingers came up to touch the collar around her neck, and the intensity of her quest came back, almost as jarring as parrying the Hunter's blade. Imer's fingers danced down her arm, squeezed her hand and then he stepped away. The lack of his warmth left her feeling bereft but rubble crunched as Ingram walked up. The dragon alighted on his shoulder with a squawk, then tucked in its wings.

Ingram's eyes narrowed as he glared at them. "The Hunter has fled but he came too close. Next time we might not be so lucky."

His gaze turned on Maeve and she dropped her eyes, aware of the frustration Ingram felt with her but relieved he did not voice it.

"The treasury is close," Maeve pointed in the direction of the waves and the ruined castle.

"Aye, up against the coast," Imer murmured. "A day or two will bring us there, and then we search."

Ingram frowned. "It's time we find the blade and kill this Hunter, once and for all."

Maeve did not say it aloud, but she wondered to herself, *If the Hunter walked the face of the land, what other foul creatures might the fae awaken once they collected all seven shards, put the crown back together, and broke all curses? What nightmares waited for them?*

"Should we rest for the night?" Imer suggested, looking from Ingram to Maeve.

"There are some broken statues a few paces from here," Ingram gestured impatiently.

"I'd rather move on from this spot," Maeve interrupted.

Ingram nodded. "Let's move north."

They set off at a run, but this time, instead of rage, a vague sensation of doom swept through Maeve.

9
TREASURE OF CARN

The next day and a half passed without mishap, pulling them deeper into the desolation until they arrived on the side of a cliff where the ruined castle of Carn perched. A tightness came to Maeve's chest and her throat went dry at the sight of the crumbling towers. Her fingers closed into fists as she took in her home. This was where she was born, where she'd grown up during her early years. But what could she hope to find in this abandoned structure? And what did she want to find? It was true that the quest for the seven shards had brought her here, but there were deep reasons why she'd stayed away, had chosen to forget, instead of treasuring her memories of Carn. *Why? What else could there be aside from the wicked ways of the Carnites? The brutal death of her mother and her own tortured beginnings? Who had called the orcs from across the sea? And what were the origins of the magic the orcs used? Was it of Carn?*

The swirling runes on her arms, shoulders, and back

began to itch underneath her stolen orc clothes and Maeve swallowed hard, eyes burning.

Ingram gave a low whistle as they stood in front of the hallow entrance, staring into gloom. "This is it?"

Maeve shrugged. The words: I don't remember, died on her tongue as memories returned, twisting and turning like lost shells in the sea, tossed and turned by the relentless waves.

Wide stones made up what had been the castle, towering high above the cliffs which dropped down to water's edge, giving them a magnificent view of the churning sea and white beach where shells and crystals sparkled in the sunlight. The smell of decay and rot was blown away by the fresh sea breeze, and the tide rolled up against the beach, scattering treasures across the lonely strip of land. Maeve imagined the waters were purifying, but when she looked down at the sea-foam, faint memories danced around the edges of her vision. She recalled running down the beach shrieking with laughter. Collecting shells in a bag and, later, wearing a necklace made of shell and seaweed. She recalled standing in those waters, the coolness rushing up against her ankles and then frightened shouts as someone much larger than her swept her away from the perilous mouth of the sea.

Her eyes went wet at the happy memories. So there was joy, before all this devastation ruined her life. Maeve blinked, hoping Ingram and Imer did not notice her emotions, and scanned the area.

Green algae and gray rubble covered the once white stones of the castle, and, although no new life grew, there were still remnants of carvings chipped into the stone. The images told the story of the Carnites, powerful beings who had fallen from grace. Instead of defending the world, they welcomed the evil that plagued it and thus were destroyed.

"Do you know where the treasury lies?" Imer asked.

Maeve avoided his gaze, knowing she would see concern behind those dark eyes. As if answering his question, the Finder's Stone pulsed against Maeve's chest, pointing the way. If it were up to her, she'd turn and run away from the old, painful memories. But she recalled the way the fae had treated her when she hid the third shard from them, and although her bruises had healed, she would not welcome being bullied by them again.

"It's through here," Maeve pointed to the dark entrance. "The Finder's Stone will lead the way."

Imer's fingertips brushed the markings on her shoulder, soothing the burning flesh. "Aye. Go, we will follow, use your instincts to seek. But be careful, although we need not worry about the Hunter during daylight, there are other shadowy beings that might dwell in ruins."

Maeve rubbed the back of her neck, unable to fully grasp his kindness. It was difficult to understand why the brothers traveled with her and yet did not want anything from her. Was there such a thing as true friendship? Even Caspian had needed her blade and desired to be with her for other reasons. Perhaps it wasn't her he truly wanted, but the way she made him feel. And if that were the case, what was love? Just a sensation? A hope?

Tapering down her spiraling thoughts, Maeve crept toward the dark opening of the castle, heart beating in her throat. Behind her she heard the hiss of flames. Light streaked her face as Imer held out a torch, his gentle words calming her fears. "Here, use this."

Gratefully she took the burning branch and held it in front of her as she stepped over the broken threshold into her former home. Motes of dust floated in the gloom and it took a moment for her eyes to adjust to the semi-darkness. Daylight streamed in through breaks in the stone where the ceiling was missing, and she had to walk carefully to keep from tripping over stones and loose rubble in her path. What had once been a great atrium was now covered in broken stone. She ducked under fallen archways, unsure where she was going. The need to keep moving before memories overwhelmed her drove her onward. She fumbled for the Finder's Stone and held it out in front of her as she walked, letting it guide her toward the treasure.

The brothers of fire followed a few paces behind, but she noticed they gave her enough space to seek on her own, and for that she was grateful. Their presence disturbed the fallen castle which creaked beneath their feet, creating small avalanches of rubble, and yet they went on, twisting and turning their way deeper into the castle.

At last Maeve reached a set of stairs leading down, still intact. She waved the torch over them as though she could find answers just by searching. The Finder's Stone glowed brighter and, swallowing her reluctance, she ventured deeper into the underground. Her footsteps echoed in the gloom, and above her she heard the soft steps of Ingram and Imer.

The air was thick as she descended and the darkness pressed in until it felt like fingers, choking the breath out of her. Fighting down the sensation of panic and desperation to get back out into fresh air, she continued down into the depths. The air smelled of mold and Maeve shuddered as visions of the Dungeon of the Damned filled her memory. She would find the shard and give it to the fae to prevent herself from returning there. Another thirty days locked away would kill her.

The constant drip-drip of water filled her ears, and when she took a step, her bare toes brushed against something wet. Was sea water leaking in? She raised the torch to cast more light across the cavernous room. Shallow water—tinted green—flowed over the stones. It was no more than a few inches, at least where she could see it, but the water glittered like jewels.

Maeve tilted her chin and called up to the brothers. "The treasury is down here, but watch your step, some parts of it are flooded."

"Ah, treasure," Imer said, a hint of excitement tinged his tone.

"We are searching for the blade of a celestial," Ingram rebuked him. "Not records of a lost civilization."

Imer gave no answer and soon Maeve heard them slosh through the waters, light reflecting off water as they moved.

She couldn't be sure, but she thought she heard a whisper and something chattered in the waters. Holding the torch over the room she looked down, but there was nothing. Unease made her shoulders tense but she kept moving down into a wide hall. Treasure chests were stacked on shelves against one wall, and there was a holder, still intact, for a torch. She used it to free up her hand and checked the Finder's Stone. It glinted brighter as she moved toward the wall of chests. The shard lay here?

She examined the treasure chests, but each looked like the others. Once they had likely been beautiful chests, but now they were covered in dust and dirt without any distinguishing elements. Maeve pulled the first one free with a grunt, coughing as a cloud of dirt plumed into her face. There was no lock and it came open without a sound.

Her eyes went wide at the riches that lay inside. They were gifts for royalty, much like what she'd seen in the lair of dragons in the Draconbane Mountains. Her fingers shook as she examined the contents of the trunk. A string of beads, pearls she assumed, one larger than the other. A golden goblet with swirling designs on it. A crown, so heavy she almost couldn't lift it.

Was all this hers? Her inheritance? If only she'd known before the fae captured her, she could have been wealthy, perhaps even wealthier than kings and queens. She shuddered at the thought. She would have returned earlier to claim her wealth, but now everything was different. With the scourge of the fae, she wasn't sure what she wanted anymore. Freedom? Defeat the fae? And then what?

The whisper came again, and then a splash. Something moved among the ripples in the shallow water. Was it the brothers? Maeve glanced back down the hall but it was impossible to see them. She closed her eyes, stilled her heartbeat, and listened. In the distance she heard their mutters and light reflected off the water.

There was something inside the treasury with her, she was sure of it. Opening her eyes, she went back to work. Her fingers moved faster, yanking open chest after chest. The contents spilled out around her. Precious gems, ornate weapons, cups, glasses, sealed bottles of liquid, and clothes. Yards and yards of soft fabric. With a quick glance back at the entrance to the hall, she pulled out a shift that would fit her and a new breast plate. There were shoes, gauntlets. Carnite armor.

Without thinking, she put down the Finder's Stone and stripped out of the disgusting orc clothes and tossed them into the water along with her old breastplate. Her skin prickled with awareness as she stood, naked in the treasury. Tossing aside her shift the fae had ruined, she tugged on the new one. It smelled musty and slightly damp, but it fit perfectly. It was thicker than her old shift and fell just past her knees, giving her plenty of room to run, kick, and bring her legs up without ripping the fabric.

Next, she strapped on a new breastplate. It was surprisingly light and molded to her body as though it were made specifically for her. Finally, with a sigh of relief, she pulled on new shoes. Instead of sandals, these covered her feet and the straps came up to her knees, sealing in the gauntlets she put over her shins. Her hand went to her trusty sword, but no, her sword had been with her for a long time. She wasn't ready to get rid of it. Just as she was putting her crown with the ruby on her head, a small voice interrupted.

"What are you doing?"

Maeve slapped a hand over her mouth to muffle her squeak of surprise. Her eyes tore down to the shelf beside her where a tiny man stared back at her out of curious eyes. He was about three feet tall, stood on two legs, and looked at her out of a round face with eyes as gray as stone. A fat brown bundle was tossed over his shoulder, and his skin sagged off his bones, as though he'd once been a plump little man.

Defiance replaced surprise and Maeve lifted her chin and crossed her arms over her chest. "I'm taking what is rightfully mine."

The man's beady gray eyes locked in on the markings on her arms and he pursed his lips. "I believed the Carnites were dead, but I was wrong." He shrugged and studied the water, likely gauging how far he'd sink if he stepped into it.

"Who are you?" Maeve demanded.

The gray eyes studied Maeve and focused on her sword. "Naught but a humble raider, but since this is yours," he waved his hand, indicating the hall, "I'll be on my way. No need to steal from the living."

"Just the dead?" Maeve challenged, well aware she could overwhelm the little man in a moment, but she was unsure whether he was a threat or not. "How did you get past the orcs?"

"Orcs?" The man shrugged. "Who says I passed orcs?"

Maeve huffed. "Never mind, be gone with you."

"As you wish," the little man said. He stepped one foot into the water and grimaced.

Maeve narrowed her eyes. There was something about the way he moved, something about the way he held both of his fists closed, as though . . . but the thought escaped her. With a shrug, Maeve finished dressing, and a sensation of satisfaction went through her. Finally, something was going right for her. Despite the death and deception surrounding her, clean clothes were a relief.

She reached for the Finder's Stone. But it wasn't there. She frowned. Sure she'd set it down on the shelf while she dressed. Spinning, she dug through the treasure chests again. Had she knocked it over? She'd been close, so close to finding the fourth shard and now it had simply disappeared? A streak of panic went through her and she fell on her knees, upending chest after chest as she frantically searched. Her throat went dry and then a curse left her lips as realization dawned on her.

The little man! His fists were tightly closed and there had been the glimmer in the water. Gold for the Finder's Stone and blue for. No. The shard. The fourth shard. He had both of them!

Maeve sprinted out of the hall, her eyes tearing wildly around the treasure. Where had the little man disappeared too? But he was nowhere, not out in the water nor on the stairs. It was almost as if he'd disappeared into thin air. How? Why? She dashed back to the treasure chests and tore through them again. But there was nothing. Pent up frustration made Maeve's throat go tight and a strangled cry burst from her lips.

10

STOLEN TREASURE

"Maeve?" Imer sloshed across the water and peered into the nook of treasure chests. His eyes went wide for a moment and then his brow furrowed in confusion. "Who were you talking to?"

Maeve's head shot up. Heat flared across her face as Imer took in her appearance, his sea-blue eyes scanning the length of her body. He nodded in appreciation but when his gaze returned to her face, his dark eyes still held the question.

Maeve waved her hands, flustered and frustrated, she found herself shouting. "There was a little man here, a gnome, a dwarf of some sort. He called himself a raider but left as soon as he realized who I am. He said he only stole from the dead, not the living."

Imer's eyebrows shot up. "A raider? Aye, they often pillage ruins for lost treasure which they can sell for a profit, but here? I thought all the raiders would have taken their pick already, especially since the wealth of Carn is legendary. No matter, what else happened?"

"He stole the Finder's Stone and the fourth shard. I'm positive I saw the glimmer of it in his hand, but I don't know which direction he went."

Imer pinched the bridge of his nose. "By the Divine, why would this happen?"

Maeve punched a shelf in frustration. Pain shot through her hand but she ignored it. "We have to find it before the night of the full moon. When the fae return they will be vicious."

"We'll be with you," Imer stepped forward, stopping short of placing a hand on her shoulder.

Maeve bit her lip. She was too angry for Imer's comfort. "It doesn't matter whether you're there or not, the fae will do what they like. Besides, you can't pick a side. They know about you, but they haven't captured you. I'm the last Carnite, the last of an evil people . . ." The knowledge of the corruption of her people sat heavy on her heart and bitter words came out of her lips. "I'm not worth saving."

Imer's voice went hard with anger. "Don't say that, don't self-flagellate yourself. We would not be here if you weren't worth saving."

"I need that shard," Maeve snapped. She stomped out of the room, water sloshing around her ankles. Imer followed but she ignored him. A sensation of suffocation went through her as though she were back in the Dungeon of the Damned, waiting for her sentence. She could not face the Master again and disappoint him. The punishment last time had been both humiliating and painful.

"Imer!" Ingram's voice rang out, laced with excitement.

Imer pivoted.

"Go on," Maeve encouraged. "I can still take care of myself."

He turned away and Maeve regretted her harsh words. She was taking out her frustration on Imer who had done nothing to deserve it. With a sick feeling in the pit of her belly, she moved up the stairs, hoping to catch a hint of where the little man had gone. There was no way the dwarf could be faster than her, unless he was able to open and close portals.

The thought stuck with her. Her knowledge of portals and magic was poor, yet perhaps there were other beings aside from the fae who could open portals across the world. And if the raider had done so, she needed to know where he lived and who he might sell the shard to. She had to find it—or at least another shard—before the night of the full moon.

Heart pounding in her throat, Maeve left the brothers behind with the dragon, assured that the Hunter would not hunt them in the daylight.

Each step took her further into the heart of the castle and bitter memories surfaced, one as unhappy as the other, a reminder of what she'd lost, why she was alone, and what had driven her to become who she was. Maeve of Carn. Not a warrior, but a killer. Yet, she didn't believe the words she'd angrily tossed at Imer. There was redemption for her, she simply needed to find the way.

After searching the ruined castle for a while with no results, Maeve gave up and returned to the atrium, shoulders slumped. The first three shards had cost nothing more than a fight. It was ironic that the moment she returned home, the fourth shard evaded her. Why was it that as soon as she found peace, chaos and turmoil tried to betray her? She thought about sliding to her knees on the cold stone and praying to the Divine. At least she would feel better about what was happening to her.

"There you are," Imer's relieved voice broke her thoughts.

Maeve looked up as the brothers walked to her. The dragon perched on Ingram's shoulder, as usual.

"I could not find him," Maeve offered, all the fight driven out of her. "The raider took the shard and stone and disappeared without a trace."

"We'll find him," Imer affirmed, determination streaking his voice.

Maeve shrugged. "It doesn't matter if we do, I just want to leave. There's too much grief and sorrow in this place. It's haunted with it and the sensations are sinking into my bones, bringing me grief. I just want to hide, to lay low for a while, and forget about the shards. All this time I've played into the hands of the fae, doing what they requested without defying them. Now the shard is gone and they will punish me anyway, but not if they can't find me, can't reach me."

Ingram's face darkened. "If you don't find the shards, eventually they will come for you, or worse, find someone else to complete your task. Is that what you want? For yet another innocent to perish?"

His words weren't meant to be unkind, yet something about them jarred Maeve. Before she could respond, Imer spoke up. "It might not be a bad idea to go to the temple in Isdrine. We know the priests and priestesses there, and once we're there, we can use their knowledge to find out what habits raiders tend to keep. And we might find the next shard during our travels."

Although the words were meant for her, Maeve couldn't help but notice the pointed look which Imer gave Ingram. She decided not to comment on it. Was it just her mind—fraught with weariness and exhaustion—that made her second guess the brothers? They were fae after all.

"Will we make it to Isdrine before the night of the full moon?" she asked.

"It is debatable," Ingram frowned. "There are many orc camps between us and Isdrine. It might be better to travel south rather than directly through their lands."

"Do you know the location of the next shard?" Imer asked gently. "We might be able to find it before the next full moon."

Maeve shook her head, and even as she did so a memory invaded her vision.

"TAKE IT WITH YOU," the man urged. "You have to hide it. If our enemies find it, Carn will fall."

"Carn is already falling my love. Why must you send us away?"

"You know why," his voice was firm, edges of unkindness seeping around it. "If worse comes to worst, she has a chance at surviving."

"I don't understand, you've never cared about prophecies,

they don't affect our blood," the woman wailed. "Wouldn't we be safer here with our guards?"

"Go," the man squeezed the woman's arm and almost pushed her. "No more words, and take the sword. Hide it well."

"Mama?" a wail rose out of her throat at the shouting.

Then the angry man was beside her. His piercing blue eyes bored into hers and he lifted her chin to his. "You are brave, Maeve of Carn. Remember, you are stronger than all of them, perhaps you will be spared."

THE MEMORY BLINKED AWAY and Maeve's eyes misted over. A sob rose in her throat. What darkness had claimed the Carnites?

"Did you find the sword of a celestial?" she asked, this time addressing Ingram.

"Nay," Ingram's brows lowered. "For a moment I thought we had, but we found nothing but lost relics. Why do you ask?"

"My memories are returning," Maeve whispered. "Slowly. It is not here, not in this treasury, because it is the first place an enemy would look. When my mother and I fled, we took it with us."

"The sword? Where?" Imer breathed, his voice laced with hope.

Maeve closed her eyes, searching for the memory. "South is all I know. If we travel that way, I might remember more."

Ingram studied her. "What of the dark fae and the shards?"

Maeve shrugged. "You both were willing to help me with the Hunter on your trail, the least I can do is help you."

Ingram's one good eye widened in surprise and his nostrils flared.

Imer nudged his brother and then stepped toward Maeve. His dark eyes smoldered and despite the frustration of the day, Maeve's breath caught. His fingers touched her wrist and suddenly she wanted nothing more than the warmth of his lips pressed against hers, again, igniting the passion that had passed between them only a few nights ago. But she also knew once they started, she wouldn't be able to stop, their passion would be like the first flames of a wildfire, spinning out of control.

"Thank you." Imer squeezed her hand.

Somewhere in the distance came a rumble of falling rock. The dragon squawked and spread its wings, almost striking Ingram in the face. Maeve looked up, almost expecting the ceiling to cave in.

"We should leave," Ingram suggested.

As one they dashed for the exit.

II

Map of Ink

Waves pulsed up against the coast and the ruins shifted as a storm wailed out on the sea, driving rain sideways and battering the coast. A fierce wind howled and lightning struck the buildings, knocking stones onto the ground. As Maeve, Ingram, and Imer ran through the onslaught searching for a place to hide, memories flickered through Maeve's mind. Storms like this were common, and at first they frightened her. She'd heard servants claim the celestials were unhappy with the Carnites and were punishing them, which is why the storms came, destroying crops, killing peasants, and driving fish up on the shore to flop until they died. When the sun came up the next day, hot and intense, the meat was spoiled and bellies were hungry, except for those who lived in the castle. At times the guardians were called forth to battle the storms and they went to the shore with boldness, to chant against the uprising of the waves. But to no avail.

As superstitious as Mama had claimed the servants were, perhaps it was true. All of Maeve's memories, good and bad, led her to the conclusion that the Carnites had been destroyed because they incurred some kind of Divine wrath, and when their enemies closed around them, there was nowhere for them to go. The combination of an earthquake and being violated by the fae brought them to their knees. There were things Maeve did not understand: Why was she saved? For what reason? The brothers of fire claimed they did not want to use her for anything, but was it true? What induced them to stay with her? There had to be a reason, other than at Sandrine's request.

The cold rain lashing against her face brought reason back to her. After all she was in Carn, the place where mysteries would be revealed and her questions should be answered. Enough of hiding from the truth, she needed to know.

"In here," Ingram shouted, pointing to two slabs of darkness that towered above them.

They rushed into it, seeking shelter under the odd structure. It looked like a pyramid except hollow at the edges and sat snug against a hillside where the damage from the storm did little to harm the integrity of the structure. Maeve took in great gulping breaths as she stood underneath the high ceiling of the place, listening to the ruthless storm echo outside.

This place, she had been here before, she was sure of it.

Imer held up a hand, a flicker of fire on his fingertips as he lit up their surroundings.

The ground was made of stone with runes carved into it,

where water pooled, giving a glimmering sensation to the ground. As Maeve looked down she recognized some of the symbols, for they were the same ones that matched her neck and shoulders. A shiver rippled up her spine, not simply from the cold but there was something else, a vague sensation like déjà vu. There was something here she needed to remember and she closed her eyes, waiting for the memories that evaded her to come back.

"Over here," called Ingram, his voice almost swallowed up by the storm. "It looks like a firepit, or an altar."

"This was some kind of temple," Imer whistled, his voice deep in wonder and curiosity.

True, Maeve had to agree with him as he held up his fingers to the sloping walls. Symbols and pictures covered them; this place was important. But why? And why did Maeve have the sensation that she'd rather spend the night out in the wild storm instead of inside the ruined temple?

She didn't realize she was holding her breath until she let it out, small and shaky. Imer moved to her side while Ingram dried out the firepit and tried to light it.

"We'll have a fire soon," Imer said, water dripping down his dark head and pooling around his neck.

"It's not that," Maeve told him, blinking moisture out of her eyelashes. "It's this place. I've been here before and I don't like it."

Imer's face crinkled in concern. "Do you remember anything?"

"Not yet, it's more of a sensation than anything else."

"Maybe some time here will help," he offered.

Maeve nodded but chewed her lower lip.

The storm raged around the slanted walls of the temple throughout the night, and Maeve tried to sleep, but each flash of lightning brought fragments of a lost memory, something she knew she could not remember, for she hadn't been awake for it. Yet she shared her mother's memory as she watched what happened take place, like a vision.

A man held her, his arms about her waist, trapping her arms and penning them down. "The child must be inducted if you want her to live."

"She's too young!" the scream tore out of her throat. "It will surely kill her. There must be another way."

"No. The blade must hide and she must return to find it. It will be impossible if she does not have a guide."

"Write it down," she shrieked, "a piece of parchment, please, not her skin, she's pure and innocent."

A raucous laugh shook the room, although it was filled with malice. She cringed in his arms, realizing how powerless she was as they lifted the sleeping child onto the altar, stripped her, took up needles, and began to draw. A map of ink covered the child's arms, shoulders, and chest. Blood spilled out onto the stones but the child lay in her drugged slumber, unaware of what was happening to her.

"But the pain," the woman sobbed.

"She is your blood," snarled the man, "she will heal quickly."

He let go of her suddenly and she fell, knees scrapping

against the stones, bruises forming on her arms and legs from where she'd fought them.

"Take her away," barked a man. "Let us work in peace."

Maeve opened her eyes to darkness and sat up. Grief swirled through her, not mere sadness but a grief for her people, the Carnites and what they had become. From her memories and visions, she'd gathered that she did not come from a civilization that was upright and noble. They'd abused power, been corrupt, and turned on each other. She'd shut her mind to what her mother must have experienced both as the queen and as a nomad. The king, her father, had forced them to flee into doom, and it was their undoing. Even though the hope had been to save her, it was a proud, selfish wish and cost more in blood than she'd ever know. She was Maeve of Carn. Queen of nothing. Yet she still believed despite her background, she could change things, seek redemption, become noble. She would not follow the legacy of her people and run into darkness, now that she was aware of who they were and what they had done, she could seek a noble path and change. It seemed the fae had done the world a favor by destroying Carn, but why did Imer look on her with reverent respect? If Carn was evil, what did it make her? The last Carnite?

Her eyes drifted to his prone form and, as though sensing her thoughts, he stirred. Maeve blinked and her fingers rose up to the runes that traced her skin. It was a map to the blade. The blade of a celestial? She let the thought hang. Had Imer known that, did he understand her runes?

"Imer," she whispered into the darkness.

Outside the thunder and lightning had ceased, leaving only the relentless rain pouring down in torrents as though Carn were the wash basin of a giant. Maeve reminded herself that Carn sat on a hill, high above the sea, and they had no fear of being washed into the waters. Still, the storm left her feeling uneasy.

The golden eye of the dragon opened and glared at her, as though she were partly responsible for the storm and for waking it up. Maeve stared back, wondering if the dragon had the knowledge to realize it, too, was in the same predicament she was. The last of an evil civilization, born out of wickedness and yet saved. Would it morph and shift into human form? Would it speak to her as it grew older? Despite her lack of knowledge about dragons, she was glad she hadn't given in to her warrior instincts and killed it.

"Maeve?" Imer sat up.

The faint glow from the firepit lit up his profile and an ache grew in Maeve's heart. She and Imer were more alike than she'd thought. Their stories were dark, tragic, and yet Imer and his brother continued to live and fight.

"I had a dream, vision, memory," she blurted out, stumbling over the words. "The runes on my skin are a map, a way to find what was lost, or hidden. I believe my mother brought me with her when she came to hide a blade."

Imer stood and held out a hand to her, helping her to her feet. His fingers traced the pattern of runes on her arms, moving up to where they were hidden beneath her shift.

"Can you read the runes?" Maeve whispered, intoxicated by his presence and yet trying not to be swept away. They had a task to complete but once they were safe in Isdrine she would allow herself to let go of restraint and take him, wholly.

Her blood pulsed hard and an ache began between her legs as desire coursed through her veins. Heat flamed her face and she was glad of the low light, so he wouldn't see what his touch did to her.

"Aye," came Imer's low voice. "But reading runes of Carn is a sacred art. I do not understand the full meaning, but if the runes on your skin are a map, then it makes sense that the pattern of runes on you will match a pattern we find here." He waved his hand around the expanse.

Maeve glanced around at the darkness. She didn't want to wait until morning but doubted she'd be able to fall back asleep again.

"Ingram and I will light up this place," Imer waved his hand. "Ingram will stand guard, but . . ." he ran a hand through the ends of his black hair. "We run a risk that the Hunter finds us before we find the blade."

"Don't use your magic," Maeve shook her head. "There has to be another way without drawing the Hunter to us."

She shivered at the memory of the creature's tongue against her throat.

Imer nodded. "It will be slow going then, but we will find that sword."

Maeve's fingertips tingled. "And kill the Hunter."

"Agreed," Imer echoed.

His touch left her skin and he turned, calling out to

Ingram. Groggily, Ingram awoke but it was the dragon who spread its wings and lifted into the air. Smoke poured out of its snout as it settled on Maeve's shoulder. She coughed and waved smoke out of her face, but the dragon wasn't done. After gripping her shoulders with its claws, it leaped again and flew high into the air. After a moment, Maeve saw a spark of light illuminating the temple, and then another and another. Throwing back her head she watched, eyes wide, as the dragon lit up the temple as though it had heard her wish all along. Her jaw dropped but when she looked back down, what she saw made her wish they were plunged in darkness again.

12

TEMPLE OF CARN

Bones littered the ground, bent at awkward angles and there were bowls of dried ink, splashed up against the altar, creating a grim appearance. Maeve's throat went dry with awareness that she had been one of the sacrificed, one whose blood was spilled on the sacred stones.

"Maeve," Imer's gentle voice drew her back to the present, away from those horrid memories which made her shudder. "Where do your runes begin?"

The heat of his gaze sent tingles down her spine and she wanted nothing more than to show him, come bare to him. Maybe it was the strength of his magic, the gentleness of his voice, and how he was unlike any other she'd met, but she wanted him to see.

With a quick glance in Ingram's direction she lifted her short shift, and pulled it over her head, then turned her back to Imer.

His breath hissed inward as he took in her naked body,

some parts of it still hidden in the shadows, but the runes glowing brightly. With reverence he traced the line of runes from the middle of her back up to her shoulders, murmuring under his breath.

Even though it was cool inside the temple, Maeve did not feel it, for Imer's touch on her skin warmed her as though there were a fire in her belly, heating her from the inside out. She was aware of the pads of his fingers, every touch, every graze, and the sensation spread into her loins with the awareness that if Ingram were not nearby, she would take Imer then and there.

"I have an idea of the pattern," Imer whispered, a thickness in his voice. His hands brushed her hair out of the way as he took her by the shoulders and turned her around so that he might better see the runes on her chest. His fingers traced lower, almost to the swell of her breasts.

Maeve closed her eyes and tilted her head back, enjoying the attention to her flesh. *Oh, Divine One, why did she feel like this? Why was she distracted from the task at hand by mere carnal lust?*

"Here," Imer touched her hands, "put your clothes back on before my brother sees."

Maeve's eyes came open and her lips parted. For once she wished Imer were not a gentleman and would take her. Alas it was not to be. Eyes darkening with disappointment, she pulled her shift back on and fell in step with Imer. "Where do we start?"

Imer turned slowly, searching through the temple. "I've never seen anything like the runes you have, they are more symbolic, almost spiritual, with swirls, leaves, and feathers, almost as though it points towards nature."

Maeve took deep breaths to calm her arousal and tried to listen to Imer's words instead of thinking about his broad chest underneath his pirate garb and the way his lips felt on hers. Nature. She needed to focus.

"Nature makes me think of the earth, the ground," she told him, "but feathers make me think of winged creatures."

Her eyes sought out the dragon who flew above, stretching out its tiny wings. Maeve was surprised at how quickly it had taken to flight, although she knew nothing about the growth of dragons. It circled around Ingram who tossed it hunks of meat, watching the dragon dive to catch them, or squawk with displeasure when it missed and pieces fell to the ground. Ingram did well with the dragon and Maeve did not know why it frustrated her. Was she jealous?

Imer's eyes narrowed. "Given the destruction of Carn, it makes no sense to hide a treasure up high. It would be the first place to be compromised during the earthquake, unless they knew what was coming and how to secure it. Do your visions . . . memories . . . give you any indication?"

Maeve chewed her lower lip, unwilling to dive back into those unhappy memories. When she thought of what had happened to her there, her runes itched, as though she were being inked all over again. "No, except it seemed as though they wanted me to find it."

"Wait," Imer moved forward a few steps and knelt, brushing away dust and dirt with his hands. "Here it is, the symbol of a feather, it matches yours."

Excitement rushed through Maeve's veins and she joined

him, avoiding the white bones nearby. “Here’s another,” she cried, weaving around rocks and stones to find the next one.

“It’s a path,” Imer exclaimed. “Ingram,” he called out. “We’ve found the path.”

“It’s about time,” Ingram grunted. He stopped playing with the dragon and joined them.

The dragon landed on the altar and made a strange sound in its throat. Maeve chuckled. “Ingram, I believe the dragon wants you to keep playing.”

For the first time, she saw a small smile curve around his cheeks and a softness come to his eye. And while he said nothing else, Maeve felt as though she might be able to get along with him after all.

Imer waved his hand for them to follow him and pointed to a feather and then a pattern of swirls. They followed the runes deeper into the temple, which was much larger than Maeve imagined. There were halls and doors, a broken-down bunk room and then stairs which ended in a pile of rubble. They continued the path of swirling runes until they came to a low archway.

Imer ducked inside first and froze. Maeve followed him and Ingram came last, with the dragon on his shoulder. Torchlight lit up the interior of a concave hollow with low sloping walls. But what lay in the center of the small room made Maeve’s heart freeze. Her breath hitched and the walls of the room closed in around her. She was in a tomb. The air was dense and close, aged as though fresh air hadn’t touched the room in more than a decade. Swirls and runes covered the walls, glittering red as the torchlight brushed over them before they turned blue. As if noticing the lack of air in the room, the flame of the torch sank lower.

A rectangular coffin sat on a raised dais in the center of the room. Runes covered it but on top was a carving of a man, lying as though in sleep or death with a sword in his hands. Maeve swallowed hard and a ringing came to her ears.

The runes on her arms and back itched like never before and she knew, despite her fear of disturbing the dead, she could not leave without finding out what was in the tomb.

As if reading her mind, Imer pointed to the symbols. "This is where they end. Although I do not want to desecrate the dead, I believe we have to look inside."

Ingram touched the statue, bits of dust and dirt streaking his fingers. "It's made of stone. We'll have to slide the slab off."

Maeve rubbed her arms, wishing the itching would go away. Ominous words from Sandrine infiltrated her thoughts. What she found in Carn was supposed to be devastating. But what could be more devastating than the knowledge that she came from a line of evil people? Her father was corrupt, her mother had died trying to protect her, and the orcs and fae had destroyed Carn. What else could there be?

They lined up on one side of the crypt. Maeve reached out, her fingers touching the surprisingly warm stone, as though it were a beast hibernating instead of the soulless stone, hiding the long-dead body of . . . of what? Or rather. Of whom? Was it a king of old or a member of the temple?

Together they pushed, muscles straining. The stone gave way with a low groan. They pushed until it slid out of the way and a wave of decay rushed out like thirsty prisoners, eager to escape from confinement. Maeve leaped back and covered her mouth and nose with one hand, unready to breathe in the diseased air. Indeed a withered corpse lay inside, nothing but old bones and other objects that had long ago faded to dust. The importance of whoever was in the tomb was lost on Maeve as her eyes widened.

Almost hidden by the skull was a blue object, glowing gently. One of the lost shards! It was the biggest piece she'd come across, almost as long as her forearm and it would be just as difficult to keep hidden. The moment she laid eyes on it she felt that same magnetic pull and her runes ceased to itch as though they'd found the object of their desire. Out of the corners of her eyes she noticed the brothers step back, both of them looking to her.

Holding her breath, Maeve leaned over the tomb and her fingers closed around the relic. As she did, visions danced before her eyes. Blue fire, runes dancing away in the wind, and balls of magic surging forth. And then she saw herself as a child, standing before a priest who held out the shard to her. He touched the shard, then touched her shoulder, but she was frightened and pulled away, crying.

The vision vanished, leaving nothing but the shard which lay heavy in her hand. The colors were dazzling, brilliant, but there was something else beyond them. Deep in her core she knew it was the magic of Carn, and the ugly thought that she'd been saved for such a time as this whispered through her mind. Her mother, father, even the priests of the temple knew they were saving her for a reason. Was this it? To put the seven shards back together?

A wave of dizziness passed over Maeve and then faded.

The shard. She wanted to keep it for herself and perhaps she might be able to, if they could reach Isdrine before the night of the full moon.

"Maeve?"

The question in Imer's tone turned her attention back to the tomb. In the open hands of the skeleton lay a sword, but not one stained by rust or years of neglect. The blade was pure, beautiful and glistened as though someone had sharpened it recently. The hilt was silver with elegant carvings on it, but it was the runes on the blade that caught Maeve's eyes. They glowed, as though they were alive and wished to impart a secret to her.

Crippling thoughts raced through Maeve's mind as her speculations conjoined into one fluid thought. It was no accident she was here, that the fae had chosen her. She was fated for this quest, to find the seven shards, to make whole the crown of Erinyes and to find the blade of a celestial. A torrent rushed through her, but she could not deny the explicit zing of pleasure of anticipation that filled her as she reached out and took hold of the sword.

13
FLIGHT TO ISDRINE

After finding the sword of the celestial, Maeve and the brothers fled the ruins of Carn, racing to reach Isdrine before the night of the full moon. Now, the city of Isdrine rose before them like the open arms of a mother welcoming home a long-lost child. Sloping fields rolled toward the great temple which lay in the middle of the sprawling city. Unlike the Contresea, the capital of the known world, Isdrine had no walls but the people who lived there protected it from outlaws and mercenaries. From time to time there were attacks. The priests and priestesses—although they lived a life of relative peace—were not afraid to take up arms and defend what they believed in.

Maeve breathed a sigh of relief when she saw the city, and the fear that the fae would catch her again disappeared. A lightness entered her body, for the night of the full moon was tomorrow night, and they'd just made it in time. She would be able to hide in a holy place, away from the wild lands, and enjoy a solid meal, a bath, fresh clothes, and actually sleep indoors, in a bed. Rubbing her chilled fingers together she glanced over at her companions.

Ingram walked ahead, his stride fast and sure. There was a lightness to his steps as though anticipation kept his feet moving. He and Imer had joked with each other all morning long, and a pang of envy went through Maeve as she realized they had a home to return to. They had people who loved them, because they hadn't alienated everyone by killing them. Still, she was grateful for the brothers, although her eyes strayed to the dragon who flew ahead. In just a few weeks, the beast had grown to the size of a large cat. While Maeve wanted to hide it from curious eyes, she was also proud of the strange creature. She, Maeve of Carn, had the last surviving dragon, and it was magnificent.

Frost covered the land, turning every blade of grass into an icy knife which crunched under their feet. The ground turned to cobblestone beneath their feet as they entered the city. The flat landscape sprawled out around them but Maeve's eyes were pulled to the temple. Its strength and height rose like an imposing giant, staring down at its land and admiring what it saw. The stones were a golden-brown and three tiers of rounded towers reached to the sky. Intricate carving and archways decorated the outside of the temple and there were five giant stone steps leading up into the courtyard. There was something sacred about the place. After the vague evilness of Carn, it was an honor to walk into a blessed land.

Maeve couldn't help but wonder, was this where Caspian fled after the fae found him? Was this where he had come to ease the darkness in his soul? If so, it was slightly ironic that he'd come to the home of two brothers he hated to seek forgiveness. His death still sat like an old wound close to Maeve's heart. Yet as time passed, she was healing from the grief. As much as she hated the fae, the past months had been eye-opening. She'd learned more about herself, her past, her dark history, and her strength than she'd ever known. Plus the celestial blade lay heavy on her back. She'd insisted on carrying it and the shard, for holding them both close reminded her there was untapped magic in Carn. A magic the fae had not been able to get their hands on, and for that very reason, she was proud to be able to escape from their clutches and hide from them. Even if she were fated to become a pawn of the fae, she'd found a way to escape. For now.

Ingram's boots crunched on the frost covered ground as he made his way up to the wide staircase leading to the temple. Arched columns revealed a walkway where two could walk around the entire temple, side by side. The structure gleamed as though it were polished gold and the walkways were clear of frost as though it had recently been swept clean.

Double doors, twice the height of a man, swung open with a low purring sound. Two priests wearing fur cloaks walked out, clasped their hands together, and bowed.

"Ingram, Imer," one murmured in a deep voice as rich as chocolate. "Welcome home."

Turning, they led them into the temple.

Maeve followed in awe, gazing up at the sloping archways, columns and lit halls, disappearing into the intricate maze that was the temple of Isdrine. The scent of cooked meat met her nose and a low growl of hunger passed through her belly. Eating well on the road was tough and with the coming winter, Ingram had not been so lucky with hunting.

But now warmth filled her as the double doors were pushed shut behind her. Daylight faded, leaving only the muted firelight. Maeve's eyes returned to the entrance of the temple before being drawn to the fireplace in the middle of the room where others were gathered around it, wearing tunics and looking at the strangers with peaceful, yet curious expressions.

It was the first place she'd gone to—aside from the Village of the Lawless—that felt like home. It struck her hard between her breastbone. She was welcome here. There was no scheming, conniving, or warring; she was welcome.

"What is that?" A child of no more than ten pointed at the winged creature that perched on Ingram's shoulder.

He grunted at the weight, but his lips curled back into a smile, a real one. He winked at the youth. "One of the many interesting beasts we found during our adventure."

Imer removed his hat and ran his fingers through his hair before replacing it. "Where is Priestess Mariah?"

The priest who had welcomed them waved his hand, his rosy round face beaming. "Coming, we saw you from the ramparts, she will be glad to see you alive and well, and who is this?"

Imer reached for Maeve and she stepped up, lifting her chin in the old habit of defiance. If the priest was intimidated by her, he did not show it.

"This is Maeve of Carn," Imer said gently, as though he were proud of her. "She is seeking refuge here."

"Ah," the priest beamed. "You are welcome here for as long as you need."

Maeve's throat went thick and, unable to speak, she simply nodded as she took in the meaning of his words. She could stay here without being driven away.

There came a cry and a woman ran into the room, arms outstretched as she made for Ingram. The dragon took off from his shoulder with a squawk and the women threw her arms around his neck. He responded by lifting her off her feet and holding her tightly, his face buried in her neck. When she pulled back, she framed his face with her hands and laughed. "Ingram!" she cried. "It's about time you returned."

Maeve stared as his face lit up, and then he kissed her, full on the mouth, in front of everyone.

Heat flared up in Maeve's face and despite all she'd seen, she hadn't seen such love and affection between two people.

"Come," Imer grinned at her. "Priestess Mariah is here."

A stately woman walked into the room without a smile on her face. She took in the group huddled by the fire, Ingram kissing a priestess, a creature flying around the room, and Imer and Maeve. Her blue habit flapped as she shook her head, although there was the slightest twinkle in her eyes. "The two troublemakers have returned," she said, her green-eyed glare going directly to the dragon. She paused. Her eyes widened a fraction, likely because she realized it was a dragon, then her gaze swept toward Maeve.

Physically Maeve took a step back, as though the power of the priestess pushed her. The woman was just as tall as her, wearing a light blue robe that swept the ground. Her hair was covered with her habit and her face was older yet wise. A serenity emitted from her, as though she'd found peace beyond all understanding, and knew, with age comes wisdom, and that is what gave her solace through life. Maeve instantly wanted to know her and admired her inner strength as she took charge of the situation.

"Brothers," she addressed the priests, "please ensure our guests are clothed and fed."

"Priestess Mariah," Imer grinned, his face lighting up with mischief as he stepped forward and enveloped the woman in a hug.

She frowned over his shoulder and made no move to hug him back, but Maeve spied a wetness in her eyes. Was she crying?

She wondered if she'd imagined it but the priestess pulled back and patted Imer's cheek. "You need a bath," she told him.

"I wear the smell of the road so you will know where I've been," he retorted.

Ingram walked up, his arms threaded around the younger priestess who smiled up at him as though he were the only man left in the world.

"Disgraceful," Priestess Mariah scolded. "Behaving that way in front of guests, at least wait until you're in private."

The younger priestess blushed and bent her head, yet her expression said she was not ashamed at all.

"Come along then," Priestess Mariah turned and led them down the hall.

Maeve followed, unsure whether to laugh or remain serious. In some way, Priestess Mariah reminded her of Sandrine, and yet there was a kindness to her instead of the rude way that Sandrine treated her. Maeve pushed away thoughts of her quest. She was safe. For now. And she would enjoy it as much as she could.

14
REVELATION OF THE DIVINE

Nightmares plagued Maeve's dreams until she woke, sweating, chest heaving as she struggled to catch her breath. Unlike the nightmares she'd had before Carn, she had no memory of this one after she woke, just the last remnants of horror clung to her. A warning that penetrated her sleep.

She sat up on the bed and pulled her knees up to her chest. After meeting Priestess Mariah, she'd been bathed, dressed in borrowed clothes while hers dried, and enjoyed a warm meal. With a full belly, she'd been led to one of the large rooms in the temple where the novices slept. There were twenty beds lined up in a row on one side of the room and another twenty on the other. It was like a large hall and a window high above them let in moonlight.

The light was pure, as white as snow as it shone in. Yet its beauty sent shivers down Maeve's spine. The night of the full moon. The fae were searching for her, and would be furious because of her treachery. She'd taken the shard and hidden in a holy place where they could not touch her. A corner of her mouth tugged up in a sly smile, quickly replaced by another shiver. Her fingers touched her lip, still scarred where the Master had split it with his claw. How could she sleep when the fae were loose upon the world, likely ripping it apart as they searched for her? She recalled the Master's warning when he'd given her the quest. If she disobeyed . . .

Shaking the thoughts away, she rose and picked up the cloak the priestesses had given her. They were generous and yet she had questions for them. Questions which Caspian said they could answer regarding the path of the Divine. Would they be up at this hour?

Barefoot, Maeve tip-toed down the row of beds where novices slumbered, unconscious of what horror awaited outside the temple. The floor was cool under her feet and although her cloak was warm, the torrent of emotions mixing inside her kept her from feeling the warmth nor the cold. The temple was quiet at that hour and the intricate walls lit only by torchlight every few feet, casting small pools of warmth for those who might walk the halls in the dark.

Was it a mistake to leave the swords and shard behind? Tucked under her borrowed bed? But the walls of the temple filled her with peace, and the nightmares of old faded away.

Eventually, she came upon a room with a peaked rooftop. The double-doors stood open but the room was curiously empty aside from the front where a short flight of steps led up to an altar. Above it was a window and pure light shone down on the altar. Instead of fear, a sense of wonder came over Maeve, and she took a step into the room.

As she did she saw a shape, a mere shadow standing just out of reach of the light.

Maeve hesitated. Was she intruding?

The shadow moved and a woman's voice spoke up. "The night of the full moon is a restless night indeed."

The woman stepped into the light, and Maeve saw it was Priestess Mariah. "Come in," she beckoned. "If it pleases you. The house of the Divine is a welcome respite for all."

Maeve took another step into the room. "If I am not intruding . . ."

Priestess Mariah moved into the moonlight and sat on one of the broad steps. "There is no intrusion here. All are welcome to come worship, but I sense that is not why you have come."

Maeve twisted her hands in front of her, at a loss for words. "I am conflicted," she admitted, perching on a step below the Priestess, her back to the moonlight.

"I sensed that within you," the Priestess replied, her voice gentle, welcoming.

The hardness Maeve carried inside of her gave just a bit at the Priestesses' tone. No wonder Ingram and Imer returned here again and again, if they were welcomed this way. There was acceptance without any need or reason to prove herself. Maeve was used to taking up her sword and using her strength to prove her worth. But in the temple she was accepted for who she was. Yet she found herself wanting to share her past, and secretly she wondered if she were looking for a reason to be rejected from a life of peace.

"I am not worthy," Maeve said, eyes directed toward the stone floor. "I was born into darkness. The people of Carn were evil, ruthless, and I believe for that reason they were destroyed. The darkness of my people called out to the fae like a beacon of light, and they came along with the storm, and in their wrath wreaked destruction on my land. I am the last Carnite; there is nothing I have done to deserve life. My actions attracted the fae." Her hand went to her neck where the collar lay heavy, a reminder of her fate. "Yet the Divine hears me, and when I pray, peace overwhelms me. I don't deserve to be heard. Why? Why does the Divine hear me?"

"Understanding the ways of the Divine is not simple. Someone who is so much greater, so much bigger than all of us, with infinite knowledge and wisdom, is impossible to truly understand. That is why you must have faith, belief, even though you do not comprehend the reasons why. There are many who seek the ways of the Divine and give up, because they do not understand. The reason the Divine hears you is because of your heart. You have put the past behind you, and the things you did in the past, the way of thieves and mercenaries, is not a life you will return to."

Maeve searched her heart and knew it was true. The blind killings she'd taken part in stung and she was aghast at her past actions. Nay, she would not return to that life, but it also meant there was only one path forward.

"But how can you trust in what you do not understand? And why do I have this peace that fills me when I'm in the most trouble and I reach out to the Divine? How can the Divine forget what I have done? I do not forgive myself, why should the Divine forgive me?"

The Priestess smiled and shook her head slightly. She folded her hands and placed them on her knees as she leaned forward, her expression earnest. "Many ask this question, and when they ask, they do so in blind ignorance. But it is not their fault. They assume the Divine is like us, like those who were created, but the Divine, nay, all the celestials are far above us. Their ways are not our ways; when they look, they don't see past, present, and future in a linear way like we do, they see the past and what the future will bring, and potential. All of us have the potential to be something great, but we have to make a choice to fight our darkness and choose the path that will bring us into redemption. In your heart, you have already chosen, and the Divine who sees and hears all understands your intent. When you make that choice, the errors of your past are forgotten. It's just like taking a bath. The dirt and grime from the road were with you so long, you barely noticed, but when you wash yourself clean, you are made new. Aye and when you go forth, more grime will cover you, but you can wash clean again. That's what praying to the Divine is like, when you believe in your heart, and have faith, even though you cannot grasp the enormity of all the Divine sees and knows, your past will be washed away."

Maeve blinked as the knowledge sank in and the words the Priestess spoke whispered into her mind as first simple words, then understanding, and finally knowledge. Tears sprang to her eyes and she was surprised at her emotion. Her lips trembled when she spoke next. "It is gracious of the Divine to forget my past, but I do not deserve it."

The Priestess squeezed her shoulder. "None do, and remember, that is the grace of the Divine. You may not forgive yourself, you may not believe you deserve forgiveness, but you must have faith and put the past behind you, learning what you have learned. Imer told me of your past when I spoke with him earlier. You have a good heart, Maeve of Carn, perhaps you were saved for a reason. For such a time as this when darkness threatens the land. You are a defender; you can help turn the tide. Perhaps this is what you were fated to become."

Maeve went rigid, eyes still moist, and yet the thought of expectations, of someone wanting something from her did not frighten her anymore. It was difference of intent. The fae wanted to drag her down into darkness, with mind games and torture, laughing at her misfortune, drunk on her pain and fear. But the brothers of fire were different, instead of using her past against her they only had hope for her future. They wanted her help, desired it, but not to use her, but because they saw her for who she could become.

The stiffness evaporated from her back and Maeve reached out, her fingertips grazing the ruby on her crown. Maeve of Carn. Queen of nothing. But she could become something. The choice lay before her and as she thought about it, she realized it was easy. Becoming the last defender would use her skills with the blade, and, although she did not need to, she wanted to atone, to do something to make herself feel better for what she had done. Even though the Divine did not hold up her past like a mirror, using it against her, she wanted to do something to ease her frustration and the uncomfortable pinpricks of doubt in her mind.

A memory called out to her as she sat in silence, recalling the night she'd spent with Caspian at the Bawdy Sailor in the Village of the Lawless. He'd said she'd need to speak with a priest or priestess to understand the revelation of the Divine, and he was right. She would not have liked this knowledge coming from him, wouldn't have believed it. As odd as it was, it took a stranger, a benevolent stranger, to remind her that she was not a lost cause. She could stand firm and fight back against injustice and cruelty. Now she understood why Caspian had changed who he was; the revelation of the Divine had reformed him, and she, too, felt the transformation seep through her. A warmth filled her, like two arms wrapped around her and peace surged through each corner of her mind. When she looked up, the night did not seem frightening nor the moonlight cause her to flinch in fury and pain. Even the cool metal of the golden collar against her throat did not make her cringe. She had found something greater.

A tear slipped down her cheek and she brushed it away without shame as she faced the Priestess. "I feel it," she said, awe and wonder striking her voice. "I can't explain it, but maybe I don't need to. But I feel the revelation of the Divine here," she touched her heart.

"Praise the Divine," the Priestess murmured, and her eyes shone. She reached over and pulled Maeve into a hug, arms tightening around her as though she were a child.

It was then that a sob almost touched Maeve's heart, and a memory stabbed through her peace. Her mother used to hug her like this and the reminder of that comfort, of being a child with someone to protect her almost overwhelmed her. Now she was grown, but she was not alone. The fae had given her a gift, had sent her careening into people who cared about her, regardless of her past.

The sound of footsteps echoed down the hall and a sharp, female voice called out. "Where is she?"

Maeve pulled free of the Priestess's embrace and stood tall, eyes wide at the sudden commotion and the voice, she knew that voice. It was dry and feminine but brisk with irritation.

"Maeve of Carn!"

Maeve's heart thudded in her chest as she crossed her arms and her nostrils flared. A moment later, two apologetic priests hovered in the doorway, pushed aside by none other than Sandrine the Scholar. She planted her hands on her hips and scowled up at Maeve. "There you are! Don't you know there's nowhere you can hide?"

15

FATE AND FAITH

A hand squeezed Maeve's shoulder and she glanced at the Priestess. "It's okay," Maeve said, "you can leave us. No one can hurt me here."

She hoped the words were true, although if Sandrine could hurl daggers out of her eyes, Maeve did not think she would hesitate.

"Are you sure?" the Priestess glanced from Maeve to Sandrine.

Maeve nodded and the Priestess moved toward the entrance, holding her arms out to wave away the priests. "Give them some time to resolve their disagreement."

They left the room, leaving Maeve alone with Sandrine.

"Well?" Sandrine snapped, her gray eyes flashing. "What do you have to say for yourself?"

Something gave within Maeve, and the fear and uncertainly she'd felt throughout her captivity by the fae faded, replaced by sheer determination. "I am aware it is the night of the full moon, and the fae expect the next shard." Maeve spoke calmly, without fear, but purposefully leaving out the part about the magic she'd discovered in Carn. She still did not know what to think about it, and she wanted to make up her mind before discussing it. "I believe there were two shards in Carn. One was stolen by a raider and the other I found in the hidden temple in Carn, along with a celestial blade."

Maeve waited and was rewarded by the movement of one of Sandrine's eyebrows, but she quickly recovered from the surprise and gestured for Maeve to continue.

"But the fae are cruel and unkind, the last time I gave them the shards, they attacked me. So I came here, a holy place, to hide from them until I decide what to do."

Sandrine gave an exasperated sigh. "Tell me, girl, have you decided what to do?"

"Not yet," Maeve refused to be cowed. "But I will no longer serve the fae. I will not be their slave or their pawn. But know this, I will find my freedom, and find a way to destroy them."

Sandrine tilted her head, and her eyes glinted as she raised a finger. "These are the smartest words I've heard you say since we met. But how will you destroy the fae? They dwell in the Fae Underground until the night of the full moon, and even the moonlit nights do not give you enough time to sneak down into their lair and destroy them. They are many and you have no army. How do you propose to destroy them?"

"Don't you want to be free too?" Maeve stepped toward Sandrine. "Don't you want to stop them?"

Sandrine's eyes went cold. "I've told you before and I'll tell you again, if you wish to destroy the fae, you must be wise about it, and I believe I have found a solution."

Maeve's breath caught and she wondered if she'd heard correctly. Sandrine was on her side? She'd found a way?

"Tell me," she begged, breathless.

Sandrine quirked an eyebrow. "I'm not sure you are ready."

Maeve stilled, realizing that begging would not work for Sandrine. Turning, she sat down on the broad stone step again, folded her hands in front of her and waited.

It seemed odd to be in a temple, a holy place, on the night of the full moon, of all nights, discussing the demise of the fae with Sandrine. But she'd returned for that very reason, hadn't she?

Sandrine was not forthcoming, she paced back and forth, the moonlight highlighting the silver in her dark hair. Finally, with a sigh she moved closer and sat down on the other side of Maeve. "I returned to the Fae Underground for one reason. Knowledge." She tapped her forehead. "I've worked for the fae a long time."

Maeve nodded but did not add her thoughts. She assumed Ingram and Imer were close to her age, which meant Sandrine had been a captive of the fae for around thirty years, give or take. More than enough time to learn about the fae and grasp an idea of what would bring them down. It was also enough time for Sandrine to make up her mind. Which side was she on? Pushing the thought to the back of her mind, Maeve focused on Sandrine's next words.

"For years now, the fae have collected knowledge in the

form of scrolls and old books, stolen from the kingdoms, cities, temples, and homes of the wealthy. I have been their agent in this, for knowledge was always my purview. The missing piece to both the freedom and the demise of the fae is the Crown of Erinyes. Once the seven shards are put back together, then, and only then, will it be possible to destroy the fae for all eternity."

Maeve frowned. It sounded utterly convenient, a ploy, a plot, a trick. If the way to destroy the fae and gain her freedom was by doing what they wanted her to, how could she walk free? How could she ruin them knowing she was giving them the ultimate gift? Breaking all curses in the process. But Sandrine's words seemed to align with what she'd learned in Carn. A scowl covered Maeve's face and she glared at Sandrine as she rose to her feet. "Do not play with me, I deserve to know the truth and you come to me with these lies?"

Sandrine shrugged, unbothered by Maeve's outburst. "It is like I said, you are not ready."

Maeve groaned aloud as a streak of anger flared up and then disappeared as she recalled the words of the priestess. Faith. Faith without understanding. Yes, she needed to be wise but...

"I can't comprehend why you are treating me this way," Maeve returned. "What did the fae give to you that is better than helping one person? You've served them for decades and yet you want the Prophecy of Erinyes to come true. Don't you know what it will unleash?"

Sandrine crossed her arms and her eyes went dark. "No one truly knows what will be released. Yes, all curses will be broken, but do you think I know the curses that took place before the beginning of time? When the Divine crafted this world out of words? Nay, but if there is one truth, the fae cannot be wiped from the face of the world until they are free."

Maeve narrowed her eyes, trying to shut out the memory of blue magic shimmering under the surface, untapped, unused, but waiting. "Why?"

"What else will you do. Girl. You. The last defender. The last Carnite. Will you sit here in this holy place, growing old and bored while you hide from the fae? They have long lives, unending lives and unless they choose to kill themselves by walking in daylight—which they will not—they will go on, scheming and planning. Eventually they will gain all seven shards and put together the crown. May it be years from now or decades from now. You are in a unique position to stop them, because you have a unique power, your strength. Those who know about the Crown of Erinyes often think about the seven shards, for they break all curses, but that is because the crown is blessed, blessed by the celestials. If you would be there, when the shards are reformed into a crown, you could take it, take the Blessing of Erinyes and slay the fae. It will not be easy, but if you can kill the king, they will be crippled. He single-handedly holds the fae together, and if they run amok, they will not become a fearsome army. They will run through their portals, and if our allies are ready, they will be slaughtered as they flee."

Sandrine ceased speaking and her chest heaved as she gulped in air.

Maeve stared, surprised at Sandrine's passion and fever.

She'd never seen the scholar so sure of herself, so steady, and on the edge of desperation. Decisions warred with Maeve. Yes, it would be much easier to hide in the temple of Isdrine, but she was collared, her strength gone. Returning to a holy place on the night of the full moon each month sounded tedious, as though she were chained again. There was no freedom in running and hiding. Just like she'd told Ingram and Imer they'd have to face the Hunter, she needed to face the fae once and for all. Sandrine's words made sense. It was risky, desperate, dangerous, but what if it was the only chance they had? The only chance *she* had?

"Is this why you wanted me to go to Carn? To prepare myself for this conversation? Knowing that you would have me doom the world for my own freedom?" she asked, voice hollow.

"You would save it," Sandrine hissed. "Do not make the mistake of thinking you are the only one who has been wronged by the fae."

Maeve lifted her chin, unwilling to be cowed by Sandrine. "But what would be unleashed? What might happen to the world?"

Sandrine shook her head, jaw tight. "Have you heard the Prophecy of Erinyes?"

"The Goblin Queen told me—"

Sandrine cut her off. "Did you hear it in full?"

"I wouldn't know," Maeve shrugged.

Sandrine stood up and turned her back to Maeve and the moonlight. Words came from her lips, in a sing-song manner. "A day will come when curses will be broken. The lost shall be found, the found shall be lost, and the rift between mortal and celestial will cease to exist. The dragon queen of old will rise, freed but hidden in disguise. The last defender will come forth, and the sword of justice will purify."

A shiver went up Maeve's spine as the hushed words filtered through the air, stabbing it with potency. The runes on her skin began to itch again, just like they had in Carn, and memories of magic filtered through her mind. Was it true that she had something greater than her inherent strength, something that lay dormant within her, waiting for the Prophecy of Erinyes to come true?

Mortals and celestial. Dragon queen. The last defender. Those words had a deeper meaning, Maeve was sure of it, but also, the depth of the prophecy bothered her. She both desired to know and longed to run away, to leave her fate in shatters. It was easier to delve into darkness, slaying without a conscious than realize she had a primary part to play in shaping the history of the land.

Sandrine faced Maeve. "Those words mean more, so much more than taken at face value. It is thought that when the seven shards are put back together, the celestials will return to this land and wage a great war against evil. Therefore, it does not matter what is unleashed, for the celestials will be here to deal with it, and on their side, the last defender will fight, with the sword of justice."

Maeve slumped. She did not have a choice in this. Did she? She was fated for such a time as this. "The people of Carn," she faltered. "They were known as defenders, but they turned their backs on the world and gave into their wicked ways. Does . . ." she paused. Did she want to know? "Does the prophecy mean that I am the last defender?"

“Does it?” Sandrine quipped. “This, I know. Prophecies come true. If you do not take up your place, another will.”

“Do I have to decide tonight?” Maeve asked, knowing she would not be able to fall back asleep, not after what Sandrine had shared with her.

“If you were wise, you would leave this town and run, leave sacred ground and give the lost shard to the fae.” Sandrine sniffed. “But it is too late for that. They will deal harshly with both you and I when the next night of the full moon comes.”

Maeve stilled, recalling her last encounter with the fae and the bruises that had faded away. “Did they punish you?” she asked, unsure why she cared, why the guilt squeezed around her heart like a giant squeezing a soft fruit.

Instead of answering, Sandrine moved toward the doorway. “Think well, Maeve of Carn, and decide well. I shall see you in the morn.”

Sandrine disappeared, leaving Maeve alone in the room. She pulled her knees up to her chest and lay her head on them, too tired and worn out to think, or even pray. It had been a long night and the things she'd learned blurred in her mind, rolling into two words. Fate and faith. What should she choose?

16
LIQUID GOLD

"Maeve?" A surge of warmth went through Maeve at the sound of Imer's voice. "My lady, what are you doing out here?"

Imer joined her on one of the balconies of the temple, overlooking the town where they could see for miles. After a restless night, Priestess Mariah had finally found Maeve and told her some fresh air—although cold and windy—would do well to help clear her mind. The wind danced around the borrowed robes Maeve wore and tried to tug her braid of dark hair free.

"I needed some air," Maeve shrugged. Pain pulsed behind her eyes when she spoke and frustration mounted. Why was she in this situation again? With the sensation that she was trapped with only one way out?

"Did you sleep?" Imer pressed, his intense eyes roaming over her face, compassion written in his eyes.

Maeve shook her head. “Nay. Sandrine returned last night.”

“Ah,” Imer said, lifting his head and ran his hand over his black hair. “I take it she was none too happy.”

Maeve pursed her lips. “No, but she was more understanding than I assumed and then . . .” Maeve faced Imer and again felt that pull, that indescribable tug toward him. Pushing away the cloud of desire she chewed her lower lip. She needed to make a choice. Perhaps Imer could help. “Imer. What do you know about the Prophecy of Erinyes?”

His blue eyes narrowed as he stepped closer to her, until she was forced to look up into his handsome face. Gold flecks danced in his eyes and her breath caught as he took her hand, palm up, and lifted it to his lips. Delicious sensations rippled through her, until he spoke. “Maeve, we talked about this before. I told you what I know about the last defender. Did Sandrine say something to make you falter, to change your mind?”

Tugging her hand free, Maeve turned from his penetrating gaze and stared back out at the town. It was quiet, asleep under a blanket of winter. She shrugged. “It’s just that Sandrine wants the prophecy to come true. It’s almost as if all these years she’s been working on finding the shards. It has been her sole focus, and somehow she persuaded the fae it would be their salvation, when in truth it is both their salvation and demise. I don’t know if I can trust her word.”

She rubbed the back of her neck and kept her eyes on the village before forcing out the question she did not want to know the answer to. “What do you believe?”

Imer leaned against the balustrade, angling his body so

he could clearly see Maeve's face. His voice was low but calm. "Maeve, I wouldn't lie to you. I believe what Sandrine believes. The world cannot continue as it has been, and there is no way to defeat the dark fae without help. If they grow reckless, careless in their freedom, we have a much better chance of destroying them, rather than infiltrating the Fae Underground. Either way, both options are risky, frightening, but we have to take a chance."

Maeve's fingers curled around the balustrade and fury rose up in her as she gripped it. "Is this why you came with me? Why you followed Sandrine?" Bitterness rang out of her tone. She knew it was unfair and yet she wanted to blame someone else for her predicament. "Why you stayed with me through the ruins of Carn?"

"What are you implying?" Imer's tone was cold with an edge of fury.

"You are fae, aren't you?" Maeve shot back, glaring at him and wishing she hadn't.

A flash of anger crossed his face and his eyes shone almost gold as though his glare would turn into liquid fire and consume her.

"I'm sorry," she said, words tripping over each other as she reached for him. "That was unfair of me. It's just that . . ."

Imer stood tall and stepped back as though she'd slapped him. "Just that what? You're the only one who has been wronged by the dark fae? The only one who has been forced to do something you do not want to do? I've been plain with you from the start. My brother and I are fire mages seeking the sword of a celestial to slay the Hunter who wants to kill us for our magic. Nothing more. Nothing less. We also believe the seven shards should be reformed into a crown, but I forced you to do nothing. That is up to you. If you choose to leave now, so be it. Just leave the sword so we can kill the Hunter."

With those last words, he turned on his heel and strode away.

Maeve wrapped her arms around her waist and stared out at the city, unseeing as her stony gaze reminded her that she'd made a mistake. They were only trying to help and yet she'd lashed out, unwilling to accept that she was safe, secure, and had people who would fight with her. She should have known better; the brothers of fire were not like Sandrine. Why did she throw the word "fae" in Imer's face? His transition had been instant and complete. She'd thoroughly insulted him. How could she forgive herself? How could *he* forgive her? And how could she treat him that way when deep down inside, she cared.

The knowing frightened her. So quickly she'd grown to care about him which instinctively made her want to push him away. Her fingers went to the collar around her neck. She had to be free, at all costs and deal with what came afterward. And oh Divine, she needed to sleep without nightmares chasing her. Shivering with both cold and guilt, Maeve made her way back inside, wishing she'd held her tongue.

Shadows fell around the temple and at sunset the priests and priestesses drew together to pray, the swell of their chant filled the temple and peace washed over Maeve. She'd slept, ate, and found Sandrine. After telling the scholar she'd return to the quest, Sandrine had then demanded to know what she'd said to put her grandson in an ill mood. Cowed, Maeve had taken the sword she'd found in Carn and made her way to the chamber where Imer was staying.

A lump settled in her throat as she approached and the scent of tobacco smoke wafted through the air. As she neared, she heard the low rumble of voices and then laughter. Was Ingram with him?

She hesitated as she neared, noticing the door was cracked open as though they were expecting someone. No, she would not interfere now but come back later.

As though guessing her thoughts, there was a squeak and the door to the room swung open as the dragon flew out. Despite herself, a smile came to Maeve's face and she reached out for it. The beast settled on her shoulder, almost slapping her in the face with its wings. The dragon was much heavier now and its claws ripped through the robe Maeve wore.

"Maeve of Carn," Ingram's lazy voice drawled.

Maeve's head snapped up. He stood in the doorway, leaning, rather heavily, on the door. The low light made his eye patch look less menacing and his gaze rested on the dragon. In one hand he held a mug. He tilted his head back and took a long gulp, then grinned as he wiped ale off his face. Turning, he tossed words over his shoulder. "I told you she'd come looking for you."

A flush spread over Maeve's cheeks and she backed away. "I did not mean to intrude."

Ingram shrugged and held out his arm and whistled. The dragon flew off Maeve's shoulder and rested on Ingram's outstretched arm. Maeve saw he wore leather on his arm, effectively protecting his skin from the dragon's claws. "Evening prayers are almost over," he drawled. "I have a priestess to find."

He winked—not so subtly—at Imer and brushed past Maeve, leaving the smell of ale behind him. Maeve's tongue went wet. Ale. What she would give for a mug of it.

Left alone, with Imer on the other side of the door, and likely still frustrated with her, Maeve sucked the inside of her cheek. It was easy to draw her sword and fling herself into battle. But when it came to matters of the heart—a mere apology for losing her temper—she wanted to back away. Sandrine's sharp tongue was easier to handle than facing Imer.

There was no sound from the other side of the door so Maeve took a deep breath and stepped into the doorway.

The room was small and dimly lit with a lantern perched on a side table with a chair, askew beside it. A jug—perhaps filled with ale—set beside the lantern, a damp spot slowly spreading across the wood. Imer sprawled on the bed next to the table, propped up on an elbow while his other hand pulled the pipe from his mouth and pointed it at Maeve. His hat sat on the pillow and his pointed ears were clearly visible.

Maeve took a step toward him, and his dark blue eyes met hers, deep, intense, and yet welcoming. There was no anger there, no judgement, and then a crooked grin covered his face as his eyes swept down Maeve's body.

She froze. "I thought you'd be upset?"

"My lady," he retorted, a wicked glint in his eye. "I thought you came to apologize."

Maeve sighed and held up the sword. "I did . . . I am . . ." her tongue stumbled over the words and she dropped her gaze to the floor. "Imer, I'm sorry for what I said up there on the balcony. It was unfair, and wrong of me. I'm used to everyone expecting something from me, but that is no excuse. I just want to be free, but there's a cost. I think I understand that there will always be a cost, that perhaps this is my fate. When we were in Carn my memories led me to believe I was saved for this quest, and that there is magic in my blood that will awaken when the seven shards are put back together. And so I will accept this fate, but I brought you the sword of the celestials so you can kill the creature who hunts you. I'm selfish, I am aware of my faults, but you don't deserve it."

"Maeve," Imer sprang from the bed in one bound, the scent of pipe smoke floating around him as he tossed the pipe on the table and towered over her in two strides. "Thank you. I suspected as much but, it's good to hear the words from your lips."

Imer wrapped his hands around the sword, his fingertips grazing Maeve's as he took it from her. "What makes you think I will leave you now?" he whispered, his voice deep and husky.

Maeve studied him, noticing the smoldering of his eyes. He backed away, leaning the sword against the table.

"I assumed," Maeve twisted her fingers together, wishing

she had something to do with her hands. She did not do well being inactive. "I thought you and Ingram would stay here since it is your home. Sandrine will want to leave soon . . ." she trailed off, embarrassed at her rambling words.

When she glanced up at Imer, he winked and ran a hand through his hair. "Maeve of Carn," he whispered. "What do you do to me?"

"Nothing . . . I . . ."

"I could never stay angry with you," he crossed the room again, wrapped his arm around her waist, and swung the door shut with his free hand.

Maeve's pulse quickened. The warmth of his body drew her in closer and she leaned into him. Sensations swept through her, a thrill, a lust, a wanting. A moan escaped her lips and her mouth opened, craving him, desperate for more.

17
DELICIOUS SENSATIONS

"Imer," Maeve whispered.

A flush came to her face as she pressed her hands against his chest. His body was lean and hard underneath his shirt. She brought her hands up to his shoulders and dared to meet his gaze.

"Tell me," the arm around her waist tightened and his free hand tip-toed across her face, brushing her cheek and then drifting down to her bare neck. "Did you have a vision about the magic of Carn?"

His eyes were close, oh so close.

Maeve's breath hitched and she tilted her head. "Aye, when I touched the shard I saw magic stirring within it. Nothing but a blue shimmer but the runes on my skin responded to it."

His eyes drifted down and his fingers touched the patterns of swirls at the base of her neck. "And you waited to tell me?" He reproached her.

Maeve's voice dropped to a breathy whisper. "I was frightened by what it meant. The Carnites had magic and power, and yet they fell to nature, the orcs, and the fae. Who am I to survive? And why did they put a map of ink on my skin if I am not the one fated to find the seven shards of Erinyes and put the crown together?"

Imer's fingertips grazed her shoulders and his eyes bored into hers. "Because, my lady, you were meant to set things right. But not alone. Never alone."

Something loosened inside of Maeve at his words and the tension that held her rigid melted away. When he captured her lips with a slow, steady kiss, Maeve leaned into him, then pulled back. She searched his eyes and he arched a brow. "I am still getting used to this, used to you," she admitted.

"It is time," he murmured. "You're going to need allies if you plan on destroying the dark fae."

He was right but how could she ask him to come further, when nothing but punishment from the fae awaited her? "Imer, I'm serious," she fixed him with a look, trying, and failing to keep the hunger out of her eyes. "You shouldn't come further with me. It's my quest, my fate, and there's no need for you to get involved too. You've done so much for me just by accepting me for who I am. I appreciate that about you, and I cannot ask for more. At least, not right now. When the seven shards are put together and turned into a crown, there will be war, and perhaps then we can unite again."

"Maeve, don't say such things," Imer tilted her chin up and silenced her with a kiss.

He tasted like tobacco and smoke. Maeve longed for more. Heat surged through her core like a fire had been ignited within her body. The turmoil of her predicament lessoned and peace replaced her budding anxiety at the upcoming continuation of her journey. It faded away under Imer's touch.

Imer angled his head as his tongue slipped into her mouth. All she could think of was even though she did not deserve him, she wanted, nay, desired more. So much more. It had been too long and any self-control she might have had was swept away by desire. But when would she see him again?

She had to have him. Now. It would be impossible to leave without one memory to refer back to when her journey became challenging. Desire hummed under Maeve's skin, and for once her thoughts did not drift to Caspian.

Imer was the only one she saw, the only one she cared about. His hand on her skin was as hot as a brand and she longed for the heat of his touch to brand her everywhere, like the swirling ink that covered her skin. She pressed her hands against his bare shoulders. The muscles were hard under her touch, his skin smooth.

Imer made a sound in his throat, a guttural sound of longing. His hand roamed down, touching the swells of her breasts beneath her garb and then his fingers closed on the material around her waist and began to pull it up, inch by inch.

A strangled cry came from Maeve's lips as she gave in to the delicious sensations of pleasure. Their noses bumped and the kisses turned from gentle to rough. Teeth nipped flesh and Maeve broke the heated kiss, gasping for breath. Imer took advantage of the moment to lift the robe over Maeve's head. He stepped back, a devilish look in his eyes as he tossed the clothing on the floor. His eyes traced the swell of Maeve's breasts, the way they moved up and down as she breathed and the darkness between her legs. He shrugged out of his shirt and his pants quickly.

Maeve felt a wetness between her legs as she studied his naked body. She moved toward him, unembarrassed, unashamed.

Sea blue eyes studied her. "Maeve, you are beautiful," he whispered as though he were saying a prayer.

And then he was upon her, arms wrapped around her. "If you think I will let you out of my sight, you are wrong," he whispered, peppering her face with kisses. Cheek, nose, ears, neck, nothing escaped his attention. He maneuvered her to the bed and drew her down on top of him, his hands dropping below her waist to squeeze her buttocks. Maeve writhed above him, spreading her legs, ready for him to take her.

"Imer, please don't make me wait," she kissed him. "It is dangerous."

"Dangerous you say," he groaned and then the wicked glint returned to his eyes. "I'll show you dangerous." He rolled on top of her and lifted himself up on his elbows.

Maeve arched her back, thrusting her breasts up toward his naked chest. His fingertips danced across her bare skin, tracing the runes before he cupped her breast, thumbing her nipple with his fingers. His mouth followed and then his tongue, sucking, licking, tasting, then gentle bites, first one breast and then the other.

Maeve's hips rolled up, pressing into his hardness and a cry burst from her lips as her passion mounted. One of his fingers traced her slit, gathering the wetness there and rubbing although there was no need, she was already wet and ready for him.

"Imer," she begged him, desperate for more. "I need you," she whispered.

His eyes went soulful at her words and he paused, staring into her eyes, his voice husky. "Need, my lady, it is a powerful word." He traced a finger down her belly. "I can't promise I will always be with you, even though I want to. But I sense time is of the essence, and we have this stolen moment now, so your wish is my command."

Maeve closed her eyes and let all thoughts drift away and gave into nothing but delicious sensations as Imer took her to great heights of pleasure she'd never experienced before.

18

THE JOURNEY SOUTH

Maeve, Sandrine, Ingram, and Imer stayed at the temple in Isdrine for another thirty days, and then, the day after the night of the full moon, they set off. The brisk winter wind had settled to a cool chill. Maeve blinked against the frost and was thankful for the warm furs and fur-lined boots which had been given to her. They were much warmer than her warrior garb and while ineffective for battles and sparing, at least protected her from the elements. She carried her pack on her back underneath the furs, giving her the impression of a hunchback. Not that she cared what others thought, for she was warm and a playful smile touched her lips. Warm and happy. She stole another glance at Imer who traveled ahead with Ingram by his side. When they'd left the temple, one of the priestesses had held Ingram's hand and cried, begging him to return. He gently embraced her and made promises, but his face was a mask of fury and frustration as they set off. Again, Maeve questioned why he couldn't stay. Why Ingram and Imer, specifically, were fated to continue the quest with her. And then her eyes went to Sandrine, who kept pace with her, using a walking stick although she did not need it. Her hair was pulled back from her face and her lips pressed together, tight, as though she were keeping something inside of her from coming out.

The dragon landed with a squawk on Maeve's shoulder, the sudden weight almost making her stumble. She righted herself and turned to her silent companion. "Where are we going, Sandrine?"

After speaking with Priestess Mariah, she resolved to be calm, patient, and understanding with Sandrine's twisted words. Now that she knew there were greater things happening, things she could not have anticipated, she knew to be aware, to ask deeper questions before assuming everything was all about her and her fate. Although understanding she was the last Carnite, the last defender, helped her make her choice, she was still terrified at what was about to happen. Was it right to destroy the world in hopes of redemption?

"South to the grove," Sandrine spoke quickly, evenly without any anger in her words. Or fear.

It was one trait Maeve admired in Sandrine. She stood tall, sure of herself, even though she was betraying the fae. Would Maeve be like that? After she'd lost everything it was difficult to find something to hold onto, something to believe in, but she thought she'd found it again. Had Sandrine? Was her belief why she was driven to complete a task they were unlikely to survive?

"And there is another shard there?" Maeve asked to keep Sandrine talking.

“A shard, yes,” Sandrine hummed and then lowered her voice, as though the wind were listening to their words. “A shard but more importantly, the tribes of the grove. They are dark-skinned and dangerous. They will not take kindly to us entering their lands, nor will they give up the shard easily. If anything, they are even more suspicious because each month the fae have been raiding them and they are prepared to fight at any moment. So far, collecting the shards has been easy.”

Easy! Maeve kept her thoughts to herself but frowned at Sandrine. There had been nothing easy about finding the first shard, and she'd ended up losing one to the raider as well as the Finder's Stone in the process. But Sandrine had sighed instead of scolding her about it, and Maeve realized that Sandrine took some responsibility for not being there and allowing the quest to go awry. At least she understood why Ingram and Imer were there. Although she already knew the world was wide and dangerous, she could protect herself. But without her strength she couldn't protect both herself and Sandrine from the situations they might find themselves in. Traveling with the two fire mages was smart, and Maeve was hopeful that the next time the Hunter thought to fight them, they'd actually be able to kill it.

After that night with Imer, she hadn't taken the sword back from him and now he carried it, tall and proud. A sensation swelled in her breast when she glanced at him, and at that moment he happened to look back. Their eyes met. He tipped his hat and winked. Anticipation tingled on Maeve's fingertips, she wanted to touch him, taste him again. Her ears went pink with that knowledge and she turned back to Sandrine. Even if Sandrine told her nothing, she couldn't be angry with the Scholar, not after Imer and the way he made her feel.

"The tribes of the grove," she repeated. "What are we to do? Befriend them?"

Sandrine pressed her lips together. "I have a gift for them, which might give us time to find the shard and leave before our shaky alliance turns bad. There's something else you should know about the grove."

A sinking sensation went through Maeve as she met Sandrine's gray eyes. "What is it?"

"The grove used to be the kingdom of the fae, before they were banished from the land. Deep in the woods lies their kingdom, and it is thought, should the Crown of Erinyes be restored, the fae will return there to reclaim their land."

Fear jolted through Maeve's nerves and then faded. Her throat went dry but the fae were still banished. For now. "Why are you telling me this?" she asked, breathless.

"You should know, because it pertains to you." Sandrine shrugged, then changed the subject. "Tell me about Carn."

Maeve faced her, surprised the woman was actually making an effort to keep the conversation flowing. Darkness pricked the edges of her vision and she swallowed hard. "It is difficult to talk about."

"I know," Sandrine said. "Many things are but it is important to know your past, to understand it. The past often informs the future, and knowing what you know now about Carn and what happened to the city, what happened to you, is helping you make choices. You may not think you have changed, but I've seen it. There is a boldness growing in you, for you are no longer a victim of circumstance. You know what happened and now you are taking steps to amend and change it. That is an admirable quality."

Maeve stared, open-mouthed.

Sandrine frowned in return. "Don't just stand there. Keep walking. We have a long journey ahead!"

Maeve shook her head as she followed Sandrine, a small smile playing about her lips. The scholar would never cease to amaze her.

THE COLD WINDS lessened as they moved south but a chill stayed in the air. The dragon often soared above them, growing day by day. Its wings lengthening and hardening and its scales glowing. Those eyes, at first wild and disrespectful, turned canny and thoughtful. Intelligent. Once it became the size of a small wolf, it began to hunt, even though wildlife was scarce during the winter. Yet there were still small woodland animals who risked leaving their burrows and shelters to venture out into the cold in search of the last remnants of food. It was those the dragon found and tore limb by limb or swallowed in one gulp.

Maeve watched in admiration, for the dragon would grow to be a fearsome beast, and she had hopes that when the time came, it would fight with them and help them wipe the dark fae from the face of the land. That is, once they were free to return again. Maeve pushed conflicting emotions away, now was not the time to speculate on whether she was making the right choice. She'd ignored the fae for one month, one month of bliss and warmth, learning about the Divine and taking time to make love to Imer. Out in the wild though, things were different and while Imer looked at her with his intense eyes, there was something else.

Every now and then, he and Ingram would pause and lift their faces to the wind, calmly watching. Once, Maeve saw a white bird fly high above and drop a feather. It drifted down and Ingram picked it up, ran his fingers over it and said something to Imer, who nodded. Maeve watched in confusion, aware there was something they were not sharing with her, and wondering if she dared ask or should wait for them to tell her themselves.

Maeve and her companions moved toward a dark smear on the horizon that became clearer as they traveled. The dragon called out and soared into the air, almost out of sight. Maeve watched it as an unfamiliar concern settled in the pit of her belly. "Will it come back?" she asked, her words blowing out like a pillow of mist.

"He always does," Ingram said. He'd been gentler as of late, less furious and more patient with Maeve.

She assumed it was because of their sojourn in the temple of Isdrine, and the fact that the Hunter seemed to no longer be on their trail.

Maeve chewed her lower lip. "The dragon is a male, how did you know?"

Ingram smirked. "It has what all males have."

Maeve's face reddened but she refused to give in to her slight embarrassment. "Ah. My concern is not for the dragon's return, but what the people of the grove will think when they see it."

"And what they will do to it," Ingram nodded. "Dragons are not invincible and this one is too young. We should keep it in the wild lands, but Imer is not ready to leave you yet."

Yet. The word stung although Maeve should have known it was inevitable. The brothers would leave and she could continue on with her damned quest. In fact, it sang of reason. It was her, and her alone who was tasked with the deed, and it was her and Sandrine who should be there on the next night of the full moon. The fae would be spitting with anger at her deception but it was a relief not to see them for more than sixty days.

Imer walked up beside Ingram, a sly smile on his face as he winked at Maeve. "Discussing dragons?"

Maeve shrugged. "I don't know what to do with it. What if the people of the grove try to kill it?"

Imer sighed. "Sandrine can tell you more, but although the people of the grove are dangerous, in their own way, they also have a deep respect for the laws of nature, which makes them unlikely to kill a creature born of nature. I think they would ask questions first."

"Capture first, ask questions later," Ingram agreed.

"Do you know much about the people of the grove?" Maeve asked Imer, falling in step with him.

Ingram hung back, still watching the skies.

Imer touched her fur-covered arm. "I've studied many of the races of the known world. They are curious, their histories and traditions, their beliefs and their magic."

Magic. Of course he'd want to know more about those with

magic. "But where did you study?" she asked. "Surely not in the Contresea? It seems it would be too dangerous for you. And I did not realize the temple of Isdrine held such books."

Imer went still. "You'd be surprised," he said, adverting his eyes.

Maeve's heart sank. There *was* something he wasn't telling her.

"What is it?" she almost whispered.

Imer's eyes flashed, the muted colors of winter highlighting the deepness of his blue eyes. "Maeve," his voice went low as he touched her arm.

She met his gaze, unsure what to feel. As usual, his proximity drew her inward and she longed to be entangled within his warmth again. Memories of their lovemaking made her desire more. Why was it that once she got a taste she yearned for more and more, as though making love once would never be enough.

His fingers brushed her cheek and she closed her eyes, leaning into the warmth of his touch. "Imer," she whispered. "I want to be angry that you're withholding things from me. But I don't have a right to be. You can have your secrets as long as—"

He silenced her with a kiss, warm, gentle, almost apologetic.

When he pulled back, his eyes were dark with desire and his voice came out rough. "That is kind of you Maeve. I would tell you, but for once, it's not a secret for me to tell, or for Ingram to tell. There are many lives at stake and on pain of death we've been asked never to reveal this secret. But, when the quest of the seven shards is complete, I would like you to come home with me. To my true home."

He kissed her cheek and then pulled back, taking all the warmth in the air with him. A smile crossed his face at the look in her eyes, one of curious surprise. "I've said too much already. Come. Sandrine will never forgive us if we lag behind."

Maeve let him take her hand and studied him as they walked. Each time she thought she had him figured out, he revealed another layer, another depth. He was full of secrets and perhaps she'd never know them all.

19
THE GROVE

A few days later, they reached a thickly wooded forest. Old trees towered above their heads, blocking out the light yet welcoming them to sacred lands. Maeve felt the shift as soon as they stepped underneath the first bough.

The wind faded away, leaving nothing but a damp sensation of cold, an ache that climbed into her bones. The dragon landed, quiet for once, and sniffed the ground, walking along it as though it scented something or someone, and was hunting for them. Matted leaves covered the ground, the last remnants of fall, all pressed down to protect the life underneath. The air smelled of pine and oak but there was a richer scent, deeper, stronger, a sort of hazy scent that reminded Maeve of a fire. Yet it wasn't that. What was it? She couldn't quite put a finger on it.

Sound was muted in the woods, as though the trees were listening, waiting for them to make a misstep or to utter a foul word in the sacred grove. Discomfort crept through

Maeve like the clammy fingers of mist and fog. What was this place? If she had come here alone, she would have turned around and left. She glanced at Sandrine who walked ahead, striding silently as though she knew where she was going.

Indeed, a road opened up before them with arched branches interlocking overhead and the thick trunks of trees guarding the road, allowing none who entered to venture back.

They walked quietly. Even the dragon did not fly but walked on its four legs, its belly dragging against the leaves on the ground.

The oddness of the grove sat heavy on Maeve's shoulders and an itch tingled at her fingertips. Fighting was better than the relentless travel into nothingness and the anticipation that something bad was about to happen. Her fingers were more inclined to drift toward the hilt of her sword than wait and watch in a haunted land that once belonged to the wicked fae.

But nothing happened.

Hours passed, high noon came and went, and the forest went on endlessly, a reminder they were in a place that was not common.

"There are tales about the grove, aren't there?" Maeve finally whispered to Imer.

Although she did not walk too close to him, the heat of his body called out to her, instinctively drawing her closer.

Imer grinned, a reminder of his flirtatious personality. Once again, he looked like the rogue pirate she'd met on the odd ship. As if to confirm the reminder, a flash of blue appeared between his fingers. "There is a reason that tales from the grove are mysterious and unconfirmed. Methinks this place has many secrets it does not wish to share."

As though Imer's words were magic, they appeared. Shapes stepped out of the trees, surrounding them on all sides. They were both male and female, a tall and slender people with long limbs like willowy trees and golden-brown skin as though they spent many days bathing in sunlight.

Imer drew in a sharp breath and nudged Ingram. Although he kept his voice at a whisper, Maeve still heard what he said. "Willow must be from here. But she never said . . ."

Willow? Who was Willow? A twinge of jealousy went through Maeve. She shook it away.

The people who'd stepped out of the trees carried spears, held down so they were not pointing at them. Their faces were still as stones and their eyes dark as berries. They were breathtaking and beautiful, with shiny long hair, some black, others brown, and some gold like sunshine. Each wore clothing made out of skins with a belt of leaves, some woven into their hair and others around their waists or arms.

Maeve's fingers dropped away from her sword hilt. She couldn't remember the last time she'd been sent out with a delegation to meet a group of people and befriend them. It had happened once or twice, and those delegations often descended into a blood bath. Guilt racked her mind. It would not be the same here, not if she could help it. Spending time with Ingram and Imer had taught her to seek friendship first and use violence as a last resort.

The dragon hissed, shattering the tension. One of the males gripped his spear tighter, the sharp point aimed down at the dragon. In the distance, Maeve thought she heard the deep boom of drums playing a hypnotic rhythm.

A woman stepped forward, weaponless. Her black hair hung in a thick braid over one shoulder and trailed down past her waist. Her eyes spoke of her age, even though there were no lines on her face. She was about Sandrine's height and moved toward her as though gliding over ice. "Strangers to the glade, I sense your intentions. You are searching, seeking, but why have you come here? To us? What do you want?"

Sandrine placed a hand over her heart and bent her head. An odd gesture that was quite unlike her.

"We are searching and have brought you a gift in exchange for knowledge. It will be up to you to determine whether to accept the gift and assist us in our quest."

A flash of displeasure crossed the woman's face for a second before it became impassive again. "What gift did you bring?"

Maeve stood behind Sandrine, so she did not see the object which Sandrine pulled from her robes and held at her waist, just enough to allow the woman to see. The woman's eyes studied it for a long time, as though by staring at it she would keep expressions from forming on her impassive face.

Then she raised a hand, palm facing away from them.

Maeve did not see it happen but a moment later there was a pin-prick of pain and warm blood sluiced down between her thighs. She groaned as the wetness covered her legs, her sight went dizzy, and she fell backward on the path. The trees towered down upon her and it seemed as though they had faces and spoke, arguing with each other about her fate. Voices whispered, not to her but above her.

"Who do they think they are, entering the sacred grove?"

"Bringing weapons of the old enemy of our people. They should be punished."

"We are not called to punish those who break our laws, only to protect."

"What is the difference?"

"There is a reason they are here. I can smell it on them."

"Agree, and what of the gift?"

"The test, we should give them the test."

"If they survive, it is because they are meant to be here."

"The test. The test. The test."

Words faded away as Maeve gave into the darkness. In her dreams, or unconsciousness, the Hunter showed up again and again, except this time he was stronger. He chased her down, fought her with a mad intensity, and then, at the last moment, when she thought she had him, he stole victory from her fingertips and crushed her with darkness.

Maeve's eyes came open and she sat up, staring around in confusion. She was no longer on the path but somewhere else, a kind of opening in the middle of a circle of trees. There were great rocks around her, the kind used to encircle a fire to keep it from escaping. Then she realized they were the only barrier between a roaring fire and herself. Nothing bound her to the circle and when she turned, she saw Imer sitting on one end, rubbing his head, while Ingram groaned, then frowned when he saw they were surrounded by a ring of fire.

Sandrine was the only one who did not seem surprised. She moved to the center of the ring. "Quickly," she whispered. "Maeve, keep your eyes on me. Ingram. Imer. You know what to do."

A wave of heat surged around Maeve and in confusion she glanced around the flames that surrounded them. Then her eyes went to Sandrine who stood tall, lifted up her hands, and started to chant.

Words in a language unknown poured out of her mouth. Although Maeve kept her gaze on Sandrine, just beyond she saw the people of the grove, gathered in a circle, watching them.

The test.

A surge of hate went through her. What right did these people think they had to burn them alive, just to see if they would escape? And from there grant them with some kind of gift?

Maeve's finger went to her sword hilt, and alarm slammed through her as she realized her weapon was gone. Along with her furs.

Her fingers shook and all the things she'd learned at the temple of Isdrine flew from her mind.

The fire flared up higher, hot tongues reaching for the sky. Then suddenly it misted into white smoke, hiding Maeve and her companions from the villagers. From behind the cloud she heard gasps and shouts.

Sandrine ceased chanting. "Join me," she whispered, her words clipped and urgent. "What happens next will determine whether we live or die."

Die. Maeve was not ready to die and yet, her fists clenched. How could she fight without her weapons or her strength? She glanced at Imer, whose face contorted with fury. Anger blazed from his eyes. At least he felt the way she did, ready to burn down the people of the grove for what they had done.

A wind blew, gently at first and then stronger, as though the trees recognized the victory over fire and used their branches to blow away the remaining smoke. When it cleared, the people of the grove stood with their spears cast down.

The same woman who had spoken to them on the road stepped forward. "It has been decided," she said, her voice hard. "You have powers beyond what should be controlled, powers which call darkness to you. Leave. Now. Before the darkness reaches us and destroys us."

Sandrine lifted her chin. "Not without the shard."

The woman stiffened, this time unable to hide her surprise.

Sandrine continued. "We will leave as soon as the shard of Erinyes is in our hands. We have come to find that which was lost, and to make darkness answer for its deception. If you do not give us the shard, you are dooming your people. You have seen what has happened here. And you know you cannot kill us. It is your choice. Do this peacefully or bring war down upon your people."

20

Name of Justice

The woman recovered quickly. "The shard. The lost shard of Erinyes? If you wish for it, you are beyond hope. If the seven shards are found and put together, you know what will happen. War will cover the lands, a war we cannot stop nor hope to win. The celestials will return to fight and the gates of hell will open, but who will lose the most in this war? We do. The people who have dwelled on this land and our ancestors before us since the beginning of time. If you believe that war is the answer, you have been deceived. Who convinced you to hunt for the seven shards? Who told you that war is the only way? They were wrong. The seven shards of Erinyes should never be put back together. The crown must not call forth the celestials and devils to this land, to reign over us and slaughter us in the crosshairs of their eternal battle. We will never give up the shard."

Maeve felt as though her heart would stop at the words, words she'd considered herself, were said out loud. The same twisted sensation she'd experienced at the temple washed through her. Perhaps it was wrong, and although she wished she could stand firm in her decision, she was also aware of the danger of the seven shards, of turning the land into a battleground. If she had her strength, she would be able to fight, and the brothers of fire and anyone else who was a mage could step forth and fight. But—and she couldn't believe she was considering for the first time—what about the innocent? Flashbacks took her back to the destruction of Carn where the loss of life was great. That's what it would be like worldwide unless the fae—dark fae—could be stopped. Would it be enough and would they be the ones able to stop the dark fae? Her fingers went to the collar around her neck. She had her doubts but then her gaze went to Imer and again she was reminded of his strength.

Sandrine spoke up, standing tall, her back straight as an arrow. "You have doubts, but you will lose either way. If you give us the shard now, we will go peacefully, and the war on your people will be postponed. We are here to give you fair warning so that you have time to prepare and draw up alliances. Even now those who look into the future see what is coming and are preparing for the war, preparing to protect the people. If you go to them, you may be spared and some of you will survive, although I cannot guarantee who will live and who will die. Listen to me and you will have a chance but if you do not, war will rain down on your heads. The fae are gathering, growing strong in the Fae Underground. They hunt the shards without remorse. If they find you still have the shard, on the night of the full moon, which draws nigh, they will sweep in and slaughter you and your people, killing each and every one of you until they uncover the shard. And then, when you look up at the full moon, and see the bright blood of your people covering the grove, you will have wished you had listened to us, listened to me, and handed over the shard before darkness swept your land."

Fury covered the woman's face and spittle flew from her lips as she spoke. "It is because of you, Sandrine the Scholar. I know who you are, I've heard tales about you, tales I thought were untrue but now you stand before me, strong and determined to have your way. Until the bitter end. Murderous woman, but you wouldn't stop there, and you won't stop until everyone is destroyed, until everyone feels the same rage and murder and hate that you felt. When I first heard your story, I felt sorry for you but now, seeing you here, threatening my people and all I know, there is no more empathy for your plight. You know this, truer than I know it. We all have a choice; we all can choose the path we walk down. You choose the path of darkness and now you seek to draw the entire world in with you. You will not survive."

Sandrine's lip curled and Maeve watched her, almost holding her breath, unsure what to say or to believe. Was it true? Was Sandrine the infection, the darkness that spread across the world? Was she doing this on purpose to destroy the people? And even as Maeve thought of it, she realized something else. She and Sandrine were alike, with their decisions and situations. Although she did not realize it outright, Maeve was learning from Sandrine and seeing the semblance in their attitudes. They were both headstrong and determined, but Sandrine had the advantage of more years. Years of service to the fae.

"You have always been angry with me, Mara," Sandrine's voice was quieter, if possible. "I know that what I did in the past was wrong. If I told you I am on a quest to right the wrongs that I have done, you would not believe me, nor I believe myself. I hold to what I know and what I believe in, without regret. You will have to trust the knowledge that I am a scholar, and although I do not read the future, I have seen what will happen if you do not join forces, if you do not give up your proud stance here in the grove. Is the death of all you love worth it for pride? Will you not reconsider? I've seen what happens to civilizations who do not listen, who do what they want to do without regarding others. Something bigger than our petty disagreements is at hand, something that will impact the entire world, and if you sit here in your grove, holding on to your pride, more people will die because of you. I'm not asking you to simply trust me, I'm asking you to take the burden upon yourself and save your people. That is all. By giving up the shard, by creating an alliance, you will do so. What will come will come, one way or another. It does not matter how many of you stand in the way, you will be destroyed first by the fae, then the celestials, and finally by the demons. When they return. For it is only a matter of time."

The woman folded her arms in front of her and then her gaze fell to Maeve of Carn and studied her.

"Ah," her shoulders slumped as truth seeped into her like a warm drink on a cold winter day. "You have found the last defender, the survivor of the destruction of Carn. And yes, she is collared. By the fae? Is she your prodigy? Who will take your place when you are gone? A liaison between the Fae Underground and those who live above?"

A ringing came to Maeve's head, a buzzing, and she understood what she'd never understood before. They came from across the sea, from underground, across the land, to destroy Carn and find the magic hidden there. The magic that was within her, the source of her strength. She was the last defender, the one meant to save the world. But just like the others, she had a choice. Which path would she go down? That's what Sandrine had been trying to tell her all along, her actions had consequences, both good and bad, regardless of what she did. And suddenly she wanted the people of the grove to understand what she understood and she rose, head held high and faced the woman.

"Yes. I am Maeve. Maeve of Carn. I wear the markings of my people and I am the sole survivor of my land. We fell without grace and I still have vivid memories, of blood and battle, fire and flame, and blades, driving into my skin again and again. It was horrible and if I could spare anyone such loss and devastation, I would. I was only a child, and what happened on that day has stayed with me and will stay with me the rest of my life. It defined who I am, and what actions I took and will take. But Sandrine the Scholar is right. We did not come here to take the shard. We came here to ask you to save yourselves. That is your only choice. I've seen what happens when war rains down, and it is not pretty. While my scars are hidden, there is darkness within me, a darkness that the fae exploited because it is part of me. I wish it were not but wishes are naught but folly. I am here now, because I made a choice. We will rise up strong and destroy our enemies. We will not stay in hiding, waiting for the celestials to return. We will put together the Crown of Erinyes using the seven shards and call down the celestials to help us in our time of need, and call up the demons from the underworld to answer for their crimes. And then, only then, after the greatest war the world has seen, we will have peace. But it will not be because we sat back in hiding; it will be because we stood up and took charge of our fate, charge of our destinies. And so I ask you, as one who was a victim of those who did not stand up for what was right, a victim of those who choose riches and selfishness over saving their people, will you let go of old grievances and grudges? Will you stand up for your people and save them? And will you give us the shard of Erinyes and trust us to fight, in the name of justice?"

21
THE FIFTH SHARD

Maeve held the fifth shard in her left hand, her fingers tightly closed around it. It was smaller than the one she'd found in Carn, and yet still a thick shard. She could envision the crown in her head, with the largest piece in the middle and three shards on either side, creating the semi-circle crown. The blue color swam inside the shards, speaking of power, potent but harnessed, waiting for one to unleash it, call upon those who created it, and allow it freedom.

The grove was quiet. After Maeve's speech, someone had run off, and almost an hour later returned with the shard, glowing in their hands. It had been given to Maeve and she hadn't let go of it since. From there, the people began to pack. Maeve did not understand it. Why? Where were they going? But in the chaos she'd been left on her own, swept to the side, standing there, holding the shard.

The dragon spread its wings and flew through the air, landed beside her and nuzzled her leg. The heat of its nostrils almost burned her but she did not move away. Glancing down she eyed the scales which were quickly hardening. The beast was growing and it could not come with her, not into the heart of madness. The people of the grove had not killed it, but the last dragon was a treasure, a beast others would hunt, eventually.

As she watched, Sandrine, Ingram, and Imer wove between the people, speaking and helping them pack. What they spoke about, she had no idea, but largely she was ignored aside from a few curious glances. There was still an aura of anger in the grove and her discomfort rose.

"Do you want me to leave?"

The voice made her jump. She glanced around, searching for the speaker. None of the villagers were close to her and the voice was young, like that of a child's before it came of age.

There came a sigh. "Down here, it's me."

This time, Maeve did leap back and stared, eyes widening in both horror and excitement. "You speak?"

The dragon wagged its head and its golden eyes glared at her. "You know who I am. The last of my kind. You spoke to my mother, why should it surprise you that I speak?"

Maeve's mouth opened and closed. "Your mother. The Goblin Queen? But how did you know? It was before you were born and I wasn't sure she was a dragon. How come you aren't in human form? You're. . . a dragon." She shrugged helplessly.

The dragon spread its wings. "I was conscious inside the egg, waiting. Listening. She told me to wait, and so I did. But when you took me, it became uncomfortable, cold even, which is why I had to hatch. And then I had to figure out how to speak. Ingram taught me."

Maeve's eyes flew to Ingram. *He knew? All along? He had the audacity to teach the dragon how to speak?*

"It just didn't seem important, until now. I sense you are worried about me and you want me to leave. It's okay. I will go with Ingram."

"But . . ." Maeve sputtered and her cheeks went warm. "Yes, I am worried. I don't know what the fae will do to you. And although the people of the grove did not harm you, what if they did?"

"I will not be full grown for another year, and even then I'll keep growing. But I can protect myself."

Maeve stared for a moment and then slid to her knees so that she could be on eye level with the beast. Smoke curled from its long snout and its lidded eyes glistened, wild, feral, and yet it spoke. "Why are you here? Did your mother give you a purpose? Do you have a name?"

"My mother told me I was the last of my kind and should bring redemption to my people, whatever that means. Dragons do not age like humans, we are born with the knowledge our ancestors passed down to us and then we must learn how to use these bodies. You might say I am an old soul and this body is nothing but a vessel. I've learned to fly, to speak, to hunt, to breathe fire, and now I'm growing, waiting until I will be large enough and strong enough. I am male but it doesn't matter, I am the last dragon and there will not be another. The age of dragons is gone, as is the age of the Carnites."

The dragon fell silent as though lost in thought. Maeve

blinked. Another being like her, the last of its kind waiting for full growth so it could fulfill its purpose.

"Then you will fight on our side," she confirmed.

"When the time comes," the dragon replied. "The seven shards mean nothing to me, but since I am living in this world, I'm curious to see what happens to it. My mother told me many stories, some true, some not true, well aware that she was half-mad with age and longing and frustration and the curse."

"I want to know more," Maeve told the dragon. "More about your mother and the stories she told you. Why didn't you speak to me before today?"

"You never spoke to me. I assumed you were not interested, lost in your own woes. I was able to bring you some comfort, but I was made for war, for power, and for chaos. It is in my blood, boiling, ready to be released."

"Then you are bred for battle like me," Maeve gasped.

"I shall see if these battles are worth fighting for," the dragon rejoined. "For now, I will leave, and we will meet again once the seven shards have been turned into a crown."

Maeve's brow furrowed. "But where are you going?"

The dragon jerked and closed its mouth. Maeve looked up as Imer approached. Just the sight of him, once again, made her heart flip flop, his dark wild hair and deep blue eyes made her forget her woes, just for a moment. Standing, she took a step toward him, noting that the dragon spread its wings and then moved away, as though to give them privacy.

"The dragon can speak," she told Imer, breathless with excitement.

He glanced at the creature and then smiled. "Aye, so it can."

"Did you know?" Maeve asked as Imer moved closer, invading her personal space, one arm stealing around her waist, pulling her closer.

"Ingram speaks with it, and it speaks back. Impossible to tell though whether it is friendly or has its own agenda. It's so young though and we do not know much about dragons."

"Oh," Maeve felt foolish for not being curious enough to talk to the dragon but with Imer there, her frustration did not mount as it usually did. She placed her free hand on his chest where she could feel the consistent thud, thud of his heartbeat. He smelled like fire and warmth, and suddenly she wanted nothing more than to be lost in his embrace, his fire, and feel the heat of his mouth consume her again and again.

"Maeve," his fingers stroked her cheek, "you were amazing back there. When you stood up and spoke those words, everyone listened, they couldn't *not* listen to you, and the words you spoke. You are coming into your own, what you did back there was queen-like, noble. You have the potential to become more than you realize, don't ever forget that."

Maeve smiled, stunned by his words. "It just rose out of me, the words, as though they'd always been there inside of me, waiting for the moment to arise, to speak, to let the words come forth. I did not dream they would listen but . . ." she held up the shard, her eyes momentarily lost in its beauty.

"I know. I'm proud of you Maeve. I always knew you were

strong, independent," he laughed and then his eyes went serious. "I came to say goodbye."

Then, as though words would not leave his throat again, he pulled her closer, wrapped both arms around her and squeezed her hard. She felt him trembling as he held her and something more than passion welled up within her with a strong resistance to what he was saying. *Goodbye? It could not be!*

Her fingers wrapped around his cloak, holding him tight while she tucked her face against his neck, breathing in his scent. "Goodbye," she whispered, "Why? Imer, don't leave me."

The sensation of want, of desire, of need was new for her, and the thought of him leaving hurt more than knowing her strength was collared. With him, it was easy to see a different path, to find the good in life, to see the noble, to choose the right path. It had been difficult before and something she never considered but with Imer, everything was different. A word throbbed on her lips, a word she was unsure whether she should say out loud, say to him. Was it possible she was falling in love with a fire mage who was also half fae and might be one of her enemies? Although the past few months had only proven he was charming, mysterious, handsome, and that she was inexplicably drawn to him. She wanted him almost more than she wanted to be free. She wanted to see how their lives would intersect and play out, time over time, and the shocking knowledge, so quickly, so soon after meeting him frightened her. But not enough to make her pull away, in fact, it made her want to hold on to him tighter, to never let go. If he were out of her sight would she feel the same way? Would the change that came over her still be part of her? He brought out the best in her, could she be noble without him?

"It's not because I want to," his lips brushed her ear and then he pressed a kiss there, and another against her temple. "I have too. It is time. Sandrine only asked us to come for a while, to help, and we did. We have to return and we have to help these people too."

Maeve pulled back to give herself space to look up at him. "Return where? I thought Isdrine was your home but that's not what you're talking about. Is it?"

He shook his head, his laughing eyes serious for once. "Nay, we have many homes." He twirled a finger around a loose strand of hair. "Our true home is where the last mages reside, and it will be a haven when the seven shards are put back together. You must join us, when you are free of the dark fae, after your quest ends."

Relief swept through Maeve. The separation was only for a time, hopefully a short time. The months were running out; soon the seven shards would be turned back into a crown and then she would be free, as would be the fae. She shivered suddenly. "It feels foolish to say this but I'm not ready."

Imer rubbed her back. "You feel it too, don't you?"

She nodded. "We're connected somehow."

He smiled. "I'm glad I'm not alone in this."

"How will I find you? After . . ." she let the words hang.

"Sandrine will tell you when the time is right," Imer sighed, his eyes misting over. "It is one secret I will not speak about, for the knowledge could destroy many."

Instead of anxiety and questions there was nothing but

trust. Maeve nodded. "Do what you have to do, Imer. I will find you."

This time a flirtatious grin came to his lips and his eyes twinkled. "I know you will," he said gruffly and then kissed her, hard and long, as though it would make up for months apart.

22
SECOND CHANCE

The waving trees faded from view as Sandrine and Maeve continued, leaving Ingram, Imer, and the dragon with the people of the grove as they left their home in preparation for war. Uneasiness swirled around Maeve with the full knowledge that the night of the full moon was near, and she'd have to answer to the fae after avoiding them for two months. Sandrine said nothing, but Maeve knew the fae would be furious and punishment was inescapable.

Maeve rubbed her hands over her arms even though she still wore a fur. The sword of the celestial hung at her side, for Ingram and Imer had declined to take it, saying they would be safe from the Hunter where they were going. Maeve missed Imer's presence and she was curious about the dragon. But they were both gone now, leaving her with only Sandrine for company.

"What do you know about the race of dragons?" Maeve asked Sandrine, to take her mind off her incoming doom.

Sandrine frowned. "Enough. Why are you asking?"

"The dragon I found in the Draconbane Mountains speaks. I didn't know they could talk."

"You didn't," Sandrine said dryly. "After you spoke with one in the Draconbane Mountains and yet, you assumed they could not talk?"

Maeve frowned. "Yes, talk, and change into human form. Did you know the dragon could speak? And if it speaks, why doesn't it change into human form?"

Sandrine sniffed. "Did you ask the dragon those questions?"

"No, there wasn't time."

Sandrine shrugged. "Next time you're curious about a species and you have the opportunity to talk to them, try it. It might be far more enlightening than what I know."

Maeve sighed. Why was Sandrine so difficult? "Sandrine, it was a simple question. What do you know about dragons? You are the scholar; you are supposed to know these things. Who should I ask these questions, if not you?"

Sandrine continued walking. "I do not want to talk about dragons."

Was there a slight tremor in her voice or did Maeve imagine it?

She stared at her companion for a moment, and then, "What about you? Why did you kill your husband? Love doesn't turn to hate because of one action."

Sandrine snorted but her eyebrows lifted and a hint of mirth came to her face. "No, it wasn't because he took a new wife. There were several reasons leading up to it. After giving a man nine children, I wanted more, more than a life spent cleaning up dung, wiping dirty hands, and scolding reckless children. They weren't all bad years, mind you, and I loved the children, in my own way. But I've always been selfish, and I've always loved myself more. Besides, it was an arranged marriage as marriages between nobility often are. In the beginning I was young, beautiful, and more than eager to spread my legs and make him happy. But I'm a scholar, I understand knowledge, and I have a bit of magic which allowed me to set up my own trade. My husband thought I was embarrassing him and he wanted me to shut it down. We argued." She chuckled. "Loud expressive arguing, at home, in the street, in the market, everywhere. Of course he left me, we were destined to leave each other. But then he flaunted his new wife in my face and tried to steal my fortune. He had to go." Sandrine shook her head. "I did many things wrong, never accepting the fact that someone else would tell me what to do. I've paid for my sins. Time and time again. I had one child who came after me, one out of nine. The others were glad to get rid of me, glad to forget, and I don't blame them. They are safer without me."

"What do you live for?" Maeve asked, a hollow ringing in her ears, "If you live for yourself and nothing else?"

"Now you see, don't you," Sandrine said. "You remind me of myself. Headstrong, independent, only to be taught a lesson by the fae."

Maeve scowled. "It was hard to tell at first whether you were working for the fae or for yourself."

"I had many lessons to learn. The fae show you at your

worst, force you to do things you could never imagine, and then you have to make a choice. That choice is yours, and yours alone. You can either join them, or fight them. But if you choose to fight, you must pretend to join them."

"You've pretended for so long, I see it," Maeve responded, surprised that Sandrine was finally answering personal questions. "How do you know when to stop pretending?"

Sandrine grunted. "You have to choose, which is why I tell you what you need to know, when you need to know. Because knowledge is a burden and a curse. It is the path to power and if you know too much it becomes . . ."

"I am not your friend, Maeve," Sandrine said. "I am an enemy of the fae, an enemy who had been with them so long, I understand them through and through. So if you want to defeat them, you will trust me. You will do as I say, nothing more, nothing less."

"I see," Maeve said. Determination rose within her. Destroy the fae. At all costs. That was all that was left. She was like Sandrine, her darkness called out to the fae and they took her, a willing vessel to do their bidding. It was still risky, she could see that, but she had a purpose now, a reason to live outside of her selfishness. "Where are we going now?"

Sandrine's lips thinned. "To Contresea, the Kingdom by the Sea, to find the missing shard, and then to the islands."

Maeve's head jerked up. "Contresea?"

"Aye." Sandrine scowled. "It's time I returned to my hometown, after all it's the center of trade and we can find out about the raiders."

Maeve sucked on her cheek. If she'd been more careful in Carn, they'd still have the Finder's Stone and the lost shard.

And they'd be able to avoid a detour to Contresea and head straight for the islands.

"It's my fault," Maeve admitted.

Sandrine snorted. "The night of the full moon is near, when we tell the fae, they will spend the remaining moonlit hours hunting down the raiders."

Maeve sighed, knowing it was true and yet she still felt guilty that others would suffer because of her actions. "Sandrine." The tentative thought would not leave her alone. "How come the fae have never found the seven shards before? Not even one?"

Sandrine's expression was blank. "Think about it."

"I have," Maeve retorted. "At the Bay of Biscane they were close, but I found Lord Sebastian's hiding place. I understand that they could not enter the Draconbane Mountains, more specifically, the horde of treasure kept by dragons. But the shard in Carn, although difficult to find, was not impossible. What kept them from taking the Finder's Stone and hunting?"

A mirthless smile covered Sandrine's face, just for a moment. "I know what you did in Carn, how you found the shard and rushed to the temple in Isdrine to avoid a meeting with the fae. You were wrong for doing that, and there was no need, although you were unaware that the ruined temple in Carn was on holy ground. The one place the fae could not set foot. There are obstacles that prevent the fae from gathering the shards themselves, but this is also a test. Like I've said before, they have time, endless years. Although they pine for freedom, they will continue on, long after you have died. So why not set the terms of their own release? Why not play with the very person who can release them and also bring about their demise?"

"I won't let them break me," Maeve shook her head vehemently.

"Remember your own words," Sandrine said, "for they will try."

23

WRATH OF THE FAE

The shadow of Contresea loomed ahead like a monstrous mountain in the distance. Maeve stood in the meadow with Sandrine, and a shiver went through her as the sun set. The glory of the sunset lit up the sky like a blaze of fire, reminding her of the brothers. Where were they now? Back in their mysterious home? Safe and well? At least she did not have to worry about Imer and what might become of him. He was safe from the reach of the dark fae, unlike herself.

She scratched an itch behind her neck and sighed as she glanced at her silent companion. Once again, the night of the full moon had come to plague her with terrors, but this time she could not run, could not hide from the wrath of the fae. It was time to face them, to be contrite and hope they would not be too brutal with her. At Sandrine's suggestion, she'd disarmed, leaving her swords on the ground a few paces away along with her bag. Sandrine had persuaded her that the fae would not care about her weapons, yet, heart in her throat, Maeve hoped Sandrine was right. The sword of a celestial was a priceless relic, one she would not part with voluntarily.

Sandrine's steely gaze remained focused on the setting sun, watching the lights fade into night as they waited. They'd skipped dinner, and Maeve could not have eaten anyway. Her warrior's rage was rising and she did not think she could play the part that Sandrine wished her to play. After all, she wasn't sorry that she'd tricked the fae. More than anything she wanted to take up her swords, wield them with both hands, and strike down as many fae as possible before they captured her, tortured her, and locked her up in the Dungeon of the Damned again. But even though her fingers itched for battle, she forced herself to take a deep breath, and wait, gripping the shards she held in her hands tighter.

They were a beacon, a sign of truce. She hoped. The fae had given her seven months to find seven shards, and she'd found five shards in four months. Surely they'd be pleased with her speed, if not her delivery. Although she was loath to give away the shard she'd found in Carn. She glanced at it again as the sunlight disappeared and the first stars began to shine. The shard shimmered in her hand, the blue light calling to her as she held it up, examining it. The glow inside moved, as though it were a liquid, waiting to be released. It was the key, wasn't it? The shard that the other ones responded to, the shard full of might and magic. When she held it, she could feel the runes on her skin, as though they were alive and telling her something. Battle rage burned in her belly and her fingers closed into fists, ready to fight, to destroy, to unleash ultimate destruction.

Momentarily she closed her eyes, enjoying the sensations that rolled through her like an intoxicating mug of ale. There was a burning, a longing, a desire to capture the magic that so evaded her, the magic of Carn, her birthright. Just like the orc had used its magic on her, the impossible shimmer, Maeve wanted to use the hate inside of her against the fae. But she had to wait, to bide her time. Not now.

When she opened her eyes, white moonlight shone down upon them. Dread filled her heart as she watched a purple shimmer grow, turning into a whirling vortex of nothing but light. A hum filled the air as the portal grew and then out walked tall beings. Maeve's eyes widened as she counted. Three. Aside from the king of the fae himself, there were two others with swords in their hands. They remained by the swirling portal, holding it open while the Master of the fae, King Mrithun, strode toward Maeve.

His dark cloak swished behind him and there was the distinct smell of iron and blood. His claws were out, glinting in the purple light and although his face was hidden in the cowl of his hood, she could see his fangs hanging over his lip.

Out of the corner of her eye she saw Sandrine put her hands behind her back and stand tall, staring straight ahead. Even though it was only him, Maeve held out the shards and averted her gaze.

Those clawed hands closed around her wrists, the sharp ends of the claws touching but not sinking into flesh. A hiss of anticipation of pain left Maeve's lips.

"Maeve of Carn," the deep voice of the Master growled. "You have disappointed me."

He lifted her hands higher as though to examine the shards but Maeve refused to look up, for if she did, she was unsure she could hold her temper. Her body shook from the effort and a bead of sweat trickled down her neck. Her breath came slow and shallow.

"Two months, and two shards to show for it. Yet, I recall my warnings were explicit. If you dared defy me, I would release the Underworld's fury on you. I will not forget what you did nor will I give you mercy."

Suddenly he gripped her wrists with his claws and the sharp ends dug into her skin. Maeve cried out and her fingers went limp. The shards fell to the ground as the Master lifted Maeve by her wrists and hurled her.

Maeve soared through the air, limbs flailing as her scream was suddenly cut off by the heat of the collar, choking, burning, sucking away her life force and the hope of magic. A thumping rang in her ears and then her body smacked into the ground. Pain laced up her back as though she lay in a pool of fire. Breath returned to her body and she sucked in fresh air, almost crying as it entered her lungs. Anger and hatred burned within her, and although ribbons of bright red blood flowed from the torn flesh of her wrists, she pushed the pain aside and stumbled to her feet.

But when she turned to face the King of the fae, he stood in the entrance of the portal, both shards in his hands. He raised a hand. "Maeve of Carn," his solemn voice held the edges of a warning. "When we meet again, it shall be the end. You have one month to find the two remaining shards. Or your life will be forfeit. And if you hide from me, those you love will pay the price."

Maeve spat blood out of her mouth, balled her hands into fists, and charged. She sprinted across the meadow toward the portal even though it hummed and light flashed around her. She recalled her swords at the last moment and paused to snatch one up, unsheathing it as she continued her furious dash toward the portal.

Maeve leaped, sword out as the portal closed, leaving her tumbling through the air to land in the field alone, bloody, and furious. A curse burst from her lips and she slammed a fist into the rock-hard ground, ignoring the pain that shot up to her elbow, numbing her arm.

She rose to her knees and tossed her sword in the dead grass, furious at the encounter but more at King Mrithun's words and less at what he'd done.

A shadow fell over Maeve. "Are you done?"

Maeve looked up, anger still riding her.

Sandrine held out her hands. "Let me heal you. Next time, you need to control your anger. There will be a time to fight, but that time is not now."

Maeve's lips trembled, reminding her of what happened last time. She smashed her fist into the ground again before sitting back on her knees and lifting her hands to Sandrine. "I wanted to choke him, he threatened—"

"Hush!" Sandrine snapped. "And stand up. Have you listened to a word that I've told you?"

Maeve winced as a jolt of power went through her hands. The burning sensation in her wrists faded and slowly her torn skin began to knit together. She glanced up at Sandrine who glared down at her.

"Why are you upset with me?" Maeve asked, rising to her feet until she towered over the smaller woman.

Sandrine folded her hands over her chest. "Get your swords and let's go. The city is close and I know an inn we can stay at for the reminder of the night."

Fuming, Maeve gathered her bag and swords and rejoined Sandrine who set off, moving quickly toward the road.

"Maeve of Carn," she began. "If you want to win, you need to determine when to hold in your rage, and when to let it loose. Do not unleash the wrath of the fae until it is time, the right time. Right now you have nothing, no power, no leverage, nothing but broken promises. The fae do not like you, indeed, they hoped to convert you, but you've shown your hand far too early. You can't control your own emotions, you can't hold back your rage, and that will be your undoing. Because of your behavior, you have changed the timing of this dangerous quest. We only have thirty days, and if you fail, it will be you who will be tortured and beheaded. Think on those things, think about the consequences of your actions, and next time you want to live, to actually win, you will listen to me. Don't make me regret choosing you."

A roaring came to Maeve's ears and then silence as her fury rose and then disappeared. She took deep breaths as she walked to still her trembling emotions. The words Sandrine spoke were unkind, but true. It was Maeve who had messed it up, instead of tricking the fae into trusting her, they would be even more suspicious. She gritted her teeth and her words came out hard. "I did not think."

Sandrine sniffed. "Some apology. You have to think to become more. I know you're a warrior, not a hero, but you are also the last defender. There is magic in your blood that will awaken when the Seven Shards of Erinyes are returned to their original form. By all rights, it is you, with the blood of a celestial, who should carry the crown, who should wear it. But you do not deserve it. If you want to be the last defender, if you want to succeed, you have to think about the consequences, think less about yourself and more about how others will be affected by your actions. You are in a unique position, Maeve of Carn."

Maeve's mouth opened in surprise. "Do you believe that?"

"Believe what?" Sandrine asked.

"That the Crown of Erinyes should be mine?"

"Fate is an odd word," Sandrine said. "I will not mince words. You might have been fated for this, but you still have a choice. As did I. We can go into the city together, or both go our own ways. It is up to you."

Maeve frowned and her fingers rose to the collar. Every time she thought about walking away, the collar reminded her that it would take dangerous magic to free herself. Her thoughts fled back to the ruins of Carn, the tainted memories of her young life, and the runes inked on her skin. This was not a quest she would walk away from.

24
CONTRESEA

They reached the kingdom of Contresea in the wee hours of the morning. The gates loomed, silent and shut, but Sandrine led them along the wall to a smaller door and rapped on it three times. Swearing came from the other side and then it was opened a crack. "Who goes there?" a slightly slurred male voice called.

A pool of torchlight shone out followed by a plump face. The man cursed again but his eyes lit up in recognition when he saw Sandrine. "You again?"

Sandrine held up a pouch. "We were never here."

A greedy glint shone in the man's eyes and he stepped back, holding the door wider. "Of course, of course."

Maeve raised an eyebrow and shrugged. The gatekeeper gave her a look that made her want to punch him in the face. But she restrained herself and followed Sandrine. They wove their way through passageways out into the open air of the sleeping city. It was warmer inside although still damp and cold, yet the walls blocked the wind and the buildings pressed against each other, creating a barrier.

She'd been here before, in the endless maze, section after section of the city, blocked off depending on one's class and station. There was the great castle where the king lives, as well as other nobles. There was the rich sector where the Lords and Ladies of court lived. Perhaps where Sandrine had once lived? There were the barracks where the king's army trained, the slums where the poor and homeless dwelt, the market, and various other quarters. The city was large, sprawling and it would take days to cover every inch, but Sandrine seemed to know exactly where she was going.

Maeve followed, a remote anger keeping her weariness at bay. The walls of the city reminded her of days past, of training with warriors, drinking with warlords, and fighting. Anger. Rage. Blood. The memories were powerful, a sharp reminder of what she'd let herself become and the dark path she'd walked. The city was full of those both good and evil, the innocent and pure, and the corrupt and damaged. The city of humans. Would they be next? Would the armies of the fae swallow them whole, and would they be strong enough to resist? To stand firm?

"In here," Sandrine said, ducking into a dark alley. "Watch the stairs, they are sharp."

They moved higher until they were level with the rooftops. Sandrine led them across flat roofs that linked together, one after the other. High up there, the chill kissed Maeve's ears, and in the distance she thought she saw the glint of the sea. Contresea sat at the edge of the land, butted up against the water, where the warships sat, unused, yet ready for the next quest.

Sandrine led them down again, back to cobblestone streets, quiet with sleep, the hush of night spread over the kingdom like a blanket. There came a bark of a wild dog, and then a whine as it settled down, the swift pitter-patter of bare feet scurrying to a hiding place, and, even though they were not close enough, she might have imagined the lap of waves slapping against stone.

"Here we are," Sandrine paused in front of a building separated by gaps. There was one with the sign of a bottle with smoke coming out of it. Maeve squinted. *An apothecary?*

"What is this place?" Maeve whispered.

"A shop of an old friend," Sandrine replied.

She tapped on the door three times and then stepped back.

To Maeve it seemed as though they waited a long time, and she almost asked Sandrine to tap again, when the door opened with a long, drawn out creak. The weathered face of a woman framed with wavy hair, black as night, squinted at them. A curse left her lips as she eyed first Sandrine and then Maeve. "What have I done to deserve this?" she moaned and then opened the door wider. "Well, come in then, don't just stand there, someone could see."

"We weren't followed," Sandrine snorted.

"You don't know that," the woman retorted. She peered out at the silent street one last time before closing the door and turning around to face them. "If it isn't Sandrine the Scholar, I thought you were dead."

Maeve peered around the room. It smelled both sweet

and musty, as though there were too many scents vying for attention. There was a long table on one end of the room with a neat bundle of herbs, various glass cups of all sizes, and bottles with some kind of liquid in them. Maeve stiffened. So they were at the apothecary except she had a distinct feeling the woman not only made medicines, but also poisons and various other potions that should not be named, or sold.

The walls of the room were lined with bookcases with various scrolls and books. Although it was small and packed with items, the room was neat and pristinely organized. A lantern lit up the space and the woman picked it up.

"I keep the back room clear. You may sleep there as long as you don't touch anything. I'll hear your business in the morning."

Sandrine jerked her chin. "Go ahead Maeve. Tabitha and I have some business to discuss."

The woman, Tabitha, frowned. "If you wish it, although you know business is better discussed after a night's rest."

Sandrine folded her arms over her chest. "This is urgent, but it pays well."

Tabitha glared at Maeve. "Follow me."

"I want to stay, and listen," Maeve protested, even though her feet were weary. If it was about the quest and concerned her, she needed to listen.

"No," Sandrine shook her head. "Rest for as long as you can. I will come for you when it is time."

Maeve opened her mouth to protest again but something about Sandrine's gaze sent shivers down her back. Without a word she turned and followed Tabitha into the back room. It was dark and windowless, and seemed like a sort of storage room, with packed boxes and dusty bottles. But there was a pallet and at the sight of it, weariness consumed Maeve. She yawned, and, instead of eavesdropping by the door, she fell into a deep sleep.

WHEN MAEVE WOKE, she found herself alone in the dark. A sliver of light came from under the door and she stood, gathered her things, and walked out into the main room. Sunlight streamed in from two windows and Maeve chewed her lower lip. *What time was it?*

Tabitha stood behind the table, a knife in her hand as she chopped up a bundle of green herbs. She glanced up when Maeve walked in and her eyes narrowed. "Ah. So you're Sandrine's companion."

Maeve stiffened. The way the woman said those words was both unfriendly and degrading. "I need her knowledge. Where is she?"

The woman's lips thinned and her gaze refocused on her work. "She is on an errand and asked that you meet her at the tavern. It's the next street over. You can't miss it."

Maeve walked to the door and then hesitated. "How do you know Sandrine? Did you know her before . . .when she was a noble?"

The woman's eyes went dark and she moved her knife faster until she was almost slashing her herbs. Her words came out low. "If you value your life, you should run, hide, start over without her. Doom and danger follow her and I don't know you, but from your looks, you can take care of yourself."

Maeve's fingers twitched as she opened the door. She wanted to be angry with the woman for her words, but knew they were true. Despite Sandrine telling her there was a choice, Maeve had already made up her mind. Her thoughts went back to the temple of Isdrine and what she'd learned there.

"Divine save us all," she murmured, and left.

The city looked much different in the daylight and Maeve breathed in the fresh air as she moved down the cobblestone streets. There were a few people out carrying bundles as they moved hastily about their business. The sun was overhead, a telltale sign it was around noon, and as if on cue, Maeve's stomach growled. She had a few coins and decided she would have a meal once she reached the tavern and from there decide what to do as she waited for Sandrine.

Ominous clouds hovered in the sky, a signal that a storm would be coming soon. A gust of wind whipped up and Maeve walked faster, eyeing the signs on either side of the street as she made her way to the tavern.

When she turned the corner, she reached a wide street, large enough for horses and carriages to pass through side by side. There was a circle in the middle of the street with a large fountain. A man stood in front of it, dressed in the king's livery and talking animatedly. Maeve glanced at him before hurrying on to the end, as she was suddenly reminded of her past. She'd been to this tavern many times when she was working for a mercenary being paid by the king. A lump settled in her throat as she recalled the things she'd done in the name of coin. Shoulders slumped, she opened the door to the tavern and let the chaos wash over her. The smell of ale and unwashed bodies, the loud, rough voices of the clientele and the scent of roasted meat.

What was she, Maeve of Carn, doing here? Alone? What if Sandrine had abandoned her and the quest? She could not deny Sandrine's words nor her blunt frustration at Maeve's behavior with the dark fae. With a curse, Maeve made her way to the table and ordered both food and ale.

25
STORMY FLIGHT

The door to the tavern burst open, bringing a gust of howling wind and rain hurtling into the room. The guests closest to the door leaped up, knocking over drinks and bowls.

The innkeeper strode out from behind the bar, his face red as he bellowed, "Close the door you fool! Don't let that foul weather in here!"

Maeve hunched over the table and reached for her mug of ale. It was her third one, and it was almost empty. But she'd reached a point where she no longer felt sorry for herself and instead enjoyed the warmth and absence from reality that drinking brought. Lazily she glanced at the doors to see who had disrupted the peace and her eyes went wide.

Maeve stood, the happy buzz of ale fading when she saw the unwanted guest was none other than Sandrine. She was drenched from head to toe and her eyes so wide, Maeve could see the whites around them. Sandrine clutched a hand to her chest as she staggered into the room, her eyes going from table to table, searching.

A bloom of red covered one shoulder and Maeve gasped, a sinking sensation making her stomach clench.

"Sandrine!" Maeve called, waving the scholar over to herself. Although she did not want more attention it was unavoidable.

Sandrine made her way over to Maeve, breathing hard. Her eyes went to an empty chair but she did not sit down.

"You're wounded," Maeve reached for her.

"There's no time," Sandrine snapped, weakly pushing Maeve off of her. "We have to go. Get your things, now. They are coming."

Stemming the flow of words, Maeve snatched up her bag. When she spun back to Sandrine, she was drinking the last dregs of ale. Maeve cursed, surprised at nothing now and reached for Sandrine. "Do you know where to go?"

The guests stared as they made their way outside, into the driving rain. Maeve dared to glance back and heard the thunder of footsteps and rough male voices shouting.

But there was no time for words. Despite her wound, Sandrine ran, ducking into an alley and moving through the maze of the city as though she knew the path by heart. Maeve followed. "I can fight them," she shouted over the rain, even though she had no idea who was after them or why.

Sandrine did not answer but kept moving, leading them deeper into the maze of the city. Cold rain poured down, soaking through Maeve's furs to her skin. Her fingers went numb and plumes of cold air burst out of her mouth. Sandrine stumbled and leaned up against a stall, knocking over a basket of fruit. A man came around the corner, cursing as he tried to pick up bruised fruit and ended up tumbling down on them. Long-legged children ran out, taking advantage of the situation while the man shouted and fumed. Maeve reached for Sandrine's arm to steady her and they moved on, darting down alleys and weaving around buildings until at last, Sandrine slumped under a ledge, giving them a momentary respite from the storm.

Rain dripped off of Maeve's eyelashes and she took deep breaths, studying Sandrine and wondering what had happened while she sat at the tavern, bored and feeling useless. This was her quest after all, it should have been her out there, fighting and getting into trouble. Not Sandrine. And why did she suddenly feel protective of Sandrine?

The scholar had done her no favors and had been tough with her time after time, and yet a sinking sensation gripped Maeve as though she were caught in the talons of a fierce bird. "What happened?" she demanded.

Sandrine just shook her head and her eyes were slightly glazed. Reaching up, she touched her shoulder and pressed her lips together. Her face went white.

"You need to rest," Maeve pressed.

Sandrine pointed. "We have to get to the shore. A ship leaves for the islands soon, we need to be on it before the storm clears."

Maeve paused. The islands. People were skeptical about them, calling them cursed and the people who lived on them had a strange sort of magic. But the islands were on the trade route for Contresea and because they were small, posed no dangers. It was worthwhile for Contresea to enjoy exotic treasures from the islands and merchants often grew wealthy off of the riches they brought back. But a ship going to the islands in the winter seemed odd. There were the winter storms and word that monsters often rose from the depths of the sea to the surface to hunt where it was easier to find food. Surely a ship would not travel to the islands, especially with the risk. There had to be another reason but Maeve took a deep breath. Now was not the time. Instead, she asked the one question that was burning on her lips: "Did you find it?"

A glint came to Sandrine's eyes and her lips jerked before she winced in pain again. "Aye, girl. Keep moving."

Sandrine pushed off the wall, uttered a low curse, and trudged off into the rain. Maeve trotted at her side and together they wove their way through the city down to the docks.

As though heralding their arrival, the storm abated somewhat, even though the ships bobbed in the water and the waves rushed up on the beach as though they would drown the city.

The docks smelled sour and Sandrine leaned heavily against Maeve as they moved toward the ramps that led to the ships. Sandrine waved toward one and they walked, unbothered, forward while the storm hid them from curious eyes. It wasn't until they were abroad and down in the cramped bunks that Sandrine finally relaxed, lay down, and promptly fell asleep. Maeve, left to her own devices again, had nothing better to do than pace, and wait.

"WHAT HAPPENED?" Maeve asked.

She sat beside Sandrine as the ship moved from side to side. There were footsteps above and voices shouting which led Maeve to believe the storm had abated and the ship had set off. She also had a feeling that instead of being passengers on the ship, they were stowaways and while she wanted to fight, she was aware they were grossly outnumbered.

Sandrine sat up, her hair wild. She reached for her bag and took out a bottle of liquid which she swallowed quickly. Then she reached in again and handed Maeve a wrapped bundle.

As Maeve's fingers closed around it, she knew it was another shard.

"I stole this from the raiders," Sandrine admitted. "Tabitha, for all her secretive ways, is good at finding out information. I paid her well to keep this secret in the hopes that it will not be traced back to her. The raiders were in town to trade and make a profit from the shard and they had a buyer. Who it was, I am not sure, but I stole it before they could complete their deal. They will tear up the city searching for me, until the king's men put a stop to their actions. We had to escape as soon as possible."

Maeve nodded, grateful for Sandrine's quick actions and yet frustrated with the situation. She was always in trouble with the law, hunted, never rewarded for her actions. Nothing had changed. "And this ship?"

"Ah," Sandrine grunted and lay back again, folding her hands on her belly. "This is an expedition ship. They will travel close to the islands, hunting for sea monsters. If they capture enough and bring them back to Contresea, they will be rewarded handsomely. But we will leave the ship once the islands are in sight."

Maeve groaned and put her face in her hands. "Are we stowaways?"

"Sleep," Sandrine commanded. "We will need our strength for later. The islands are wild, and although there are people who live there, they will likely be hibernating through the winter. However, there is a dormant volcano where they hide their treasure. It is likely that the shard is there but it is a two-day journey down into the core of the volcano. You will need your rest, and your swords."

Maeve sighed but it wasn't up to her. She would sleep and bid her time, for the final shard would be in her hands soon.

26

Night of the Dark Fae

The island air was warm, windless, and eerily quiet. In less than a month it would be spring and celebrations of surviving the winter would begin. There were various festivals in the cities as people celebrated the change from the barren dead of winter to new life springing forth. It was a celebration Maeve usually found herself enthralled in, eating, drinking, and grateful that there would be work again and she wouldn't have to freeze her fingers in the bone-numbing cold. But now everything was different.

A few weeks prior, they'd stolen a boat, escaped the ship, and rowed to the islands where they spent days in a dormant volcano, hunting for the final shard. Through the entire journey, Maeve found herself surprisingly calm. She glanced at Sandrine who stood hunched, as though a bitter wind forced her shoulders to bend. Sandrine was quiet, glaring into the unknown while they waited. She'd said few words during they journey and tended to favor her shoulder, even though she was a healer. But instead of animosity, Maeve finally felt as though she understood the scholar.

Regardless, she missed the warmth of Imer's presence, and the knowledge that he had her back in every way, but she was glad he had returned to his mysterious home. The brothers of fire could not be snatched up by the dark fae and forced to endure what would come. They had a more important role to play in the long-term war and this was Maeve's battle to face.

Her fingers twitched, aching for the sword on her back but she held her fingers still. Not now. Not yet. The time would come for blade to break skin and bone, but now she must be patient, use what she learned and bide her time. Her fingers tightened around the shards in her hands, and she shifted her feet on the grit of the beach.

Even the waves were quiet, the tides unnaturally still as though they knew life in the world was going to change from that day forward. Maeve opened her mouth and closed it, unsure whether she should dare to break the silence. As she'd learned from the past few months with Sandrine, there was a reason for everything. She understood now why the prophecy had to come true, why she was involved, and why the darkness that had haunted her life needed to be eradicated. It did not mean she liked it but instead of sulking in her own bad luck, this time she would stand firm, determined, courageous. She was Maeve of Carn, a Defender of the People, and now that she knew who she was, she could walk in that knowledge without doubt and hesitation.

Sandrine straightened under the light of the full moon. It cast a silvery hue over her shoulders and highlighted the strands of white in her dark hair. “We all have a part to play in this madness,” she said, eyes still on the waves and her voice hard. “When my time comes, do not play the hero. Do not try to save me.”

Maeve’s brows went up and she faced Sandrine, but the woman refused to look at her.

“Know this, Maeve of Carn. When the time came to find someone to take up the quest to find the shards, it was I who found out who you were, your birthright, and fed you to the fae. Keep that in mind, should your heart soften.”

A lump swelled in Maeve’s throat although she should not be surprised. Sandrine was playing a game. Her own game and Maeve was just a pawn, and yet more important than a pawn. She was small enough to be overlooked and when her time came, she knew what she would do. She took a deep breath to still the panic rising up her throat and the impulsiveness that made her want to lash out. There was no need to punish Sandrine, she already knew, already understood why Sandrine had done what she had done.

“I forgive you,” she whispered, her voice loud in the stillness.

Sandrine snorted. “Indeed. I prefer your anger. When the time comes, act, Maeve of Carn. And do not fail. Do not let this quest be for naught.”

“I will,” Maeve said, for how could she not act? When the Seven Shards of Erinyes were put back together and turned into a crown, all curses would break, including the one that held her captive, collared. When her collar broke, her strength would be returned to her. A shiver of anticipation went down her spine and as it did, a glow appeared on the horizon.

It appeared like a fallen star, a streak of light glowing brighter and brighter, shooting toward them until the swirl of colors became almost impossible to see. The portal opened up, a yawning mouth of darkness, and out of it walked the dark fae.

There were ten of them, dressed as though for a banquet. The minotaur with a two-headed axe in one hand and what looked like a shield around his waist. The rest of his body covered in thick black fur looked as though it had been brushed until it gleamed. Seven warriors dressed in full battle armor complete with a combination of shields, swords, bows, arrows, and staffs followed the minotaur and created a circle, surrounding Maeve and Sandrine.

Maeve forced herself not to flinch and attempted to keep her expression blank as Nathair, master of the whip, marched out of the portal and leered at her, crooked teeth gleaming. He coiled the whip back and his arm twitched, as though he wished to entangle her flesh in the cords of his whip. And finally out stepped the Master of the fae, King Mrithun, wearing clothes black as night. His face was covered in the cowl of his cloak but his clawed hand was held out, ready to take action should Maeve choose to flee.

Gritting her teeth, she stared into the darkness of his hood where his eye should be and held out the shards. The mere act displayed utter submission, something the fae would believe she'd learned after months of doing their bidding. Fighting was futile, it was better to behave and save herself the pain. Out of the corner of her eye she glimpsed a disappointed twitch from Nathair, who delighted in pain and humiliation.

King Mrithun stepped forward and his claws grazed her skin as he took the shard from her. Maeve sensed a vibration coming from him as his eagerness pulsed out of his skin and seeped down into the beach. He could not deny his excitement and yet he controlled himself. Instead of speaking to Maeve, he turned to face Sandrine. "Sandrine the Scholar, you have done well. Enter the Fae Underground and prepare for your final task."

Without a word of acknowledgement, Sandrine turned and headed to the portal. She disappeared into darkness before Maeve could protest. She took another deep breath to steel her nerves. King Mrithun stood in front of her and his voice dropped. "Maeve of Carn, you have fulfilled your bargain. Come, watch the ceremony and then walk free, in the daylight, as we will."

Maeve stiffened. After their last meeting she was surprised by his words, and doubted he meant for her to walk in freedom. He likely had a nasty surprise waiting for her down in the depths, and although her feet willed her to flee, she forced herself to take a step. Her hands went clammy and she stole another glance at the moonlight for strength. She did not want to walk in darkness.

"Wait." King Mrithun held up a claw. "Since you are still a prisoner, you should return in chains."

He waved a hand toward his warriors, and in a moment, they were upon her.

Rage boiled in Maeve's belly as the claws of the fae touched her and she gritted her teeth to keep from lashing out. Hands touched her inappropriately, taking her arms and putting chains on her wrists and ankles. The swords she wore on her back were stripped away, just as she expected. Sandrine had warned her and yet the sting of it ached her. *How dare they touch her swords, especially the sword of the celestial?* But she also knew they would take them to the Underground, and she needed her swords to be there. Her fingers clenched into fists and when one fae trailed a finger up her leg she lashed out, kicking. She knew they were not interested in her body and yet she could not help it, the touch reminded her of Imer, his fingers and tongue trailing up her body and the fury he would unleash if he could see the fae with her now. Before she could fight more, the collar around her neck flared to life, cutting off her breath and knocking her down.

Maeve cursed as weakness came over her, she was so close to freedom and yet the fight would not leave her. Her bones went limp and she lay still, just as the fae wanted. This would be over soon, she just had to close down her mind, be still and wait. But it was harder than she'd thought, to give in to their demands, to submit to the fae. Her feet were linked together, giving her just enough room to hobble forward if they forced her to walk. Hands twisted into her hair and yanked it back. Spit gathered in her mouth as she looked up into the face of Nathair. A grin of mockery covered his face and he whispered, low, his face blurring into the shadow world just for a moment. "You're not free yet . . ."

Maeve's eyes flashed. When she was free, his neck would be the first she'd strangle. "But when I am . . ." she growled at him through gritted teeth.

A blow struck her back and she closed her eyes against the kiss of the whip. The fury inside of her rolled and then abated as she was dragged to her feet.

The gaping mouth of the portal loomed, looking into a vast darkness where horrors lay. Against her will, Maeve was dragged forward and flashbacks invaded her mind, of being locked in the Dungeon of the Damned once again. But this time instead of utter helplessness and horror, a surge of determination rose in her. Even as the lash of the whip snaked around her bare legs, drawing red drops of blood from her flesh, and the fae jeered as they shoved her ahead of them, laughing as she stumbled. Maeve had something else, an inner strength. She lifted her chin, come what may, the fae would be sorry, for she was both their salvation and their demise.

27
THE CEREMONY

Smoke from torches filled the gloom with a hazy glow and the smell of incense hung heavy in the air. Maeve paused before the gates of the Hall of Judgement, recalling the last time she was there. Much had changed in less than a year, including her own attitude and yet her resistance was still there. Even though she wanted to see the Seven Shards returned to a crown, she also wanted to flee as far away as possible from the consequences the fae would unleash upon the world.

The whip kissed her flesh again, hissing as it withdrew. Fire laced up Maeve's legs and she resumed her hobble, well aware that Nathair sought a reaction from her. King Mrithun had left them as soon as they entered the portal and part of her wished he were still with them to hold Nathair in check.

She was led to a column and as she walked, she saw the Hall of Judgement was full of a strange mixture of fae and human. A small green creature with pointed ears glared at her out of red eyes and opened a mouth full of razor-sharp teeth. A furry winged creature paced back and forth on four legs, waiting for the festivities to begin.

The fires were lit and all were dressed in their finest garb. Moans and howls rose up from the creatures chained to the columns, winged monsters, some with three heads, others with abnormal limbs, long teeth, and claws.

Despite her bravery, Maeve shivered as she stood in her shift, back where the nightmare had started. Columns towered high above her and in the shadows oddities and horrors peered out.

All eyes were riveted to the middle of the room where a dais had been set up. In the middle of it lay the Seven Shards of Erinyes, glowing with their unearthly brilliance. There was a hum in the room, a magnetic presence and Maeve felt compelled to gaze upon the beauty of the shards. Just as she had when she'd found them, she wanted them as her own, to touch them, to look upon them and, more than anything, to put them back together. Yet she was only a prisoner, like many others, chained to the columns, awaiting the ultimate judgement.

King Mrithun swept in, his robes grazing the ground and the hall fell silent as he walked. By his side strode a winged creature, a woman with hair as vivid as the sunshine and dark wings folded on her back. She wore a tight garment which emphasized her curves and looked as though it might be ripped away if she moved the wrong way. When she walked, her eyes glided over Maeve's and a shiver went through her. There was something about the woman that was oddly familiar, and Maeve's heart thudded in remembrance. It was in the Draconbane Mountains where she met the Ariefluer, the Goblin Queen who warned her about Drakai, the Dragon Queen. Her sister. This had to be the Drakai, for there was a family resemblance.

A lump settled in Maeve's throat and a deep foreboding went through her. The Dragon Queen. Maeve was missing something, wasn't she? But no, if she stuck with the plan she and Sandrine had discussed while traveling through the dormant volcano, everyone within the halls of the fae would perish.

From a dark corner came the sound of drums, a deep throb echoed through the halls like the pulse of a heartbeat. It was slow and steady as the fae king and his queen walked the length of the hall, as though they were in no hurry. King Mrithun led his queen up to the dragon throne but instead of sitting, they took their places on either side of it.

The pace of the drums increased and a wail rose through the air, as though a spirit were crying out for release. Maeve's heart beat in time to the drums and she strained against her bonds, her feet wanting to move, to run, to join the fae and gyrate in a frantic dance as she awaited the unveiling of the crown.

The beat continued, harder and faster until King Mrithun held up a hand and silence descended on the court of the fae.

He stretched out his hands, as though he were one with great power who would bless his people. Maeve supposed it were true. After years of humiliation and hiding, the fae were about to be free from their curse and walk in daylight again.

"I will keep this brief," King Mrithun's voice rolled like thunder, capturing the room with his words. "Tonight is a great night for the fae. A night we have waited for, the end of the curse, the end of captivity, and the moment when we will take back the world. The world that is ours by right, a world which has gone on without us. But no more. The fae shall rise again and everyone will know our names, will fear us, and honor the fae. This quest, this feat, would not have been accomplished without the knowledge of the scholar, so without further ado, let the curse be broken and the festivities begin!"

A roar began, deep and dark, as creatures growled or howled their assent. The volume rose and then died down as a woman moved toward the center of the room where the crown lay in pieces.

Maeve sucked in a breath when she saw it was Sandrine. She'd changed clothes and wore a simple white robe, like the priests and priestesses, with a belt around her waist. She'd let her hair down and it flowed in waves past her shoulders. She moved with grace, an indication of the noble woman she once was. Her lips moved as she walked and when she reached the table she continued to chant as though she were the only one in the room.

Leaning forward, Maeve strained her ears, but she could not catch the full pronunciation of the words nor understand their meaning. Sandrine continued to chant and the boom of a drum rang out, so instant and suddenly it made Maeve jump. Her chains jingled as she moved and a stir of anxiety twisted through her gut. When her collar melted off, would she be strong enough to free herself from her chains?

Sandrine lifted the first shard. Blue light shone across the table and lit up the floor in front of her until her entire body was encased in blue light. She held the shard high for all to see while her ceaseless chant continued. It was the largest piece, thick and long, the one Maeve had found in Carn, the one that shimmered with magic. The runes on Maeve's skin began to itch and she felt that same familiar burning sensation. Was it magic within her, begging to be released?

The shard was almost too large for Sandrine to hold with one hand, and yet she held it up high and added a shard to it. The broken pieces clinked as they met and then fused together as though Sandrine were the welder putting the crown back together.

Maeve assumed the linking of the pieces had something to do with the chanting and the potent magic swirling through the air. Sandrine added another piece and another, her words growing louder and stronger as each piece fused together. Her body swayed and her eyes gleamed as she held up the crown. The last shard remained, the smallest piece to complete the half circle of the crown.

Despite Sandrine's chanting, the tension in the Hall of Judgement was potent. Hairs rose on Maeve's neck as though she felt every breath the fae drew, the anticipation beating in their hearts and the moment many of them had waited for—some for hundreds of years. The energy in the room seeped into Maeve and almost without realizing it, she, too, was leaning forward, straining on her bonds, holding her breath, waiting for the final moment.

As if she knew, Sandrine moved slowly, almost painfully slow as she lifted the last shard. The journey of the shard from the table to the crown lasted an agonizing eternity. Maeve thought she detected the slightest tremor in

Sandrine's hand as the last shard fused into place and she held the Crown of Erinyes with both hands.

All sound ceased like a wind blowing out the final flame and a sinking sensation rose in Maeve's throat, clawing to the top as though all hope were gone, leaving nothing but empty terror. The way she felt was mirrored in Sandrine's eyes even as she stared at the blue glow, there was nothing but absolute and pure terror. Then Sandrine's mouth came open and she began to scream.

The high-pitched shriek of agony echoed through the hall and the columns reverberated with her cry. Maeve almost choked on her breath and reeled back in surprise, slamming her head against the column. Her ears rang as the howling increased and suddenly others were joining in. Chains slammed against stone and fists beat first flesh and then stone as the eerie cries rang out again and again. The wolves the fae kept howled, joining the melody of anguish but it took Maeve a moment to see why.

Blue light leaked out of the crown in the form of flames, and they licked up Sandrine's arms, burning her alive. Blackened flesh fell onto the table and then the stone floor, hissing. A wind came up out of nowhere, fanning the flames until the blue fire burst and entrapped Sandrine in its vengeance. Her entire body went up in flames, licking the white robe, burning her dark hairs, and the smell of burning flesh and cloth and hair filled the room with an acrid tang that even the incense could not get rid of.

Maeve's mouth was open and she did not realize—until her throat went raw and hoarse—that she had joined the melody, screaming and yanking against her chains, determined to break them, get to Sandrine and snatch the crown from her hands. But it was too late, far, far too late as Sandrine's body turned to ash and the crown crashed down on the stone table. All seven shards glowed with an unnatural brilliance. The light continued to grow, shining brighter and brighter until it exploded with a boom and light burst across the hall.

Maeve squeezed her eyes shut and bowed her head as the light struck her, and silence descended upon the Hall of Judgement.

28
THE DRAGON THRONE

Charred smoke filled the air and Maeve opened her eyes. Tears dripped down her cheeks, both at the horror of Sandrine's death and the stinking of smoke in the air. She moved her hands and instead of staying bound at her back, they came free. Quickly she wiped her face with her hands and looked down. Her bounds had come undone, the chains open. Hardly daring to believe it, her hand went to her neck and felt the broken ends of her golden collar. She tossed them on the ground as relief surged through her. She was free! Then rage. Now was time to make the fae pay for all they had done. But first she needed the sword of the celestial.

Her eyes drifted to where Sandrine had stood, now nothing but a pile of ashes, but there was something else. Unless her eyes deceived her, there was a flicker of silver underneath the ashes. Tears brimmed in Maeve's eyes, remembering Sandrine's last words to her. *Do not play the hero.* Had Sandrine known that putting the crown back together would bring her death? And even so, had stolen Maeve's sword and brought it to the Hall of Judgement?

Blood went thick and Maeve's eyes narrowed. Now it was up to her, and she would not fail.

She turned her attention to the hall where the fae seemed to be coming out of the same comatose state she had been in. The prisoners who had been chained stood tall, realizing their bonds were gone, and then all eyes went to the Crown of Erinyes.

Maeve swallowed hard and dared glance down at the Dragon Throne. King Mrithun and his queen stood together, hands clasped. He took a step, she let go of him. Maeve, seeing their intent, began to run.

Maeve's heart thudded in her throat as she dashed past the flickering torches. Smoke rose from the ground and stung her eyes. A roaring sound came to her ears but she ignored it as she ran. A prone human lay in her path and she leaped over him, almost into the arms of a fae drawing his sword. She ducked from the blow, throwing herself off balance and almost crashed to the ground. But in the blink of an eye she regained her balance and continued her determined flight toward the Crown of Erinyes.

From the perspective of the fae, it appeared like she meant to steal the crown, whisk it away and enjoy the blessings it bestowed solely on herself. Bah. Let them think that, the fae had their way of destroying life and decimating hope. She needed to fight and make them pay. She heard the voice of the whip hiss out of the darkness and suddenly it was there, the slick golden ends flying toward her arms, ready to wrestle back the freedom she'd gained.

Quick as a flash, Maeve dropped to the ground, using her hands to support herself. Her thick braid of black hair whipped around her shoulder and she closed her eyes momentarily as the whip flew over her head, striking nothing. A thrill went through her but without wasting time she leaped up and kept running, a growing boldness surging within her. Her strength was back, and so were her reflexes. She was a warrior of warriors again.

The round stone table loomed as did King Mrithun, although for some reason his queen had not joined him. Maeve had no time to look around as she slid to a stop, ducked under the table and, cringing as she did it, placed her hands down on the ashes where she'd seen the silver glint. Hard, cold steel meet her hands and she almost sliced her fingers as she touched the blade. Her fingers danced down it, scattering ash, her mind crying out as she did. This was no way to honor Sandrine, but she promised herself she would, as soon as she finished her task.

Finding the blade she leaped to her feet just in time to see King Mrithun lift up the crown. His cowl had fallen back and his face appeared, chasing away the shadows. His eyes were red and his mouth was open, showing off a row of sharp fangs. Maeve cringed away from the sight and horror filled her heart at his appearance. She hadn't known what she expected him to look like, but not this terror which seemed a mutilated cross between man and beast. He lifted the crown up on his horrible head and blue energy surged out of it, surrounding him, but unlike Sandrine, it did not burn him.

"My people!" King Mrithun shouted. "We are free! Go forth into the land above us and make haste to our kingdom!

Slay all those who interfere." His head came down and his eyes glittered as he studied Maeve who still crouched below the table. "Our prisoners have been set free," there was humor in his voice, a lightness as though a heavy weight had been lifted off his shoulders. "Show them freedom from life with death."

Howls and roars echoed through the halls and suddenly there came the scurrying of feet, the click of claws, the pounding of boots, and the rush as fae fled the halls, moving toward the portals and the exits. A slow chant swelled through the air, "King Mrithun, King Mrithun, King Mrithun!" only punctured by screams as prisoners were stabbed in the belly or throats slit.

The air turned thick with the scent of blood and through the haze Maeve rose to her feet, lifted her chin, narrowed her eyes, and held up the celestial blade.

King Mrithun's red eyes met hers and a sinister glare covered his malicious face. "Ah, I see the scholar left you a gift, yet I doubt she shared the true power of the crown. Or perhaps she did not know. This is your end, your demise, Maeve of Carn. Prophecies can only go so far, the price of what you have done is chaos."

Maeve gritted her teeth, although it was hard to ignore the blazing brilliance of the crown. "I would curse you," she retorted, "but you will get what is coming to you."

King Mrithun grinned. "I will, there is much coming for me, but more coming for you. Kill her!" he roared.

Maeve leaped and at once the power she'd lost came surging back like a current of rage filling her. She barely noticed as she stood up on the table, towering over King

Mrithun, nor that the fae rushing toward her, shouting and laughing.

Nathair's whip curled out of the air and Maeve swung the blade, slicing it in half. The ends fell with a sizzle and a cry of outrage burst from Maeve's lips. King Mrithun faded into the throng as the fae surrounded her.

The blade sang in Maeve's hand as she parried and thrust, blocking the weapons that danced toward her, eager to draw blood from her flesh. She leaped down from her perch on the table into the throng of fae which seemed endless. Furry and winged creatures cried out in combinations of fierce glee and fury as they surged around her, some peeling off to escape through the portal while others gyrated in bloodlust, slaying the prisoners where they stood, even though some screamed and called out for mercy, there was none.

Five of the fae hemmed in Maeve, but she was fast and strong. Her double-edged sword was meant for parrying and thrusting and the fae, although they were dressed for battle, her blade sank into flesh, ripped it from bone, and sliced open their necks. A river of blood splashed around her but she cared not, she had to get to the crown and smash it into pieces.

Sandrine had told her that the Crown of Erinyes had the power to break all curses, but it was destroyed for a reason. Only a celestial blade could destroy the crown again and rend it so that it could never be put back together. While it would not undo the curses, at least no one could abuse the magical power of the crown. At least, Sandrine assumed the crown held power, but she had not been able to find scrolls about its power. Either she had been betrayed by the fae, or there were none. Betrayal was likely, since it seemed the fae knew putting the crown together would kill the one who did it, although Sandrine's sacrifice had seemed willing.

A blow to the head almost dazed Maeve and she stumbled, righting herself at the last moment before a blade sliced her arm. Out of the corner of her eye she saw Nathair shift out of shadow form and laugh as he pulled back for another blow. With a slash, Maeve blocked the blows of the two fae in front of her, dropped to a knee, and thrust the sword up into a gut, then yanked it out with an arching slash that took down the second fae. They fell dead at her feet and when Maeve spun around, she was alone. The other fae had backed away. Noting her ability with the sword, they thought it better to flee than fight.

Shaking the grime from fighting off her skin, Maeve ran toward the dragon throne where King Mrithun had returned to his bride. Sword in one clawed hand he leaned toward her and her fingers came out to touch the crown, but instead of yanking it off his head, she grabbed hold of the largest shard and closed her eyes.

Maeve cocked her head and another blow smacked into her ear. She went deaf for a moment as her left ear absorbed the impact of the blow, but instead of reacting, she forced herself to remain still. Again, out of the corner of her eyes she saw a murky shadow. Nathair. Coming to laugh at her again. He had a new whip coiled around his arm and he lashed out with it. Maeve leaned into the blow, opened her mouth, and screamed. Rage centered around her core and she charged toward Nathair with unnatural speed. At the last second he sidestepped, disappearing in a blur but Maeve was ready and guessed where he would be. Her sword came out, pointed at chest height and she slammed it into nothingness. For a moment she thought she'd missed, and then she felt the blade sink into flesh and grind against bone. Nathair appeared again, shock on his ugly face. His hands went limp, the whip dropped away, and his eyeballs rolled up in his head as he dropped to the ground like a limp fish. Maeve slid the sword out of his body. "Never again will you hit me with your whip you worthless coward!" She spit and a glob of it landed on his cheek.

Maeve stepped back, a surge of satisfaction swelling through her. She set her sights on King Mrithun and his queen, just as the ground began to shake.

29
CHAOS UNLEASHED

Maeve's eyes went wide. All strength left her and suddenly she was a young child again, holding on to Mama as the ground shook beneath her. She heard shouts, moans, and cries as steel struck steel, then flesh. Blood and fire filled the air and she screamed out, terror shaking her body. Her feet ran and ran but she couldn't find Mama and then came the blade which drove into her back over and over and over again. Pain laced up her side and then her eyes came open and she was in the Hall of Judgement while the ground shook. She stared and a surge of fear went up her spine. She was too late, it was all over and everything within her shrieked for her to get out before she became a tragedy in the Fae Underground, another prisoner who could not escape in time. The torches tumbled onto the stone floor, some going out, and great boulders fell.

Tears slide down Maeve's cheeks again. Was all she'd done in life only to lead up to this moment? Destroyed by the earthquake? Was death what her heritage had fated her to? What she'd been doomed to face in life. "Oh, Divine One," she whispered. "What have the fae done? Save us all."

And then she saw it. Just to the side was a purple light, flickering in and out. A portal. Everything in her screamed to run toward it and hurl herself into it, regardless of what came, anything to escape the downfall of the fae. Wasn't this what Sandrine had warned her about? *All* curses would be broken, which meant the underworld, the real one, full of demons, had been released, and when they came forth, they would swallow the fae.

And yet there was the Crown of Erinyes, still on the head of the fae king. As Maeve's eyes were dragged back toward the dragon throne, ice filled her heart at what she saw.

King Mrithun was gone, vanished as though he'd never been standing in front of the throne moments ago. Instead, the queen stood on the dragon throne, her dark wings fully outstretched, her arms open, head lifted, and eyes closed. Blue light swirled around her body and Maeve realized with shock that the queen had discarded her clothes. There was a flash of light and then the dragon throne began to move. The scales shone brighter and then skin of a dragon morphed and shifted, growing, changing, moving as though it recognized where it belonged. For a moment it swallowed up the queen, hiding her from sight, and then the shaking turned violent.

Even as Maeve fell to her knees, she realized the shaking was coming from the dragon throne. It wasn't the underground vomiting the demons into the known world, it was the dragon queen rising. An acid-filled roar belched out of the queen's throat. Impossibly large wings spread wide open, with claws on them. The head of a beast rose out from between the wings, the head much bigger than Maeve herself. Then the wings began to beat, revealing four legs, long teeth, and the shining gold and black scales of a monstrous dragon.

Maeve's head went back as she stared up at the magnificence of the dragon queen. Her wings stretched out at least ten feet on each side of her enormous body. It stretched and grew, filling the hall, knocking over columns, and swallowing the darkness with her bulk. And yet, despite the horror of the monster there was something both fearsome and beautiful about the dragon. Understanding dawned on Maeve. The fae weren't the only ones who had been cursed, and the Crown of Erinyes was intended to set them free, but more important, set free the last dragon.

The last dragon.

A lump settled in Maeve's throat as she recalled the dragon the Goblin Queen had given her. The Dragon Queen would swallow it in two bites, and if such a monster was unleashed upon the world, there would be no hope. A surge of determination twirled through Maeve, a beacon of hope for the world. Even as her feet stumbled in the quake and rubble rolled around her, she pushed her panic to the background and set her sights on the dragon. If it escaped . . .

A bellow of putrid breath almost sent Maeve reeling. To the side of her stood the warden and he snarled at her as he lifted his double-bladed war axe. Maeve paused. The warden. He'd been part of her demise, part of the group of fae who humiliated and beat her. The ground shook. Maeve stumbled but the warden held fast and bellowed out a challenge again, then he charged.

Bringing the sword over her head, Maeve ran and swung in an arc. Her blow sliced through the minotaur's side and as she spun she kicked out, slamming a foot into the minotaur's back. Combined with the shaking of the ground, the warden tipped forward, roaring as he went. Maeve followed through by driving her sword into his skull, pushing and screaming until the tip of her blade hit stone.

The minotaur went limp.

Maeve yanked her blade free and got up, dashing toward the portal while stones tumbled down around her. When she looked up, a cascade of dirt almost blocked her vision and she saw impossible cracks covering the high ceiling.

She gave a furtive glance at the portal which seemed so far. Would she make it?

Then the dragon threw back its head and bellowed.

A belch of fire spewed out of the dragon's mouth, igniting the torches which had gone out. A sharp crack rifled through the air as the dragon moved. Great claws gripped the stones, scratching them with a high-pitched sickening screech. The dragon lifted off the ground, wings spread wide, flapping as they gained traction and created a stale breeze.

Maeve forced herself to look away—no easy feat—and quickened her pace, speeding toward the portal where hundreds of the fae had already fled. The dragon roared again and the hall buckled.

Columns crashed down and the crack on the ceiling split open. Maeve almost held her breath as she dived for the portal, risking one look back. The dragon was in flight and shot up among the rubble. A rift appeared in the Fae Underground, spilling in dust, stones, and moonlight.

A shudder shook Maeve's body and she balled up her free hand into a fist. She'd failed to grab the crown and destroy the fae. Now they'd been unleashed upon the world and the dragon queen had regained her ferocious form. Maeve watched a heartbeat longer as the dragon soared into the air, bellowing orange flame and roaring, a cry of victory, a cry of freedom.

Maeve's hand trembled as she lifted it and touched her neck. Freedom had been gained. But at what cost?

NOBLE

NIGHT OF THE DARK FAE BOOK THREE

I

SHADOWED ISLAND

Maeve dove through the portal, purple lightning flashed around her. Legs burning, she scurried out on the other side, heart thudding in her throat. Her mind reeled with what she'd seen in the fae Underground. She'd succeeded in finding all seven shards, but Sandrine the Scholar had given up her life creating the Crown of Erinyes. The sight of her melting under a fatal blue fire had been horrific enough, but more so was the knowledge she, Maeve of Carn, the last defender, had doomed the world. She'd had the chance to snatch up the Crown of Erinyes and put it on her head, but thoughts of revenge and bloodshed gripped her mind, so she'd dived for the Sword of Justice. Now King Mrithun wore the crown and had used it to free the Dragon Queen. What else would he do with its power?

Bile filled Maeve's throat as her thoughts flickered back to the monstrous black dragon who'd burst out of the fae Underground, seconds before Maeve dived into the portal to save her own life. Hot flames of fury rose within her, but it was useless. She'd failed once, but now all she had to do was fight through the fae, find the crown, and destroy it. Her hands went to her neck where the collar used to sit. That foul brand was gone. No more was she subject to the whims of the fae, no more would she bow down to their demands, or wait in fear for the night of the full moon. Waiting for them to abuse her to their own delight. She was free, stronger than before, and she vowed to kill them all.

A niggling sensation drew her eyes to her surroundings. She paused and turned around. The luminous purple portal had disappeared. But instead of the magnificent trees of the grove, and the castle she expected to see, there was nothing but rock and rubble under a dark red sky. Her fingers tightened on the hilt of her sword. Where was she? This was not the home of the fae. Had she gone through the wrong portal? Had they changed the location at the last minute? Her brow creased. Nothing made sense.

Rubble crunched beneath her sandals. The night sky glowed like the red eyes of a monster, without the familiar light of stars or moon—which she found odd, for it was the night of the full moon. Vague shapes dotted the shadowed landscape. A ripple of red lightning shot through the sky, illuminating the boulders that loomed like giants, their craggy surfaces chipped with holes, as though they might have eyes.

Shivering, Maeve racked her mind, even though it was useless. She'd never heard of a place like this, nor could she guess where she was. As far as she knew, she was standing on a shore of rocks, even though she did not hear water. Swallowing hard to hold her panic at bay, she whirled, searching for a path, a road, any indicator that might lead her out. Oh Divine One, she could not stay here. She had to make the fae pay and then find Imer and his secret home. Even before her death, Sandrine hadn't given her any clues where to find the fire mages. And now this?

A shape moved behind a boulder. Maeve went still, pointing her sword in its direction. Memories of the Hunter rose. Fingers cold as death against her throat, evoking an ancient fear that made her want to run, not fight.

A wild cry echoed off rock, followed by the distinct smack of a body hitting rubble. A shape ran toward her on two legs like a human, but in the darkness Maeve made out a shadow with red eyes, and little else. As the shrieking creature drew near she took up her battle stance, legs apart, feet pointed out. She swung her sword in a wide arc, slicing at the creature's waist. Her sword struck, hard and true, and with a wail of frustration, the creature disintegrated into dust.

Maeve stepped forward and tilted her head, listening for more cries. Again came the thump of feet slapping rock, and another shadow hurled out of the darkness, a hand shaped into a claw. It sliced at Maeve's face, but she jerked back, almost tasting the wind as the claws missed. She drove her sword up hard into the chest of the creature, then yanked it out. Rock crumbled around her and a crescendo of shrieks rose.

Glancing over her shoulder, Maeve saw a blur of shadows, some scrambled down from the boulders, others thumped against rock. A flash of red showed her an army of shadow creatures behind her, and ahead of her loomed a mountain. Without waiting to be attacked again, Maeve sprinted across the rocky ground. If she could reach the mountain and gain high ground, perhaps even hide in a nook or cranny, she could fight off the creatures, one by one, until they stopped, or slept. Morning had to come in this damned place and she would find a way out. No need to panic.

Snarls echoed off stone, and shadows leaped in front of Maeve as she fled. She slashed with her sword, knocking the creatures back into the ground, shattering them to dust and rubble while she fled. Tiny stones kicked up, embedding themselves in her skin, stinging her bare legs and knees. But she cared not. Her breath came short and fast as she ran and then slowed down into a rhythm, keeping pace with herself. Her warrior training was all coming back, along with the newfound strength she was imbued with.

The mountain loomed above her, and as she drew closer a niggling sensation went down her spine. It looked familiar. And when the next streak of red lightning lit up the darkened sky, she knew why. It was no mountain, and she'd seen one before. The last quest she and Sandrine had taken was through a volcano, down into the heat where the path turned into liquid lava as they attempted not to get burned. The volcano had been inactive, and she hoped the same was true of this one. For she had no Scholar to guide her, to tell her what was truth and what was false.

Maeve parted her lips as she ran, and her breath whistled out. Her heart seized as she thought of Sandrine, surprised she'd grown used to her grumpy companion. Did she dare grieve for someone who'd played a hand in her misery over the past few months? If not for Sandrine, the fae would never have captured her and forced her on the dangerous quest to acquire the Seven Shards of Erinyes. But then, she never would have returned to Carn, discovered the magic that sang in her blood, and learned the truth about why her family, nay, her people were destroyed. And if not for Sandrine, she never would have met Imer, and fallen in love with him. Love. The word stung her, and she ran faster, pushing the thought to the back of her mind. Her insecurities and lack of confidence in love and how the Divine saw her could not distract her now.

Another shadow creature leaped from a boulder, and this time, Maeve wasn't fast enough. Arms encircled her neck and dragged her to the ground. Maeve rolled hard, teeth gritted to keep from biting her tongue, and came up fast, even though the creature clung to her neck, biting down on her shoulder. With a scream, Maeve bent forward, flinging the creature off her back. It landed in the rubble; the breath knocked out of it. Two more ran up but Maeve slashed at them, returning them to stone and as she did so, she saw a pile of rocks rattle together and form another shadow person.

The pit of her stomach dropped. What was this accursed place where the very ground turned into warriors to fight against her? With all haste, she slashed at another creature and ran. If they could rebuild themselves, she'd be there all night, fighting until she was nothing left but an empty husk. She couldn't help but think the fae had led her astray on purpose. Someone wanted her here and hoped she'd find her own ruin in this damned place. Was it an island somewhere near the kingdom of Contresea? She hoped so, for as soon as daylight broke, she'd swim for land. If she could survive the night.

The screams of the rock creatures echoed around her as she gained the base of the volcano and slowed her pace to an even trot as she moved uphill. With each streak of light she searched for a place to stand, to hide, to fight. But the walls of the mountain sloped upward, smooth and even, leading to the summit until Maeve was afraid there was only one place to hide. Within the very volcano itself.

2

THE GUARDIANS

Maeve climbed, heart pulsing in her ears, the shadow creatures hissing at her heels. Darkness floated around her and a thick fog claimed the sky, blotting out the red glow. She knew it was still night, but the incessant darkness gave her no sense of time. She continued until the shadow creatures withdrew, snarling as they sank into the mountain, as though they were part of it. A glimmer of gold flickered on the edges of Maeve's vision and she slowed to a quick walk. She needed to save her strength for there was no knowing what lay in wait at the summit. The air was warm as though she walked close to a furnace. Beads of sweat dripped down her neck, and deep within the mountain she thought she heard a bubbling sound. Perhaps nothing more than the shift of rock on rock. She assumed the volcano would rumble and shake if it were close to erupting, but there were no tremors, nothing after the shadow creatures disappeared.

Rounding a curve, Maeve came to a halt as the summit of

the mountain opened before her. The path continued, running in a zigzag pattern around a great rock with words carved on it. The words glowed on the stone as though illuminated by a light within. Maeve's hands tightened on her sword and her throat went dry as she took in the giant who stood just beyond the rock.

He looked like a man, but the resemblance ended there. He stood ten feet tall and golden armor covered his bronze skin. His face looked as though it had been carved from stone and his gloved hands rested on the hilt of an unsheathed sword, shining in the darkness as though it were made of light.

A breath escaped Maeve's mouth in a long, drawn-out hiss. Every inch of the man's body was covered in thick layers of muscle. His round head was bald, eyes deep-set, and lips full and serious. His was a mouth that never smiled. But it wasn't his size, nor the golden armor, or the naked sword that drew Maeve's eyes. It was what lay on his back. Golden wings that swept almost to his feet arched from his back, with long, golden feathers. An aura of light danced around him and as Maeve gawked, a sudden knowing came over her, a fear. She fell to her knees and cast her sword on the ground.

As she did, a flash of light lit up the sky. Instead of bowing her head, her eyes were drawn upward as another winged creature descended. She, too, was clothed in golden armor with great, swooping wings on her back. Sparks of light danced around her as she landed beside the man. A shimmering circlet, much like Maeve's, was around her head, but it was plain, with no jewels. Her yellow hair was pulled back from her face, but the ends of it were loose and settled over one shoulder as she landed. Her skin was a deep bronze and her eyes a blend of green and gray. She faced the man but followed his gaze down the path.

Ragged breaths tore out of Maeve's throat in fear and wonder and astonishment. Were these the beings spoken of in age-old stories? Were they the ancient celestials, the ones who would fight against the demons?

The woman spoke first, her voice like music of the night as she conversed with the man in a language which Maeve did not understand. He answered, his voice rumbling like thunder on the edge of a storm.

Head down, Maeve listened, her thoughts whirling. While she had no doubt they would assist her in some way, she was woefully unsure of the protocol for standing before celestials, those blessed to spend eternity in the presence of the Divine. And somehow, their very existence made the old guilt and shame she thought she'd beaten rise within her. A shiver went up her spine and wormed its way up to her mind. She was not worthy to stand in their presence.

"Rise, oh warrior, defender, Carnite," the woman's voice rang out like a bell, strong, commanding.

Taking a deep breath, Maeve rose to her feet, sword in hand, and faced the celestials.

The solemn expression on both of their faces had not changed. Maeve was reminded of her days as a mercenary, when she would stand among warlords and comrades, discussing their next task. But she was a sellsword no longer and her decisions were born out of both revenge and hope. Hope that her actions would erase the darkness of her past.

"Better," the woman said, pressing a hand to her heart. "I

am Yael." She bowed her head. "This," she extended an arm toward the man, "is Asim. We are the guardians."

Courage returned to Maeve as the woman spoke and she pressed a bloodied hand to her chest, aware of how dirty her clothing was and her lack of armor which the dark fae had ripped from her. "I am Maeve of Carn. The last defender."

The last phrase she spoke had an odd ring to it, but she added it, because it was true and at last she'd decided to walk in the way of the prophecy.

"Well met, Maeve of Carn," Yael admonished her. "Tell us, are you the one responsible for the Crown of Erinyes?"

Maeve opened her mouth and faltered. Responsible? Her brows knitted together. "I am not sure what you mean. The king of the fae has the crown."

"Currently, yes." The woman frowned. "But you are the one who found the seven shards? Are you not?"

Excuses flooded Maeve's mind. Yes, she'd found the seven shards but only because she was collared, forced. And at the end, she'd believed Sandrine, that it was the right thing to do, the only way to destroy the fae once and for all. Except she hadn't succeeded. They'd escaped, and she was here, in some forsaken land with golden guardians glaring down on her. Was this judgement for her actions? "Yes," she said, her voice hushed. She wanted to say more, but it seemed imprudent.

"And you have taken it upon yourself to fulfill the prophecy and become the last defender?" Yael's tone was sharp, insistent.

Maeve lifted her chin. "Yes."

"Then I bid you welcome, Maeve of Carn." Yael smiled.

Maeve almost sagged to the ground in relief, but kept her

position, feet apart, head held high. "Why am I here? What do you want from me?" she asked, glancing at Asim, who watched her out of unreadable eyes.

Yael's eyes widened. "We require nothing from you, it is we who will assist you."

"We are the Guardians of the Gates," Asim spoke for the first time, thunder in his booming voice. "The crown has been restored, curses have been broken. The fae run free, the last dragon has taken her true form and the gates of the underworld will not hold. War is coming to this land, a great war between demons and celestials, humans, hunter, orcs, and fae. Your strength, your skills are needed if good should win against evil, and this world continue with those who can survive what is to come."

A chill went through Maeve. Despite the warmth, she shivered. "I am not a leader," she admitted. "I don't know where, or how to begin. I went through a portal, following the fae, and found myself here."

Yael nodded. "You are exactly where you need to be. For now. The fae passed through here, but they are gone, likely home, or wherever they can cause chaos as they celebrate their newfound freedom. Your journey begins at daybreak, for now we will retire to our watchtower lest the gates of the underworld swing open earlier than we expect."

Asim spread his wings, and Yael held out her hand to Maeve. She took a breath and stepped forward. This was her destiny now, her path. Lifting a hand, she took Yael's and suddenly they were airborne.

3
WATCH TOWER

Maeve closed her eyes and opened them, but it made no difference in the stormy sky. Clouds of mist hovered around her, wet and clammy, and the bolts of lightning that zigzagged across the sky were so close she thought the heat would burn the skin on her neck. But Yael avoided the lighting. Soon the clouds broke and the red glow appeared, vibrant and pulsing. Another mountain loomed before them, twice as high as the volcano Maeve had stood on mere minutes ago. As they neared, Maeve saw a tower had been built into the mountain. Yael landed on the top, which was flat, without walls surrounding it. Maeve felt a surge of vertigo as she stood in the open, buffeted by the winds that howled above them. The moment they landed, a light rain began, quickly turning into a heavy mist.

Instead of letting go of Yael's hand, Maeve clenched it tightly, trying to get rid of the dark fear that the storm would sweep her over the edge, down into a darkness she could not fathom. But she need not have feared. Yael dragged her across the open space to a trapdoor and flung it open. "After you," she shouted over the roar.

Maeve fumbled for the ladder and started down it, moving quickly to warm herself back up from the driving rain. Wet strands of hair flopped on her back and a mixture of dirt and blood slid down her legs. When at last she reached the last rung, she stumbled onto a stone floor and looked around. She stood in a wide-open hall. Unlike the fae Underground, this hall had arched windows that overlooked the dark valley, and the rain beat upon them, creating a steady rhythm.

Instead of torchlight, an inner glow came from the gray stone walls. Maeve turned in a slow circle, gazing at the ceiling which rose high above her. She looked for a door, but there was none, only other trapdoors, and a staircase curving down. The tower was a perfect circle on the inside and Maeve imagined if she took the staircase down she'd find another level much like the one she stood on, if only wider.

Yael landed beside Maeve, and Asim came down with a thud. His boots rang out with low echoes as he crossed the room toward the windows. "We have much to discuss," he said, waving at Yael and Maeve to follow him. "The night grows old while we delay and the gates weaken."

Maeve joined him and took a sharp breath. Even the driving rain could not hide the view, for down below the tower a cliff dropped off into a void. Just beyond the void was a mountain. At the base of it, a red glow shone, like a star on a bleak night. But the glow was violent, angry, like the stain of blood spreading across a pure white fleece. Maeve knew, before she asked, what she looked at, even though she could not see the gates beyond the glow. "What is that?"

"The underworld," Asim explained. "We guard the gate, for if the demons should come forth, we are the first who shall stand against them, and keep them from overrunning the world. And if we fail. . ."

"Divine help us all," Yael murmured.

Maeve examined the far off glow, and as she did, a wave of exhaustion passed over her. She wiped her face with a grimy hand, realizing it had been a long day, and her body hummed with a torrent of emotion. Sorrow and horror for Sandrine's death, guilt for not being able to halt the dark fae, and surprise at the rise of the Dragon Queen. She shuddered to think of what the Dragon Queen was doing now. Flying across the Sea of Sorrows? Setting fire to everything and everyone she saw as she exalted in her freedom? Or maybe, like the fae, the Dragon Queen was shrewd and would wait, once again, biding her time. How many years had they already waited, hidden in the fae Underground, waiting for the seven shards? Surely they had a plan, but would they risk an all out war?

"Where are we?" Maeve asked. The very sight of those gates made her fingers tingle and itch to rip out her sword and run forward to slay the demons of the deep.

"The Island of Hades," Asim said. "Set north of the Sea of Sorrows and beyond the watchtower over the fae Underground, this is an island no man can find, and the dangers of sailing here are far too perilous. Those who do arrive soon find themselves consumed by the rock creatures. They blend with shadow and rise out of the ground when the living come near. This is the last stronghold, and as guardians, we serve here, waiting until the last battle."

Once again, Maeve wished for the knowledge of the Scholar. Sandrine would have heard about this place and could have explained it, but Maeve fought to wrap her mind around the fact that the Island of Hades even existed.

"This is the valley of volcanos, and beyond," Yael pointed, "is the bridge to the gates."

Maeve followed the direction Yael was pointing, but she saw nothing.

"The clouds and mist hide it, but it is there," Yael dropped her hand back to her waist. "Long have we waited for this day to come, but you should not tarry here long."

"Where am I going?" Maeve frowned, confused at what was happening to her. "I need to find the fae, get the crown. . ." she trailed off as another flash of lightning split the skies. This time she saw it, a high, arched bridge, leading down to the deep ravine where the hellish gates awaited.

"You will return to the world you are familiar with," Yael proclaimed. "A hidden city of mages awaits you, and it is there you will find your allies. They have great magic and an army waiting for this day. The mages will help you find the fae and regain the Crown of Erinyes. But be warned, now that the relic is in the world, among the living, there are many who shall seek it. Not just the orcs, but humans, and. . . others. The fae are cunning, you will need all your wits to win against them."

Maeve's fingers tingled as excitement rose within her. The city of mages. Was it the true home that Imer had told her about? Her eyes went dark as she considered warring against the fae, and a thrill of blood lust surged within. She squared her shoulders. "I am ready. How will I find the hidden city of mages?"

"When the storm clears, one of the winged beasts will fly you through the portals." Yael glanced at the skies, pressed her lips together, and shook her head. "It is dangerous to use the portals with the fae nearby, the taint of their presence stains this land and beckons the demons. But we have no choice. After you have regained the Crown of Erinyes, you must return here and use it to shut the gates, should they open. And when the gates are shut, the Crown of Erinyes will be destroyed. Once and for all."

Asim shifted his impressive bulk toward her, and the gold on his armor flared brightly. Maeve blinked against the light and shielded her eyes. "Do not make the mistake of believing you can accomplish all of this alone," he thundered. "Allies are given for a reason, and when the celestials return, they alone will choose which side to fight on. Do not give them reason to doubt you."

"You aren't the celestials?" Maeve blurted out, looking from Asim to Yael.

"Once," Asim replied as Yael lifted her chin, her expression unreadable. "We were graced to dwell in the presence of the Divine, but we are needed here. Guarding the gates is not a task to be taken lightly, and we are honored to be the first to assist the created land."

Maeve couldn't be sure, but she thought his hand tightened around his sword hilt, as though he held back his anger. She wondered what it was like to be banished from the presence of the Divine. But she didn't want to know, not anymore.

The guardians were fearsome enough with their stone-like faces, impassive expressions, and unnatural height. They were giants, and their words made her feel insignificant. If they were not the celestials, who would come to assist them?

"Your journey will be long," Yael warned. "We have a fast mount that awaits you, but she will not stop. You have enough strength, so this ride will not kill you, but you must rest and recover afterward."

"Kill me?" Maeve's eyes went wide. How could riding on the back of a beast possibly kill her? Now she was frightened.

"Just as we are not of this world, nor are the beasts who assist us," Yael said.

Dread coursed through Maeve's veins. Why was she always thrust from one impossible situation into the next? Why should she be the unfortunate one? She rubbed the back of her neck, eyes stinging. She would do this without complaint. "What kind of beast is it?" she asked.

Yael glanced at Asim. "Is it safe?"

He inclined his head. "It is."

"Follow me." Yael set off down the stone hall. "I will prepare you for your journey."

Without another word, Maeve followed, aware this was a time of war, and rest might be long in coming.

4

SWEET SUMMONS

Yael did not offer any further explanation, and Maeve followed her silently down the spiraling staircase until they arrived at another level. Once again, a golden light lit up the concave room, displaying rows of swords, shields, mail, bows, arrows, and more. Maeve turned in a slow circle, gazing in astonishment at the vast armory. There was enough armor to equip hundreds of soldiers.

Yael studied her, her gaze running the length of Maeve's body. "We have little for someone of your stature," she admitted, her fingers brushing the shelves as she walked. "You will need to be covered, for touching the beast could prove. . ." she paused, searching for the right words, then gave up as she pulled a smaller suit of armor out. "Dress quickly, the storm will cease soon and there will only be a small window before it begins again."

Maeve did not see how the storm could end because of the way it roared and wailed. Rain struck the window as though instead of raindrops, they were pellets of tiny stones, seeking a way to get inside. But she had no choice, and the extraordinary turn of events still left her mind reeling as she attempted to process everything that had happened to her.

She pulled on a new shift, the soft material cool against her body. Then came the gauntlets for her arms and legs, which covered all of her exposed skin, but were flexible enough to allow her unrestricted movement. Yael handed her a golden breastplate and a helm for her head.

"Make sure you tuck your hair in," she said, "if you want to keep it."

Maeve hesitated, worry flooding her. "What kind of beast is this?" she asked as she finished dressing. The armor felt light on her and although it was not too restricting, she still felt as though she were encased in a metal box. Her heartbeat increased, and quickly she reminded herself that she was not collared or trapped, nor was she in the fae Underground. She was free, about to return to the world, the city of mages.

"She is the oldest creature, the fastest, the strongest, the best. We call her Enya."

Taking a breath to still her nerves, Maeve tried to think of a meaning for the name: Enya. But nothing came to mind. Instead, she followed Yael back the way they had come until once again they stood in the hall with Asim keeping watch over the gates.

"She is ready," Yael announced.

"I will summon her." He lifted a silver horn and blew upon it.

A sweet, tinkling sound filled the air, and a rush filled Maeve. She took a step forward before she recalled the horn was not meant for her and did not call her to that place. Above her head a dark shadow swept over the skies, and just as Yael had said, the storm relented. The rain slowed, as though it begrudgingly had to stop. The sporadic lightning was no longer followed by great rumbles of thunder, and then something landed on the top of the tower with a harsh scraping sound.

Dread filled Maeve's heart, but regardless, she followed Yael to the ladder.

Light filled her vision as she climbed on top of the tower, unnerved, once again, by the lack of walls or anything else to hold on to. Her breath left her body as the dazzling light lessened and she saw the most beautiful creature she'd ever seen. Bright orange feathers, the color of flame covered the creature's broad back. Curved claws rested on the gray stone of the tower while the beast looked down at Maeve and Yael, bright eyes examining them while a red glow pulsed on its chest. It spread its wings and cocked its head. Maeve stepped back. The bird towered a good five or six feet above her with a plume of red and orange feathers crowning its head.

"Eyna is a firebird." Yael pressed a hand to her heart. "She will take you as far as the city of mages but be wary of her fire."

Firebird. Phoenix. Like dragons, Maeve had heard of them in old tales, and assumed they were not real, only a legend. How wrong she'd been once again. But she couldn't help the fear that wrestled in the pit of her stomach. Legend held that the creatures burst into flame when antagonized, but were also known for their rebirth, for a firebird could never truly die. Still, how ironic was it that she could not escape from fire. The dragon. The fire mages. Now a phoenix?

"Take this." Yael pressed a bundle into her hands. "Now go with grace. We will meet again."

Maeve paused as the firebird turned its back to allow her to mount up. "Once I've found the crown, how will I find you again?"

"Find a Master of Portals," Yael instructed. "One should dwell in the city of mages, and now that all curses are broken, the torn magic will work again."

Maeve had no idea what that meant, but regardless, she mounted up. Warmth filled her body as she settled into the nest of feathers. The firebird spread its wings and lifted her away, leaving the dark gloom of the Island of Hades behind.

5
FIRE MAGES

Black clouds rolled across the night sky, shutting out the light. A sharp wind blew with a sour tang to it. Imer fidgeted on the battlements and felt for his pipe. A quick smoke would help soothe his nerves, his frustration at doing nothing.

Three days ago everything had changed, he'd felt it in the marrow of his being. The magic of the world had shifted and with it came the dense, dark clouds. Every night was black, hiding the moonlight and starlight. Imer couldn't help but wish to know more about what had happened that fateful night. The night of the full moon.

His thoughts went to Maeve and his fingers tightened into fists at the thought of her suffering abuse in the hands of the dark fae. He hadn't meant to fall for her, flirt, aye, but actually care about her? He knew it could come to no good and hated the very thought of leaving her collared, with only Sandrine's unpleasant attitude for company. But he also understood that they played a long game, and his place was at the wizard's tower with the other mages, waiting.

But he hated waiting, not knowing what had happened, and whether Sandrine and Maeve would return, or whether they were dead. If they returned with the Crown of Erinyes, war would come. And if they did not, war would still come. But whether the mages set forth or stayed in the tower's shadow would be determined. Soon.

Turning his back to the wind, he hunched over to light his pipe, using his fingertip so the wind would not easily blow out the flame. He took a long drag, losing himself in the fragrance of tobacco. Pipe smoke reminded him of a time when he and Ingram snuck off from the temple of Isdrine where they were raised. They discovered a pond, hidden in a grove of trees, where a boy about their age sat fishing. They'd joined him, shared their first pipe, and caught many fish together. A calm adventure it had been, but necessary, to remind them that all was not dark and evil. Despite the death of their parents and their secret magic, there was still good in the world, and opportunities to find pleasure in the mundane.

"More come." Ingram's deep voice broke Imer's thoughts.

His brother leaned over the battlements, taking sips of ale as he watched those down below go in and out of the wizard's tower. The eye patch across his bad eye flapped in the breeze and he frowned as he took a small sip from his pouch. Imer noticed that while his brother still drank, he never let himself go beyond getting slightly tipsy, which was a good thing. A drunk fire mage would not do well in battle. Imer knew his brother was just as antsy as him, if not more so. He'd left his priestess in Isdrine. But would it be safe if the orcs marched forth and took down city after city? Were the people strong enough to fight back?

Imer followed Ingram's gaze. Down in the cobblestone city, people moved in groups, making way for a battalion that crossed the streets, sweeping toward the gates of the tower. "Are those. . ." Imer trailed off as he studied the battalion. They wore shiny helmets and they all carried bows and arrows, much like the people of the grove. Except, they weren't a tribe of the grove. From the distance, Imer could not see any more details, but a rush of excitement filled him.

"I think they are elves," Ingram confirmed.

Imer took another tug on his pipe and crossed one arm around his chest. "Elves haven't been seen in these parts in an age. If so, they've come up from the south because they, too, sense the change in the wind."

"And they've come to fight with us," Ingram agreed. "But we need news, this waiting, this not knowing is. . ."

"Difficult," Imer said. "It's only been three days but it feels much longer. Perhaps you should ask Willow." He grinned at his brother.

Ingram snorted. "She took up with the wizard while we were gone."

"But she has a soft spot for you," Imer protested. "You might find out more from her."

Ingram frowned, then lowered his voice. "Word is, there was a curse upon this tower, and now it is broken. The wizard was bound to this place, but now he can leave. I don't think it will be long before he has a plan. I don't know how many years he was bound here, but he must wish to see the world for himself."

"Interesting." Imer had heard the same rumor.

"Aye, just like Maeve of Carn." Ingram took another sip. "What is it about her that you're drawn to?"

Imer stiffened, surprised and irritated at his brother's question. "Since when were you interested in my love life?"

Ingram shrugged. "Since it affects me."

Imer gave his brother a rueful grin. "How? We did what we set out to do, did we not?" He held up his fingers, ticking them off. "We found Sandrine and protected her through the mountains. We tested our ship against the eels, evaded the Hunter, and found the celestial blade in the ruins of Carn. My affections for Maeve hadn't held up our plans at all."

Ingram pressed his lips together and took another sip. "And now? If she returns and war wrecks this land, how will you make clear judgements? You'll side with her and only her every time. And what if her decisions aren't what's best for us, what's best for Imperia?"

Imer shrugged. "You know I would never willingly put us in harm's way, nor go against the wizard. I know what he did for you and me. He has my loyalty, I won't forget it. But Maeve is different, she has strength, resilience, and a willingness to change. She's not a victim. . . " he trailed off. "Remember when we went to Isdrine and you met Priestess Selene?"

Ingram frowned. "Don't bring her into this, she serves the Divine. She's not a warrior with a dark past, searching for a way out of a situation she got herself into. She is true and pure and honest."

"Righteous," Imer grunted. "Don't make me angry. You believe Selene is too good for this world, yet you've corrupted her and leave her time and time again."

"She is safe in the temple. As we were," Ingram protested. "I'm just asking you to watch yourself, because of the Prophecy of Erinyes. If the last defender returns, all eyes will be on her. She will have choices to make, and what if those don't include you? I'm just asking you to prepare yourself. Don't go rushing in as though you could have a normal life. We are brothers of fire, nothing is normal. We weren't meant to settle down, or marry. We were meant for battle, to protect and defend, not to enjoy."

Imer crossed his arms over his chest to keep his anger from burning into his fingers and exploding into fire in his hands. He faced Ingram, his words cold. "Do you think so little of me, brother?"

"As your older brother, it is my duty to have your back in all things. It was different when we were on the road, harmless, but if you're serious about Maeve, you need to prepare for what is to come."

Imer frowned and opened his mouth to respond, when a flash of light caught his vision. He turned his face toward the dark skies, eyes darting back and forth as he searched. It came again, a brief flare in the sky, but not of lightning. Throat dry, he watched the pulse grow nearer. Flames leaked out of the sky and flashes of orange as a creature far larger than he'd ever imagined, crossed the sky. It wasn't a dragon, that he was sure of, but something else. It wheeled closer, and he clearly saw a tail with red, orange, and yellow feathers, bold and bright, starkly visible against the bleak sky.

With each turn it came closer to the tower and a cry burst out of its mouth, a warning. It circled once more, then turned on its side, showing him the impressive span of its wings and a being, encased in golden armor that rode on its back.

"By the Divine," Ingram whispered beside him. "Is that what I think it is?"

"A celestial bird," Imer responded. "A firebird. Is it, possible?"

He didn't see his brother's shrug but heard it in his tone. "All curses have been broken, all things are possible now."

"What do you think it wants?" Imer went on, attempting to translate its cries.

Below in the streets he heard people gasp and cry out, pointing at the magnificent creature that wheeled above them. An aura of surprise and hope filled the air, as though the magic of the firebird could chase away the dark clouds and stop the storm from coming.

Instead, with one last swoop it wheeled about and turned, so violently the armored being on its back fell with a scream. It was only perhaps ten feet, maybe more, but the scream echoed in Imer's mind. A strong suspicion hit him. He had to know. The body landed with a thunk on the lone tower above him. The wizard's tower.

"Come on." He threw the words over his shoulder to Ingram as he dashed toward the door.

6
WARM AWAKENING

Maeve opened her eyes as she regained consciousness and immediately wished she hadn't. Every muscle in her body ached, her throat parched for water and beads of sweat covered her skin. The armor was tight on her body and more than anything, she wanted to strip it off. During the long flight on the back of the firebird, she'd sweated endlessly and with each sip of water, her thirst increased. The guardian, Yael, had been generous in giving her six water pouches. And while Maeve had tried to ration them, her thirst got the better of her.

They'd flown high above the clouds and throughout the long flight she felt as though she couldn't get enough air or enough water, not to speak of food. Now, hunger gnawed through her stomach, making her wish she could eat an entire chicken. Wherever she was, she hoped a feast was about to take place. She'd forget her thirst and forego a cooling bath just for a good meal.

The glare of her shield stung her eyes and made her head pound. She struggled to move her hands to rip it off when the ground beneath her shifted and cracked with a splitting sound. It gave way and she fell for a second time and landed with a thump. This time, she was too weary to cry out but all the same she struggled to her knees.

"In here!" someone shouted.

"Bring her down," another voice cried.

And then she was surrounded, arms reaching out to lay her on a pallet. Dimly, she struggled against them as she was taken, downward, she thought, and came to a rest again.

"Who is it?" a woman's voice said.

"Open the helmet, gently," a man's smooth voice instructed. A loud banging on what must have been a door interrupted him. "I'll see to this, interruption." His voice sounded amused.

"Water," Maeve whispered, her tongue almost too dry to speak. She'd screamed when the firebird dropped her, and that had drained the rest of her energy.

Pressure pounded around her head and the helmet slipped off. Light filled the room, firelight, she assumed, and she blinked up at the face of a woman bending over her. Her heart-shaped face was youthful, her skin dark and her almond-shaped amethyst eyes full of curiosity and concern. Before the strange woman could say anything, doors thudded open and the sound of booted footsteps rang across the stone floor.

Maeve turned her head, struggling to see where she'd fallen. Was this the city of mages? Wide windows let in the gray light from outside, and at one end of the room she glimpsed what looked like a throne. When she turned her head the other way, she saw feet running up to her. A man knelt beside her.

"It's Maeve!" he exclaimed, and then his face peered over hers.

She couldn't help the tired smile that came to her lips at the sight of Imer. As she studied the crooked grin on his face, her heart flip-flopped, but she couldn't miss the guarded caution in his eyes. Something had changed.

"Water," she mumbled again.

"Don't move." Imer lay a hand on her shoulder.

"She needs to be taken to the infirmary," a woman's voice rang out. "We will speak with her when she is feeling better."

Maeve caught a glimpse of the woman's face as she was lifted and carried on the pallet. She closed her eyes as the rocking sensation took over, and it wasn't too long until she was set down again. In the distance she heard voices talking and someone pulled off her boots and started unfastening her gantlets. A water skin was pressed to her lips and she drank deeply, relieved to be out of the air, back on solid land where the warmth of the firebird did not touch her. A weariness overcame her and her eyelids closed, even though she tried to fight it. Her last thoughts were that she was thankful to be in a safe place, once again.

When Maeve woke, disoriented and confused, her golden armor had been piled up on a nearby table and shined until it glistened. Her sword lay with it and she blew out a breath. Swinging her legs over the side of the bed, she stood up, snatched the water pouch off the table, and drained it dry. The pounding in her head was gone and the heat that inflamed her skin had passed. She still wore the sheath but noticed additional clothes had been laid out on the table beside the bed. She ignored them and ducked out of the room.

The next room was larger, lit with torchlight and a woman stood by a table, folding white linens.

"Hello," Maeve said.

The woman gasped and a hand flew to her mouth. "Oh, my lady, you're awake. We did not expect you to get up so soon, I must tell the others."

Maeve held up a hand to keep her from rushing out of the room. "Where can I find some food? I am half-starved."

Eyes wide, the woman pointed to a basket on the table. "Eat as much as you like. I'll have something hot brought from the kitchens. Don't go anywhere." She held up her hands as though she could keep Maeve in the room.

Ignoring her, Maeve went for the basket. Inside were cheese, grapes, and bread that smelled as though it had been baked a few hours ago. Sitting down, she tore into it while the woman fled from the room. She chewed and swallowed, wondering whether a flagon of wine could be had to wash down the food. As she ate, she recalled all that had happened to her, and her next task. How long had she slept? There could be no delay. A sense of urgency made her stand while she shoved cheese into her cheeks.

When she turned to the doorway, Imer leaned against it, watching her with an unreadable expression on his face.

Cheeks bulging, she froze, and confusion churned within. Imer. She had to admit, she'd thought of this moment, imagined their reunion many times. But not like this. She'd been frustrated when he'd left her and missed his calm presence, his firm belief in her quest and their passionate lovemaking. But now that they were together again, an awkwardness hung like an invisible curtain between them. She didn't know how to behave around him.

When they were hunting for the shards what was between them was different. She was desperate to escape the fae and he had answers about her past. But now, no more mystery surrounded him. Her desire for him was still there but it had changed. Was it the distance? The finale of the quest? Or the impending war? She wasn't sure, but her feet did not run to him, and although she would welcome his kisses, she did not need them. What had happened?

Maeve finished chewing, although she would have rather spit out the food, her hunger gone. Imer, sensing the tension in the air, broke it with a lazy smile. "Maeve of Carn."

The familiar tone of his voice sent a tingling sensation through her veins. Her thoughts twisted in confusion. Perhaps she was simply exhausted and still trying to wrap her mind around what she was feeling as the world changed around her.

"I am glad to see you well, and whole, unbroken. When

you fell. . ." he trailed off and ran his fingers through the waves of his dark hair.

"You should know that Sandrine did not make it," she told him, her fingers forming into fists at the memory of blue fire licking up Sandrine's body.

His mouth set in a grim line. "I understand."

A tight ball of disappointment formed in the pit of her stomach and she wasn't sure if his words meant he understood about Sandrine's death or the tension between them. She took a step toward him, aware that she smelled of heat and battle. Her hair was frizzy and she wanted to soak in a hot bath before touching anyone.

Blinking hard, she changed the topic. "This is your home?"

His eyes were hard although his lips retained the smile, his secret weapon against the world, the mask he wore to keep others from reading his true thoughts and sensing his feelings. "Aye, my lady."

The term warmed her and a flush came to her face. The old Imer was still there after all.

"We returned here after we left you in the glade." He rubbed the back of his neck. "It's been a long few months, waiting, and now war is coming. The wizard will want to speak with you, and I assume we will march to battle."

Maeve bit her bottom lip, longing for a touch from him, something other than words, an action, a gesture that would encourage her. She shook her head. "It went all wrong down there." She recalled the fae Underground, being chained up as the ceremony began. "I wasn't fast enough. The dark fae have the Crown of Erinyes, and worse, the Dragon Queen is free. Imer, she's coming."

Imer's face paled and his hands dropped to his side. "You cannot blame yourself." He moved toward her.

"But, I do," she replied, frowning.

"And yet, you are here, because although you try to carry the weight of the world on your shoulders you cannot. War was always coming and now that we stand on the brink of it, everything will change."

He didn't stop walking until he was right before her. His knuckle brushed her chin and a shiver of arousal touched every inch of her skin. She took a deep breath before she met his eyes, deep blue with the golden flecks. A reminder of why she'd fallen in love with him in the first place broke the fog of her thoughts. It wasn't simply because of the way he made her feel, although that was part of it, but also the way he encouraged her, reminding her she wasn't a lost soul and the past was behind her.

"Imer." She touched his wrist, intending to explain but he tilted his head and gave it a slight shake.

"You don't have to explain yourself to me," he told her. "Much has happened in the last few months and it is normal to question everything, especially as alliances form. I have my own motives, but I would have you know that I am on your side."

Then he leaned forward and brushed her lips with his. The kiss was slow, sweet, and full of promise. Before Maeve could react, he pulled away and strode out of the room.

Maeve stood stock still, the kiss burning on her lips. She

wanted to stand there and bask in it. But a moment later the woman returned.

7
POWERFUL RULERS

After a bath and a warm meal, Maeve returned to the infirmary. The woman had relayed a message. The mages of the tower desired to speak with her, but they would allow her to rest for another day. Maeve took advantage of the time to sleep, although her fingers tapped with anticipation. To her regret, she did not see Imer again nor have any other visitors; it seemed they wanted her to spend some time in solitude, recovering from her flight.

But when she went to the door, she could hear murmurs, whispered voices, hasty footsteps. As Imer had mentioned, they were gathering. Alliances would be chosen and they would march.

On the morning of her second day there, she dressed in her shift, pulled on a belt with her sword in it and left the infirmary in search of answers. She'd barely set foot outside the door when a voice called out, "You must be Maeve."

She turned, and a woman strode toward her, the same

one who'd pulled the helmet off her head when she landed. She was taller than Maeve and her appearance was striking. The woman smiled and her amethyst eyes lit up. She had a heart-shaped face with a small pointed nose, almond-shaped eyes, and curly black hair that complimented her brown skin. Her hips swayed when she walked and she wore a sleeveless blue gown which almost swept the floor. The scent of raw magic filled the air, and Maeve had a feeling the woman was both powerful and dangerous. She could be her best ally, or worst nightmare.

"I'm Willow," she said, extending a hand.

Maeve hesitated and then took Willow's hand. Willow. Ingram and Imer had mentioned a woman named Willow, and Maeve saw the resemblance. She had the same features and coloring as the people of the grove.

"Welcome to Imperia." Willow pressed Maeve's hand.

Maeve had the distinct sensation the woman was reading her, and she wasn't sure if she liked it. "Imperia?" she repeated. The word felt beautiful on her tongue.

Willow let go of her. "The city of mages. We heard about your quest to find the seven shards and reform the Crown of Erinyes." Admiration filled her voice. "You succeeded, and we are grateful."

Maeve cocked her head and alarm bells rang within her. "We?"

Willow smiled. "We are mages who serve at the pleasure of the wizard. The gathering is soon, and there are many who would like to meet you, but first I would like to introduce you to the wizard. Follow me."

Willow walked down the hall, and Maeve had no choice

but to follow her. This time when questions swirled through her mind, she was sure that she'd have answers. Soon.

The tower she walked through was magnificent, open and airy with the light scent of herbs. It was clean, calm, and even though footsteps echoed off the stone floor, it did not have a harsh ring to it. Eyes wide, Maeve slowed down to take it all in. Rich tapestries hung on the walls and when they moved up a spiraling staircase, the smell of ink and old parchment hung in the air. They passed others, men and woman who nodded at them, a few with pointed ears, dressed in armor. A slender youth dashed down the stairs, almost running into them, his mouth open as he stared, then set off again.

Imperia. Maeve thought of the word again, and a longing began in her heart. So long she'd run, calling no place home. At times she'd desired one, but it seemed best to stay on the move. She was used to running away, but now she understood it was because of her past, because of what had happened when she was a child. And now she'd found people like her, with power, those who were looked upon for their special abilities and fought over by those with power. Except, there seemed to be no malicious intent here. When the war ended, would this be her home?

But she was getting ahead of herself. She had yet to meet the wizard.

Willow led Maeve up to the top of the tower to a set of double doors. Without knocking, she lay her hands flat on the doors and pushed. They swung inward and Maeve gasped. She was at the top of the tower in a grand hall covered with multi-colored prisms. She blinked against the array of colors, struggling to determine where to look. The colors faded and her heart pounded in anticipation as a man whirled toward them, eyebrows raised to see who dared interrupt him. He carried a thick book in his hands and stood at the window, reading the text. His expression warmed as he lay eyes on Willow, and Maeve wasn't surprised. She crossed her arms as she examined the room, looking for the wizard, for the man who strode toward them couldn't be him. He had a youthful appearance with black hair, a trimmed mustache but no beard. Maeve studied him, and he returned her stare with eyes deep and magnetic that gave away nothing.

"Thank you, Willow." He held her gaze, a soft smile playing around the corners of his mouth.

Maeve pressed her lips together and drew a sharp breath as she realized, nay, was she wrong? *This* was the wizard?

"I am Jacq the wizard," he introduced himself. "Welcome to Imperia. We heard of your deeds and are pleased you have joined us."

Maeve's eyes darted from Willow to Jacq. Both of them had a faint glow about their bodies, a spark of magic. She sensed their power, just standing there, and recalled the words the guardians had spoken to her. She was supposed to return to the city of mages to lead, but they already had leaders with far more power than her. She wanted to ask them why she was there, but she was the one who'd fallen out of the sky, she was the one who needed their help.

Jacq paused, but Maeve could not think of anything to say to him, so he went on. "Will you tell us what happened? When the shards were reformed into a crown?"

Maeve didn't miss the curious glint in his eyes, although

he tried to bury it. She sensed his need for power. Her brows furrowed. “How do you know about the quest?”

Willow moved to stand beside the wizard, so they both looked down at Maeve. Uncertainty rose in her, and she took a step back.

“Ingram and Imer told us of their adventures when they returned,” Willow said. “Of meeting you and the scholar in the Village of the Lawless, traveling to the Draconbane Mountains, hiding in orc territory and being chased by the Hunter. They shared how the last dragon came to be with them, and the sword that was found in Carn.” Willow glanced at the sword at Maeve’s waist. “And finally, they brought the people of the grove here, to form an alliance with us.”

Maeve studied the ground, wondering why she felt so hesitant. Ingram and Imer trusted the wizard of the tower and called Imperia home. She should do the same, for it was only her past that made her instinctively wary of others. She took a deep breath, and her tale flowed out of her. “Hunting the seven shards wasn’t my choice. But after spending thirty days in the Dungeon of the Damned, I saw no other way to gain my freedom.” Her fingers went to her neck, remembering. “I used to be a sellsword because of my strength, but the dark fae collared me so that I would do their bidding.”

Anger churned within and her fingers tightened into fists. She told Jacq and Willow about finding the final shards, watching the ceremony where Sandrine voluntarily gave herself over to death, and the chaos that broke out in the fae Underground. She shared about the rise of the Dragon Queen and running through a portal, only to find herself on the

Island of Hades where the guardians lent her a firebird to ride back to the city of mages. When she drew breath, they stared wordlessly at her, waiting. "I have to fix my mistake. When the Crown of Erinyes was reformed, my instructions were to take it, for it holds powerful magic. Instead, the King of the Dark Fae escaped with it. I have to find them, find him and bring them to justice."

Jacq and Willow turned to each other as though they could read each other's minds. Maeve watched their silent communication. A slight twinge of regret pinched her as she thought of Imer. Where was he and what was he doing? Would they become close once again?

Jacq nodded. "Then you shall go. I have called for a meeting of the alliances, but I believe it will be best to meet over a meal and discuss our plans this evening. Rest from your journey, and well done, Maeve of Carn. We are honored to welcome you into our midst."

Maeve bowed her head, for it appeared the wizard and the mage were powerful rulers and deserved her loyalty.

8

GRAY BATTLEMENTS

Maeve left the audience chamber with more questions than she'd had when she first arrived. It perplexed her that they treated her like a hero for finding the seven shards. The Crown of Erinyes was dangerous, for it doomed the world. And yet, she couldn't help the irritation that went through her. It seemed the mages agreed with Sandrine's point of view. They wanted all curses to be broken, they wanted war and death and devastation, and she did not understand why. Personally, she wanted to see the downfall of the fae, to take revenge on them for what they had done to her. But why did the mages want the crown? Was there another piece to the puzzle she'd missed?

"Hello."

She jumped and spun. At the foot of the staircase stood a boy, bouncing up and down on the soles of his feet. Curly black hair covered his head and he was lanky for a youth. He grinned at her. "I'm Jordan. Are you. . .?" he trailed off, waiting for her to answer.

"Maeve of Carn." She wondered what he wanted.

"They said you're the one who found the shards." His eyes went wide with admiration.

She frowned. "I was forced."

Some light went out of his eyes, but he shrugged. "Still, it was brave of you. Anyway, I'm to take you to the battlements."

"Why?" she asked, aware she was being unfriendly, but she didn't care.

"Imer's there. . ." he said hopefully.

Imer. Her shoulders relaxed. "Okay, I'm following."

Jordan led her down the staircase, back to the main level and through a series of halls to another flight of stairs. They wound their way to the top and he held the door open as she ducked out into harsh light. Maeve's eyes were drawn upward, to the dark clouds that hovered over the tower before sweeping across the gray battlements. She was halfway up the fortress, and above her she could see the domed top of the tower and perhaps the audience chamber she'd just been in. The smell of pipe smoke drew her attention back to the battlements. Soldiers in full armor stood at the edge, looking down and watching, as though they expected a battle to erupt at any moment. Dread made her shoulders tighten, and she forgot to thank Jordan as she strode around the curving circle toward the smoke.

"Imer?" she called as a halo of smoke drifted up into the cloudy sky. Through the gloom she could see the sparks from his pipe, the light glowing as Imer took another drag. He turned in her direction and a cocky grin lit up his face.

He opened his arms. “Finally, you decided to join us.”

Imer’s light-hearted greeting brought a smile to Maeve’s lips. She walked into his open arms and took a whiff of his scent as she hugged him. His heart pounded slow and steady, and Maeve relaxed as she rubbed his back. This was a much better greeting than the awkward one earlier. She pulled back and tucked her hair behind one ear, wrinkling her nose at him. “Imer.” She lowered her voice, although no one was close to them. “What’s going on here? Everyone acts like I’m a hero for finding the shards, for being there when the. . .” Maeve bit her lip and glanced around to ensure no one was listening. “The crown was reformed. But I don’t understand why. My actions doomed the world. Why are they celebrating?”

Rubbing the back of his neck, Imer sighed and took another drag on his pipe before responding. “They aren’t celebrating. *We* aren’t celebrating, just admitting that a change has come. A long-awaited change. Besides, rumor has it the wizard of the tower was cursed, and now he is free. You see, even though the world is doomed, there are others who have benefited from this.”

Maeve crossed her arms and backed away, shaking her head. “I don’t like it.”

“Do you want some advice?” His eyes laughed at her. “This is the wizard’s tower, full of powerful mages. You have thoughts, but keep them to yourself, for now.”

Maeve frowned at him.

“Trust me, Maeve.” He squeezed her arm. “If you have

opinions, tell me. This is a place where you are free to come and go, as long as you obey the wizard. He is powerful and has the best interest of the mages who dwell here in mind. I know little else. I came here because I needed a haven, and this is home. Don't destroy it."

He kept his expression light and that cocky smile on his face. A warning whispered around Maeve and she pressed her lips together to keep her initial response from bursting out of her lips. Instead of responding immediately, she took a moment, her eyes darting out across the landscape.

To the south a cloud of mist hung over a shimmering lake, like a mother bird guarding her nest. To the north rose a mountain. As the clouds moved, she made out the pointed shape, and then a beast whirled, scaly wings flashing out of the gloom. For a moment, her heart thumped in her chest and bile rose to her throat. But it wasn't the Dragon Queen, but a smaller replica with orange wings. Her dragon. She drew in a sharp breath as she watched it circle and disappear again, and an idea came to her mind.

"Imer." She faced him again. "I wanted to find the seven shards and put the crown back together so I could destroy the fae. That hasn't happened, instead, I lost the crown and Sandrine died. I don't know what the gathering is about, nor what the alliances will decide, but I can't stay here. I have to leave as soon as possible and find the fae. Do you think the people of the grove will help? Can they find the old kingdom of the fae?"

A glint of mischief hung in Imer's eyes. "I knew I liked you." He grinned. "You're trouble."

"Well?" Maeve prompted as she smiled back, warming to him again.

Tracing the swirling symbols on her shoulder, he turned his face to blow a whiff of smoke over the wall. "Listen, the meeting of alliances is tonight. After it's over, come join me in my chambers and we will discuss this further. It's a good plan, but likely what the wizard will instruct us to do, anyway. For now, I want to show you Imperia and hear how you escaped and secured a ride on a phoenix."

Maeve shook her head, already feeling better about her situation. "It wasn't my choice. It was the guardians, Imer. They are real. I thought at first they were celestials, but they said they weren't. They guard the Gates of Hell and it glows. The demons might break through and invade this world."

Imer took her hand and blew out his pipe. "Hush, Maeve, we don't have to talk about it now. You're going to save the world, I feel it. Tonight, you'll understand the desire to see something magnificent. To bring back the ancient powers, to have the celestials come down and right the wrongs of this world."

Maeve squeezed his hand. "Show me Imperia."

9
CITY OF MAGES

Imer took Maeve through Imperia. The walk around the small but crowded city was enough to calm her nerves and remind her that she was a part of something much larger than herself. They spent the midday meal at the tavern where they were joined by Ingram. In exchange for coin, they enjoyed a drink, a warm meal, and a word with the jolly tavern owner.

"I suppose you'll want to see the dragon," Ingram said.

"I do," Maeve agreed. The last time she'd seen it, it had spoken to her, and she wanted to speak with it again.

Leaving the city behind, they strode out to the fields which were naught but barren slopes of mud, awaiting the coming spring. The promise of frost hung in the air, and Maeve's eyes were drawn to the fog on the mountains.

"Where does Imperia lie on the map of the world?" she asked the brothers.

"We are south," Imer told her, "and east of the grove in a

series of mountain ranges. But this mountain is spelled by magic. No one can find it, unless they have already been here. And then they still have to look very hard. Most come here because they are the unwanted, those with potent magic the world rejects."

"But we are outcasts no more," Ingram agreed.

"And the wizard?" Maeve glanced from one brother to the other. There was something about the wizard she couldn't quite put her finger on. "He's, not what I expected. How old is he?"

Imer shrugged. "Old, I assume. Not much is known about him."

"Aye, but he keeps us safe."

"And sends us on quests, as he chooses."

Maeve took a deep breath as she watched the mist move, and a hint of orange appeared behind a dark wave. Turning, she folded her arms and faced the brothers.

Imer stopped and pulled out his pipe, pressing more tobacco into it. Ingram took a swig from a pouch, then tucked it away.

"Be honest with me." Maeve squeezed her hands into fists. "Did the wizard send you? To find me?"

Ingram snorted, opened his mouth, then glanced at Imer.

Maeve watched Imer's face tighten and knew she had offended him. Once, he'd told her, everything wasn't about her. But she'd since learned that the Prophecy of Erinyes *was* about her. Somehow, being the last Carnite meant that she had a part to play in saving the world. And now that she was free, it was up to her to decide who to trust. She saw the situation differently now. Originally, she didn't have a choice, but now she wanted to know if those closest to her were playing with her too.

"We've all known," Imer began, "when we first arrived here, the wizard made it clear what our goal should be. The dark fae were taking people, stealing them away every night of the full moon. And it was known that their actions would make the Prophecy of Erinyes come true. We didn't know it would be you, and we only guessed that Sandrine would have a part to play. We were sent to help our grandmother, to make her burden lighter. And we succeeded. For a little while."

Tears filled Maeve's eyes, and she tore her gaze away, staring off, unsure why she was upset with him. At the temple in Isdrine, he'd been clear about what he believed, and yet it seemed different, knowing he'd been sent on a quest to help make the prophecy come true.

"But helping Sandrine was only a side quest," Imer went on. "As I've told you, we were sent to find the sword of a celestial, because of the rise of the Hunter. We returned here without it, explained to the wizard why, and he agreed with our reasoning. Regardless of what happens next, we have to remember that we have enemies. The Hunter is still out there, the dark fae are free, and the orcs march."

"I know," Maeve mumbled. "I keep searching for a reason to disagree, to fight. But I know my fight isn't here, it's out there."

Ingram cleared his throat. "Are you done rehashing old arguments? For here he comes."

Maeve followed Ingram's gaze and her eyes went wide. Her arms fell to her side as she watched the dragon. He'd landed and walked on four legs with two massive wings, golden and orange, tucked behind his back. He'd grown and now stood over ten feet tall while his long tail wormed away and created a path in the grass. Maeve's heartbeat quickened as she took in how much he'd grown. The last time she'd seen him he was the size of a small wolf.

Hand out, she stepped forward, trembling as she reached out to touch his snout. Part of her felt as though she were meeting an old friend again while the other part of her felt like she'd had a child and abandoned it.

"Give her some time," she heard Imer say, and sensed the brothers of fire walk away, leaving her alone with the dragon.

"Hi," she whispered.

Golden eyes blinked at her as the beast bowed its head. "You have returned." His voice was low and deep and rumbled like the faint warning of thunder.

"I have," Maeve said solemnly. "I came back to prepare an army and go fight."

"Then I will come with you, this is the battle, the war I have been waiting for."

Maeve frowned, recalling the Dragon Queen.

"There is a problem?" The dragon nudged her arm with his nostrils.

"There is." She faced the dragon again. "I want you to come with us, but you should know that you are not the last dragon."

"I am."

"Yes, the last one born, but you aren't the last one anymore. The Dragon Queen of old has risen. . ."

"My mother's sister. So she survived." The dragon wagged his head.

"She did, and she is free. If you go with us, eventually, she will make an appearance and she is much older, bigger, stronger than you are. I worry that you will lose if you fight against her."

"A valid concern," the dragon mused. "Considering there's not much you know about dragons and even less you know about her. But she will not kill me, instead she will hope to take me prisoner and let the age of the dragons start anew."

Maeve's eyes narrowed. "How do you know all of this?"

"Most of it is speculation," the dragon admitted. "From the ravings of my mother, I gathered what might happen. But you believe she is evil, do you not?"

"I do," Maeve agreed, unsure if the dragon could read her mind or guessed at what she might say. The way it spoke, and the cadence of its speech, reminded her of its mother. She bit back a retort. For dragons were known to be wise, there was a reason they had become one of the most powerful civilizations, in their time.

"Then I will fight with you. Call when you are ready."

"Wait," Maeve called, unwilling to end the conversation. "What should I call you?"

The dragon blew a cloud of smoke out of its nostrils. "My name is Drago."

10

THE GATHERING

Late afternoon a trumpet sounded, the summons to join the gathering of leaders. Maeve followed the brothers of fire to the basement of the tower. They entered a wide, square room where a long table was heavy with roasted meats, smoked cheeses, and fruit of every kind. Maeve's eyes widened as she walked in, taking in the lantern light that cast leaping shadows on the gray stone walls. Harp music filled the room but did not cover the inaudible murmur of voices as others strode in and took their seats. Maeve recognized the leader of the people of the grove, the old woman Mara who had argued with Sandrine, along with mages she'd not met yet.

Maeve sat between Ingram and Imer and watched while light-haired elves with curved, pointed ears and pale eyes took their seats, stern expressions on their beautiful faces. Last to arrive was Jacq the wizard, with Willow, the mage, on his arm. He took his place at the head of the table with Willow by his side. Maeve noticed at the other end of the table, there was no chair. No reason for anyone else to sit at the end in a position of power.

Keeping her thoughts to herself, as Imer suggested, she studied the decorations. Candles about ten inches long stood every few feet on the table, casting a soft glow over the food. Each plate was made of polished silver with a bowl resting on top and a silver knife, fork, and spoon beside it. The goblets were full of wine and looked as though they were made from a fine crystal. White flowers rested in vases, their tiny buds open to the light. Maeve knew they were called winter flowers because they bloomed despite the snow.

Jacq stood as soon as everyone was seated, and a hush fell over the gathering. His deep, magnetic eyes studied every person in turn and when he lifted his arms, the deep sleeves of his rich blue robe fell open, revealing the swirls on his arms. Maeve gasped, surprised that he also had runes inked onto his skin. Although they were nothing like hers, still, they drew her curiosity. Was it a common practice among those who carried magic?

"Greetings, friends," Jacq proclaimed. His voice overpowering the gentle music of the harp. He raised his hands as if in blessing. "A time has come for us to unite, but before we move to discussion, I hope you will enjoy the bounty of Imperia. Unprecedented times arise before us, and we will all need our strength. Eat. Drink. And be merry."

With those words, he took his seat, raised his glass, and took a sip. It was a few moments before those at the table relaxed enough to turn to food and drink. A roasted pig with an apple in its mouth took up one side of the table, and mouthwatering scents drifted to Maeve's nostrils as someone rose to carve it. There was squash, cooked until the skin was soft and fell open with a touch. There were cheeses, some sharp, others soft, and fat red grapes that burst on touch. A warm, spicy soup filled Maeve's body with warmth. She ate and drank with relish, keenly aware of how many good meals she'd missed during her travels.

When at last everyone had settled into conversation, their bellies full, and a dessert, filled with chocolate on a bed of a flaky crust was passed around, Jacq, the wizard, rose to his feet. His very presence commanded a hush, as though he were the king of the city, and Maeve speculated on just how powerful the wizard was and what kind of magic he used. Was he like the dark fae and had magic of a similar kind? Although she did not detect the taint of dark magic, she couldn't help but worry her lower lip between her teeth as he spoke. His voice should have filled her with a comforting calmness. But it didn't. She missed the beginning of his words, and when she tuned in again, her spine went rigid.

"The seven shards have been found and reformed into the Crown of Erinyes. A feat which was commissioned by the dark fae. Long have we known that the dark fae sneak into our world on the night of the full moon, to steal corrupted souls to do their bidding."

Corrupted? Maeve stiffened even further.

"Even though we believe that all can be saved, should they change their hearts, I will freely admit that I have turned a blind eye to the deeds of the dark fae. For it seemed as though they were doing us a favor by ridding the world of those who seek to ruin it. But now the curse upon the dark fae has been broken, and not just their curse, but all curses across the known world. Now that the dark fae are free, we assume they will return to their homeland, the hidden kingdom in the grove. Although they will celebrate their freedom, it is known that they will set forth to conquer, as they once did, hundreds of years ago. Kingdoms fell at their feet as they sought world dominion. And not just any kingdom, but the powerful ones we assumed would never fall. The dragons and the Carnites. Many have speculated why they fell, but we know it was because of the influence of the dark fae, among others. But now they have returned to haunt us, in accordance with the Prophecy of Erinyes:

A day will come when curses will be broken,

the lost shall be found, the found shall be lost,

and the rift between mortal and celestial will cease to exist.

The Dragon Queen of old will rise, freed but hidden in disguise.

The last defender will come forth, and the Sword of Justice will purify.

Silence filled the room as the wizard spoke the last words, and even the music of the harp fell quiet. Maeve glanced at the surrounding faces, lips parted, hearts beating as they waited for more. The wizard stood erect, his shoulders lifted. He raised his hands. "The Crown of Erinyes is in the hands of the dark fae. The Dragon Queen of old has risen. The Gates of Hell are weak, but the last defender has come forth, and with her she brings the Sword of Justice. Maeve of Carn, will you rise?"

The request was unexpected and yet, Maeve wasn't surprised. Stiffly she rose to her feet, and all eyes examined her. Whispers filled the air and hung there. They were curious about her past, what brought her to Imperia and she was sure, what made her the last defender. After she'd had her fill of the stares and whispers, she sat again. Imer gave her hand an encouraging squeeze, but she fixed her eyes on her plate, uncomfortable with all the attention.

"Against her will," the wizard continued, "Maeve of Carn was taken by the dark fae, and we believe this reason to be two-fold. She is a warrior, but she is also the last Carnite. They have had their eye on her since birth. We believe they wanted to get to her first, which is why they assisted in the destruction of Carn, along with the orcs. Maeve had help, though. Sandrine the Scholar, another who was taken by the dark fae, decades ago, served as her guide. Our own fire mages, Ingram and Imer, helped as well, particularly during the journey to the Draconbane Mountains and in the ruins of Carn which have been overrun by orcs. Our scouts have seen movements in the ruins and believe an army of orcs is getting ready to march. To where? We have no knowledge yet, but it is likely their next conquest will be Contresea, the kingdom by the sea, the kingdom of men. If, indeed, the orcs march to Contresea, there is no doubt the dark fae will sense chaos and join them. It will be a bloodbath, and while we have an alliance between mages, elves, and the people of the grove, we must be stronger. As the prophecy proclaims, the rift between mortal and celestial will cease to exist. We hold on to the belief that soon the celestials will return and bring the power of the Divine to fight with us. It is likely the humans will also amass an army, but when the dark fae and the orcs are gone it is unlikely that they will continue to fight with us. Our ultimate goal is to ensure the Gates of Hell do not break and the demons do not surge forth. Many of you are aware the Hunter has risen and seeks our magic with relentless ambition. We have already lost a few to the Hunter, but if the demons of old come forth, only the guardians and the celestials can stand against them. We must be prepared."

Unease hummed through Maeve and she shifted in her seat. She glanced down the table, recalling those she'd seen in Imperia. If they were the ones to stand against the dark fae and the orcs, they'd surely loose. She'd fought the orcs and seen the hidden magic they used, magic stolen from Carn. The humans would not survive against them, or the fae, not unless they had a greater power on their side. But she also recalled the goblins in the Draconbane Mountains and how they had burned when the fire mages fought. Perhaps the fae would fall like that, although they weren't mindless creatures, fighting to save a horde of treasure. The fae were intelligent, with quick wit and magic of their own. But she couldn't imagine what would happen if the celestials returned.

What she'd seen of the Crown of Erinyes, and even the Sword of Justice made her sense their power was potent and dangerous. She was confident that if the celestials fought with the mages, they'd surely win. But what would happen afterward? And where were the celestials?

She'd assumed when the Crown of Erinyes was reformed,

they'd return to the world in glory. It was true she'd spent three days on the back of the firebird, unaware of what happened in the land below, but surely if the celestials were there, she'd have seen a sign. And if not her, then surely Jacq and Willow would know, for they seemed more in tune with the world than she would have expected, hidden as they were in the city of mages.

"Willow and I have laid out a strategy," Jacq went on, his gaze flickering down to his assistant.

Maeve's eyes narrowed as she watched them. Willow sat up straighter, a proud smile on her beautiful face. She was well aware of her beauty, magic, and strength. Maeve couldn't help but wonder if she'd tried to bewitch the wizard. The look that passed between them did not speak of mere friendship.

She sighed, unsure whether she was jealous, frustrated, or wanted more recognition. After all, she was the one who had been forced to hunt the seven shards. She understood that the quest had been dangerous and almost impossible to complete without the knowledge of the Scholar. But if the mages had been willing to go down into the fae Underground, or even find the seven shards themselves, would all of this be happening? They would have control, they would have the Crown of Erinyes.

"But first, as we prepare our armies, we need to take the Crown of Erinyes from the dark fae. We have little to go on, other than the fact that the fae had returned home. They walk in the shadows, they slide through portals, and the Dragon Queen of old is on their side. Maeve of Carn has volunteered to lead this group that goes into the kingdom of the fae. This is a quiet quest, quick and stealthy, but those who know about the kingdom who have explored its hidden ways should go with her. I ask for volunteers to leave in the morning to recover the Crown of Erinyes. We will need its magic if we hope to win this war."

II

DARK FAE

King Mrithun stood in the tower with his eyes closed, arms clasped behind his back. The scent of home was just as it had been, hundreds of years ago, inside the aging castle where he used to dwell. He'd visited it from time to time, each night of the full moon, but it was only a potent reminder of what was, and long ago he'd resigned himself to the dark halls of the fae Underground. But now? Homecoming wasn't quite what he had expected. Instead of a thrill of pleasure he found that he missed the dark.

The sunlight on his face was warm, penetrating, but even in the cool of winter the light touch of heat that, for once, did not burn and flake his skin, was almost too much. Who knew in the years he'd spent away from the light that he preferred the dark. It was potent and powerful, and he could listen to the madness that swirled around him without the light to distract his thoughts.

The scraping of claws came, and he heard the thump as a

beast landed, shaking the ground near the castle with the strength of its power. Moments of silence stretched and then at last came a creak as the door to his tower swung open and closed like a hushed whisper. He opened his eyes, but didn't turn around, knowing what he'd see and torn between scolding or admonishing her.

"You're still wearing it," she remarked as she glided across the room and stood beside him.

He held his neck stiffly, aware the heavy Crown of Erinyes still graced his head. The trouble was, although he should lock it up in a chest and hide the key, he couldn't bring himself to part from it. After the years of patience and planning he would wear the crown, as a reward, as a bonus to the freedom his court experienced. Which is why he'd given them free rein, to go where they desired and do what they pleased. But after three days of celebration, they were ordered to return home. To the castle deep within the grove where only twisted paths and hidden signs would lead. She was the first to return. His queen. He licked his lips and his claws twitched. His dragon queen.

"The crown fills me with power," he told her. It wasn't untrue. The blue light hovered about him, and the radiance inside filled him with a deep sensation that he was invincible. If he leaped from the tower and fell four floors down, he'd land on his feet. If he stood in the midst of dragon fire, the flame would not consume him. And if the last defender, Maeve of Carn, choose to run him through with her blade—the sword of a celestial—he would withstand the pain and heal himself. Curses were broken and magic sang in his veins.

Drakai laughed, a harsh trill as she folded her golden

wings on her back. The smaller wings, the ones she had when she stood in mortal form. Despite himself, he turned and bared his fangs at her. "Are you pleased?" He cupped her chin, leaning closer to taste her.

She gasped as his fang bit her lips, but he licked away the blood as he pulled back, running his claws through her dark hair. Her honey-colored eyes gleamed as she pulled him closer, one of her legs coming up to wrap around his waist. "Pleased does not begin to describe it," she purred. "Let me show you how pleased I am."

She rocked against him, but he held her fast. "Are we ready?"

Pausing, a frown knit the perfect skin of her brow and her eyes darted away from him. "Business first," she spat. "Are we not meant to celebrate?"

He shrugged but inwardly was glad he had taken the upper hand away from her. Just because they'd won one victory meant nothing, they had to stay sharp to win the war. "We are. We won a battle, but you know that Maeve of Carn slipped from our fingers."

The retort died on her lips, for it was she who'd failed. She'd been in the midst of a transformation, and while he understood that she had not cared in that moment, about anyone other than herself, she had to know that her actions could change the course of their destiny. "I burned the Bay of Biscane when I left," she bragged. "I will burn the last defender as well. When she comes, we will be ready. I will personally enjoy raking the flesh off her bones."

"Such violence from your lips." He sneered. "Leave her to me. I shall enjoy displaying the power of the crown."

Drakai frowned. "If you wish it, although fire would be a worthy death for her."

"Her time will come. The assassins are prepared. Now we wait."

"See." Her tongue came out, the tip of it licking his parted lips. "No more business. Come, pleasure me for the first time in your kingdom, as we once planned long ago."

12

Night of Solitude

"What do you think?" Imer whispered in Maeve's ear as the wizard dismissed the gathering.

The comfortable buzz of wine hung in her stomach and she smiled at him, noting how the flecks of gold danced in his eyes. His jaw was covered with day old stubble, and his hand seemed so warm in hers.

"I think we have limited time before we leave again." She wiggled her eyebrows at him. "Earlier you mentioned something about showing me your chamber?"

A rogue grin covered Imer's face at the suggestion. Winking at her, he took another sip of wine and stood. "Aye, follow me. You'll meet our companions tomorrow, although I'm fairly sure I could tell you who volunteered."

Eyes turned toward her as she rose, and Maeve recalled that those who gathered seemed to think of her as a hero. She nodded as she met dark eyes and pale ones. One of the female elves glanced at her, an unreadable expression on her face.

Heart pounding and heat covering her face, Maeve was grateful to escape the crowded room with Imer.

The halls were refreshingly cool, lit by pools of lamplight every few feet. Imer led her through the maze, around corners, and upstairs until he reached a row of doors. “This is the floor where the mages sleep,” he told her. “We each have our own rooms, given to us by the wizard when we decided to study under his tutelage. Those who are unmarried stay here, but those who wish it are free to return to the fields and build a house, as long as they continue to contribute to the city.”

“How long have you called this place home?” Maeve asked.

“Ten years.” Imer scratched the back of his neck. “It seems longer than it’s been, but Ingram and I often grow restless and the wizard likes to send us out on tiny quests, anything to keep us amused. Besides, we are often drawn back to the temple in Isdrine.”

Maeve recalled their time at the temple wistfully. It was the one shining light of relief in her tormented travels, the place she’d learned that she could gain peace and happiness, despite her past. “I understand why,” she murmured as they paused in front of a door.

Maeve’s eyes were drawn to the markings on the wood, and she pointed. “What is that?”

Imer cleared his throat and unlatched the door. “These are the runes that mark this room as mine. I don’t claim to read runes, but the wizard knows them, and marks each room for the mages that dwell here. This rune,” he pointed, “depicts fire and the other rune,” he brushed his fingers over the second one, “stands for wit.”

Maeve smiled and tapped her head. "Because you'd rather use your mind than your hands."

"That's the idea," Imer agreed, touching the small of her back to steer her inside.

While Imer lit a lantern, Maeve studied the room. It was much larger than she'd imagined with a square window on one side. It overlooked the glistening lake which was only a dark shadow under the gloomy lights of night. The window was open, sending a cool breeze in and Maeve shuddered in her shift.

"Close it if you like," Imer said, "I'll start a fire."

Pulling the window shut, Maeve took in the wide fireplace beside the window. Imer knelt on the hearth, stacking a bundle of wood before lighting it with his hands. On the other side of the fireplace, a tidy bed took up a corner along with a series of chests and drawers. On the other side of the room was a table, or rather, a workbench, with wood carvings, maps, pipes, scrolls, and other items covering it. "You do woodwork?" she asked, impressed with his diversity of skill.

"When I have time." He shrugged and stepped back.

The gentle glow of firelight graced the room and gave it a homey glow. Soon the scent of cedarwood filled the air combined with the dried tobacco on the table.

"Would you like a drink?" Imer perched on the edge of the table.

At Maeve's nod, he pulled a pitcher off the shelf behind the table and filled two cups.

"I propose a toast, Maeve of Carn."

She suppressed a snort. "What are we toasting?"

He walked toward her until his chest bumped hers. A

surge of liquid desire went through Maeve, replacing all the awkwardness and indecision she'd felt earlier. She assumed it was merely time and distance that made her second-guess everything. Now she'd warmed to Imer again. Deep in her heart she knew he not only cared for her, but he would have her back, despite the impending war and the hand she'd reluctantly played in its progression.

He angled his head toward hers, his voice low and dangerous. "It is our first, and only night of solitude together. Let's toast to that."

Maeve pressed her lips together, letting the teasing jest die on her tongue. "To us, then."

They clinked cups and Maeve downed the ale in one gulp, tossed the cup on the floor and kissed Imer. Hard. For a mere second he went rigid with surprise and then responded. His cup clanged to the floor and rolled until it struck the one Maeve had dropped moments before. Arms around her waist, he guided her hips backward as he deepened the kiss. Rough, passionate and oh so delicious. Maeve shivered with arousal, her fingers tearing against material, her mouth tasting, biting, refusing to let go.

Imer tangled with her, his hand slipping under her shift and pulling it up. His fingers brushed her legs, thighs, stomach until he broke all contact and slid her out of her clothes. Maeve returned the favor, relishing the glazed need in Imer's eyes as he let her undress him.

The movements were familiar from their time in Isdrine and yet new, as Maeve realized this was the first time she was free, uncollared. As though he noticed, Imer traced a line from her neck to her cheek and then kissed her throat as though his love could burn away the imprint of the collar that lay there. A strangled sound came from Maeve's throat at his passion, and unable to wait any longer, she pushed him down on the bed and straddled him. Moans echoed off the stone as he thrust into her, tasting, taking, giving. They moved together until Maeve felt as though they were one in the glow of a love that would only last for a short time.

13

TWELVE DAYS

"Here we are again." Imer pointed to the mass of darkness that rose in front of them.

Maeve shivered as she stared at the trees of the grove. It was hard to believe that only a few months earlier, she'd stood in the same spot. Only this time, instead of being accompanied by Sandrine, she had Ingram, Imer, Drago and four others.

Seven days they'd traveled, showing Maeve just how close the city of Imperia was to the rest of the world. During the quick, but cold journey, she'd kept to herself, uncomfortable with the stares. Aside from Ingram and Imer there were two elves, a female called Faelyn and a male called Eythin. Nimya and Fin were brother and sister, they were from the grove and knew the hidden paths. Maeve wasn't sure of their powers but understood why they'd come. They represented the alliance between the mages of Imperia, the elves, and the people of the grove. Two from each group had come to assist Maeve in retrieving the crown.

The scouts, Nimya and Fin, spoke in low voices and then moved toward the wood, gesturing for everyone else to wait for their signal. Maeve's fingers twitched with impatience and she paced back and forth, watching the tall trees sway, which seemed to watch her back. A cool mist still hung in the air and the trees were bare. She counted on her fingers. It had been almost twelve days since the shards were reformed into a crown and the world still hung under a cloud of gloom. There was no sign of the celestials and she wondered if they would come as she imagined, beings streaking out of the sky like fallen stars to rid the world of evil. Or would they come secretly...

"I can't just stand here and wait," she whispered to Imer. "I know we have a plan, but I need to go in and see for myself."

"My lady, do you not want the scouts to find the path so you can run into the heart of the fae kingdom?" His eyes fell to her throat. "I thought you worked with warlords, surely you are used to following a plan?"

Maeve frowned at the reminder of Caspian. Would he have wanted this? If he were still alive, where would he have fit in the events that were unfolding? The thought gave her pause, for if he was still alive, she was sure he would have damned her quest, and her decision to move forward with it. Yet, he'd kept many secrets from her, especially regarding the shard. All she knew was that she could trust herself, and Ingram and Imer. Everyone else had to earn it.

"I have," she said. "But that was before all of this

happened. When the crown was put back together, and the collar broke, I sensed something else. Power surged within me, stronger than before. I can't just stand here and wait. I have to fight. It flows through me, it begs me, it's an urge I need to release. And right now, the dark fae are my release. You know what they've done to the world, and to me. I want revenge."

"Maeve," Imer cautioned as he stepped in front of her, as though shielding her from the trees. "I saw the way you looked at the shard when we were in the ruins in Carn. When you get the crown, what will you do with it?"

Maeve paused. Instead of thinking for herself, she was still following orders. Deep inside, she desired the crown for herself, with a knowing she could not explain. But it would not be possible. She looked away from Imer, wondering if siding with the guardians went against the wizard of Imperia and his commands. He wanted the crown returned to Imperia, but it wasn't what she was going to do. Should she trust Imer with her assignment? Would he stop her or was this a chance to test his loyalty?

"I told you I met with the guardians." She bit her bottom lip as she met his curious gaze. "They asked for the Crown of Erinyes." Imer waited, his face giving away nothing. "The celestials sent them to guard the Gates of Hell. If I can steal the crown back and return it to them, they can use it to ensure the gates do not open, and the demons do not escape. It is a worthy cause."

"Worthy indeed," Imer agreed, but a shadow crossed his eyes. "And you told the wizard this?"

Maeve shook her head as a dreadful sensation rose in her.

Had she created a powerful enemy—again—by omitting the truth?

Crossing his arms, Imer frowned and studied the ground. A slow sigh came from his lips. "Maeve of Carn," he muttered. "Trouble follows you."

Maeve wondered if she should be offended with his comment. But Imer took her elbow, his lips close to her ear. "The wizard has seen fit to send us on this quest while he protects Imperia and forms alliances with those who will fight our enemies. Dark fae, orcs, and demons. We need the magic of the Crown of Erinyes to protect us. But all along, you've intended to take it for yourself, sneak off, and deliver the crown to the guardians?"

It sounded as though she were betraying the wizard, even though she hadn't planned on being part of his quest to save the world. Although they were on the same side, they had unique methods. She did not desire to stay in Imperia, hiding and waiting for the enemy to strike. This time, she wanted to be the first, to wipe out the fae and prevent the demons from invading the land. Did Imer stand with her? Or was he loyal only to the wizard? Blinking, she met his solemn gaze. "Aye, that is the truth of it. Will you try to stop me?"

The cocky grin returned to Imer's face. "I hoped you'd invite me to join you."

Relief made Maeve's shoulders sag. "Imer, I don't have much of a plan. My first goal is to get the crown, after that, I'm not sure how to return to the island. All I know is that it is beyond the Sea of Sorrows and the watchtower where the fae Underground is...was. . ." she trailed off, realizing how foolish her plan sounded.

"I have some ideas." Imer ran his fingers through his hair. "After all, the wizard only told us to take the crown, not what to do with it afterward. Regardless, for now, say nothing."

Deception. Maeve shivered and wondered how the wizard would react. If her plan worked and the world was saved from the demons, would the wizard, nay, all the mages of Imperia forgive her?

"What about Ingram?" she asked, glancing toward the other brother. Ingram stood, arms crossed, his gaze flickering between the wood and Drago.

Imer tilted his head and gave it a slight shake. "I'm not sure. He wishes to go defend Isdrine, after our task is done here."

"Alone?"

"We can take care of ourselves," Imer said. "Besides, Isdrine has an army of its own."

Maeve thought of the peaceful temple, the kind priests and priestesses, and the people who lived in the surrounding lands. Dread swept through her. How could they take care of themselves? Although north, the temple lay in the direct path of the orcs, should they choose to march directly to the kingdom.

"I didn't mean Isdrine." She crossed her arms, worrying her lip between her teeth. "I meant, if Ingram goes off alone, he will become easy prey for the Hunter. He's still out there. Isn't he? And in this chaos, he might take this moment to pick us off, should we become heedless."

Guilt edged Imer's eyes. "Actually, that is something I was hoping you'd help me with. We need to rid the world of the Hunter once and for all. My original quest with Ingram was to find the celestial sword. We did, but obviously your need for it was greater than ours. I was rather hoping you'd help me find the Hunter and slay him before he comes after us."

Maeve drew in a sharp breath and her fingers instinctively tightened around the hilt of the blade she wore. "When?" she asked. "After this quest?"

"On our way to give the crown to the guardians."

"Will not the wizard be expecting you?"

The lines around Imer's mouth tightened. "The wizard is not my master. As long as he believes I went after you to get the crown, we shall be fine."

The knowledge hit Maeve squarely in her chest. It was her. She was the one who would suffer the wizard's wrath. But she lifted her chin as the scouts came out of the wood and beckoned with fingers to their lips. The company rose and followed, Maeve bringing up the rear.

14
Fae Assassins

Gnarled branches curled over their heads like twisted fingers as the scouts led them deeper into the wood. This time, there was no anticipation of meeting the people of the grove, and bribing them to turn over the shard. Her thoughts drifted back to the item that Sandrine had given to Mara, the leader of the grove. Maeve wondered if Mara and her people thought of that day with regret, knowing war was coming.

Even though it was winter, the woods were so thick, Maeve could not see between them. The path was narrow, only a trail with barely enough room for them to walk in a row, one behind the other. They moved stiffly, weapons at their sides, shields being used to push aside dead branches as they forced their way through. Drago had flown ahead, claiming he could take care of himself. Maeve had warned him to be careful, worried the Dragon Queen would come for him.

The sound of a stick breaking pierced the silence. Maeve slowed, even though she couldn't see the scouts ahead. She looked up, but the interlocking branches blocked out the light. It came again, a slight rustling and out of the corner of her eye she saw a shape fade in and out of the shadows. "Ingram. Imer," she hissed, hoping they heard her breathy whisper.

Imer paused and tugged on his brother's shirt. They both dropped to the ground, Maeve behind them as an arrow flew out of the wood. A ragged scream filled the silence. One of her companions? A bolt of adrenaline passed through Maeve. She scrambled to her knees and drew the sword. The clang of metal rang out, giving away her position.

A whistling sound hummed in the air and an arrow whizzed over her head, so close she felt the feathers brush her hair. She instinctively ducked, moved into a crouch, then ran into the underbrush, breaking branches under her feet as she searched for their attackers. Branches scratched her flesh and tore at her clothes, like fingers trying to hold her back. Behind her she heard more cries and then shouts of "Take cover!"

More arrows whistled through the wind. An arrowhead sunk into the tree beside her and she saw a vague shape as one of the dark fae moved, weaving in and out of trees and into the shadow world. She didn't think he'd seen her, but she was making too much noise. She squatted behind a tree, gripped the sword in both hands and closed her eyes as the armed assassin drew near.

Sound rushed around her, the thudding of feet, the whistling of air and then she saw the being come out of the shadows, golden bow raised. She spun out of her hiding place, drawing the sword up at an angle. It sank into the belly of the fae and he fell with a howl, crimson blood splattering the neutral colors of the wood.

Wiping drops of blood off her face, she drew the sword out of the body before it collapsed on the ground, and then ran. The next assassin was quicker and shot at Maeve. She had the presence of mind to slap the arrow out of the air, snapping it in half with her blade before ducking behind another tree. She waited, but he did not approach her. She moved again as she dashed toward the second assassin, but he was focused on her companions. He took aim at one of the elves and let his arrow fly.

Maeve swallowed hard and stilled as she watched them, surprised she could see light and dark, the normal world and the shadow world. Blending with the shadows as though it were night, the dark fae flew in and out of the shadow world, some with wings, others with fangs, throwing knifes, arrows, darts, whatever they could to take down the company of mages. Maeve weaved between them, running them through with her blade, slicing off arms, ripping through their defenses until she was lost in the woods and couldn't see her companions anymore. Silence reigned again, but this time it was hushed, whispered as though there was someone, or something else. Waiting. Watching her out of patient eyes. A flicker drew her eye. It wasn't a rustle, but the air of a breath.

She turned and froze.

A woman stood a few feet away, out of reach of the sword, watching her. A halo of hair graced her shoulders, and she wore leather. Her red lips seemed out of place in the dead wood, but her eyes pierced Maeve's with recognition. Maeve took a deep breath. Drakai, the Dragon Queen.

"I came because I was curious," Drakai said.

She placed a hand on her hip, and even in the blended shadows, Maeve caught the glint of claws. Her pulse quickened, and she swallowed to moisten her throat as her fingers tightened on the blade.

"You must be the one they call Maeve of Carn," Drakai went on. "I've seen you fight, and you are worthy indeed. It is no wonder King Mrithun saw your value. It is a shame he had to collar you to gain your loyalty and obedience. You did well, and you escaped. But why come here? Why now? Surely you are not longing for the arms of your captor again?"

A hot rush of awareness went through Maeve at the dark desire Drakai referenced. Her lips went tight with distaste and she almost spat as she addressed the queen. "Nay, I did not come for loyalty or any reason you'd understand. I came to kill you, the king and all those loyal to you. But more importantly, I came for the Crown of Erinyes. By all rights, it belongs to me. I came for revenge. I came to take back what's mine."

Drakai gave a short trill of laughter as she raked her claws down the trunk of a tree. "I thought as much." She grinned, displaying a mouthful of knife-sharp teeth. "I hoped as much. You and I, Maeve of Carn, were meant to fight, one last battle. I'm sure you saw my transformation in the fae Underground, saw my true form, returned to me at last. King Mrithun has his failures, but he kept his promise to me all along, and for that, I am grateful. Which is why I cannot let you take the crown from him."

Maeve barred her teeth. How was she supposed to fight a dragon? The odds were staked high. "You would risk letting the demons run free in this land?" she demanded. "They will turn it into turmoil, they will destroy it."

"Do you think we are stupid?" Drakai snapped. "We studied the texts. We know about the Prophecy of Erinyes, for my fate, and your fate are both bound to those words. We knew about curses, and what would be broken when the crown was reformed. Why do you think we wanted it?"

"Because you are strong enough to beat them?" Maeve couldn't help the question, even as she wondered what, exactly, was in those texts.

"No." Drakai shook her head, a wicked glimmer in her honey-colored eyes. "Because we want chaos. Endless chaos. It is only when the kingdoms of this world are razed to the ground that we will come forth in victory and rebuild."

"I don't want to rebuild," Maeve said. "I don't want endless chaos, I just wanted my freedom, and your actions have made me your enemy. I will not stop until you are dead, and I am free from the threat of your rule."

Drakai pointed a claw at her, unbothered by Maeve's anger. "You seem to forget, that was the point. We wanted to control your power, to see you fight, watch your rage and anger drive you. But now, there's something different about you. You did the unexpected down there in our dark halls, and I only expect something unexpected from you now." She paused, her nose wrinkling as she sniffed the air. Licking a finger, she held it up. "Unexpected," she whispered, so low that Maeve had trouble hearing her. "What did you bring with you?" Drakai demanded.

Maeve took a deep breath to calm her racing heartbeat, wondering if she could run fast enough to drive her sword into the queen while she was distracted.

The sound of branches snapping came from above. Maeve thought she heard the faint whirl of wings. Heart in her throat, she took off running just as a bright shape hurled itself out of the sky. A scream ripped from the Dragon Queen's lips, quickly turning into a manic laugh.

Her eyes turned to Maeve, reptilian and dangerous. The golden wings on her back stretched out, heedless of the tight-knit trees around them. "So. Not only did you go to see my sister," she uttered. A hiss came out of her mouth and she raised a hand. "She left you a present."

Maeve leaped over the bramble and dashed for Drakai, sword out as a rain of twigs and branches poured down on her head. Vaguely she heard someone yelling, but she didn't understand the words as she swung the sword. Above her, she knew Drago was diving, his claws outstretched to rip the Dragon Queen away from where she stood, one hand outstretched.

Victory hung in the air, barely an arm's length away, and time slowed down for Maeve. She drove the sword toward Drakai's stomach, but the queen brought up a skeletal wing to protect herself. Her hand in the air transformed into a claw and she butted Drago away. He fell. Hard. Wings fluttering as they snagged in the woods.

Maeve saw the claw hurling toward her, and she ducked, but not fast enough. The powerful arm of a dragon, hard and scaled, slammed into her head. Her vision was replaced with a white haze, then a searing pain rocked her skull. She stumbled, hand still on the sword, but she could not see as she fell forward. Something heavy landed on her back as she struggled for consciousness. The forest spun when she opened her eyes and at first she thought she was back in the Hall of Judgement. She needed a moment, just a few seconds to recover herself. Already the surge of power within her was bursting forth to provide her with enough energy to stand again.

A hand twisted through her hair and yanked her head up. "Maeve of Carn," came the whispered voice of the Dragon Queen. "I could kill you right now, tell me why I shouldn't?"

Maeve thrust back with her elbow as hard as she could to give herself more leverage with the sword. A satisfying grunt came from the Dragon Queen and she let go. Maeve blinked as the edges of darkness crept away from her vision. She could just make out the blurry figure of the Dragon Queen and raised the sword, cursing herself for not having any daggers to throw. The scent of birch and burning wood rolled through the forest and Maeve forced herself to her feet, although her vision swam. She gritted her teeth. She was a warrior. She could handle whatever the Dragon Queen threw at her. Lurching forward, she swung the sword, but it seemed to arch so slowly.

"You've been warned," Drakai shouted.

She moved, and before Maeve's vision could follow, a block of wood came hurling out of the darkness. Maeve dodged it and stumbled. Reaching for the trunk of the tree to hold herself up, she paused for a moment, letting her senses return. When she stood upright again, Drakai was gone.

Maeve turned around, but the woods were quiet, as though no one had ever been there.

Heart in her throat, Maeve stumbled to the place where the underbrush was thrashed, where Drago had gone down. But he wasn't there either. Cursing, Maeve spun in the wood, frustrated. But she was alone.

15
SHROUDED KINGDOM

"Maeve?"

She pivoted toward Imer's voice and held up a finger, still watching her surroundings. Her head was clearing, and she squinted, trying to see where they had gone. A gaping hole in the trees where Drago had come through let in more light, but the shadows still blended and moved, hiding from each other.

"What happened?" Imer whispered as he joined her.

Maeve quickly filled him in. "And you?"

Imer shook his head, his face set in a grim line. "Nothing but surface wounds."

Maeve cursed. "They knew we were coming."

Imer gave a frustrated nod.

"How close do Nimya and Fin think we are?"

Imer rubbed his forehead with the back of his hand, leaving streaks of soot across his forehead. "Very close. But we could wander in a circle and it could be under our very nose. I smell the magic in the air."

Maeve sniffed. Was that what she'd been smelling? "We can't stop now, especially since they know we are close. Tell everyone to be on guard. We have to go forward."

It was what she recalled from her past missions. Focus on the prize and then deal with what happened when it was over. Something flashed across Imer's face, but instead of waiting for his reaction she pressed on, watching the wood. Soft mist glimmered in the low light and she thought she detected the flicker of wings. Keeping as silent as she could, she crept toward it. While she did not have much experience with magic, something told her if she could find the glamour that hid the kingdom of the fae, like a blanket, she would succeed.

And then she saw it, the edges unfurling. She glanced back for Imer and saw the rest of the company. They crept out of the trees, staying low, their eyes wide as they watched for more assassins.

Maeve waved to get his attention and then pointed at the ground. It was so tiny, just a flicker, but she hoped she was right. Using the edge of her blade, she nudged it. Mist covered her face, cold and clammy, and an odd sensation went through her, almost as though she were flying through a portal again. Her stomach flip-flopped, but she took another step and another until the mist cleared and she walked out into a grassy meadow with a kingdom set on a gently sloping hill.

Maeve's jaw dropped and a surge of anger went through her as she stared. Green grass rose around her feet as though it were spring, or summer. The scent of herbs hung in the air, tantalizing and fresh. Sunlight shone through the gray clouds, warming her cold skin. A castle rose in front of her, gray and wicked, with towers shooting toward the perfect sky. But the aura of it was ominous, a thousand memories trapped within it.

She could almost hear hushed whispers in the grass and see the vague mirror of mist that surrounded the castle. Memories of screams, blood, and terror, rose and faded. She guessed the crown was within and the runes on her arms itched as though they were drawn to power.

Behind her, she heard the audible gasp as her companions stepped across the threshold into the kingdom of the fae. She looked up. But no dragons barred the way, and a wide path led up to the castle.

"Keep an eye out," she whispered to the others as someone passed her the shield she'd dropped earlier. She took it, grateful for a cover, and led the way into the shrouded kingdom.

Maeve stilled her heart as she crept through the blades of grass, some still bowed over with dew. Her eyes scanned the perfect horizon, but there was no sign of flying beasts. What had happened to Drago and the Dragon Queen?

A shadow moved in one of the towers.

"Shields," Maeve called back to her companions, purposefully keeping her voice low.

They retaliated, lifting their square shields, ready for arrows to fly out of the castle. But none came. A nagging sensation rode up Maeve's spine. Something was wrong here, wasn't it? She glanced back at her companions, but Imer shrugged and motioned for her to keep going. She bit her bottom lip as she walked. This silent behavior was unlike the fae. They enjoyed laughing and preening, fighting, and showing off, taking enemies and torturing them in front of others. If they saw a small group stride into their realm, vengeance would come quickly. Wouldn't it? Arrows should fly, fae should flicker in and out of the shadow world, and dragon fire should consume them. But it wasn't.

Dread filled Maeve's heart, and she stopped. "We have to go back," she said, out loud, facing her companions.

Ingram's brow furrowed and Imer opened his mouth to protest, when a horn sounded. Maeve pivoted toward the sound and lifted both sword and shield to ward off what was to come. The sound of drums resounded across the forest, a deep and mellow boom, followed by the sound of marching.

"It's a trap!" she screamed.

"Circle up," Ingram ordered.

"Move toward the castle, if the doors open we can take cover inside," Imer called.

Maeve's gaze shot skyward as she cursed herself for not realizing the game was more treacherous than striding into the dark fae's kingdom and stealing a crown. It would be the first place they'd expect her to look. But if the dark fae weren't home, where were they? Bile filled her throat and her thoughts were torn in two. Would the fae seek to destroy the kingdom of men or the city of mages?

The rhythmic throbbing of the drums continued, and then the double doors to the castle swung wide open. Maeve's fingers tightened around her hilt and she glanced down at her already bloodied blade. *Let them come.* Anger gave way to rage, but she was still taken aback as an army of orcs swarmed out of the castle. Their sweaty bodies were covered in mail and they waved battle axes in the air, thick blades, hatchets, and spiked bats. The stench of their unwashed bodies soiled the meadow and suddenly the brightness of the clear skies seemed nothing more than a mockery.

"Fight!" Maeve screamed, and, without waiting for an answer, dashed forward.

She struck the shield of an orc hard with hers, shattering it, then lopped off the head. Blood spurted in the air as she swung her sword in an upward stroke. It slid into the side of another and she ripped it free, spilling blood and guts as she did so. She sensed an orc behind her and spun, bashing it with her shield. The orc fell back, stumbling into another and Maeve leaped, sword raised as she plunged it through its eyeball. It sunk through and slid into the orc behind it, only nicking it. The creature fell with a howl but Maeve was already up and kept moving, her blade singing as she whirled and kicked, bringing death with every blow. Behind her she heard the grunts of her companions as they fought and the scent of burning flesh filled her nostrils. Eyes stinging from the smoke in the air, she continued her forward fight, slicing and dicing as she went until she reached the broad steps of the castle.

A single row of orcs stood at the top of the steps. Instead of armor they wore long robes of mail, and their eyes glinted with an odd light, as though there was something wrong with their minds. Maeve dashed toward them as they lifted their hands. A memory of what had taken place in the ruins of Carn came back to her and she lifted her shield as a crackling sound filled the air. Balls of light slammed into her shield, one after the other. The impact was hard and solid, as though stones were being thrown at her. She gritted her teeth but couldn't help but cry out against the impact. Even though it wasn't painful, her arm went numb all the way up to her shoulder.

The scent of tainted magic hung in the air, and a curse rose on her lips. She had to be smart. Last time, she'd unknowingly walked blindly into their magic, but this time, she wanted them dead. She knew where it came from, magic stolen from Carn, magic that should have sung in her blood, but she did not know how to use it. Her birthright had been stolen from her and it rang back bitterly. Maeve of Carn. Queen of Nothing. Pawn of the Dark Fae. Once again she'd fallen into their trap and she could almost imagine King Mrithun's evil laugh.

No more. She swore and dashed up the steps, even though another rain of magic slammed into her shield. One of those balls of power smacked into her leg. She tripped and crashed down hard on her shield. A scream tore out of her mouth but she leaped to her feet and hurled herself at the first orc mage.

A gurgling sound came from the orc's throat as it waved its arms, attempted to make another ball of magic. Maeve was quick. She thrust her sword up into its neck and the orc's hands dropped to its side. It fell with a sickening thud and a wave slammed into Maeve's back. Eleven orc mages turned to face her, and she brought up her shield, but not fast enough. She crouched as magic flew around her and her back burned. Pain radiated up and down her spine, but she remained in position, teeth gritted to keep herself from crying out, so they would not see how much they hurt her. Just as suddenly, the storm relented, and she was up on her feet, driving her sword into the side of a mage and slicing off the head of another. She willed her feet to move faster while their power regenerated, but just as she reached the third, those balls of magic brightened in their fingers.

Maeve raised her shield as a wall of flames slammed into the mages. Three of them went down, screaming as flames rode them and the remaining stepped back and turned their attentions to the battlefield. Maeve followed their gaze and saw Ingram, his eyes dark, his fingers charred. He nodded at her before turning, fire glowing on his hands.

Thankful for the distraction, Maeve fought through the remaining mages, slaying them before they could deal out any more damage. When the path to the castle was clear, she glanced at the open doors. They tempted her but she wasn't sure if she should rush in. It was clear the fae weren't there. They were likely laughing into their hands as she went the wrong way, thrown off by her desire for the Crown of Erinyes. She glanced at the castle again and then backed down the steps. They had to leave before something else happened.

The small army of orcs was quickly defeated, and they regrouped among the steaming pile of bodies, chests heaving, clothes covered in blood. Maeve blinked back disappointment.

"We have to go," she pointed toward the trees, where they could still hear the hollow beat of drums.

Imer nodded. "The dark fae fled."

"It is clear they used a portal, can we follow them?" Faelyn asked.

Maeve shook her head. "It's too late for that. I imagine they went to Imperia, if they know the way, to wipe out the mages while they can."

Distressed expressions crossed her companion's faces.

"We need to go," Ingram growled. "Now!"

He sprinted toward the edges of the grove, back to the forest. But before they could leave the dark fae's kingdom, an army of orcs stepped out of the woods.

16
ALARM BELLS

Willow climbed the stairs and opened the hatch into the wizard's sanctum. Together, she and Jacq had rebuilt the glass dome that hung over it, shattered when Maeve of Carn dropped through, covered in golden armor like a celestial herself. She was different from what Willow had expected. She'd thought a warrior would come, bold and relentless. Maeve of Carn was just that, a warrior, but she carried a shadow of distrust behind her eyes. After what had happened to her, Willow could not blame her. But Maeve of Carn had to learn that all those with magic weren't evil.

"Willow," Jacq said, without facing her.

He stood with his back to the door and gazed out over the land. Magic hummed in the room and Willow once again caught that taste of power and deep, undeniable arousal. She wondered if the other mages felt it, the magnetic pulse of power and the way it thrummed when used together. The way it awoke desire. When she and Jacq used power together, it was almost more erotic than the very act of lovemaking. Part of her was torn, for although she longed to use her magic in war, she also wanted nothing more than peace. While she yearned to see Jacq in his prime, using the highest of his power, she did not wish for evil to befall him, even though she'd done enough to become his successor. He'd let her in, partly for her power, and partly because he saw her potential. In her past, none believed she'd amount to anything, but she'd proven them wrong.

"Do you sense it?" Jacq went on.

Willow joined him. He took her hand, clasping it tight in his broad one. A surge of power made her senses tingle and she closed her eyes and waited. The voice of the wind reached out to her, humming a warning. An itch began on the top of her head and her limbs trembled. She couldn't quite see it, but she heard, and she knew.

"They are coming," she whispered, wondering how it was possible.

Imperia was supposed to be a forgotten city, hidden by magic. Yet they came anyway, likely spurred on by the power of the Crown of Erinyes. Instead of fear, excitement raced through her veins. For a chance to fight, for a chance to display their united power.

"Aye," Jacq confirmed. "We must prepare for war. Ring the alarm, have them bring the women and children to the tower, secure the walls. All mages must take their stations and defend Imperia."

"We can take them," Willow said, the hiss of anticipation bursting out of her throat.

"Do you sense how many?" he watched her.

Willow suspected he guessed that her power was growing stronger than his. Closing her eyes, Willow listened again. "No, it is masked, somehow."

Jacq nodded but did not show any emotion. "It is likely that those we sent to the kingdom of the fae are walking into a trap. We need them to return, but perhaps it will be too late for them."

"And no sign of the celestials," Willow finished, disappointment lacing her voice.

She'd thought they would have arrived by now, streaking out of the sky like bright comets, come to save the world from doom. But perhaps they had changed their minds, and the world was past saving. Perhaps they determined to leave the world to its doom.

"Time is of the essence," Jacq lifted his hands. "Ring the bells."

Willow left the sanctum, calling out orders as she went. Within minutes, the tower was a buzz of activity. She ran, peering out to the battlements where the mages took their positions. She went down into the infirmary where the healers prepared, and finally to the bottom level, where the woman and children without magic gathered. There were a few men, elders who joined the women and children. They had food, water, and blankets, enough to last for months if they rationed carefully. Willow praised the Divine that the tower had everything they needed, even if she'd never thought a long siege would happen.

Trumpets sounded and the thump of marching feet dispersed the air. She watched it settle and the scent of ink and scrolls was lost as various kinds of magic swirled through the tower. Tense and ready to be used. Willow picked up her feet and fled toward the wizard's sanctum once again. When she reached it she stilled before she opened the doors and froze on the landing. She had to know.

Stilling her mind, she closed her eyes and called out to her hawk, Kel, who shared her mind. The bird was already whirling around the tower and it flew higher at her request, and then toward the mountains where mist covered the marching army. Clouds blew past her, but her feathers were warm and steady. She blinked, beady black eyes, watching. The vineyards were quiet, the farmland untilled, waiting for the icy breath of winter to blow itself out before the spring planting began. She flew beyond that, to the meadow where the baby dragon had flown as it grew, chasing down deer and goats as it hunted, its hunger endless.

The mountains split, opening into a hidden valley, and that's where they marched, an unending river led by none other than the king of the fae. A crown shimmered on his head, the blue magic luring her closer. She swooped, wondering if it would be easy enough to dip down, to use the element of surprise to snatch the crown off the king's head and fly back to the tower with it. A risky thought though, and instead of acting upon it, she studied the army, quickly realizing it wasn't just fae. Among the flag bearers and half beasts with chains and mail and sword and steel were other creatures, with marks on their helms. A shiver of repulsion went through her. Orcs. Distaste thick in her mouth, she flew higher, and as she did, one white feather broke free. It swooped down, eased by the wind as it drifted here and there. It landed on the arm of the fae king. He looked at it, pausing his mount while he picked it up. Sniffing, he let it go free, and his gaze turned skyward.

Kel wheeled in the air, rising higher, but a flicker just above showed off a shadow that seemed as big as a mountain peak. A musky scent filled the air and then the sound of wings in the breeze. Kel flew faster, using the wind to dart through the air, but the dark shadow above was faster, bigger. It flew in a direct line and nowhere Kel flew was fast enough to escape it.

Willow almost pulled back, terror constricting her heart, but she had to look, had to know for certain who their enemy was. With a cry, she spun just as the mist cleared. Above her flew a monster, with a tough obsidian hide, scales glittering in the low light. Wings beat against the air as though it were nothing, and the length of that lizard-like body stretched away beyond what could be seen.

Kel dived, but the dragon was faster. Lidded eyes opened and pounced. Teeth sank into flesh and feathers. There was a snap and then Willow felt a searing pain, as though someone had snapped her bones in half. A scream ripped out of her mouth and the connection snapped. "Kel!" She shouted, her body trembling as she spun, wild-eyed. But the connection was gone, she was herself again and Kel had been eaten. Anger, grief, and fear moved through her in waves. She burst through the doors of the sanctum, almost hurling herself into Jacq's arms.

"She's here," she moaned. "The Dragon Queen of old is here."

17

ORC ARMY

"Hurry into the castle," Ingram rasped, waving frantically toward the doors.

Maeve paused, unsure what he intended, and then saw why. The army of orcs marched into the glade, and although two lines of them surrounded the castle, another came, weaving through mist and shadow as though they waited only for the opportune moment. As Ingram, Imer, and the others rushed toward the castle steps, Maeve moved into the hall. There was only a short entryway and then a wall of stone. She crept around it, waiting for something, anything to jump out at her from the other side, but nothing did. When she reached the other side of the wall, arched windows let in translucent light and she saw a set of stairs, curving up into what she imagined was the heart of the castle. Halls branched off from the initial court room, too many to count. Were they alone in the castle? Or had the fae left them a nasty surprise.

"Close the doors!" came a cry, and then a shadow of darkness came along with the sharp thump of the castle gates shutting. Maeve wondered how long they would hold, although she could see no way to defend them. Perhaps if they stood at either corner of the walls while the orcs burst through, they could stem the tide and fight on their own terms. But there wasn't a way to hurl fire from the castle and slay them all. Briefly, Maeve's thoughts flickered back to the Draconbane Mountains and the goblins. Ingram, Imer, and Sandrine had defeated the horde, although she was unsure what part Sandrine had played. The Scholar had always held her power closely, never sharing what hidden benefits she might possess. But now Maeve wondered. Was it only fire?

"We have moments to prepare," Ingram said as they gathered in a circle.

Imer stood with his feet apart, studying the court room. His eyes flickered to the passageways. "Are we alone?"

"I haven't seen anyone." Maeve shrugged.

"Listen," the female elf, Faelyn, said. She stood a few inches taller than Maeve, her silky hair pulled back in a long braid. Her hair was almost whitish with a dark yellow tint to it. The color of wild daisies in a field. She wore a helmet and carried a thick spear, carved with designs and a pointed tip at the end. Her pale face was almost bloodless as she spoke. "We need to go above and find a way to stop them that way. It's likely the dark fae left something here. Anything we can find and use to barricade the doors or throw at the orcs will be effective."

"I'll go with you," Ingram offered. For an instant, flames rose from his fingers, then faded.

Nimya balled her hands into fists. "My arrows are spent and I cannot refill until I'm outside. If you can break the magic that binds this place, I can speak to the trees and ask for assistance."

Fin nodded. "Aye, if they assist, there will be a way."

Eythin frowned. His eyes were hard lines, deep-set in his angular face. Unlike Faelyn, he did not wear a helmet, and his light hair flowed across his shoulders. "You will need an incantation, or ceremony to awake the trees, it's still winter and they are deep in slumber."

Nimya lifted her chin. "I am aware, but it is possible. The grove used to belong to my people."

Imer held up his hands. "Let's not argue. The orcs will be upon our doorstep. We will hold the doors, and if, only if, there is an opening, you can make a sacrifice to the trees."

Maeve couldn't tell if he was making fun of them or agreeing. She had her own opinion. It seemed foolish to rely on the trees when she had her strength. It was only an army. With fire and ice and strength, they could take them. Unless. The thought poked at her. Unless the orcs had once again brought more mages with magic she did not understand.

"Watch his back," Imer told Faelyn, pointing at Ingram.

She frowned. "He can watch his own."

"Let's move," Ingram said. "The orcs will be on the doorstep soon."

Ingram and Faelyn ran toward the staircase and Maeve took up her stance on one wall, Imer and Fin behind her.

Eythin and Nimya moved to the other side, and they watched the door, ready. Waiting.

The sound of marching continued, and Maeve counted

her breaths as she listened to the drums and the marching. She squeezed her fingers around the sword and closed her eyes. Her thoughts twisted away to her first job with a crew she did not know. *Guard the door.* They'd said. *Make sure no one comes through.* Then they whisked away to do dark deeds and she'd stood, sword in hand, watching the door. It wouldn't be her first fight, but she hated the wait, the not knowing what would happen. She longed to surge into action, to face her enemy, head-on. Not stand in a corner, waiting for the drums.

Opening her eyes, she pivoted toward Imer. He wasn't in a battle stance but slouched against the wall, fumbling with his pouch of tobacco. Maeve immediately envied his cool approach to battle, the way he stood as though an elf would stride through the door, they'd have a pleasant conversation and nothing else. But when she met his eyes, his gaze went somber.

A thud broke the sounds of marching, and the door shivered. The remaining dust that had been clinging to it from years of disuse gave way. Fine, white powder crumbled across the stone floor. Maeve's eyes shifted toward it and back to Imer. She licked her lips, and he stood tall, eyes on the door as he held out his hands.

Another thud slammed into the doors. And another. And another. Each boom rocked Maeve to the core and beads of sweat trickled down her back. The waiting, the endless waiting was the worst. The doors gave way with a resounding crack and the orcs poured through with a yell. Some of them slammed into the stone wall and backed up, dizzy, as a wave of fire crashed into them.

Nimya lifted her hands, but behind her, Eythin was faster. Bolts of ice shot from his fingers. The orcs screamed and shouted in the fray, but quickly mastered themselves and moved. The heavy scent of musk hung in the air, but Maeve leaped forward, swinging low to take the orcs off guard and knocking them off their feet. She spun, slicing and hacking, her sword rising and falling as though it were a dance and she was the wielder who sang out the music, who kept it going. The orcs darkened the doorstep again and again, and they took them down, until the bodies stacked high and rivers of blood poured down the steps. And in the thick of the confusion, Maeve dared to hope that it would be enough.

18
Hopeless Victory

The last body fell with a thud and Maeve stood still, at last. The Sword of Justice dropped from her slippery fingers, coated with blood and grime, and landed without a sound on the ground. The ringing in her ears would not go away, and her arms were stiff and sore from swinging the blade. Tears gathered in the corner of her eyes, from exhaustion, frustration, or grief, she did not know. She stood in the glade, outside the castle, hating the thought of returning to the house of death.

Two of her companions had succumbed to their wounds. Eythin had fallen, his eyes glazed over as frost covered his limbs. Fin had multiple stabs, and Nimya held his hand and rocked back and forth, wordlessly.

Even though she did not know them, Maeve could not face her companions. For the first time since finding the last shard, she wondered if she'd made the right choice. Chaos had come and death ruled. Worst of all, the celestials showed no sign of coming and she couldn't find the fae or the crown.

The glamour had faded from around the castle. Maeve briefly considered whether they could find traces of a portal, but even if they did, she did not possess the magic to reactivate a portal. The battle had been easy for her, despite the sheer numbers, it seemed her strength increased as the days passed. But she could not be everywhere at once, it was not enough.

Shoulders slumped, she thought of water, and perhaps a brief rest. Turning, she faced the castle. Ingram and Imer were coaxing fire from their charred fingers to burn the bodies. Faelyn paused and put a hand on Nimya's shoulder, acknowledging her grief. Streaks of char and grime and blood covered their clothes, and although they still carried their weapons, Maeve could see the hopelessness in their eyes.

"We should leave," she said, her voice hollower then she'd expected.

Faelyn stepped up, leaning heavily on her staff. She and Ingram had found a perch above to rain down fire and hail on the orcs. Their actions had burned the outer rim of the army, forcing the orcs to retreat or fight desperately to enter the castle. Still, Maeve assumed using magic exerted energy, too much energy, and they all needed to rest. But not here, not in the halls of death where the fae might return at any moment.

Faelyn spoke. "We need to find water so that I can send a message to Imperia."

Maeve glanced at her. Although the elves were nature bound, using water to communicate with others was more of a rudimentary magic. Maeve had seen the scrying bowls in the wizard's sanctum, but thought nothing of it, until now.

Ingram turned to Nimya. "I know you are grieving, but do you know a place?"

Lips tight, she nodded.

Without any more words, they weaved a path through the bodies. When they entered the forest again, Maeve's eyes widened. The impact the orcs had made as they marched was clear to see. A muddy path was strewn with broken branches and bushes and brambles ripped out by their roots.

A heavy tension hung in the air and Maeve felt numb. Her thoughts went back to her first visit to the grove. Sandrine had demanded that they give up the shard, but it wasn't until Maeve spoke up, that they'd changed their minds. And now? Guilt weighed heavy on Maeve's mind. It was too late for the people of the grove. They'd been afraid of the consequences and they'd been right. Maeve, in her desire to be free from the scorn of the fae, had rained down punishment on the heads of innocents. Now the fae were on a mad campaign, for war, for victory, for endless chaos. They weaved in and out of shadow and portal, certain no one could stand against them. Maeve was beginning to wonder if anyone could.

Nimya led them away from the ruins of the forest into thickets and brambles, and finally to a watering hole. A vine hung from a tree and she pulled it, letting down a bucket.

One by one, they used it to dip water out of the pool and splash it over themselves, cleansing the signs of battle away. When at last she was clean, Maeve bent over the pool and scooped water into her mouth, the sweet coldness of it filling her with strength once again. She sat back on her knees and watched as Faelyn knelt on the other side of the pool and began to chant.

Although Maeve could not tell what was happening, she watched, curious about the proceedings. Her brief stay in Imperia was her only knowledge of magic, and she was unsure whether to fear it or learn about it. But the aura of the incantation drew her, and she watched Faelyn's face as she studied what was there. A cry left her lips and she pressed a fist to her mouth, turning away.

"What did you see?" Ingram demanded.

"Imperia," Faelyn gasped, her pale eyes dark with sorrow. "It's been attacked and it burns." A sob broke her voice. "The Dragon Queen of old has risen, and she comes with the flame to crush all."

A curse left Imer's lips and he paced, his fists tight.

"We should never have left," Nimya wailed, her fingers sinking into the mud. "Everything brings us grief and sorrow. None of this should have happened."

Maeve swallowed hard as Nimya's eyes met hers. She was the one to blame, the one to point at when things went wrong, because she hadn't fought to stop any of this. In fact, she'd failed her mission and this was the pestilence cast upon her.

"It's not her fault," Ingram said quietly.

Maeve's lips parted in surprise. She hadn't expected

Ingram to defend her. And a surge of anger went through her, nor did she need him to.

"We all wanted this," Ingram went on. "We knew it would turn to war, but the idea of war and the reality of it are quite different from what one expects. Sorrow lingers, like something that can never be let go of. But we have a choice, to let ourselves wallow in grief, let it take over our lives and lead us, or we can put it behind us. What we do next is of vital importance. We were saved from Imperia's burning for a reason, and perhaps there are others who were saved as well. Hope is not crushed on the edge of a knife. Yes, we were taken by surprise, beaten down, but this is only the beginning, our first battle. If we let ourselves fall this quickly, lose hope this easily, we shall never win the final war. So take tonight, cast your cares down, grieve, rant if you must, but when the morning comes, leave your sorrows behind. We have a task, a quest, a mission. We have the last defender and the Sword of Justice, and perhaps, even the celestials. We need the Crown of Erinyes, and if it is where the dark fae are, we will find them."

Maeve's jaw dropped as she studied him. Ingram was hard, unrelenting, and full of surprises. She sat back on the bank, realizing he was right. This was only the first battle. "We will go to the kingdom of men," she said firmly. "The dark fae will want to crush all kingdoms, and it is next."

Ingram met her eyes and nodded. "Onward then."

And once again, hope pierced her heart and she hardened her hands into fists. She would not give up or give in, not now. Not ever.

19
BATTLE STRATEGY

The days were calm as they traveled, hearts beating with an unnamed panic. Each day they lifted their eyes, searching for the black dragon who ruled the skies with flame. And at night they huddled together without a fire, using each other's body heat to stay warm. They slept in turns with at least one keeping watch for what might come.

Ingram pushed them hard, running during the day and resting for brief stints at night, each taking turns keeping watch. Sometimes, Maeve thought she caught a glimpse of a shadowy figure following them. The Hunter? If so, she'd gladly welcome the opportunity to run him through with her blade. Although a chill went up her spine as she recalled the tales of the Hunter, the Gates of Hell, and the likelihood that demons might be worse than the Hunter.

As they traveled, Maeve waited, heart in her throat, for signs of Drago. One day when she heard the beating of wings and saw a flash of orange in the sky, she almost wept with relief.

"Drago!" she called, running to him. "I was worried, what happened?"

Drago perched on the ground and wagged his head while folding his wings on his back. "I sensed your concern, even from afar," he said, a low rumble in his throat. "The Dragon Queen chased me through a portal which is why you could not find me. We returned to Imperia and that's when the attack began." He dropped his head. "They fought bravely, but Imperia was overrun. I stayed to help as much as I could, but the wizard bade me return to find you. He is headed to Contresea with those who escaped the siege."

They had escaped. Warring feelings twisted through Maeve and she nodded. "Good, we are headed to Contresea as well. And what of the orcs, did you see any as you flew here? We were attacked by a detachment in the kingdom of the fae, but they seem to have vanished now."

"A large force marches toward Contresea," Drago said. "The wizard believes the city will fall if we do not arrive in time."

Maeve clenched her hands into fists. If they arrived in time, she could find the Crown of Erinyes. She nodded at Drago and sat down. "I need to think."

"Think." Drago nodded. "But not too long. The city is near."

Maeve crossed her legs as she sat in the dust, watching her companions build a bonfire. "It's just that I can't figure out how to get close enough to the fae king to take the crown," she puzzled.

"You spent time with the fae and know their habits, yes?" Drago asked.

Maeve shook away unpleasant memories. "Time, yes. But I wasn't studying their habits. If I could be like them and make myself invisible, slip in and out of the shadow world, it would be easier."

"Think on it," Drago advised and spread his wings. "I must hunt."

It wasn't until he was nothing more than an orange dot in the sky that Maeve realized she'd forgotten to ask him one pertinent question. The thought occurred to her time and again, if the Dragon Queen could shift from dragon, to human form, why couldn't Drago?

Standing, Maeve walked farther away from her companions, mulling over the crown. Finally, she knelt in the dust, surprised to taste hints of spring in the air. Closing her eyes, she whispered a prayer to the Divine.

Comfort warmed her body as she prayed, and when she finished, unclasped her hands and rose, a thought came to her mind. It was no more than a whispered hush. She had an idea of how to find the crown. But she needed to be alone. Would her companions agree to her plan? She thought not, and although she did not want to leave them in the wild, it was necessary. She knew, for certain, the dark fae wanted her dead, but they would not come for her if she were surrounded by mages.

It was not that she wanted to leave but she knew she had to do something to halt the fae. Especially since Imperia was gone.

Returning to the bonfire where meat roasted she stood,

looking at her companions. Imer handed her a portion of meat and she squatted as she ate it, keeping her eyes on the flame. "We are close to the city, and I need ideas on how to get close to the fae king and take the crown. But before we go on, I'm warning you, it is something I need to do alone."

"Why?" Faelyn tore strips of bread and placed them in her mouth, chewing slowly.

Maeve took a bite, wondering how to explain the sensation that sat heavy on her heart. "It will be easier to take the crown if the fae are distracted." She said finally, the words rolling off her lips. All the years of fighting with others had prepared her for this moment. "War is in the air, we can taste it. If the fae are in Contresea, they are in the heights of blood lust and magic. We can only hope after their victory in Imperia that they are distracted and will not be as cautious as they once were. I will find a way to disguise myself, or hide as I slip past their defenses. They might notice a few, but one can get through. I will find the king and take the crown, but I need to escape, and quickly."

Ingram grunted and crossed his arms, cheeks bulging as he ate.

Maeve ignored him and continued. "I need your ideas for a strategy, how to escape. Originally, I'd hoped to use a portal, but even if we find a Master of Portals, the fae could follow us through."

Nimya nodded, her brow furrowed. "Kill the king," she said at last. "With the king dead, the fae will need to regroup."

"True," Maeve puzzled. "But I'm more worried about the

Dragon Queen. If she is there. . ." She shook her head. How could they defend against dragon fire?

"I will distract her," Drago volunteered.

Maeve blinked at him. She opened her mouth to protest, but there was no other way. The Dragon Queen had had a chance to kill both her and Drago, and they were still alive.

Imer broke a bone and tossed it into the fire. His dark gaze met Maeve's. "You are the last Carnite, if you wear the crown, the power will flow through you. After all, it is in your blood to rule."

20
SHADOW WORLD

It is in your blood to rule. The words stayed with Maeve as they traveled. As soon as they were in reach of the city, they parted ways. Drago to search for the Dragon Queen, and Ingram, Imer, Faelyn, and Nimya to search for the army. Maeve was left alone with her thoughts, left alone to enact her plan to kill the king and steal the crown.

Magic sang in her blood. The realization washed over her and visions of her past flashed before her eyes. The soldiers in Carn, the crown with the ruby stone her mother had pressed into her hands. Its significance had been lost on Maeve all those years, but now she pulled the band from her head and studied the ruby. At first it seemed just a jewel, but as she turned it she saw a glimmer, a shimmer of power, untapped, untouched, bottled behind it. She'd treasured it all those years because she'd assumed it was all she had left. A token of Carn, a relic of who she once was. Daughter of the king, Princess of Carn, Queen of Nothing. Her heart beat faster as she ran her fingers over the stone, searching for a sign, a clue that would assist her.

An itching sensation made the hair on the nape of her neck stand up straight, and her body hummed with need. Her breath came short and fast as the runes on her neck and shoulders swirled. She hadn't known, how could she have known? There were no memories of the stone and the sleeping power it carried. No one had ever tried to steal it from her.

It was a risky gamble, but she had to know, even if she ruined the only token she had of her past. She placed the crown on a stone and drew the Sword of Justice. She positioned the tip over the stone and froze. How could she do this?

Beads of sweat trickled down her face and the muscles in her neck went tight as she gritted her teeth. What power of Carn would be released when she plunged the sword into the stone? She squeezed her eyes shut, reminded again of her mother's embrace, and then the earthquake that shook the kingdom, bringing it to its ruin. Again she recalled the smoke, the screams, and the terror as people ran, and the soldiers came. But this time, it wasn't simply the kingdom of Carn that was being taken down. It was the entire world. First Imperia. And now the kingdom of men. What would fall next if she did not take a risk, take a chance and stop it all?

Her fists tightened around the sword and she plunged it deep. For a moment, she thought it hadn't taken, but then the ruby gave way and liquid poured out. It rose like a sacrificial fire, the smoke stinging her eyes as she breathed it in. She coughed as sensations rode through her, fire, ice, but more importantly a knowing, pure and true. The world faded around her, turning into a shadowy semblance of itself. Maeve blinked as she held out her hand in front of her. It waved back and forth as though she were under water. But she wasn't. What was this? Could it be the shadow world?

She turned and a sense of urgency filled her. The city was burning and she had to find the fae king before he stepped through another portal and left her behind. Before she set off, she swept the broken shard of the ruby into an inner pocket and placed the crown back on her head. Hefting her shield on one arm, she set off at a run.

The hills and pastures flew by on either side, nothing more than a blur. Even the shouts and cries of war, the clash of blade and shield had faded, as though they were far off. She was dimly aware that she ran by people fighting, and yet no one saw her, as though she were invisible. She followed the river of blood, weaving in and out of battle, ducking from arrows. Everywhere the fae fought, their mad laughter adding fuel to her fire of revenge.

When she reached the city, a horned creature leaped into her path and swung. The blade bouncing off her shield. A snarl left the creature's lips and it tried again, but Maeve drove her sword in and out, aware the fae who were in the shadow world could see her. The power drove her on with a frenzy she did not comprehend until at last she reached the middle of the city, the king's tower. Far above stood King Mrithun. His arms were outstretched, as though he were the one who ruled the wind and commanded the waves. Perhaps he did, she couldn't be sure. His hands moved and Maeve hurled herself through the door of the tower before the gate-keepers could sound an alarm.

Bodies were strewn across the staircase, some face down, others face up, but all dead. Bodies had been hacked apart, arms and legs mangled in a devastating array of death. Hatred seethed through Maeve as she ran, and the words burst from her lips: *No more.*

She increased her speed, determined to take King Mrithun by surprise, it was her only hope, her only chance to snatch the crown off his head, to repay him for what he'd done to her.

The tower was high and the curving staircase went on endlessly, but Maeve pressed on, her breath coming in gasps as she felt the first edges of the shadow power begin to fray. *No*! Her mind screamed at her to hurry and she pushed forward, ignoring the burning sensation that crept up her legs like flame taking to a wood.

When she reached the top, a circular platform kept her from falling over the edge. The wind was strong and she sensed the tang of sea spray in the air. In the distance she could just make out ships, their sails aflame. But other than fire, there was no sign of the Dragon Queen. Maeve dashed around the circle and almost stopped short when she saw King Mithrun. His back was to her and the Crown of Erinyes glimmered on his head like a beacon. She only had one chance, a very small one before he sensed her presence and turned to face her.

Dropping her shield to free her hand, she pressed on, leaving her thoughts behind and giving into warrior instinct. She ran up behind him and leaped, one hand stretching out for the crown while she held the sword across her body. Her fingers closed around a hard, cold shard just as the fae king turned. A claw swiped the air, ripping through the bare flesh of her shoulder. Frissons of pain clouded her mind but her reflexes carried her through.

She tugged. The crown tore free. But it was much heavier than she expected. Her arm swung back and she lifted her blade as a snarl burst out of King Mithrun's throat. He lifted his fingers, but she was collared no longer, he could not steal breath from her body. His backhanded assault knocked her off balance. She tumbled toward the ground—unwilling to let go of the crown or the sword to catch herself. She kicked, knocking King Mithrun down with her.

His elbow landed in her unprotected stomach and she grunted in pain, then lifted the crown to smash it across his head. He didn't react to it, only moved until his body weight trapped her legs and those claws came out, deadly and dangerous, to rip her flesh away. She brought up a hand to protect her face and his claws slashed through her arm. Bright red blood dripped out and Maeve screamed, more in fury than in pain. Her sword was facing the wrong way. Regardless, she brought the butt of it up. There was a satisfying crunch as the bone under his chin broke and Maeve lashed out again, breaking his nose with a sickening twist.

A snarl broke from his lips and Maeve pushed against him as hard as she could, trying to free herself. The dangerous glint in his eyes made her want to hurry. The shadow world drifted away, leaving her in daylight, all her senses writhing at the pain which billowed through her.

"King Mithrun," she said through clenched teeth. "I

resent what you have done to me and I defy your wishes." The blade twirled in her fingers until the edge pointed right at his heart.

Even as claws closed around her throat, Maeve drove the blade upward, into his heart. "Die," she said, "like the beast you are. I take my revenge and I will undo everything you have done to this world, to my people, and to me."

She twisted the blade. A low moan and then a choking sound came from the king. His fangs curved up and his jaw went slack. His eyes remained open in his hideous face and Maeve lay still, panting.

She'd killed the king and stolen the crown.

21

HUNTER'S FIGHT

A surge of relief flooded Maeve as she caught her breath, her bloody fingers still holding the crown up. Rolling to her side, she stood, glanced at King Mithrun's body, and spat. Her fingers tingled as vengeance swelled in her breast. She, Maeve of Carn, had single-handedly destroyed the king of the fae. A cruel smile covered her lips as she took his place, standing on the top of the tower, overlooking the battle between fae, mages, human and orcs. The screams and shouts of the dead and dying rang in her ears, now that her hearing had returned to normal. Flame flickered and smoke billowed.

The Sword of Justice dropped from her fingers with a clang as she used both hands to place the Crown of Erinyes on her head. Her runes tingled, her breath caught and her pulse pounded widely as the celestial relic formed to her head. The tingling increased, burning through her body while her fingers shook. Waves of magic poured into her like a cold river and fullness came to her belly. As she removed her fingers from the crown, she thought she might shatter with the weight of what she held. The current of magic continued, twisting into her and winding tighter and tighter until her breath came short as though she were on the verge of explosion. The scream that burst from her lips was wild and hoarse, like the cry of a beast, and not herself. Her vision went hazy and an intense pain rolled through her as the magic exploded.

A blue wave erupted from her body and surged across the kingdom, shaking foundations, snuffing out flame and flattening every solider, every warrior, every mage who dared stand on the battlefield. Maeve was thrown violently against the unforgiving stone of the tower, and she heard a sickening crunch as she landed. Shapes blurred around her and then there was nothing.

A SLURPING SOUND WOKE HER. As consciousness returned, a wave of pain washed over her. Her ears rang and she arched her back, holding back the cry of pain. Every muscle in her body ached, but the pressure on her chest gave her pause. Something was on top of her. But what?

She blinked against intense light as her blurred vision cleared but only saw a vague darkness rising above her. She tried to kick out, but her legs wouldn't move and were heavy, as though something were on top of them. She wiggled her fingers and tingles of pain shot through her. This wasn't right. She had the Crown of Erinyes, she had magic. Who dared restrain her?

Relieved she could move her arms, she reached out, fingers stretching blindly for the Sword of Justice, unsure where she'd dropped it. Around her head she still felt the pressure of the crown yet her vision had not recovered. Squirming, she continued to reach, and a hand closed around her neck. Pressure built and she squirmed, straining harder for the sword just as her vision cleared.

She choked on her own spit and her cheeks bulged as the hand pressed harder. Above her loomed the dark shape of the Hunter. Despite the light, his face was hooded, a pit of endless darkness, and his boney fingers gripped her throat, squeezing as she struggled. Now her restriction made sense, for he sat, pinning her legs while his bulk hovered over her, holding her down.

Questions raced through Maeve's mind and she struggled widely as panic took over. She strained against him, trying to buck him off. But he wouldn't budge. Her eyes rolled back in her head as she struggled, all the while his hands tightened around her neck, choking away the pure air, her last breaths. She kicked as best she could, aware that she was using up too much energy in her panic. But evil pinned her down and the Crown of Erinyes plus her strength seemed to be no match for the Hunter.

Her grasping fingertips landed on steel, and hope fluttered in her chest. The sword. It had to be her sword. She reached again, fingers dragging across the hilt and inching it toward her, just as Hunter leaned forward, cutting off her breathing. The world spun slowly as the darkness closed around her, and an intense smell filled her nostrils. Death, decay, and much more. A tongue licked her cheek, drooling slowly down her face as though he could taste the magic on the pores of her skin.

Maeve gritted her jaw and made one last reach. Her fingers closed around the sword. She swung it up and drove it into the Hunter's heart. The sword sank through, coming out the other side.

At first, nothing happened. The fingers tightened around her neck and Maeve's mouth opened and closed, gasping for air that did not come. Her nostrils flared and then a roar came, quickly turning into a high keening sound as the Hunter rolled off her. He landed on his back and the sword scrapped against stone with a sickening screech. Maeve coughed and gasped, one hand going to her crushed neck.

She sat up, even though her body protested and rolled to her knees. The Hunter writhed on the ground and smoke poured out of his chest where the sword was. Maeve reached out a hand and then stopped herself, eyes wide as she watched. The high pitched screaming sound went on and on until she wanted to cover her ears, but the Hunter continued to thrash as his body disintegrated. Maeve watched him burn until his body was nothing more than ash and the Sword of Justice clanged down unto stone.

Cold fear gripped Maeve. What had happened to Sandrine had just happened to the Hunter. What power did she carry? With trembling fingers she picked up the Sword of Justice and sheathed it, then snatched the Crown of Erinyes off her head. What a fool she'd been, enchanted by a lust for power, a power she did not understand nor could control. Now she understood why the crown had been destroyed, mortals, nay, not even immortals should have a power to rule others through such impossible magic.

She ripped off King Mithrun's cloak and wrapped the crown in it, then turned to the stairs of the tower and limped down them.

22

GOOD AND EVIL

Maeve staggered down the stairs and ducked under the arch of the tower. The silence after the battle was almost haunting, and numbly she took in the faint murmur of waves and the flicker of tiny flames, fighting to stay alive even as the sea breeze blew them out. Death and destruction left the great kingdom of men in nothing but shattered ruins. Aside from the tower, nothing else stood tall.

Maeve took in the crumbling buildings, their foundations still secure, and the dust that covered the ground. The cobblestone roads were paved with rivers of blood, and everywhere she looked she saw the dark fae. They lay, strewn among the rubble, as though the fall of their great king had ruined them all. Even though she should have been rejoicing, Maeve limped numbly onward, glimpsing soldiers from the kingdom, mercenaries who fought with them, and more upsetting, women and children who died defending themselves, weapons in hand. Memories flashed through her mind, although she tried to push them away, regretting that she'd remembered when it was easier to forget. The Kingdom of Contresea looked like the ruins of Carn. The dark fae had done their worst, and even though she'd tried her best, she was still too late to save anyone, other than herself.

When she reached an open marketplace in the city, she slumped to her knees. Leaning back on her heels, she lifted her face to the skies. "Why, Divine One?" She begged. "Why this? Why this death and sorrow and destruction? Why didn't you stop this from happening?"

Her shoulders shook with emotion and as tears filled her eyes the dense darkness of the clouds parted. Beyond the gray she glimpsed blue skies, white clouds, and the glimmer of yellow, like the twinkling of stars.

Maeve blinked, not understanding what she saw as the glimmer grew brighter, like a falling star. Her heartbeat quickened and she stood to her feet, mouth dry as she watched. Were the celestials coming?

But. . .hope rose and died within her. It was too late, wasn't it?

She quickened her pace, searching as she went and losing her way more than once. There was no place left untouched in the city and the ball of guilt twisted tighter and tighter in her gut, until she reached the gates.

Although they had been bashed in the walls stood firm, chipped, and crumbling in some areas. Beyond the gates Maeve saw a muddied field with white and blue tents covering the hill just outside the city. Her heart lurched and she dragged herself forward.

Crossing the ground she saw people moving around the

tents. Someone saw her and pointed, and a shout went up. Survivors. There had been survivors after all. But who were they?

Maeve moved faster, aware of the grime that covered her body. A woman left the tents and strode toward her, a carved blade at her side and curly black hair blowing in the breeze. Her sharp amethyst eyes took in Maeve and she hurried forward. "Maeve of Carn."

"Willow?" Maeve returned, surprise bringing her to a stop.

"Praise be to the Divine, we thought," she shook her head and paused before Maeve, as though she'd like to hug her.

Maeve clutched the crown to herself. "Where is everyone? Who survived?" she begged, her thoughts flickering to Imer, Ingram, Faelyn and Nimya.

"Come," Willow nodded. "Those who escaped the burning of Imperia are here. The healers are taking care of the injured. Come, and rest. You should see a healer once they are finished with the life-threatening wounds. Besides, the wizard would like to hear your tale."

Maeve swallowed the lump in her throat, noting the way Willow's eyes lingered on the crown. Would she and the wizard try to take it from her? Hesitantly, she followed Willow into the encampment.

Maeve washed in the privacy of one of the tents. It was little more than a simple structure, with a wash bucket and cloth. Stripping out of her soiled clothes, Maeve poured the bucket over her head and washed out as much blood as she could. The stench of death seemed etched onto her skin and no matter how hard she scrubbed at it, it clung, unwilling to come free. Using a brush, she scrubbed at the dirt and blood under her fingernails. There wasn't anything else to wear, so once again she pulled on her short shift, breastplate, and sword.

She'd forgotten her shield and hadn't had the presence of mind to snatch it up when she left the tower. Her fingers went to her neck and felt the marks where the Hunter had pressed against her skin. There wasn't a mirror, but she knew it was rough and red, yet she couldn't hide. Holding her head up, she braided her wet hair back, thankful that at least it, her breastplate and sword were clean. Free from the remnants of war, even though low moans and hushed cries surrounded her.

Ducking under the flap of the tent, she stepped out, once again, into daylight. Blinking, she flashed a glance toward the skies, searching for the twinkle she'd seen. The words of the priestess in Isdrine came back to her, the words of the Divine. People were given free will to live as they wished, to do as they pleased which ultimately led to corruption. But out of free will was born the purest love, devotion, and strength.

"Maeve?"

Imer's quiet voice made her pause and her determination crumbled when she met his eyes.

One of his arms was in a sling, and although he looked weary, there was a spark in his eyes.

His gaze flickered to the object wrapped in the cloak and he glanced from it back to her. "Is it. . .?" he trailed off as though the words were too potent to say.

Pressing her lips together she nodded, holding back just a moment before falling into his arms.

He pressed her close, holding her tightly and she leaned into his strength, both relieved he was still alive and frustrated that she cared so much.

Wasn't it what the mercenaries warned against? Relationships that made you care were a weakness, for others could use them against you. But not if they were part of the same raiding party. The truth warmed her body while she held him, pressing her face against his neck and breathing in. He was steady, dependable. He listened to her and more than anything, she wanted him by her side during the war. She was used to being alone and frustrated, with no one to rely on. Yet he showed up again and again, without judgement or reservations, regardless of her frustration, her anger and, most importantly, her mistakes.

Perhaps his love for her was a reflection of the Divine, that relentless love that saw past all mistakes, that offered forgiveness and second chances when no one else would. Her hardened warrior exterior was giving way under his love and she was beginning to see the world anew, through his eyes.

"I thought. . ." he trailed off again, as though emotion choked his words. "When we saw the explosion I thought there was no way you would survive it."

She squeezed his uninjured arm as she pulled back and gave him a slight smile. "Haven't you heard? I'm Maeve of Carn, I did not come this far to fail."

"I know." His fingers stroked her throat, his face tight. "What will you do now?"

Maeve sighed. "I shouldn't have done it. I shouldn't have put the crown on. Its power is too strong for me. There's a reason why the shards were never put back together and now

I understand why. I have to go to the Island of Hades and give it to the guardians. They will know what to do with it."

Imer nodded, his eyes grave. "I'm coming with you."

Maeve pulled back and studied Imer's face. His skin was pale and there were circles under his eyes. For the first time she understood the toll that war and endless battle took on others. Especially those close to her. It was unfair to ask him, nay, to allow him to come further into the darkness with her. She shook her head. "No Imer. You don't know what it is like to be on the Island of Hades, where the rubble turns to shadow creatures. They won't relent, not even for fire. For a great volcano stands there and rivers of lava pour out. They aren't afraid of fire and brimstone, they are like the Hunter, pure evil." She shivered.

Maeve did not realize she'd instinctively brushed her neck until Imer touched her fingers. "Did the king of the fae do this to you?"

A flash of rage crossed Maeve's face.

Imer flinched but did not let go.

"No. It was the Hunter. The wave of magic must have called him," Maeve shuddered. "I passed out and when I woke he was sucking on the fae king's dead body, and I was next."

"He is dead then," Imer confirmed.

Maeve nodded. "This is too much, Imer. Too much grief and sorrow and pain. It reminds me of the last days of Carn. When the soldiers came, and the orcs, and the fae, and all was lost in one horrific night. Soon the world will look like this, and I cannot let it be so."

"But the fae are dead, I saw it," Imer protested.

Maeve sighed and a heaviness made her shoulders slump. "All of them?"

Imer pressed his lips together. "We can't be sure, but it seemed the wave of magic killed them all."

In her heart, Maeve hoped it was true. She blew out a breath. "The orcs still run wild, raiding and pillaging, I assume. And the Dragon Queen is still out there, bent on revenge but where, where is she?"

Imer shrugged, grimacing when he moved his bandaged arm.

"We don't know, but Drago has returned."

"Will you take me to him?"

"Follow me," Imer agreed.

Maeve fell in step with him as they weaved between the tents.

"What happened to your arm?"

"I wasn't as diligent as I should have been, watching my surroundings. One of the orcs snuck up and twisted it behind me before I could kill him. I fared better than many."

Maeve raised an eyebrow. "Snuck up on you? That doesn't sound likely."

Imer's tone dropped. "The orcs brought more mages with them, I don't know how or why, but the magic keeps flowing from them. We took out as many as we could."

"And where are the orcs now, I did not see any when I left the city."

"They fled when the wave of magic came, but if they return tonight we shall be woefully outmatched."

Maeve frowned. "Who is keeping watch?"

"The army has been decimated, not many are left. The mages are weak and have exhausted their magic."

Maeve stuck her tongue in her cheek. The remaining mages needed protection from the orcs, they needed a tower, a city, food, water, supplies. The winter rations had likely been destroyed, food was low, what would they do? But she had an inkling of an idea. The wizard would want the Crown of Erinyes, he would seek to use its magic to put all wrongs to right. Should she let him? But it would only delay her journey to the Island of Hades, and what if the Gates of Hell had opened and the demons were leaking out into the world? There was no way to tell until she went and discovered for herself. And who was to say that after she closed the gates using the crown, it could not be used again.

But in her heart, she knew the guardians would ensure the crown was shattered.

"I sense your conflicted heart," Imer said as the row of tents ended. "You are too hard on yourself Maeve, you saved us all back there by taking the crown."

Maeve tugged his wrist, pulling him to a stop. She bit her lower lip and gazed off at the horizon. "I know that's what you think, but when I saw the crown, a compelling desire overcame me. I wanted it, like nothing I wanted before, and my entire body responded to it. It was a feeling I felt before, when we found the shard and the sword in the temple of Carn. The runes on my skin sang, and my blood felt it, this magic, it means something to me. Something much more than just power and domination. With it, I can see like I've never seen before, I can feel like I've never felt before. My heart belongs to the magic and it overrules all logic. I put the crown on my head as though I were a celestial myself, as though I were one who would rule, and all I wanted was more. The darkness in my heart crept up again, that lust for power and to control the fate of all. When I look at the crown, I lose myself in it. Despite the pain and humiliation I suffered when I was collared, I learned many lessons: how to have empathy for others, the strength of my feelings for you, and what it feels like to let go of selfish concerns. I care about the fate of the world, not just for myself, but somehow, the crown corrupts it all. . ."

Maeve trailed off and shrugged. She held up the crown, still hidden under cloth. "I can't look at it Imer. I don't think all curses were broken because the Crown of Erinyes is good. I believe it's because it drew all that darkness into itself, into those shards, and a malevolent power seeps beneath it. I am not worthy, no one is worthy. The celestials need to come down and deal with this." Her gaze flickered back to the sky. "But why don't they come? Where are they?"

"Perhaps because we never asked." Imer glanced toward the sky. "Have you noticed, the clouds are finally clearing?"

"I saw light in the skies," Maeve agreed.

"Perhaps the tides have turned and they are coming after all," Imer said. "The celestials aren't like us though, they will move in their own time."

Maeve nodded, glancing at the sky once more, trying to catch a flicker of golden light. A foreboding sensation told her something more was happening, something she did not understand yet.

23
GATHERING OF KINGS

The white flap of the tent moved. Maeve's fingers relaxed on her sword hilt when she saw Imer's handsome face poke through. His eyes were calm and he offered her an encouraging smile. "It's time," he said.

Maeve nodded, swallowing to keep her nerves from showing on her face. Gingerly she picked up the tightly wrapped Crown of Erinyes and tucked it under her arm. Despite being wrapped in the thick cloak, the proximity of the relic to her body made the runes on her skin itch, as though they longed for magic to fill them. Maeve's jaw clenched tight. *Never again.*

Ducking outside of the tent, she joined Imer. He'd taken time to clean the mud off his boots, his pants and tunic had been washed. No signs of blood and battle showed on his clothes. Tucked into his belt were two knives and he wore his cloak over one shoulder, hiding his injury. Once again, a hat adorned his head, concealing his pointed ears. He glanced at her under the brim of the hat and touched her wrist. “Are you okay?”

Maeve felt disheveled next to him. She tried and failed to relax her tight shoulders. “I’m nervous, is all. We are in the middle of an encampment that grows daily. If we should disagree on what should be done with the crown, it will not be easy to escape.”

A sly grin crossed Imer’s lips, but Maeve didn’t miss the guarded look in his eyes. “This is naught but a peaceful discussion, we will not come to blows.”

Maeve shrugged but offered nothing else. In her experience with warlords, tempers ran high after a heist or battle. Arguments about treasure, how to divide it, and where to store it often led to blows. It was wise to carry a weapon and have a plan should the discussion go against Maeve’s personal plans.

Self-consciously, she brushed her neck. In the few days since the battle, her bruises were already healing. Soon there’d be no sign of the Hunter’s attack on her, just the memory, burned into her mind like the others. They were still raw, especially memories of Carn, but when she looked at them, the rawness faded, bit by bit, leaving her with nothing but determination. She, Maeve of Carn, would not be like those who came before her, turning a blind eye to the madness of the world. To the darkness and corruption that swept over it, to the greed of kings, lust for power, and selfish concerns of nobility.

While it seemed arrogant that she, Maeve of Carn, could make a difference, she reminded herself time and time again, who she fought for and why she fought. This time it wasn’t for herself, to rid her body of the cursed collar, this time it was for her childhood self, abused and torn away from the grasp of her parents. Her blood was used to create runes, a path to the Sword of Justice, and her skills, pitted against others, innocents, to fill the desires of blood-thirsty men.

But now, as the sins of the world caught up with it, she understood there was no place for selfish motives. If she hoped to survive, and for the world to survive, she had to work with others and stand for truth and justice. It was the only way, for she had no doubt if she succumbed to her dark desire for power, the demons would run free and life would cease.

"After you," Imer broke through her thoughts.

He held open the flap of the largest tent in the middle of the encampment. It was a royal blue with golden fringes around it and a dome-shaped top. Maeve ducked and took in the assembly. A table, chairs, and a bed had been moved to the side to make room. Those who'd already arrived stood in a semi-circle with Jacq the wizard in the center. He looked slightly bent and this time Maeve saw streaks of silver in his hair. Briefly her thoughts went to the burning of Imperia and wondered how much magic he'd used, trying to save the city.

By his side stood Willow, shoulders straight, her wavy black hair tossed over one shoulder. In her hands she held a scroll, her dark eyes giving away nothing as she studied each one who came through. Ingram was there, dressed in fine clothes like Imer, clean and fresh along with his eye patch hiding one eye and a pirate-like hat on his head.

Maeve's eyes were drawn to the surviving mages she'd traveled with. Nimya and Faelyn were both there, standing in full armor. There were a few other elves, one with sharp features and a crown on his head. The king of the elves? Here? But Maeve had no time for speculation as two soldiers walked in behind her and took their places. They were big, brute-like men. They took off their helmets and Maeve's mouth went dry as she took her place in the circle. Men, elves, mages, and the people of the grove.

Jacq the wizard held up his hands. "Thank you for coming," he began. "I believe not all of us know each other. I'll take the liberty of introductions."

He began, introducing each person and their talents. None of it was surprising to Maeve, but her heart pounded faster. Kings had gathered, for the fate of the world was a matter for kings.

"We have gathered today to discuss next steps for our people and our world. And, most importantly, to discuss what must be done with the celestial relic. The Crown of Erinyes."

He extended his hand toward Maeve, as though he would take the crown from her. Ignoring him, she held up the wrapped crown, and confidence surged through her. It was Yael the Guardian who'd told her that she should lead. Which meant she couldn't sit back and wait for an opportunity to arise, she had to stand up and speak out for all to hear.

"Aye, the Crown of Erinyes," her voice rang out. "Many of you have heard my story. I spent the last months in the service of the dark fae, hunting the seven shards to break all curses. Against my will, the dark fae saw fit to curse me with a magical collar, and I was their servant until the crown was restored. Since then, my quest has been vengeance, to destroy the dark fae and their mark on this world. They were the ones who slew the dragons and killed an old, knowledgeable race. They were the ones who marched on my hometown, Carn, and brought it to ruins. Those of you who are older will remember Carn in its day, in its prime, with its magic, magic that was wrought with darkness. I am the daughter of the king, next in line to rule Carn. But I don't stand before you as nobility, nor a representative of Carn. I stand before you as a warrior, one who has come face to face with darkness, who understands the lust for blood and power. I've seen the evil creatures that lie in wait, waiting for us to fall on our swords, fall on each other and give the world, our world, over to their hands. They are patient, and they will wait, especially now that all curses have been broken. We've seen the effects of the dark fae's desire for power, but I stand before you with the crown. The crown that belongs to my people. I made a mistake when I killed the king of the fae and thought that I could wear the crown. It answers to my blood, for the blood that runs in my veins is none other than celestial blood. It is why I am fast, strong, why the fae sent me after the crown in the first place but collared me so that I could not take what is rightfully mine. But now I see, the crown should never belong to a ruler, there was a reason it was broken into seven shards and scattered across the known world. It does not belong with us, it does not belong in this world. If you look upon it, it will sway you, make you desire it and the possibilities of power. But the Crown of Erinyes was put together for one reason. To ensure the Gates of Hell do not open. When I escaped from the fae Underground, I went to the Island of Hades where the guardians dwell and saw it with my own eyes. Evil grows relentlessly there, and if you think what happened when Contresea fell was terrible, you would not last against the demons. They are dark, foul beings with no souls, no remorse. They will come and kill and dance on our graves. We cannot allow such evil to enter our world. When I was there I saw the gates were weak. Time is of the essence. We must go to the Island of Hades and use the power of the crown to shut the Gates of Hell once and for all."

She held the crown above her head, still wrapped in the cloak although she could sense it responding to her words, sense the energy that pulsed from it. Her chest heaved as she spoke, and she glanced at each person in turn. "What say you?" She demanded. "Are you with me or against me?"

"The floor is open for discussion," Jacq cut in, his voice calm despite the passion in Maeve's words. "I would agree with Maeve of Carn. Willow and I have listened to the whispers in the wind, to the prophecies of old and I have seen how the tides of war have shifted and turned. I have made up my mind to join Maeve in her quest to the Island of Hades, but it is only with great deliberation, for there must be those who keep this land safe. The orcs still march and their numbers swell, they will return to pick off those who have fallen. Those left behind must rebuild and stand firm, should we not return."

"I will join," Willow said, her fingers tightening around the scroll.

"And I," Ingram agreed.

"Aye." Imer nodded.

Maeve took a deep breath, and a wave of relief washed over her. She'd expected violence only to be received with agreement. It was true indeed, the tides had changed and perhaps war was bringing them closer together, making them like-minded as they fought for one cause.

The king of men grunted, shattering her illusions. “I don’t see what all the fuss is about, if we have such magic, such power in our hands now, why not use it to drive back the orcs? Kill them all, like the fae were killed, and then, once we have secured our forces, go forth to a foul island.” He waved his hand, his face red. “If they are real. All this about prophecies and magic is nonsense, we should fight what we can see. Not the intangible!”

The elven king lifted his chin, his voice cold as ice. “I am inclined to disagree. While we must fight what is unseen, there is a greater harm if the demons are loose. Once, the fae were naught but a mystery, invisible creatures who came on the night of the full moon, causing mischief. But look what they did, when we assumed they were trapped in the fae Underground for all eternity. They bade their time and came forth to laugh on our graves. Such misery is only because of them and I regret the day I did not take my army and sweep into their underground, killing them once and for all. I will call upon the armies of elves and trees, and we shall fight the orcs and drive them back across the seas.”

The king of men glowered and crossed his arms but did not say more.

“I will finish what I started.” Faelyn bowed to the elven king. “With your permission I will go to the Island of Hades as a representative of the elves.”

“Granted,” the elven king said.

“Then I will stand for the Grove,” Nimya said. “My people

are displaced because of the dark fae, we broke a vow to never give up the shard and we have paid for it dearly. The dark fae are dead but it is not enough."

Maeve stared around at the gathering, realizing there would be seven of them, to face the darkness and hold back the demons. And once again, she desperately hoped the celestials would fight on their side. "You go to face evil," she told them. "Your deeds will not be forgotten, even if there is nary a return for us."

Jacq held up his hands, indicating the gathering was over. "We must prepare a ship."

24
A VOW

"That went much better than expected," Maeve said as she and Imer left the gathering.

He took her arm and pulled her further away from the royal blue tent, where raised voices were lifted. "It did, you have the power of persuasion. Others listen to you when you speak up," he said admiringly.

"And you?" Maeve touched his chest and drew closer still, dropping her tone to an enticing whisper. "Do I have the power to persuade you?"

He kissed her lightly, then pulled away, eyes scanning the horizon. "Drago should return with word on the ships. I need to visit the healer's tent." He grimaced as he gestured to his arm.

Nodding, Maeve pulled back, understanding that it was an inappropriate time for stolen trysts. The buzz of anticipation in her chest settled to a steady heartbeat and she turned her attention back to the quest.

"You'll rule one day," Imer said before he walked away. "You'll see."

Maeve's brow furrowed at his sudden departure but she set off toward the rise of the hill where Drago kept watch. Others were frightened of his bulk, but understood he was a fearsome enemy, should the orcs venture near again. She found him eating the last bits of some fallen animal, his eyes lidded with the pleasure of a full belly. Maeve sat on the hill beside him, upwind of his rotten breath. "The gathering went well," she told him. "Seven of us will go to the Island of Hades."

"I sense this pleases you," Drago said, stretching his wings and refolding them on his back.

"It does." Maeve patted the crown. "I expected a fight yet it was all resolved peacefully. What did you find when you flew over the city? Still no sign of the Dragon Queen?"

"It is as though she disappeared into legend," Drago said. "The skies were clear as far as I flew. I haven't traveled west to see what became of the orcs, but I'll do so tonight. As for the ships, they are almost all burnt, but there is one that fared better than the others. Aside from replacing some sails, it looked seaworthy. If you are in luck, you might find that it was being prepared for an expedition and fitted for travel."

Maeve recalled her sea journey with Sandrine. "Can seven sail a ship?" she mused more to herself.

"I know nothing of ships, only of sea and sky. But I have decided to come with you."

Maeve turned and studied the bulk of the dragon. "How?" she sputtered. "I want you to come with us but. . . You're almost big enough to sink a ship. How will you rest when you get tired? How will you hunt?"

Drago paused and chewed slowly. "There are things I haven't shared with you yet," Drago admitted. "But I have a way to change forms, although I hope you will never see me in anything other than this form."

Maeve waited. So he could shift. She wondered if the Crown of Erinyes had lifted the curse on dragons and allowed him to use his full abilities. When he said nothing more, she went on, cautious not to offend him. "I would like you there, although it is dangerous. I thought I'd lost you once, when the Dragon Queen attacked. I wasn't sure what had happened to you but I still feel responsible for your fate."

"Because you made a vow to my mother?"

"No." A slight wind whipped up and Maeve tucked loose strands of her black hair behind her ears. She stared out at the lonely horizon and touched her chest as though she could feel the aching hole that grief left. "It's more than just a vow. You and I are the last of our kind, given up by our mothers, lost and lonely. I see a reflection of myself in you, except you've had the opportunity to make the right choices all along. And you have. Despite the tales, the knowledge your mother shared with you, you did not join the dark fae or the Dragon Queen, you choose us." She spread her arms to indicate what she meant. "The humans, the mages, the elves."

"But I am still a dragon. When this is over I can return to the mountains and make my home there, once again."

Maeve bit back her reply. When it was over. She hadn't thought about the future, except to do what she always did when a quest was finished: Sit down in a tavern and have a drink. She recalled those drunken nights, laughter, ale sloshed over the tables, throwing darts, waging coin, and then the fights. Although, no one bothered her after learning she'd break a nose, a leg, or arm, whatever was closest. A wry grin came to her face and faded. Everything was different now, she wasn't sure if there would be taverns to return to, especially since the Dragon Queen was loose, burning everything in her path.

"I haven't had a home," she admitted. "I've always gone from one job to the next. I feel restless when I slow down or stop. I don't think I could be like the peasants. I am a warrior, that's the life I've always known and I'm not sure if I want any other."

"Think on it." Drago lay his head down and closed one eye. "It is what Imer thinks of. He's not sure what a future with you will look like."

Understanding rushed through Maeve and her face flamed with heat. Was that what he thought of? Did he want a future, with her? Children and land? Suddenly she didn't know what to feel. She stood, pacing back and forth. "I'll think on it," she grunted.

But Drago closed his other eye and went to sleep.

25
LEGENDS AND TALES

As Drago had said, one of the ships escaped the burning of the harbor and floated just off shore, held in place by a weighty anchor. Using one of the unburned long boats, Maeve and the other six who would travel to the Island of Hades rowed out to the ship. Ingram and Imer—who were the ship experts—studied the vessel with glee, making remarks to each other which Maeve understood nothing about. Instead, she paced, wondering if it would be wise to go below decks and find a place to hide the Crown of Erinyes. Although the mages claimed they were with her, she did not want them to be tempted with the crown. If they so much as looked at it, and felt that same need and desire she felt, their voyage might be undone. She felt their eyes on her as she opened the hatch and navigated down the ladder into the gloom.

They set sail that afternoon, for Willow claimed the wind was with them. She stood at the helm, eyes closed, arms uplifted as she listened to hushed whispers. The wizard stood by her side, staff in hand, as though by their power they could control the winds that bolstered the ship forward. Maeve, after hiding the crown, leaned out, watching the evening sky shift and fade. This voyage was much different from her previous ones. It was true, she'd set sail on great ships before with blood-thirsty mercenaries, intent on gold and glory. Those days she'd had to fight to maintain her honor, and the last couple of voyages, she'd been stuck below decks. But now she watched the waves rise, choppy as the ship moved up and down, as gracefully as a fish swimming. A darkness hovered overhead and a smile came to her face as she looked up and caught sight of Drago, wings spread as he soared over them.

A pang struck her heart at the reminder of their conversation the previous day and her eyes were drawn to Imer. He was closer to the mast of the ship, taking a break from his duties and smoking his pipe. Earlier, she'd caught him whittling a new pipe out of wood. Now, she walked over to him.

"Maeve." He smiled and his dark eyes reflected the midnight blue sky.

She jutted her chin in the direction of Jacq and Willow. "Can they really sail the ship with their magic?"

Imer grinned, a sign of his old cockiness coming back. "The wind is with us and we are set on a good course. I attribute that to the skill of Ingram and I." The grin melted away into seriousness. "But yes, they can speak to the wind. It will assist us, especially since we don't know where we are going. No one has sailed to the Island of Hades."

Maeve picked at a piece of wood on the railing. "No, I

imagine not. But the phoenix flew straight and true, it can't be that far beyond the Sea of Sorrows."

"That accursed place," Imer's hand closed into a fist. "I assume the spirits trapped in the Sea of Sorrows are free now, laid to rest when all curses were broken."

"I didn't think of that," Maeve gasped, her thoughts returning to her mother's spirit. Was she at peace at last? No longer tormented with loss, grief, and betrayal?

"No? There are many stories of the cursed ones, some fables, others truth," Imer went on.

"Will you tell me a legend? Distract me from what is to come? I don't want to think about the island, nor demons. Not tonight."

Imer touched her shoulder, the gesture both arousing and pleasant. She stepped closer as the scent of tobacco filled the air briefly, then quickly rushed away by the cool wind. Tugging her cloak tighter around her neck to protect against the chill, she smiled at him.

"When I was a young lad, living in Imperia, I liked to hear the stories of the celestials. Did you know that in the early days, they dwelt in the world among the mortals?"

Maeve shook her head and moved closer, sharing her body heat with him.

"It was also in the days when all creatures spoke, and the mortals thought the celestials were too strong. So they spread rumor of a great treasure to the north, enticing the celestials to travel there. Then the mortals went to the bottom of the sea and asked the monsters to try their best to sink the ships of the celestials. They sent the great sea serpents, who were unsuccessful, and the many-legged squids and octopuses to blow ink in their faces. They sent the great blue jellyfish with a poisonous sting so intense the celestials should have passed out. But nothing made them relent, instead, the celestials became so frustrated, they cursed the monsters of the deep to keep them from rising again in the northern sea. And legend says that when the curse is broken, the monsters who have been held back for time unknown will rise to the surface and fight against the celestials for freedom."

"It's not much of a story." Maeve made a face.

"It's a legend, a fable, but some believe it, others don't. Regardless, it did its duty. People talk about the north, where treasure abounds. But is there really treasure? Or it is simply a trick of mortals? I've always been curious to discover, what lies in the north."

Maeve's thoughts drifted back to her fight with Lord Sebastian and his words. He claimed to have sailed north and found the treasure of treasures. Had he found the lost shard somewhere in the north? "North," she repeated, dark thoughts surging. "What if it is nothing but a trick?"

Imer grinned and faced the sea. "But wouldn't you like to know? We are living in an unusual time."

"Yes, the world could end in a matter of days."

"True, but we have an opportunity before us. I don't believe the prophecy was foretold so we could lose. It was foretold so we would know what to do to win the greatest battle fought between mortals, immortals, celestials, orcs, and demons. The battle to determine the course of our world and destiny as we move forward. Perhaps the celestials will come down and join us, fight with us, and restore the world to how it once was, in days of old, when everything was young and pure. Wouldn't you want that? What will you do if you don't have to be a warrior?"

"I don't know." Maeve sighed. It wasn't a conversation she was ready for but clearly it was what Imer wanted. To discuss what would happen if they succeeded and had endless time to themselves.

She crossed her arms over her chest, pulling away slightly. She did not know what she wanted. She'd never been lucky enough to dream or desire. With the world war-torn and ruined, she didn't know how Imer could speak of the future when so much disaster surrounded them. First, they had to rebuild what they had before they could look for more.

26

EVIL STORM

The days passed quickly, one after the other mixed with wind, mist, and the dark sensation that something was about to happen. One afternoon, as the ship rocked up and down in the waves, and Maeve was tired from the constant motion, she saw a spot on the horizon. It was far to the east, but black like a void, a mouth opening and closing. Her heart hammered in her throat as she stared at it and knew with a certainty, they were close.

Leaving her perch she stumbled up to the helm, cursing her lack of sea legs she reached for the railings to steady herself. "There!" she pointed. "Do you see that?"

Ingram held the ship firm as he steered toward it while Jacq and Willow turned in the direction Maeve pointed.

Willow pulled herself upright and shielded her eyes. "Aye, tis a storm," she said.

"Not just any storm," Maeve countered, hoping Willow

could translate the whispers in the wind and explain what it was. "It's the island, isn't it?"

"I sense darkness, evil," Jacq said, lifting his face and closing his eyes. "I hear the sounds of battle, of death, of pain."

Willow lifted a hand, palm out as though she could touch the air. "It blows toward us, full of malice." She spun, alarm on her face. "Ingram, what must be done to ready the ship for a storm?"

"Everything is tied down," Ingram responded. "We sail straight and true but ready yourselves to fight, we know not what comes out of the deep."

A sinking suspicion rolled in Maeve's gut and she fled down the steps toward the hold. "Prepare for battle!" she shouted as she went, before tugging open the trap door. Above her head she heard the pounding of footsteps as her companions took their places. There wasn't much a group of seven could do, but she hoped they could survive the storm and whatever came with it. They were close, oh so close to reaching the island, but the crown was what she needed.

Stumbling through the hold, she found her hiding place and pulled out the crown. It was still wrapped in the cloak, but she couldn't fight and hold the crown at the same time. Her eyes landed on some rope and she grabbed it, making knots as fast as her fingers could and tying the crown to herself. She wrapped the rope around her waist twice until she was sure it was secure. Even then the runes on her skin itched, and a sudden longing thrummed through her. She could almost hear whispers of desire. *Take out the crown. Wear it.*

Shaking away the sensation she turned toward the ladder. The ship lurched as though it had struck something. Hard.

Maeve lost her balance and stumbled, slamming her shoulder into a wooden post. She hooked an arm around it as she caught her balance, struggling to stand as the ship pitched wildly. Above she heard faint screams and shouts and then the roar of heavy wind and the slamming of rain against wood. She listened to the drumming, her heart pounding loudly in her chest. For a moment she glimpsed a shaft of light above her, then the door to the hold closed with a boom and everything went black.

Maeve blinked at the sudden darkness and a panic washed over her. Holding her hands out in front of her, she lurched toward the ladder. Her fingertips grazed the edges of it just as the ship rolled wildly to the other side. A raw shout left Maeve's mouth and her hand flapped even as the movement of the ship pitched her backward. She landed on her bottom and struck her head against the boards. With a curse, she rubbed her head and, thinking better of walking, rolled to her knees. Crawling forward with one hand out, she found the ladder again, just as screams echoed above her, and then there was silence.

She climbed as quickly as she dared in the dark, still hearing the roar of the wind and the onslaught of rain. But there were no more footsteps. Just silence. What was happening? She had to know.

Pressing her hand against the door, she pushed, but it was wedged shut. Had someone trapped her below? She pushed again and felt the door give way. Suddenly it sprang open with a boom but she had to hold onto the ladder as the ship pitched again, as though it were traveling through a whirlpool. A loose piece of timber flew across the deck toward her and knocked into the door, slamming it shut. Maeve swallowed and ducked into the darkness. Perhaps it was better to wait out the storm.

She clung to the ladder for what seemed like hours while the ship creaked and tossed, pitching back and forth so relentlessly she thought she'd be sick. Her grip on the ladder tightened as she heard boards come loose. Waves crashed and barrels of goods rolled back and forth behind her. She did not know what time it was when a crack of lighting split through the darkness, revealing a hole on one side of the ship where water sloshed in beneath her feet. The roar of thunder that followed wasn't so much like a roar but the bellow of a fierce giant, preparing for war.

Fear made Maeve's fingers shake. Fear not only for herself, but the fate of her companions. She reached up to push at the door, but it was trapped, sealed shut once again. A cry of frustration burst from her throat. Were they alive? Had they lashed themselves to the mast to keep from being washed over? Were some lost to sea?

And what of Imer? The thought of losing him made her chest burn. She wanted to explore a future with him, should they survive the Island of Hades, and she hoped her chance hadn't been ripped away. The fleeting thought had no sooner left her mind when there came a thunderous, cracking sound. One moment she was holding on to the ladder, the next she was airborne. Maeve's fingers snatched at raindrops and air until she landed with a terrific splash in ice-cold water.

27
Island of Hades

The waters dragged Maeve down, like fingers of ice were clasped around her ankles. She kicked and struggled, seeking the surface, her lungs burning for air. Her memories flashed, drawing her back to her most recent journey under the waters. The Sea of Sorrows where darkness drew her down, and visions of her past tried to ensnare her. But this was different, cold, unkind, as though someone wished she'd drown rather than face what was to come. With thoughts of her companions, she broke the surface, shivering and shaking. Immediately she dropped her hands to her waist to ensure both the Crown of Erinyes and the Sword of Justice were still with her. Both were, but it only brought her a slight relief. She turned in the waters, still rough with the effects of the storm, although it had faded as though its sole mission was to hurl Maeve and her companions from the ship.

Around her, planks of wood drifted, the last remnants of

the shattered ship. She swam toward one and held on to it, letting her laden legs weave back and forth while the coldness threatened to turn her body stiff. In the water, she saw no sign of her friends. A chill shook her and she turned. Her jaw dropping as she saw the island.

In the dimness, it was impossible to tell how far away it was, but it glowed like a red monster. Trepidation rode through Maeve but she had no choice. The island was where she wanted to go, and in her present condition, warmth was what she needed. Using the wood to balance herself, she moved her feet under the water, kicking her way toward the island.

The trip was long, lonely, and as she neared the island, the smell of burning sulfur filled the air. Her nose twitched and the waters warmed around her. Her legs and arms tingled as sensation returned to them but she wouldn't let herself rest and continued, kicking against the waves as the shore rose before her. It was nothing more than rock and rubble, more of the same that she'd seen when she first visited the island. But now, although heavy clouds hung over it, creating a constant gloom, she could make out the features of the island.

Rocks and mountains dotted it, and a wall of cliffs rose, sharp and stiff. It was much larger than she expected. As the ground turned firm beneath her feet, she stood and splashed through the shallows up onto the shore. Bending over, she caught her breath as she determined what to do. The answer was clear, she had to find the guardians, but she was unsure where to begin.

There were no paths, but uphill she assumed she'd have a

better view of the island and could gain an idea of where to go. There was no light to guide her but she had faith the guardians would find her, as they had before. Did they not fly across the island daily? Keeping watch?

Despite her predicament, she was more concerned about what had happened to her companions. Turning her back on the island she shielded her eyes. The waves were high but showed nothing but broken pieces of the ship. No friends. No dragon. Shuddering she turned around just as the sound of a whip crackled through the air. Her thoughts went to Nathair, master of the whip, but no, she'd killed him.

Her hand went to her blade and she drew it, remembering where she was. She had no friends in Hades.

"Are you lost?" a female voice asked, a cruel lilt to her voice.

Maeve jumped and pointed her sword in the direction of the voice, which seemed to be coming from all around her.

A mocking laugh came, but instead of high it was deep, as though a multitude of creatures were laughing. A winged creature landed on the bank above her and folded four pairs of wings on her back. She had six arms, the body of a female from the waist up, naked with large breasts bouncing as she moved. On the ends where her nipples should have been were the pointed tips of spears. From the waist down, her buttocks and legs were covered with hair, like that of a goat, and she had hooves for feet. Her eyes and mouth were black and patterns had been inked in swirls across her skin.

Maeve shivered as the woman snapped the whip again. Was she face-to-face with her first demon?

"Who are you?" Maeve demanded, weary of being accosted wherever she went.

The demon grinned and stalked toward her, cracking the whip with every step. "I am hungry, for your soul."

The sinister voice sent a shiver through Maeve. Without answering, she dashed for the creature, anticipating the fall of the whip. When it came she snapped it in half and brought the sword up to block the next blow. A fist sank into her stomach. The blow knocked Maeve backward and a grunt escaped her lips. Six arms. She wasn't prepared. She blocked the blow to her head and slashed toward the creature's hairy thigh, to no avail. Bringing the sword up in an arc, she slashed at the creature's belly, drawing a line of blood, dark as ink.

The demon screamed and pulled back. Although Maeve did not think the cut was anything more than a mere scratch, it began to smoke, as though it were burning the demon from the inside out. The demon screeched and moved further away, soulless eyes darting toward the sword. Boldness surged through Maeve and she rushed at the creature. Arms and wings came up as the demon defended herself. But the Sword of Justice sang as it struck true, and smoke furled, filling the air with the deep intense smell of burning flesh. In two moves, Maeve lopped off the demon's head. It fell to the ground with a smack. The hideous body waved back and forth before falling flat on the ground while the hissing of smoke burned it to ash in a matter of moments.

Maeve held up the Sword of Justice, grim satisfaction encouraging her as she took in the sight of the clean sword. It was as though darkness could not touch it without destroying itself. Recalling the Hunter she moved up the bank. Beware to the demons who choose to attack her, for she could take them all, as soon as she discovered which way to go.

A moment later she heard the swoosh of wings and something landed behind her. She whirled, sword pointed at the new intruder, but a sigh of relief made her shoulders sag. "Drago!" she gasped.

She rushed down the bank to greet him, questions rising and falling as he tucked his orange wings on his back. "What happened to you? Do you know where everyone else is? Did you fly through the storm?"

Drago lifted his head to scan the skies, which were clear except for the strange clouds. "She's here," he said.

"Who?" Maeve demanded, a chill creeping up her spine.

"The Dragon Queen," he wagged his head. "I don't believe she saw me, but she's out there. She's the one who helped the demons escape and she's leading them out, giving them passage to the world. We've come just in time."

Maeve's brow furrowed. "How do you know this?"

"I've been speaking with the guardians," Drago said.

"You met the guardians? Are they close?"

"I flew ahead when the storm struck, seeking shelter. The winds whirled me around and around but ultimately drove me here. I saw shapes flying in the darkness, demons I think, with many arms and wings, and long tails. They were headed toward the ship, but the wind blew my fire back into my mouth before I could burn them. I think they came for the others. But how did you escape?"

Maeve's hand went to the crown tied on her waist and

guilt rode her. She should have been there, she might have been able to stop the demons from taking her friends. "I was in the hold, securing the crown. Did you see where they took them? We have to rescue them!"

"Rescue," Drago repeated. "I thought you might suggest such an action. But Maeve, don't you see? Your path is different. I will work on rescuing them, but in order for this battle to end, you must use the crown to seal the Gates of Hell. That is your task."

The familiar itching returned to the runes on her skin, and Maeve flexed her fingers, wanting to scratch the itch, but knowing it would not help.

"I don't want to," she said, blinking back tears. But it was a useless answer. She had to, whether she wanted to or not. Biting her lip, she glanced at the waves rolling toward the rocky shore. "I will," she squared her shoulders, her voice loud and strong. "But I don't know how. I need to get to the guardians, if you would but show me the way."

"I will," Drago said. "And there is something else you should know."

He blinked slowly and Maeve had the strange sensation he was preparing her for something unusual.

"What?" she almost whispered.

"The celestials are here."

Maeve spun, her eyes darting across the barren embarkment. There was no one there, of course, no shimmer in the air, no sparks of glory. Nothing. How could they arrive so quickly, so silently? She'd assumed that when the celestials came they'd shoot from the sky, wings spread, swords in hand, with a shower of glory.

"They are battling the demons," Drago went on. "But they have no hope of winning until the crown is used to close the gates."

Still, Maeve's heart beat faster, she wanted to see. "Take me, Drago," she said. "I need to know."

"On my back then, just this once," Drago said, and spread his wings.

28
INTO THE DARK

The flight on Drago's back was quite different from the hot ride aboard the back of the phoenix. The air was still stifling and stiff and the smell of brimstone and sulfur hung in the air as though it would suffocate the life from that place. Even the surrounding waters and the thick clouds which hung above the island did nothing to dispel the heat.

Maeve watched the uneven landscape as they swept over it. Drago flew low, his clawed feet almost scraping the low range mountains that shot up, sharp and craggy, nothing but rock on rock. Maeve had the feeling she was too heavy for him, young as he was, but he did not utter a complaint.

The land rose up steeply from the shore, as though it were one giant volcano. The water was left far behind, hidden by the clouds, and after a little while, Maeve blinked against the strange motes in the air. She held out her hand. Something soft and gentle landed on her wrist, and then a stinging sensation flared up her arm for a brief moment. She gasped and pulled her arm away, but more filled the air and rained down. Tiny motes of ash, stinging as they landed on bare skin. Maeve hissed in displeasure and annoyance.

Drago's scales were thick, and he did not seem to notice the rain of ash as he flew. His pace slowed as he reached another mountain and Maeve glanced down, surprised to see lava flowing out, slow and steady. The volcano was not exploding but it brimmed, a bubbling lake of lava. Smoke poured out of it and Maeve swallowed hard. It was only a matter of time.

She tensed as Drago wheeled and squeezed her legs around him. In the distance she glimpsed the pulsing red glow she'd seen, and then what looked like black ants, crawling across the slope. It took her eyes a moment to adjust in the gloom as she realized what she saw were demons. An army of them, thick and black, like a multi-headed serpent, crawling across the land. Her eyes widened as she stared for they were everywhere, stretching as far as the eye could see, coming from that infernal glow.

Fear made her go cold. The Gates of Hell had opened after all. Drago was right. Even though she believed him, it was another thing to see, with her own eyes, the wicked creatures that came forth. And even though she was too far away to see them clearly, the stench of death stretched across the entire island. She blinked rapidly. If the demons had her friends, how could they survive? Her heart seized as she thought of Imer and herself, and their unsure future. War ruined everything, for how could she think of a future when she was flying into the jaws of death? And how could she love Imer when everything she'd ever cared about had been ripped away?

Regardless, she pushed those thoughts away and suppressed her emotions. She was free of the dark fae, but not from the consequences of their actions. Not yet. It was only when the Gates of Hell were closed that she could dream of a future. If she survived.

Drago turned in the air once more and began to rise. Each pulse of his wings sent a blast of acrid heat toward Maeve. She hunched down on his back as the guardian's tower came into view and relief surged through her. Drago landed with a heavy thunk on top of the tower and Maeve slid off his back. "Thank you," she said, shaking off the ash that landed on her skin. It was thicker around the tower.

"I hope you succeed," Drago said. "I would go with you to their halls, but I can do more damage out here."

Maeve nodded. "Be safe," she told him, just as she heard a whooshing sound from above.

She looked up to see a dark shape hover over them, and then the Dragon Queen swooped into view.

A roar filled the air and the strength of it slammed through Maeve like a heated flame. She felt the anger, frustration and rage that pierced that roar, and she thought she understood it. The Dragon Queen had had everything she wanted, and for moments she'd been winning, before Maeve came along and took everything from her. King Mrithun. The Crown of Erinyes. And now she was back, out for bittersweet revenge. Maeve understood that fear and frustration and her hand went to her sword just as Drago pounced on her.

Maeve fell, anger rising before she realized what Drago was doing. She lay flat on her belly, the Crown of Erinyes digging into her flesh as Drago spread his wings, covering her from the onslaught. Dragon fire burned across the platform, the heat of it deep and intense. Maeve couldn't help the scream that ripped out of her mouth as she closed her eyes and tucked her head into her arms, as though it would protect her.

The heat blistered around her, sucking the moisture out of the air. Maeve gasped as another hail of fire poured out just as she heard a cry. Pure and loud. A shrieking filled the air but she lay still, heart pounding in her throat as she waited for what was to come.

A moment later, Drago rose off her with a gust of wind. Maeve lifted her head and saw the dark shape of the Dragon Queen launch herself upward, and above her head were orange feathers, a burst of crimson in the bleakness. Maeve gasped. The firebird had come to fight the Dragon Queen. Hope filled her heart just as the trapdoor opened.

Yael appeared, glanced toward the sky, then at Maeve and waved. "Come. You are late," she said, her mouth set in a grim line.

Maeve rose to her feet, crying out as her hands hit the heated stone of the tower. She ran across it, trying to ignore the burning sensations that danced up and down her legs. She reached the trap door and climbed down.

Yael moved quickly, striding into the wide hall which was much the same as Maeve had seen before. It was hard to believe it was not so long ago that she'd been there.

"The last defender has arrived with the Crown of Erinyes," Yael called as she strode across the room, golden wings folded on her back.

Maeve looked and saw seven guardians stood in a semi-circle, arms crossed, wings folded on their backs. Each wore glowing armor and some were male, others female. They looked at her with unreadable expressions. Maeve reached for the crown with the sudden realization that she should pull it out and show it to them, no matter how she felt about it. They gazed at her with expectant faces and her fingers trembled on the knots.

She bit her bottom lip. "Will you show me how to close the gates?" she asked, looking from one face to the other.

Asim lifted his head and his face was grave. "The first of our defenses has fallen to the demons. Although the celestials have come to fight with us, we are in grave danger of being overrun. As the last defender, it is up to you, Maeve of Carn."

His words sent a chill through her. For he spoke as though she, and only she, could stop the onslaught of demons. But all she had was the relic, the Sword of Justice, and a changed heart. A heart that desired to help, to right the wrongs, and let justice and truth reign again. The dark fae were nothing compared to the darkness the demons brought, the stench of death and the vicious onslaught without regard for humanity. If they overtook the world they would bring a hell on earth that would be unbearable. She understood that fact and yet, she looked to the guardians for help while they looked to her, as though she were the very one who would help them.

Yael spoke up. "We will lead you to the entrance of the tunnels. They run down to the gates, and it is an entrance which has not been overrun yet. We will guide you down there, but when we arrive it is up to you. You must break the Crown of Erinyes and use the shards to seal the entrance. There is a rune over the gates, a place for each shard. Once the Crown of Erinyes is used to seal the Gates of Hell, they will never open again."

"Or so the legends say," Asim said, a hint of warning in his tone.

"Come," Yael said, "we have delayed long enough. But be on your guard, demons are full of tricks. We know not what awaits us in the tunnels."

Maeve nodded. "I am ready."

Yael led the way, and the other six brought up the rear, their footfalls heavy as they moved across the stone floor to the ladder leading down. Maeve followed Yael down into the keep where she'd gotten the armor from, and realized, with some embarrassment, that it was a gift she'd left behind. Not because she was ungrateful, but she'd assumed she wouldn't have a need for it again. How wrong she'd been. Yael glanced at her and then picked up a round shield and handed it to her. "You might need this. The shields here are fireproof for we know not what we might face."

Maeve took it and nodded. The shield was light and she slid it onto her arm before following Yael. They descended, past other rooms, some with color, others with the scent of food, and yet others with the smell of blood and iron.

At last the stairs ended and Yael came to a stop in front of a door made of gray rock. It was solid and wide and stood about fifteen feet high with runes and arcane symbols carved across it. Maeve shuddered as she stared up at the immense door, detecting an ancient age vibe to it, as though it were as old as time itself.

Yael turned to the side and stood back. The other guardians followed her example, standing tall with chins raised on either side of the door. Asim remained standing in front of the door with three guardians on either side. His eyes were troubled as they met Maeve's. "This is the end," he rumbled, his deep voice making goosebumps rise on Maeve's arms. "Once the path to hell is open, it cannot be shut. Are you sure?"

Maeve met his solemn gaze and pushed her shoulders back with the awareness that she was sure of nothing, only her own emotions as she lifted the Crown of Erinyes. She'd managed to free some of it from the cloak, and the blue shimmer shone across the carved stones like a torch. "The dark fae did this," she told the guardians. "They took me and collared me and forced me to do their bidding. I will not let them release hell on the world when I've just gotten free, and I haven't begun to live yet. Others deserve to know what I know, to understand there is hope and redemption for all, despite how dark our deeds are, or how wrong the world is. We deserve to fight for it. Come if you wish, or stay here and guard the way, but I am going regardless."

As she spoke, her thoughts drifted back to the mages she'd traveled with. Of Jacq the wizard with his odd magic and youthful appearance, and Willow, his assistant, with her desire to use power to eradicate evil. She thought of Ingram and Imer, the brothers of fire, and how they used the unfortunate circumstance of their birth and death of their parents to find a way to ruin the dark fae. And finally the others she did not know well, Faelyn and the elves, and Nimya and the people of the grove. Although they were swept into battle, each had their own motives which drove them.

She watched the blue shimmer of the crown and thought

of her mother's death by fire, and her father's decisions to send them away. Darkness ran in the blood of Carn, would it always be that way? Did she have a choice when she was fated to become the last defender, to stand against the demons and to carry the Crown of Erinyes only to destroy it for all eternity? Her choices led her down a path of no return, but she would complete her quest, finish her task, to ease the guilt on her conscience, and to give peace to those who deserved a second chance.

Asim broke through her thoughts by producing a key. It hung on a heavy chain around his neck and was as large as one of his broad hands. It was a sickening bone white, and Maeve's thoughts flew to the bone tools she'd seen the fae use for torture, deep in the fae Underground.

The key turned in the lock with a loud crunch and a wave of dust filled the air as the seal on the door broke. It opened inward, yet it took three of the guardians, pushing and straining, to shove it open. Maeve's heart sank as the opening revealed a gaping black hole, like the yawning mouth of a beast. Her courage disappeared as she looked into the gloom, with a darkness that seemed to stir and breathe, as though it were the essence of pure evil.

Yael stepped forward, holding something that looked like glowing sticks and tossed them into the opening. Immediately it lit up with a low glow, showing off the low, sloping walls, roughly cut into the mountain. The air was old and stale and Maeve pulled the shield closer to her chest, as though she could protect herself from the darkness.

"These are the catacombs." Asim pointed. "There are many paths and terrors, but only one leads to the gates. The signs are likely carved into the rock. Be cautious, watch your step, and stay on guard. You should arrive before daybreak."

Maeve nodded, realizing he was not going with them. Three of the guardians stepped forward with lit torches, leading the way into the darkness. Maeve swallowed hard and followed them, feeling quite alone and helpless.

The other guardians brought up the rear and as the door swung shut, Maeve wanted to call out, to ask them why they did not fly straight to the Gates of Hell, but she already knew the answer. The demons would overwhelm them and steal the crown, and even though the Dragon Queen was distracted by the phoenix, she would burn them alive. Maeve whispered a prayer to the Divine for the safety of her friends and followed the guardians into the dark.

29
SEVEN HALLOWS

Maeve felt alone in the dark, even surrounded by the six guardians. They were tall giants, solemn and steady, and the pace at which they moved did not encourage discussion. The darkness pressed in on both sides, and despite the light, visions of the fae Underground haunted Maeve. The air was still and stale, as though they were the first ones to breathe it, and the tunnel went on and on. Every now and again, the guardians would halt and hold up their torches, examining the walls and the runes written upon them. After a quick examination, they'd move onward at almost a run.

Maeve trotted in the middle, her breath settling into a rhythmic flow, although the heat intensified the further they went. Her hair stuck to her neck, and her clothes were soaked through and felt heavy on her body. Even the light shield grew sweaty on her arm, as though it would slide off. A faint glow came from the cloak. Even though she'd re-wrapped the crown, the symbols on her skin itched.

At long last, vestiges of light pierced the gloom, along with the intense smell of fumes, so dark and evil, tears sprang to Maeve's eyes. She was reminded of the aura of the Hunter, but as they stepped into the light, red and intense, she saw where they were. They'd crossed the great canyon and come up the other side. The tunnels ended in a shallow hollow, below the gates where the demons poured forth, howling, shrieking and keeping up an infernal noise that made the fae Underground seem like nothing at all.

"Wait," Yael grabbed Maeve's arm and pulled her back from the glow. "They will see us as soon as we leave this opening. We must be prepared. Look." She pointed toward the red glow. "Just above the gates is a place for the seven shards. The Crown of Erinyes can hold the power of Hades in check. Once we leave the catacombs you'll have to run straight and true to the rocks near the gates. Climb the jagged stairs to reach the top and lean out over it. I will come with you but the demons will be upon us as soon as we leave the catacombs."

Maeve tilted back her head and sure enough saw the red glow gleaming like an evil eye. Beside the glow she could make out rough stairs, and above them were small hollows, spaces for the seven shards.

Yael went on, a hand going to her broad sword. "You'll have to use the Sword of Justice to break the Crown of Erinyes. Once it is broken, you must press each shard into its place and that will close the gates and destroy this island."

Maeve went stiff. "Destroy this island?" she repeated like a fool.

Yael nodded. "It is the prophecy. When the seven shards are used to close the gates, the Island of Hades will be no more. Hell will sink under this world, never to rise again."

Maeve's heartbeat slowed. "What about everyone who is fighting here? What about the guardians? The celestials?" But what she really meant to say was: *What about my friends?*

They had to be rescued, saved, before everything shattered.

"If you want to save the world, this is your path," Yael's tone remained firm. "We all have sacrifices to make."

Maeve pressed her lips together, wondering what sacrifice Yael had made to become a guardian. She blinked back tears all the same. This wasn't what she wanted. When she imagined the celestials coming, she'd thought they would save the mortals from having to fight and give up their lives. But she realized now the world belonged to the mortals, the celestials only came to assist. If she were not willing, would they still save the world from the demons? She understood the two-sided choice she was presented with. Either she could fight to save the world or find her friends, but she could not do both. She could save a few or save many, keep the demons from rising or let them flow into the known world, killing and torturing all they could find. And the orcs, they were infiltrating the world too.

"Okay," she nodded at Yael, pushing away her frustration. "Tell me when to go."

"Now," Yael replied.

Maeve bolted from the shallow pit and leaped up onto the

ash. The ground was warm, almost hot beneath her feet, and the rain of ash stung her skin as she ran. She dashed toward the stairs, sword out, swinging at the demons that shrieked and laughed as they leaped into her path, red mouths open, wicked teeth glittering. But the guardians were swift and cut them down, wings spread, twirling and spinning as they drove their blades in and out of the drooling demons. If Maeve had had the time to watch them, she would have thought them beautiful, but urgency carried her toward the stairs and she dared not glance back.

The air was dense, so thick she felt as though she could reach out and touch the haze. She swung her blade but it cut through nothing. The jagged stairs rose before her as a winged creature surged toward her. Without hesitation she brought up the shield, slamming it into the bulk of the creature and following through with her blade. It sunk into muscle, ripping and cutting, almost singing as she pulled it free.

"Hurry," shouted Yael, somewhere by her side.

Maeve pushed her feet faster, legs pumping as she reached the first stair. It was more of a ledge and she had to climb on top of it, putting down the shield to give herself leverage. As she did, a dark shape swooped over the glow. She looked up and horror filled her as she saw the Dragon Queen dive toward them.

"Shields!" Yael shouted.

Maeve only had a second to react. She ducked under the shield and crouched down, jamming her shoulder into the rock wall just as a fireball burst over them. Heat surged around her and the smell of burning flesh filled the air. The ground shook and rock poured down but Maeve squeezed her eyes shut as her skin blistered under the heat. The frustrated roar of a dragon filled the air and she blinked, coughing against the smoke in her throat, almost retching as she stumbled to her feet. The rock around her was nothing more than charred stumps, and when she reached for the next ledge she snatched her burnt hand away, almost screaming at the intense pain that rode up her arms.

Grit covered her face and she glanced toward the skies to see if there would be another blast, but it was impossible to see through the rain of ash. A creature flashed out of the smoke, smacking into her, and knocking her off her feet. Losing her balance, she fell from the ledge, slamming her shoulder into a wall. A white flash of pain rocked her body but she fought against it, determined not to succumb to physical discomfort. She waved her sword in front of her and was rewarded with a shriek when the blade struck true. Regaining her balance, she stumbled to her feet and moved toward the red glow. The rock had cooled to a manageable heat and she used the advantage to push herself upward where the hollows above the gates were.

She climbed quickly as the ground shook, and war drums beat endlessly, reminding her time was of the essence. The pulse thrummed in her head and in her heart but Maeve continued to climb until she stood on a sliver of the ledge with barely enough room for her feet. And that's when she saw she'd have to have wings to reach all seven hollows.

30
GATES OF HELL

Maeve balanced on the ledge and reached for the Crown of Erinyes. Without unwrapping it, she undid the ropes and lay it on the rock, placing a foot over it to hold it steady. Her lips were dry and cracked, and when she used her tongue to wet them, it was shriveled and dry. The red glow pulsed in warning, creating spots behind her eyes, and making her vision dizzy as she fought to keep her balance. She did not know whether she would vomit or fall. A wave of dizziness passed over her and she gripped the sword in both hands and raised it up.

Shadows danced toward her. Snarling demon faces with hideous eyes, wide and snarling as they leaped at her. Sharp teeth ready to tear her apart. Something scratched at her ankle and she kicked it away, almost falling but catching herself at the last moment. A flash of gold told her the guardians were still fighting, but they were surrounded by a stream of four-foot-tall demons with arms as long as their bodies. They scampered on four legs toward her, like monkeys.

A shadow flew overhead and Maeve saw the Dragon Queen dive, mouth open, a ball of flame in her throat. There was no time to react or hide behind the shield, which had fallen to a lower ledge. She had nothing left to do other than carry on and shatter the crown. Maeve raised the Sword of Justice and brought it down in quick succession, once, twice, thrice.

There was a nasty crack and a deadly scream as the Crown of Erinyes broke and the Dragon Queen billowed into Maeve.

Maeve flailed for balance. Her head struck rock as she fell, cutting open the back of her neck. Blue light unfurled and shimmered around her and something thick and heavy closed around her neck. Her consciousness wavered, just for a moment until she heard the shrill scream.

"What have you done? What have you done? You stupid girl!"

The voice reminded her of Sandrine. A scowl rose to her lips as she fumbled for the sword, her fingers closing over rock as her vision cleared. The Dragon Queen stood on the ledge just below her, mouth wide open as she screamed in fury. But her eyes weren't on Maeve. Maeve followed her gaze to the smoking ruins of the cloak and saw the Crown of Erinyes. Except it was a crown no more, but seven shards once again, glimmering and burning brightly. And the Dragon Queen was not in her dragon form, but in the shape of a woman with long leather wings on her back.

Maeve's hands trembled as awareness washed over her

and she felt for the band around her throat. The collar was there once again which meant? She wasn't sure. King Mrithun was dead and could not control her, but all the same a sensation of dread washed over her. Had she reversed the curse by breaking the Crown of Erinyes?

Without waiting for answers she scrambled to her feet, snatched up her blade and one of the shards.

Pain laced up her arm as she leaped, slamming the shard into one of the hollows. The ground continued to tremble and she was aware of a host of noises, a deadly roar, screeching and screaming at her without remorse.

But the curse couldn't be reversed, for the demons were still free and the gates hadn't shut. If anything, the red glow seemed to have increased. Maeve reached to snatch up another shard as the Dragon Queen hurled herself forward and kicked.

"No!" Maeve shrieked, but her words were like dust as six of the shards went flying over the gate into the chaos below. Her fingers snatched at nothing but air and horror filled her. Her heart thumped in her ears as tormented emotions washed through her. Taking advantage of her shock, the Dragon Queen knocked her over. Maeve managed to keep a hand on her sword as claws scratched at her arms and a fist slammed into her cheek.

Maeve struggled against the onslaught, her thoughts going wild. Now was the best time to kill the Dragon Queen when she was in her mortal form, but each time Maeve attempted to bring up the sword, the wings stretched out, knocking it away. It was all Maeve could do to protect her face, letting her arms and chest take the brunt of the onslaught, all the while wondering how she would find the shards lost in the churned ground beneath her.

She kicked and struggled, attempting to shake off the Dragon Queen, but her merciless grip was too strong. She pinned Maeve down and used her wings to hold tight. Maeve knew she was stuck yet she continued to struggle underneath the stronger woman. She'd bested the fae king and killed the Hunter, surely the Dragon Queen would not be her demise.

Straining against the onslaught, Maeve's eye caught a speck of orange. At first she assumed it was flame, but the next moment, two claws ripped through the Dragon Queen's back. Freed from her grasp Maeve moved quickly, sending a silent thank you to Drago as he wheeled, ready to make another dive at the queen. Taking advantage of the distraction, Maeve slashed her blade across the Dragon Queen's face, pulled her arm back, twisted the hilt and drove it up into her belly.

Warm blood flowed over Maeve's wrist and arm. The horizontal, lizard-like eyes of the furious Dragon Queen turned from shock to horror as she stared down at the blade sticking out of her body. Maeve pulled her sword free and the body of the Dragon Queen slipped over the edge where it thumped on the ground. The demons shrieked as it landed and within moments they surrounded her, ripping and tearing at the flesh as they feasted.

Maeve ripped her eyes away but couldn't suppress the wave of vomit. Leaning over, she spewed over the edge and cursed as she wiped her mouth. When she looked up again, she saw a javelin fly through the air and sink into the belly of Drago. Her sword dropped and she thought her heart would stop as she watched him flap madly, struggling to keep his balance before sinking into the fray.

Maeve screamed. Her cry of horror blotted out by the sounds of demons feasting below her. The bitter tang of bile rose in the back of her throat. Ash stung her skin and pain radiated through her body from her battle with the Dragon Queen. But none of it compared to the devastation that swallowed her. Drago had exchanged his life for hers. Tears blinded her eyes. The shards were lost, both dragons were dead, her companions had been captured and the celestials had not seen fit to help them.

Tears streaked down her face and a heaviness came over her. She slid to her knees on the slippery rock, half burned and covered in blood. The one shard taunted her as it hung above her, its magic shimmering. Magic she did not know how to control, although it sang in her blood. Her birthright. Yet it all seemed for nothing. What had she fought for, and why? Since the day she was born, death and destruction awaited her.

Closing her eyes, she lifted her face to the stinging ash, and gave in.

A trumpet blared, the sound sweet yet urgent. Maeve opened her eyes as something wet touched her face. It was cool, gentle, and as she looked up, another splashed on her face. Rain instead of ash? But how?

Her eyes widened as she looked across the battlefield. Everywhere she saw golden light, wheeling through the darkness, shattering the demons who fled, screaming, back toward the red glow. Silver swords flashed. Golden beings whirled as though they were created of light and no evil could touch them. A wave of radiance washed over the battlefield and the crystal clear sound of a trumpet blared again. Hope bloomed in Maeve's heart along with anticipation. Celestials! The celestials had arrived, and with their arrival they wiped out the demons who fled before them, shrieking and screaming.

Maeve's eyes darted toward the ground, but she was too late. Three of the shards were already in place above the gates and three of the guardians were below, fighting the demons. One of them saw her watching and tossed something toward her. Maeve held out her hands and caught one of the shards. It was the largest one, the one she'd found in the ruins of Carn. Light poured out of it, surging into her even as Maeve turned toward the hollows above the gate. Wings beat beside her as two more of the guardians flew up and pressed the shards into the hollows.

A guardian caught Maeve about the waist and lifted her —she thought it was Yael—and positioned her above the final hollow. Maeve pressed the shard of Erinyes into it and the blue shimmer expanded as though it were on the verge of explosion.

The guardian holding Maeve moved upward as the ground trembled. Maeve saw Enya, the firebird, flames trailing from her feathers, eyes dark as night and mouth wide open as she soared toward the opening of the Gates of Hell. Demons screamed and fled in an attempt to escape the closing of the gates, but Maeve turned her face away from the devastation below her.

Rain poured freely out of the sky, but nothing could stop the flames nor tame the explosion that erupted as blue light shot out in every direction, like a volcano erupting. The island trembled and Maeve watched as it split in half and the tower of the guardians began to fall. The air was alight with a combination of rain and fire.

Maeve shivered. It was over. The celestials had come, the demons were gone, it was the end. The dark fae had been destroyed, the Dragon Queen slain and somehow, someway, she'd survived it all. The victorious sensation that should have erupted through her did not come, instead she only felt hollow. She closed her eyes as the guardian bore her away, daring to hope that she was not the only survivor.

In the distance she heard the break of thunder rumble across the world. Her hand went to her throat where the collar lay there again. How, and why? She had no idea but hoped wherever it was she was going, there would be answers.

31
HALL OF JUDGEMENT

"Maeve of Carn?"

A hesitant tone woke her and Maeve opened her eyes. Weariness seeped over her and every muscle in her body ached. Her head felt heavy as though it were made of stone and her eyelids refused to open all the way.

Her lips were cracked and dry as she opened her mouth, her voice nothing more than a breathless whisper. "Yes?"

"Have a drink," the voice went on.

Something touched her hand. Maeve lifted the water skin to her lips and drank deeply, greedily, some of the water trickling down her chin and dribbling down her neck. "Where are we?" she asked, as the refreshing water gave her strength to open her eyes wider.

It seemed that she was once again in a tower or a castle. She slumped on a bench, and saw that Yael stood before her. Her armor was shining as though she'd never fought and her face calm, although this time Maeve noted the relief in her eyes.

"We are just outside of the Hall of Judgement," Yael replied. "You are next."

Hall of Judgement? Was she in some dark dream? Suddenly the water did not taste as sweet, and a thousand questions buzzed through her mind. Her eyes fell to her hands, ensuring that she was not chained, but no, other than the collar around her neck, there was nothing. Still, panic rose in her throat as she wearily stood to her feet.

"Whose Hall of Judgement?" she dared ask.

But Yael closed her lips and stood tall, leading the way toward a set of golden doors. They swung open as she approached and Maeve followed.

Maeve trembled as she walked into the hall, noting the wide arches that shot up, hundreds of feet into the air. Light filled every corner and arched windows looked out on a blue sky with white clouds.

Hall of Judgement. Maeve understood in a moment as she took in the solemn faces that looked on her. Celestials and guardians alike, some with great wings, others tall with hardened bodies. But there was something beautiful and graceful about their perfection, and Maeve felt wholly inadequate as she walked into their midst.

At the very end of the hall, a soft white light glowed, and Maeve felt a fear like she'd never felt before. She was scarcely able to take a few steps before she was down on her knees, head bent, while the aura of the place swept over her. She was certain, quite certain she was in the hall of the celestials themselves. She waited while she knelt, her eyes squeezed shut as though an executioner would come and lop off her head. But the strike never came.

Instead, a voice came from that light, firm yet gentle, commanding yet understanding. When it spoke her name a peace she could not explain filled her and she wanted, so badly, to please that voice no matter what it cost.

"Maeve of Carn. Well done."

Her eyes came open and she looked up, but she could see nothing tangible beyond the light. Her fear melted away into humbleness and she kept her hands clasped before her. Waiting.

"You choose to overcome evil and fight for what is right. Regardless of the peril to your own life you choose to save the world from the influence of darkness. For that you shall be rewarded. What do you desire, Maeve of Carn? The barrier between mortal and celestial has been broken, the Prophecy of Erinyes has come true. Do you wish to take your place among the celestials? Your actions have proven you are trustworthy. Or do you wish to dwell among the mortals?"

Maeve listened, thoughts twirling through her mind. She was invited to walk among the celestials, but she could barely hold her head up in front of them. They faced forward and she was able to scan through the crowd, admiring their royal clothes, silks, jewelry and great wings. None of which she had. If she were to walk among the celestials she would always feel inferior. And what would she do in their great halls? She would be alone once again. After everything that had happened, she did not want to be alone.

"I would ask what happened to my friends," she said aloud. Her voice sounded low and weak to her own ears. "And I wish to return to the mortals. I understand they are unlike you, flawed and full of mistakes. But I have found the kindest hearts and the most forgiving souls, and I would take my chances with them, if I am granted the grace to live another life."

"Then you shall return and discover the fate of mortals," the voice said. "We name you the defender of the world, and if need should arise, call upon us, and we will come to your aid."

Maeve opened her mouth to say more, but before she could, a trumpet blasted. A hand dropped to her shoulder. Maeve looked up at Yael who beckoned to her. The doors swung open and Maeve was escorted out, while someone else she could not see was escorted in.

"Who was that?" she glanced up at Yael.

Yael shook her head. "You are not the only one who will be offered a chance to stay with the celestials or return to the land of mortals."

Maeve's eyes went wide and she glanced back to catch a glimpse of the individual inside, but the doors had already closed. Her thoughts flew to Jacq the wizard, Willow, Ingram, Imer, Faelyn, and Nimya. Were they alive and would they be offered the same deal she'd just turned down?

"Maeve of Carn?" Yael was speaking again.

Maeve jerked, and for the first time she looked down and saw the crusted, dried blood on her clothes. The Sword of Justice hung in her sheath but she was bloodied and bruised. All she wanted was to go home.

“Maeve of Carn, I will escort you back to the land of mortals. Where would you like to go?”

Maeve opened her mouth, and an idea came to her.

32
FATE OF MORTALS

Maeve stood on the shore of a barren land. The wild grasses had escaped the burning, although the village behind her was nothing more than smoking ruins. She sat down on the shore, watching the waves ripple and imagined there were eels, festering in the deep. But nothing would be as terrible as the demons, and nothing would make her heart stop like the sight of the Dragon Queen, escaping from her prison. Maeve's fingers went to her throat, where the collar came off. It was only a remnant of the curse and could not hurt her anymore. She lifted her arm to toss it into the waters, then thought the better of it.

A moment later, she heard a thump as a being landed. Anticipation surged in her chest. The guardian rose into the air and Maeve stood to watch the man who remained.

Imer limped toward her, clothes torn and bloody, but he was alive, and that was all she cared about. She ran toward him, surprised at the relief and other emotions that surged through her. He smiled at her, his eyes dark, a wry grin on his face as she threw her arms around him and held him tight.

"I was afraid you were dead," she gasped, pulling back.

Imer shook his head. His hat was gone and smudges of dirt were on his face. "I thought so too," he said, his arm remaining around her waist, holding her tight. "When the storm blew in and you went below, I thought it was just that, a storm. But it was a flight of demons, surging toward the landmass. They took such delight in terrorizing us. They killed Faelyn instantly, but Jacq was able to hold them off, despite the fact we did not have a celestial blade. Demons are very hard to kill, as we found out. They took us prisoner and flew us to the island where I suppose they were setting up a camp. They locked us up, for sport I suppose, but the guardians engaged them in battle before they could torture us. After that, we waited, using what we could to try to free ourselves. As ironic as it was, magic does not work on demons, nor fire, nor wind, nor spells. And then the Dragon Queen kept flying over, and the firebird. I heard what happened to Drago. I am sorry." Imer squeezed her hand.

Maeve bit her lip but her eyes were dry. "He saved me. Perhaps it was his fate after all, but now the last of the dragons are dead. I'm not sure I was supposed to survive either. The dark fae are no more, the demons are gone, all dragons are dead, who am I, the last of my kind, to escape their fate?"

Imer squeezed her gently. "You are Maeve of Carn, the Last Defender. Don't think of yourself as any less than you are. I was grateful when I heard of your choice to return to the land of the mortals instead of dwelling with the celestials. It gave me hope for a future, for our future."

Maeve smiled at him, grateful she actually had a future to look forward to.

"Why did you choose this place though?" he asked, staring out at the waters.

"This is the place where new beginnings take place," Maeve waved her hand, pointing at the burned Village of the Lawless. "I found the first shard here, and it set me on a journey I will never forget. It wasn't that long ago, less than a year when we were here, with Sandrine and Caspian." Maeve sighed.

Sandrine, who had been hard and brittle from her years of servitude to the dark fae. But at the last moment, gave up her life in the hope that the dark fae's rule of terror would finally be eradicated. And Caspian, who carried the first shard and never told her that he sought to change the darkness in his soul. Through it all, Maeve had learned who she was, what she desired, and how to live in a way she would be proud of.

"What of the others?" she changed the subject.

"I'm sure they will rebuild." Imer shrugged. "We left the elves and humans and the people of the grove in charge when we set sail. I'm sure they will come to an accord, now that the doom that haunted this land has lessened. If I had to guess, Jacq the wizard will remain with the celestials. Willow will be torn, but I do not believe she would give up the opportunity to rebuild Imperia and train a new generation of mages. Eventually Imperia will become a place to learn magic and I would not be surprised if we are invited to return there, one day. Ingram will go to Isdrine to ensure they survived, especially from the onslaught of the orcs. As for you and I, my lady," he quipped. "What does your heart desire?"

Maeve shrugged. "I don't want anything big or dramatic, but I would like to sit down, enjoy a cup of ale, a hot bath, and not worry about who will attack us next. I'd like to relax, and laugh, and hear stories, without my heart breaking. At long last I know who I am, but I would like to go north and discover the mysteries that are there, if there are any."

Imer smiled and pointed at a plume of orange in the sky, as the firebird moved across it. "I believe our ride is here, to take us home."

As the firebird streaked down, Maeve climbed on top, behind Imer, this time without worry that she would burn. They flew over water and ruin until the temple of Isdrine rose in front of them. Imer and Maeve dismounted and bade the bird goodbye, and hand-in-hand walked down the cobblestone path toward the temple.

A sunset flashed across the sky, rich with pinks and oranges, and a few fluffy white clouds sat on the horizon. When Maeve looked up, she could see the shades of blue in the sky, and she could have sworn that on the highest cloud a golden city hovered. Home of the celestials. Waiting for a call, if there ever should be a need. And perhaps the orcs would return, or a new terror would rise. But for now the world was saved. Still, she carried the Sword of Justice, in case she was called to defend the world again.

WHAT TO READ NEXT

Enjoyed this story but want more? Check out the Tower Knights collection: complete, stand-alone spicy fantasy romances.

Phantom of the Opera meets Beauty and the Beast in this gothic-inspired dark fantasy romance.

A haunted tower, a mysterious instructor, and the lure of the music of the night...

Get a discount on signed hardcovers when you visit angelajford.com

Acknowledgments

A special thanks goes out to:

My husband for encouraging my work and providing me with plenty of creative inspiration.

Courtney Andersson for amazing edits and going above and beyond to make this story come alive.

Raquel A. Beattie for recording the audiobook and bringing the characters to life.

Readers far and wide who enjoy these kinds of stories and send kind words and notes. I'm always happy to hear from fans. I truly hope you enjoyed this tale and are looking forward to the many fantastical stories to come.

Visit angelajford.com for more!

ALSO BY ANGELA J. FORD

Join my email list for updates, previews, giveaways, and new release notifications. Join now: www.angelajford.com/signup

Chronicles of the Four Worlds (epic fantasy)

A complete six-book epic fantasy series spanning two hundred years, featuring an epic battle between mortals and immortals.

Legend of the Nameless One Series (epic fantasy)

A complete five-book epic fantasy adventure series featuring an enchantress, a wizard, and a sarcastic dragon.

Night of the Dark Fae Trilogy (romantic epic fantasy)

A complete epic fantasy trilogy featuring a strong heroine, dark fae, orcs, goblins, dragons, antiheroes, magic, and romance.

Tales of the Enchanted Wildwood (fairy tale romance)

Adult fairy tales blending fantasy action-adventure with steamy romance. Each short story can be read as a stand-alone and features a different couple.

Tower Knights (fantasy romance)

Gothic-inspired adult steamy fantasy romance. Each novel can be read as a stand-alone and features a different couple.

Gods & Goddesses of Labraid (epic fantasy)

A complete epic fantasy duology featuring a warrior princess with a dire

future who embarks on a perilous quest to regain her fallen kingdom.

Lore of Nomadia Trilogy (epic fantasy romance)

The story of an alluring nymph, a curious librarian, a renowned hunter, and a mad sorceress as they seek to save—or destroy—the empire of Nomadia.

One Winter Night (fantasy romance)

Winter-themed spicy fantasy romance. Each novel is a stand-alone and features a difference couple.

Visit angelajford.com for autographed books, exclusive book swag and book boxes.

ABOUT THE AUTHOR

Angela J. Ford is a bestselling author who writes epic fantasy and steamy fantasy romance with vivid worlds, gray characters and endings you just can't guess. She has written and published over 30 books.

Aside from writing she and her husband own The Signed Book Shop. A one-stop shop for readers to find signed books and book merchandise.

If you happen to be in Nashville, you'll most likely find her enjoying a white chocolate mocha and daydreaming about her next book.

facebook.com/angelajfordauthor
instagram.com/angelajfordbooks
amazon.com/Angela-J-Ford/e/B0052U9PZO
bookbub.com/authors/angela-j-ford

Milton Keynes UK
Ingram Content Group UK Ltd.
UKHW012127070823
426486UK00019B/370/J